THE STREETBOYS

HUNTERS MOON

TAYLOR J GRAY

Hunters Moon

Copyright ©2021 Taylor J Gray

ALL RIGHTS RESERVED.

This book contains material protected under International and Federal Copyright Laws and Trusties. Any unauthorized reprint or use of this material is prohibited. No part of this book may be reproduced or transmitted in any form or by any means, electronic or mechanical, including photocopying, recording, or by an information and retrieval system without express written permission from the Author/Publisher.

This is a work of fiction. Names, characters, places, and incidents are the product of the author's imagination or are used fictitiously. Any resemblance to actual persons, living or dead, business establishments, events, or locales is entirely coincidental.

Cover Design: Book Cover by Design

Proofreading: Abrianna Denae

Formatting: Abrianna Denae

ABOUT THIS BOOK

Layton went to the forgotten vanilla streets to find a boy and returned with two different ones.

Their arrival will have consequences and the ripples of those will be felt in both worlds.

This is how their story begins…

AUTHOR'S NOTE

For those that have followed from the Isaac Series, I want to say welcome to this new journey. You'll get to see your friend in small moments and get updates of his life.

This new series is written with a different pace, and I hope you like long stories; with moments where it's just snippets of their daily lives to other more serious moments, with consequences.

It's a life story and sometimes, like life, it's a slow burn and sometimes it moves faster than you catch your breath and doesn't always go the way you think.

It starts with two boys and expands with the people whose lives they impact, sometimes in a small way, sometimes in a bigger way, sometimes as a ripple from their path.

Life changes people, life is sometimes fragile and life experiences and the people we meet set our lives on different paths. This is never more true for the characters in this series. Enjoy.

DISCLAIMER

This is an adult only read. It contains descriptive scenes of M/M sex, BDSM and conversations of self-harm and sexual assault.

CHAPTER ONE

JOE

What the hell just happened?

I felt like six years of street living was rushing around in my head, moments, memories swamping me, trying to make sense of what had just happened. Leo was a freak... I stopped the smile from actually getting to my lips and shook my head. How many times had I comforted him from the other street boys and their name-calling? Name-calling for fuck's sake. I was protecting him from name-calling and he was getting his fix being cut up with razor blades! I wasn't even sure if this made sense of everything that had happened over the last four years, but I guess it must have played some part... *shit his back had been...* I wasn't sure there was an answer for the state of his back. I had never seen anything like it and I had seen some shit over the last six years.

I wasn't no prude, I mean I lived on the street for fuck's sake, in the gutter with the rest of the rubbish and you saw things, you learnt things. There were customers who wanted stuff… extra stuff, kinky stuff, and I did it sometimes too. I knew about kinky BDSM shit, I did… well, I thought I did. What I had just seen, what Leo was doing… was a whole other level.

I tried to recall everything Layton had said… it was a need… like wanting a drug, a cigarette. I shook my head. I needed a cigarette – right now as it happens – but it fucking never left me needing bloody hospital. I closed my eyes trying to rein in my swirling thoughts.

Standing with Leo looking at the alley for the last time, where I had lived for the last six years, had been hard. I had prepared myself to leave, got it all straight in my head. What Layton had told me, offered me, it sounded okay. Well, it wasn't like I had any other options so there wasn't much to think about really, my time there was at an end. Six hard years of sucking and fucking, running and hiding from the vanillas and the pigs, dodging fights and drugs. Why was it so hard to leave such a fucking awful destructive and damaging place? I knew the answer.

Freedom. There was no one to answer to on the streets, only yourself, and if you didn't ask yourself any questions, then you didn't even need to do that. It could be as hard or as easy as you wanted. Hard, earned you more money, easy was safer but made no money. I had been a hard player in the beginning. Sucking and fucking seven or more times a night or less if the customer wanted an all-nighter and was willing to pay. Going off in cars, or to rooms, I hadn't cared. The thrill, the danger made it exciting, the money made it worthwhile and…well fuck, I was free to do as I pleased.

Then four years ago, Leo had turned up. A kid, just fourteen, he said. I never knew for certain but knew he was young. He was completely lost and it had taken me a few days to get him talking. His story was like many others, broken home, step-parent, disagreements, fights and arguments. Although he was so quiet, I couldn't imagine he would bother anyone. He had the remains of a black eye, which he said he'd got in a fight. I had to try not to laugh, coz this kid didn't look like he could fight a fucking fly.

I had seen it so many times before, teenage kid runaways looking for better, looking for a way out. They didn't know how good they had it. Even their worst day at home would never come anywhere close to the misery of a good day on the street.

Their teenage tantrums making them disagreeable and obnoxious to the vanillas, made them seek understanding from the streets but they didn't know what lay waiting for them there. I knew what drew them though, it was the freedom…but they never understood what came with that freedom. Even so, on this occasion, there was something a little different about Leo. His huge, stunning eyes held a sadness, the likes of which I had never seen before, not even in the boys that had frequented the streets for a few years. Drawn to him, which I put down to him being a kid, I spent a few weeks with him and the sadness seemed to fade and his eyes became a little more vibrant and bright. They were eyes the colour of… the sea? A green/blue colour that I had never seen on anyone else. I was sure the colour was called teal but it reminded me of the sea, well, one I had seen on a postcard once. I hadn't actually ever seen the sea.

I got to know him a little in those few weeks and it was clear that he didn't belong here. He was certainly not your typical street boy, he was just a kid, still shy and compliant to his elders, possibly a bit touched in the head. I liked him though, I liked how easy he was to talk to and be with.

When Layton visited, I introduced them and hoped that Layton would like him enough to help him, take him. I knew the sort of boys that Layton took – well I thought I did – and Leo sort of fitted. Layton helped kids, got them off the street and I always had this rose-tinted idea that it was for something better, that he found the young ones new homes and the feisty ones like Orion, well, he took them to be his…slaves. I was okay with that. Boys like Orion were… different. Leo was nothing like Orion… except, apparently now, he was. *Christ.*

At the time, Layton had said he was a little different but he was just young. He couldn't stay on the streets, that was clear, so I thought it was better to go back home and try and sort out his problems. So, that's what I did, I walked Leo home and told him things would get better. To be fair, at the time, he hadn't seemed bothered about going back. He seemed up for giving it another try, which convinced me I had done the right thing. Also, the guy who opened the door to him looked happy to see him, like relieved he was home so I didn't think anything of it.

I had missed him back at the alley, missed seeing and talking to him, which was silly because I'd only just met him. That was street life, kids came and went, sometimes they stayed long enough for you to know their name, sometimes they didn't.

It was a week or so later when it was getting dark and I left the safety of one of the back buildings to start my business and there he was, sitting with the piled rubbish at the back. He was bruised and a bit bloody but I recognized him immediately, his big sea-blue eyes looked at me fleetingly before they closed. I carried him inside, cleaned him up, and stayed with him until he came back. He was upset but with a little coaxing, he told me that he and Steve – his step-father – had fucked after he had found him jerking off over some old magazines he'd found in amongst the rubbish.

I had been a little taken aback, mainly, at the matter-of-fact way he'd spoken about it all. He was upset and he was in pain but he wasn't as distressed as I would have expected, like he felt like he deserved it? To me, he was fourteen years old and his step-father had raped him. No one deserved that. He refused to speak about it after I threatened to go back and sort him out, he'd got pissed about it, upset, so that's all I ever knew about it.

If I had to pick a moment when I first felt something for Leo, then that first night back with him was it or that's when I recognised something. I hadn't considered it love, I hadn't even thought about it over the four years that we'd spent in the alley. Love wasn't the sort of thing boys like me and Leo thought about. We thought about getting business so we could survive another day in the gutter of the vanilla world. A smile took my face. That wasn't true. I thought about getting business, Leo always tried not to think about it, for four fucking years he tried not to think about it, he hated the customers, yet at times, he had seemed curious and drawn to them.

No, I never considered it love. I knew I liked him, liked his company, liked watching him, listening to him, being with him. I liked sleeping with him, feeling his shivering body next to mine and feeling his skinny body under my hand as I rubbed him to warm him up. I missed him when he stopped sleeping with me. It hurt to listen to him crying alone sometimes on his makeshift bed, it hurt, even more, when he started to sleep with Ginger.

I felt the tears sting my eyes and quickly swept at them with my fingers. I looked at Kendal. "Can we stop? Just for a minute...I just need a minute."

She briefly looked across at me. "Sure, honey."

The car pulled off into a side street and as soon as it stopped, I unclipped my belt and slipped out onto the pavement. I stepped forward and threw myself back against a brick wall for support. Taking out my cigarettes, I lit one, taking a long draw on it.

Leo had changed when Ginger had arrived. Within a few months, he seemed to want to do whatever Ginger asked of him and when Ginger got pissed with him, he'd come looking for me. I kind of accepted it. Sharing Leo's company was better than not having him at all. Now I understood, well, I knew, my understanding of it all was a little hazy. Leo had been getting his fix from Ginger. I wasn't sure where that left me in Leo's eyes. That I loved him had only really dawned on me today when I tried to leave him. Now I was standing here wondering if he was going to leave or if I would never see him again. Kendal joined me, leaning on the wall next to me. I looked at her briefly.

"I'm sorry, I just needed to take a minute."

She smiled at me. "You don't have to apologise, Joe." Kendal was one of the nicest people I had met over the years. She always made me feel like I was still worth something. "I'm guessing you didn't know then? About Leo's need? What he was doing?"

I shook my head feeling a hysterical laugh building but it never materialised. "No. You didn't seem worried by it all? Do you know about this thing? Understand it?"

She smiled and nodded. "I do, yes. I sometimes wish I didn't because I find it hard to understand…even in myself."

My head swung round to look at her. "You?"

She nodded and half-smiled. "Not like Leo's need, nothing like Leo…or Isaac but I have a desire to be and feel submissive. I can ignore it most of the time, push it away but there are times, usually when I'm very tired or a little run down, that I can't move it. As soon as I know that I can't ignore it, it just gets worse, the need for it just gets bigger. It becomes something that I can't control."

"Shit." Fuck, that was meant to stay in my head. "Sorry…And the pain thing? You need that?"

She half smiled and shook her head. "No, not so much. It depends on how long I let it ask for before I give in to it. My need is mostly to feel submissive to someone, to have them take my will away. The feeling of being vulnerable to someone seems to be my thing. I've not explored anything more with anyone since…well, I've not explored anything more recently." She was quiet for a minute before continuing. "Need like Leo's and Isaac's are a lot stronger, a lot more demanding. Their control of it is very limited especially when the feeling is so strong. The more they understand it, the better they are at dealing with it, when it asks and when it's sated.

"I understand it can be a bit shocking and what you saw on Leo was not a good example of what it is. I don't always agree with the world I live in, but when I see needs like Leo's, that's been misunderstood and without any guide or control, it reminds me that our world is a good place and does good things. No one in our world suffers like Leo is suffering now and yet some of them have desires as strong as his. It is dealt with differently, with love and understanding and praise. I know it's hard, Joe, but Leo, the boy you know, has always had this need. He's still going to be that same person that you've loved over the last four years."

I gave a false smile, took a drag on my cigarette and blew the smoke out before I glanced a look at Kendal. "I didn't know I loved him, not until today, until I tried to leave him. Now, I'm not sure if he's coming. Ginger has known him better than me...why would he leave him? He gave him what he wanted."

Kendal turned to face me leaning on the wall and reached a hand out to lightly touch my arm. "Hey. Leo's need made him subservient to Ginger and he will find that a little confusing to leave behind but he always came back to you. In our world, the slaves go off to clients to have their needs satiated but they always return to their Keepers. It is their Keeper who they love and trust. The pain thing, it's just a small part of who they are.

"I know after looking at Leo's back it seems huge. And when it asks, it can take their thoughts and feelings and consume them but that's when they need their Keepers. To love and comfort them through those feelings, to see beyond it, to see the person that is lost in it but still wants to be loved and reassured. It means everything to them. You loved Leo through it all, when he was needy and when he was healing, when he was upset and low and when he felt the high of having it sated. You shared and loved him without conditions because you didn't know about any of it. He may not be able to express that to you in words but he'll know it, he'll feel it and he'll show you by coming back to you."

"I've got to take Ginger's place now, haven't I? I've got to do those things to him?"

Kendal laughed a little. "Really, really not, no and if you do, I will be pretty pissed! Ginger did what Leo requested but it was not the right thing or way. What you will do now is guide and lead Leo a better way because of your love for him. Layton will show you other ways to help him. You may find it a little overwhelming at first. You will be his safety, set his limits, and he may not always be very happy with it but he will love you for it. It is very dangerous to give submissive people everything they desire. Just seeing Leo's back shows what happens when he is allowed to lead the show."

"So, he can't have it like that?"

Kendal shook her head. "No, not like that. Eventually, you will decide what he has, whether he has to work for it or whether he will just be given it."

"Work for it?"

Kendal smiled. "Please you, serve you." Kendal touched my shoulder. "It's not all about pain, Joe." She pushed herself away from the wall and held out her hand. "Come on, at this rate, Leo will be there before us and I have to get some food ready for Isaac." I took her hand fleetingly, threw my cigarette butt into the curb and got back in the car. As I did my belt Kendal got in.

"Isaac is..." I couldn't think of a word that described him.

Kendal laughed. "Difficult to describe?" I smiled at her uncomfortably. "Isaac has been on a very long journey. He has lived most of his adult life as a slave and now sometimes finds his world difficult and confusing. He loves constant attention, be it verbally or by touch, which makes him quite demanding but he's naturally submissive which can make him very vulnerable and childlike...sound like anyone you know?"

I smiled and looked out of the window. "Are they all like that? The slaves?"

Kendal spoke as she watched the road. "No, not all, some are different, like Orion. Isaac is a masochistic submissive, like Leo, but he has been taught that it's a beautiful thing, all the slaves are taught that, that what they have, what they do, it's a gift. They are encouraged to share their need with their Keepers and clients. The more they share, the more love and comfort they receive in praise of their feelings."

"Does Isaac go to customers…clients?"

Kendal shook her head. "No, not now. Isaac is not a slave anymore; he is privately owned by Layton. Isaac's life is a little confusing to outsiders. He lives with Layton mostly but sometimes with Peter. His relationship with both of them is built on love, trust and a great deal of understanding. He lives as freely as he's able, as he's allowed to but when asked for his subservience, Isaac gives it." I frowned at her and she looked at me fleetingly and smiled. "It's not as it sounds. Isaac lives to serve, it's his nature. He wants to be loved, he wants attention, mainly Layton's or Peter's. He will happily submit and serve, and even be sneaky to have it. He finds a lot of peace in being restrained and confined, it takes a lot of worry and responsibility from him. Layton has spent a lot of time with Isaac, gaining his trust, learning to understand him so that he can live with some sort of independence. Not independence like you and I understand it, Isaac will never have that, he would never want it."

Kendal sighed. "It's difficult to explain it all quickly. People...people like Isaac, come here to be slaves. It takes away their will, their worry and responsibilities of life and responsibility for themselves. Trying to control such strong desires in the vanilla world is hard, especially when the feeling is constant. Everything is decided for them here, when they eat, when they sleep, when they play. Even going to the toilet is decided for them." Jesus Christ. "It keeps them very submissive and subservient, controlled. They want that feeling, it's part of their desires, their need. If they misbehave they get punished."

"For what? What can they do if they are controlled so tightly?"

"Rudeness, pleasuring themselves…it's forbidden, not following instructions, coming without permission – in and out of play. Some will purposefully misbehave to be punished, such is their desire for it. For Isaac to be able to live some sort of independent life, he has had to re-learn some basic life skills. Things that, to you and I, are simple everyday things. Going to the toilet on his own, walking without being led, thinking his own thoughts, although I'm not sure that ever held Isaac back." She smiled her amusement. "Layton understands that Isaac has lots of needs and because Layton has to look after his slaves that live in his house, he allows Isaac to have other relationships with people that he trusts to keep Isaac safe. He has his Keeper, Peter, who looks after him when Layton cannot be there and another friend called Marcus, who he visits occasionally."

"Peter? The guy from today?" Kendal nodded. "And he allows this relationship to go on in front of him?"

"Yes but it's not how you are making it sound." Kendal smiled. "In our world, it's understood that you can love more than one person, that you can have a different relationship with different people. Layton and Isaac's relationship is very strong. It is not just based on love, it's deeper because of their needs and their understanding of it. Isaac's devotion to Layton, out of slavery is something rare and beautiful and no matter where he is, the connection that they share is never doubted by either of them. It doesn't matter how many people Isaac loves or love him, he will always have the security of Layton." Kendal glanced a look at me. "If you had something so precious, wouldn't you want to know that even when you couldn't be with it, it was being loved and cared for, like you loved and cared for it?" It? Is that what people were here?

"Doesn't that kind of make Peter and this other guy second best?"

Kendal shook her head. "Not to Isaac. Isaac just loves, there are no levels to his love. Each relationship is not more or less than the other, just different. Layton cannot always be there for Isaac but he understands that Isaac must have someone who he trusts as much as Isaac trusts him and who understands Isaac. Peter and Isaac are like you and Leo. Their relationship is new and they are still learning about each other. There are things that they are unsure of but they try and take one step at a time. Isaac is Peter's first male love."

"Really? It didn't look like it."

Kendal sort of laughed. "Isaac is teaching him to embrace his feelings…and when you fall in love, things are natural."

I smiled trying to show my understanding even though it all seemed a mess to me. "Can I ask where we are going?"

She spoke while watching the road, flicking a look at me now and again. "To a friend's house. The house belongs to a man called Jacob. He lives with Julian, he's Julian's… friend. He is also privately owned and only submits to Julian. He has the same needs as Isaac and Leo but generally, he's not as controlled by them. He has lived a different life, one that makes him more independent. He doesn't need as much guidance as Isaac but still likes to be fussed over, mainly by Julian. With others, he's quite shy. He and Isaac are friends and have a thing for each other." Jesus, this was like some kind of TV soap.

I blew out a slow breath. "I have a lot to learn."

"You do but you'll be surprised how much Leo teaches you. We're here." I looked outside beyond the windscreen. Here, was a one-level house. It didn't look very big but as we drew up I could see it stretched further back. It was surrounded by woodland like something out of a creepy horror movie and once out of the car, I stood and looked around before Kendal joined me. "It's very safe here, Joe, no one overlooks this place, Julian owns a lot of land. He gave this to Jacob a long time ago so he would know that he was safe when he wasn't with him. Things have changed since then and Jacob is rarely alone now, he spends a lot of time with Julian usually here, sometimes at his place. Come on, I'll give you a quick tour and get you settled." I looked at her, unsure, and she smiled. "It will be okay."

I shook my head. "Everyone keeps saying that but I don't feel okay. How can I convince Leo if I don't know it? I don't think I should have left the alley, not yet, I'm out of my depth here, wherever here is. I have been in that alley for nearly seven years, living on the street… this is… overwhelming."

Kendal pulled some stuff from the car as she spoke. "I know it feels strange but that's the point of being here. It's safe and you don't have to worry about anything except Leo. You and Leo can spend some time just getting to know each other. You're not a prisoner here, you and Leo are free to leave at any time but you have some breathing space here, I would take it."

I closed my eyes and tried to breathe and think sensibly. I recalled Leo's back and winced. For now, I had little option and I trusted Kendal, everything told me she was a good person.

I blew out my breath slowly. "Is it okay if I let you guide me for the moment? I'm a little lost."

Kendal smiled and reached out and grabbed my hand. "That's what friends are for, Joe. Even someone like Layton needs the guidance of his friends sometimes." I stepped forward and we walked to the door.

"Really? I can't imagine that he ever needs help from anyone. Who does someone like Layton turn to for help then?"

Kendal looked at me and smiled. "Most of the time, believe it or not, Isaac. If it's something more involved, then Julian is his friend. He and Julian have known each other for a long while. They have both lived in this world a long time, they understand it more than most. Come on." Kendal opened the door and I stood there for a moment. I couldn't remember the last time I had been inside a house. I mean, I remembered, of course, I did, but it felt like a big thing. I stepped inside and Kendal closed the door.

CHAPTER TWO

JOE

As soon as the door closed I felt like the walls were coming in on me. The air seemed stifled and if I thought too much about breathing, it felt like there wasn't enough air. I held it together though while she showed me around, trying to keep up with everything she was telling me. I touched the walls a lot as we went around, and I wasn't sure if it was to lean on or to remind myself they were real and not get overwhelmed by them. It was so stupid. It was just a fucking wall. I just wasn't used to being so…enclosed.

"This will be yours and Leo's room."

Right, our room. Next to…Jacob's? Or was that other door Isaac's? I couldn't remember. I followed her inside. As bedrooms went, this was huge but what did I know, I hadn't had one for a few years. Maybe all rooms were like this now? Maybe this was small?… No, it was pretty big.

"There's a bathroom in the back. You are both free to roam the house as you want but it's probably not good to let Leo know that. Even though he'll be a little scared at the moment, they can get themselves into trouble pretty quick. It's probably best not to leave him alone. If his needs get the better of him and he does wander, there's not too much trouble he can get into and Peter will be around."

I could feel the panic building inside me just talking about being with Leo.

"Are you not staying?"

"I'll do both your checks, see to Leo's back and make sure he's settled. I'll make you all dinner for later but I'm pretty shattered and in need of some sleep. It's been a really long day and night." Of course. "Peter can get a hold of me if you need me. I'll only be at Julian's which isn't far from here, just through the woods out the back. I'll come back first thing tomorrow and check on him...and you." I half smiled trying to show far more confidence than I felt. "Come on, I'll show you the kitchen, you can make tea while I ready the dinner for later. I'll make Isaac a sandwich for now just to keep him going. He's a bit of a food monster."

I smiled softly. That reminded me of someone else I knew.

In the kitchen, Kendal showed me where everything was and set about preparing dinner. She filled the kettle and I gathered two mugs from a cupboard she had shown me and now I stood just looking at the cups. I couldn't remember the last time I had made tea. I mean it wasn't quite seven years ago, but it was a long time. Thinking about it, it was probably in a customer's house from when I used to go off in the cars. He had found it funny to get me to wait on him, make him tea and serve it, he said it was like 'fucking the butler'. He had done that too, a few times, well and truly. I cringed about it now but I remembered finding it funny at the time.

"Joe? Okay?" I bit my lip and turned my face to her feeling stupid.

"Erm… I haven't made tea in a really long time…" I gently bounced my fist against the worktop feeling awkward.

"Oh goodness, I'm sorry, Joe." She came over and reached for a canister on the side.

"If you just give me a quick reminder, show me where things are…" I smiled, feeling amused and Kendal smiled at me.

"What's funny?" I sort of laughed at the situation.

"Out of all the things we had to do to get by each day… we never had to make our own tea. If we couldn't afford to buy one ready-made, we didn't have one. I just found that funny." Kendal's smile turned sympathetic and I tried to ignore it, turning to see what she was doing. "Teabags… of course, and hot water." She gestured to the large double-doored fridge.

"Milk will be in there, in the door." I turned towards it as she had pretty much everything else under control. When I opened the fridge door, I was taken aback again. My eyes scanned the obscene amount of food inside. I must have gawped for quite some time as some sort of alarm sounded from the fridge, making me jump back and curse in fright.

"Shit." I heard Kendal chuckle quietly and reached around me and grabbed the milk from the door.

"If you shut it, it will stop." I closed the door and stood looking at it as silence fell again. I turned to look at Kendal to ask but she was smiling at me. "Sorry, I forgot to say. We had to have an alarm fitted on the fridge for when Isaac stays as he once spent a night raiding the fridge and then threw it all up. It was his first time away from Layton and slavery and things were just looking too inviting. It's a bit different now but we keep it on there just in case." Wow, okay. "When the kettle's boiled, just fill both cups…Oh, do you take sugar? Milk?"

I shook my head. "Erm, no sugar and yes to milk. Okay, yes… Sorry, this must seem pretty stupid but I think I remember."

"Don't be silly, Joe, this is going to be so different for both of you. Don't be afraid to ask for help, even if it feels silly." The kettle clicked off and Kendal looked at me questioningly and I nodded as I picked it up and poured it in the cups.

Wow, I was making tea in an actual kitchen. It was crazy that such a simple thing was making me nervous and I was shaking a little. Kendal was chopping vegetables and throwing them in a big pot along with some meat she got out of the really big fridge. I concentrated on making the tea, grimacing when the milk came pouring out too fast and flooded one cup. Kendal told me to not worry and to start again. It was good practice if nothing else, and I was glad no one else was here to watch my clumsiness. As I put the milk back, after making something that closely resembled tea, I turned and looked at Kendal as she seemed to be finishing up.

"What if Ginger doesn't want him to go? What if he loves Leo? He's nice to Leo, well nicer than he is to anyone else." I smiled to myself then looked at Kendal. "I think I was a little jealous of their friendship, especially when Leo started to sleep with Ginger." Kendal looked at me fleetingly and smiled as she put the big pot in the oven.

"Why didn't you ask him to sleep with you?" She washed her hands and wiped them looking at me.

"Well, he did, he used to, then Ginger arrived and he drifted away and started sleeping alone. I thought he was just getting older, you know, like a grown-up kind of thing? He used to pester Ginger to stay with him the whole night but after Ginger and he had seemed to have their… fun, Ginger always made him go away. I thought they were fucking..." I shook my head and smiled. "I never hung around, it sort of hurt to see them together. Leo would sometimes be crying quietly in his bed when I returned but I thought that was because Ginger had made him leave. Sometimes I would just leave him to cry until he fell asleep and sometimes I felt so sorry for him so I would take him outside and we would watch the sunrise together. It seemed to quieten him. If I had known what was going on I would never have left him to cry, not knowing he was in pain."

Kendal smiled and joined me at the table. "Seeing what he's dealing with now, I don't think he was crying because of his pain, well not his physical pain anyway. He was probably overcome with his need, frightened of it, confused, he wouldn't have understood it."

Jesus, all the times I had just lay watching him struggle because my feelings were hurt.

I shook my head trying to make sense of everything. "Why didn't he tell me? I've always looked out for him."

"What would you have done?"

I shrugged. "I don't know, helped him somehow, got Layton to take him."

"The exact thing he didn't want to happen, and would he have gone without you, do you think?"

I closed my eyes fleetingly, trying to sort out my thoughts. "I would have made him. He would have understood, once he got the help he needed to understand it himself." Would I have been able to do that? Words were easy.

"Maybe that's why he didn't tell you then. The only thing in his life he's ever been sure of is you, Joe, why would he want that to change in any way? If he didn't understand it, how could he tell you? Leo knows all the sacrifices you've made for him over the years, he'll ditch Ginger for you, it will be hard and confusing but he'll come. Do you seriously think Ginger will want him to stay?" She looked at me questioningly. "Seriously?"

I laughed a little. "No." I sighed. "God, it's going to be different, isn't it? For him, for us?"

Kendal smiled softly and nodded. "Good different, and not everything will change. You'll have to do for Leo what you've always done for him, make him feel secure and keep him safe. He'll need that even more so now. Layton will help guide you with his need." Kendal smiled at me as she got up and made a sandwich for Isaac. "Make yourself at home here, Joe. Help yourself to anything. There are towels and robes in your bathroom and you will find linens in the cupboard if you want a change of clothes. There are linens in there too for Leo. They are cream and yours are black. We can wash your clothes or I can get you new ones once you've settled. Once things are decided." Decided, yes. Linens? Black or cream? What? Who was wearing what?

I frowned. "Linens?"

Kendal nodded. "It's kind of a staple clothing that the Keepers and the slaves wear but they are so comfortable that the boys' kind of use them as loungewear. The Keepers or Dominants always wear black though and the subs/slaves always white or cream. It makes it clear to anyone who may visit or you see, stop any misunderstanding about places. It makes it clear immediately who holds what place... or rank if you like. Even though Jacob and Isaac live freely in this world, some rules still apply. It helps keep their minds settled too. More so for Isaac, the linens mean more to him than Jacob as he was a slave for so long.

"Leo may prefer them to his clothes as they won't bother his wounds so much. Also, it is quite natural for the subs to be naked. So, if Leo doesn't want to wear his clothes then that's okay too. The boys, Peter, Julian and Layton, when in company, usually encourage Jacob and Isaac to wear boxer shorts or linens. Jacob generally wears clothes around the house but Isaac still has an issue with them after not wearing them for so long so don't be surprised if you come across him naked." Kendal smiled with her thoughts. "Isaac's mind works differently."

I smiled back. "I kind of got that from meeting him. I wasn't that nice to him but he didn't seem to care."

Kendal smiled as she wrapped the sandwich and put it in the fridge. "A lot of clients were not nice to Isaac but he still usually got what he wanted. He is very clever at looking beyond peoples' words. He kind of gets a vibe about people which can guide his feelings, more so than what they say. If he feels safe with them he will shut out their words. Someone hurt Isaac very badly not so long ago, we nearly lost him. Layton had to work very hard with him to move his thoughts from what happened. It's a testament to how strong their bond, their relationship is, that Isaac allowed him to do that. To see him now is amazing, so we overlook some of his little foibles, outbursts and misdemeanours. Even Julian, who rarely gets involved with slaves past or present, has a soft spot for him."

Jesus, he got hurt? I thought this place was meant to be safe?

"Was it a customer that hurt him?"

Kendal shook her head as she boiled the kettle again. "No. It was much worse than that, it was someone who was meant to keep him safe. It was his Keeper. How Layton ever got him to trust again is beyond me. Taking Isaac out of this world to yours, to the street today, was a big deal. Peter was really worried. I think that's why he came to help today so he could be on hand in case Layton needed him to have Isaac. That's what Layton does for Isaac though, he moves him forward all the time. He has earned Isaac's trust, he's never lied to him, not even about the smallest thing. He encourages him to feel and share those feelings and seems to bring balance to Isaac's life." She sighed and sat with me again, giving me another tea. "I'm sorry, I'm droning on. I didn't mean to bore you or overwhelm you."

I shook my head. "You're not. You're kind of filling me with a little hope." I smiled at her. "I see a lot of Leo in Isaac, it gives me hope that I can help Leo find that peace."

It had also made me see that I had a lot of learning to do. Not just about Leo's need but his mind. It had always fascinated me, Leo's outlook on life. The things he said, sometimes random things that bore no connection to what we were doing or talking about. I had never encouraged Leo to share his feelings, when he spoke, I listened but I could see now that that probably wasn't everything that was going on in Leo's head.

The door opened down the corridor and Kendal smiled at me. "They're here."

My stomach somersaulted and I blew out my breath. There was no more thinking time.

Isaac entered the kitchen first at a sort of running pace and then slowed when he saw me. Kendal greeted him in her usual friendly manner.

"Hey sweetie, it's all ready. Where's Layton?"

Peter entered the kitchen as he answered. "He's taken Leo straight to the bedroom."

"I put them in your room?"

Peter looked at her and nodded. "Yep, that's where he's taken him."

I stood desperate to see Leo but also a little unsure.

Peter looked at me and spoke. "You should go and see him."

I nodded but didn't move. I had a million questions about what had gone on.

"Is...is he okay?"

Peter smiled at me. "He's a little traumatised and upset and has shut himself off a little. He'll come back once he knows you're with him, I'm sure."

Kendal touched the back of my neck, stroking it while I tried to make sense of everything. "Go on honey, I'll come in, in a bit and we will start sorting him out." Still, with my heart beating louder and faster than it should, I nodded and left the kitchen.

I walked to the room where Kendal had shown me earlier. The door was open a little and I stood for a moment and watched Layton with him. He had laid him on the bed and was sitting with him, stroking his fingers over his forehead.

"He's coming, Leo, Joe's coming." I took that as my cue to enter and I stepped into the bedroom, stalled for a moment and then walked straight over to them. Layton moved and I took his place on the bed and stroked Leo's face.

I looked at Layton. "Was it bad? Did he play up?" I knew what Leo was like when his emotions got the better of him, he was hard to contain.

Layton smiled and shook his head. "No, Leo struggled to say goodbye but Ginger made it easier for him. He used his alley status to move Leo on, closing the door to Leo so he understood his place was gone. It hurt Leo a little, but he did it for you both, so you and Leo can move on. Leo's a little upset and confused about everything but he'll be okay."

I nodded and looked back to Leo. He looked lost on the bed, maybe because I had never seen him on a bed before. He was curled up on his side doing the staring thing he did sometimes.

"Should I bring him back?"

Layton nodded. "Give it a moment. Just let him know you're here so he can feel a little safer."

I nodded and continued to stroke his face. "Hey, Leo. You're with me now." He didn't seem to hear me but then he seemed to take a quick breath and then tipped his head forward to my leg. I stroked my hand over his head to let him know that I was with him. I looked at Layton. "What shall I do?"

Layton sat on the end of the bed. "It's going to be a difficult time for him. You're in a strange place and he won't feel very safe being away from what he knows. The main thing is getting his wounds treated so let Kendal guide you while she sorts him out today. Once that is sorted you need to talk to him, a lot. He has a lot of things going on in his head and he's going to have a lot of questions. I know that is going to be difficult because you don't understand a lot yourself or have all the answers but if you show you're not worried, then he'll follow.

"Take this time to get to know him better but don't change the way you are with him, the way you deal with him. He's going to be unsure and a little confused but he knows you and he'll follow you. You're both safe here, you have a room, a bed, and food for a few days. I'll come back tomorrow and we can start discussing your options. If you struggle tonight, Peter will be here in the room across the hall. He's still learning but he understands a lot, he'll be able to help you even if it's just a temporary fix until I get back. He trusts you and the stronger you can make that relationship, the better it will be for when you move. Can I ask? Are you and Leo intimate? Do you fuck?"

I was taken aback by the question but shook my head. "No, we have never... I... I wanted to... but…"

Layton smiled. "It's okay. There's no right or wrong answer to that, I just wanted to know where your relationship was with him."

I nodded and looked at Leo. "I used to think he and Ginger were." I looked back at Layton. "Do you think they were? Do you know? Do people do this sort of thing and…fuck?"

Layton smiled. "If you let him, I'm sure Leo will tell you. If you ask though, you can't be angry with him if the answer is not to your liking."

I nodded. "I get that, I understand that. I would never speak badly of Ginger. I promised Leo we would talk about him, whenever he wanted. If they did, then should I...with him...? I mean I'm taking his place aren't I? Jesus Christ, I'm so out of my depth here… I didn't even remember how to make tea."

Layton held up his hand to me. "Slow down, Joe. You are thinking too much. Breathe." I took a deep breath and gave him a forced grin which disappeared quickly. Layton smiled back. "Can you do that when you're stuck? When you find yourself thinking too much, just take a breath. This time is for you and Leo to find your way and there are no set rules. This is no longer about Leo and Ginger, it's about you and Leo and…you've not had to make tea in a very long time, so give yourself a break. Being here is going to feel strange to you too."

I nodded and looked at Leo. He looked so worried. Was this really the same boy that had laid quietly for Ginger so he could inflict the wounds I had seen?

"I look at him now and wonder how he does it? It's like two different people."

Layton smiled. "Imagine how confusing it feels to him. Wouldn't you want to hide? Even though you don't understand it fully, you can still guide him. Remember, just… take a breath, let the moment pass while you figure it out."

I looked back at Layton. "Thank you for finding us this time." Layton stood and reached out, taking my head in his hand and pulling me towards him. He kissed the side of my face and stroked his fingers in my hair and then let them drop away and went to move but turned back.

"Joe?" I looked at him and he smiled. "I like that you've toned down the swearing." Jesus, did he notice everything?

I sort of smiled at him. "Well, I was with Kendal and it doesn't feel right…she's nice so…and a lady. Last I knew you didn't…you had to be polite around them. I'm swearing inside, a lot. I really need a ciggie too."

He pursed his lips together sympathetically. "No smoking is permitted here but I can make allowances, outside only. I can wait here with Leo?" I turned and looked at Leo. He wouldn't like it if I left again and I had promised him we would look at the moon together as soon as it got dark.

I looked at Layton. "It's okay, I'll wait. Will it be okay to take Leo outside later and watch the sky?"

Layton smiled. "I think he would like that. I'll see you tomorrow." I nodded and he left.

CHAPTER THREE

JOE

I turned and looked at Leo laying traumatised on the bed. Usually, when he zoned out on me he looked peaceful, he didn't look peaceful now. He was gripping the covers tightly in his hand and his bottom lip was quivering now and again. Okay, I didn't know much but I did know he couldn't stay there, like that. All the things that Kendal had told me went through my mind. Hell, I had no clue what I was doing but this was Leo and I knew Leo. I sat on the bed next to him, took his wrist in my hand and pulled his hand from the cover.

"Hey, Leo." He could hear me calling him, I could see it in his eyes. "Leo! Come on, sit up." He moved his eyes towards me and then his face to look at me.

"I'm tired, Joe." I smiled at him. He always said that.

I did not doubt that he was tired. He had been awake all night, standing with me on the edge of the alley, avoiding the eyes of the asking customers that wanted him. He had taken one customer, a guy I had chosen for him. I hadn't seen this guy before but he'd looked unsure as he had approached Leo. Leo had looked at me scared and uncertain and I had nodded to him to take the guy around back. The guy, the customer, was obviously new to this and I knew he wouldn't be too pushy about what he wanted, he wouldn't scare Leo…as much.

I had followed them, staying back so as not to disturb them but wanting to keep an eye. Leo had sucked him for a while and then the guy had leaned over and pushed his hands down Leo's trousers, gripping his arse. He had spoken to Leo, I couldn't hear what he had said but Leo had nodded and turned around on his knees and the guy had pulled his trousers down over his arse, crouched behind him and with only Leo's spit to ease the deed, tried to enter him. Leo didn't agree willingly, I knew. He never agreed. He nodded and he said the words because he wanted to be good for the customer but inside, he was scared and hated it.

I could hear Leo's pitiful cries as the guy tried to gain entry. Leo wasn't a natural bottom; he just didn't seem to be able to relax enough for it to become anywhere near enjoyable or acceptable. Luckily, the guy was so excited and turned on by it, he came quickly over his backside, saving Leo from enduring any more forceful attempts. The guy seemed unsure of what to do as he tidied himself and Leo, as always, just stayed as he was, slumped forward over his knees. The guy dropped some money on the floor and walked quickly away. I watched Leo for a moment as he sat back on his heels and then moved his hand to his arse and rubbed the soreness and wetness. I had walked over to him, picking up the pittance the guy had left and picked up a scrap of paper from the floor. Wiping the guy's cum as best I could, I pulled his trousers back over his arse and Leo, who was still distraught, leaned his head against my leg. I hadn't noticed his back even then, I hadn't been looking.

The guy had paid him a measly three quid and I called him all sorts of names in my head as I tried to soothe Leo. He was never very good at getting payment from his customers, he was always so traumatised afterwards, some even realised they could get away without paying at all and ran off before I could catch them. Last night we had sat for a while after, before going back to the end of the alley but Leo completely withdrew and waited like an impatient child for the night to be over with. At one point he had sat down and drawn imaginary drawings in the dirt to pass the time and ignore everyone. I, knowing that it was my last night with him, had wanted the night to go on for longer but a scuffle broke out between a few of the boys and some new boys vying for customers. Leo had gotten knocked to the ground, accidentally caught up in it, and I took him to the back of the alley before the night was over and we sat watching the sky for what I thought would be our last time together.

Now here we were. Not apart, but together. Nearly halfway through the day and he hadn't had a moment to sleep. I was used to it but Leo craved sleep like he craved food...and other things it seemed.

I patted his leg. "I know, but you can't sleep yet. Come on, sit up and I will take your shirt off." He looked out of it, stoned, which made me smile. He never moved. "Leo?" Now he looked agitated and unsure. "Come on, Leo, sit up. Your back will feel better without the shirt rubbing on it." He slowly pushed himself up and crossed his legs. I started to undo his boots. "Are you worried about where we are?" He nodded as I took one of his boots. "Layton has given us this room and this bed to stay in tonight." I pulled his foot from under him and took the other boot, watching him. "Did you say goodbye to Ginger?"

I wished I hadn't mentioned his name because I saw the anguish cross his face. I was a bit unsure whether I should draw him away from that feeling or continue. I had always soothed his thoughts, made him think of other things. I took hold of the bottom of his shirt and went to sweep it over his head while I tried to decide what to do but Leo pushed his hands onto mine then caught hold of the bottom of his t-shirt and held it down. I looked at him, the anguished look had gone, which I was pleased about but now he looked unsure. He looked unsure of me, which I had never seen before and it didn't feel good.

He looked down at my hand and then slowly moved his fingers to mine. I curled my fingers around his. There were always moments when Leo didn't speak much. Sometimes on the street, there wasn't much to say, and Leo always managed to convey to me his feelings without words. Moments when he would just walk away, or push his hand into mine without even looking at me or screw his face up and kick the rubbish. I knew what he was saying but that was when I thought I knew him, knew everything. I didn't know about this.

"Leo?" He never looked at me so I reached out with my other hand and touched his face drawing it up to look at me. "Doesn't it feel better without your shirt?" He shrugged and I thought that was all I was going to get but then he spoke.

"You don't like it, you don't like looking at it so I don't want you to see. I can wear my shirt, I don't mind how it feels. I don't want you to look."

Fuck. Had I made him feel that? Did he think that I would rather him sit there in pain rather than see his wounds? Was this what Kendal had been talking about? Was he trying to please me? Make this better for me? It was crazy.

While I was trying to work that through my head, he smiled at me and spoke again. "Now Ginger doesn't do it, it will all go away now, won't it? Then we can just forget it."

My thoughts couldn't keep up with him. Breathe, breathe. I smiled back at him. It wasn't a forced smile, he always made me smile when he smiled at me. I was still holding his face and I leaned forward and kissed his cheek, stroking my thumb across it. Brushing my lips to his face wasn't new, sometimes when he was distraught, usually after a customer, he would almost hide with me and I would do it then, almost as if I was stealing the touch when he wouldn't notice. I had wanted more, it just wasn't possible, not there.

I slowly let a breath out and then jumped as there was a sound of smashing plates in the house somewhere. I waited to see if it continued or if Leo was worried by it but it had seemed to pass him by so I carried on with what I was going to say. "We have a lot to talk about when we look at the sky tonight, don't we?" The thought made him smile, it always made him happy. "I said we would, didn't I? As soon as it gets dark, I said we would sit and look at the sky and the stars but we can't do that if you're not well, Leo." I could see his smile fade in confusion. "I was a little worried earlier about your back, about you too. I thought someone had hurt you and that made me a little angry, didn't it?" Leo looked at me confused and I smiled at him trying to make it better, make it okay.

I dropped my hand from his face and took hold of his other hand. "I like looking at you, I've always liked looking at you and now I know that these…things on your back are something you like to feel, it makes me feel different about them. It doesn't make me feel different about you though. I still want to look after you and keep you safe and well and make things better for you, do you understand?" He looked away. It wasn't unusual for Leo to not be able to look at me or hold my eyes for long. He did it with everyone and with the customers, he tried not to look at them at all. "I know that it will be better for you to not feel your shirt rubbing on your back, so let's take it off. I also want to make sure that you're not hurting but I don't know how to do that, so Kendal needs to come and look at them again for me."

Leo shook his head. "I don't want her to touch them again, I didn't like it."

I smiled at him. "No, I know. Let's do one thing first, let's take off your shirt so it feels better okay?" Leo nodded and held his hands up like a child would be undressed. I swept his shirt slowly up and over his head and threw it on the bed. "Good boy." My words got an immediate look from him and this time he held my eyes for a while. It made me smile. "That must feel better?" He half smiled and shrugged. I put my hand on his head and ruffled his bald head, smiling at him. "I know you're tired, and I know that there are lots of confusing things happening but I'm here with you and I'm not leaving, okay?" He nodded.

There was a knock at the door and as I turned, it opened slowly and Kendal stepped in. "Hello, boys."

Leo took my attention back by gripping my hands tightly. I turned and looked at him and he was shaking his head in panic. "No touching, no more bloody touching."

I had seen this panic when he had had enough of customers and didn't want to go back to the end of the alley and wait for more. I put one of my hands to his face.

"Hey, hey, Leo!" He was breathing heavily but he looked at me and then looked down. "Okay, okay, calm down. Just...sit here with me for a moment." He looked up at Kendal then to me and then back to Kendal before looking down again. I called his name again to draw his eyes back to me. "Leo! Kendal just wants to talk to me. Just sit here while we talk." I watched him a moment to see if he was going to flip out again but he sat quietly and looked down. I turned to look at Kendal. "He's had enough, can this wait? He's upset and confused, he's in a strange place..."

Kendal looked sympathetic but shook her head. "I know, Joe, I'm sorry, but it really can't." She moved closer and I felt Leo become unsettled again and I looked back at him.

"Hey, enough now, sit still."

Kendal moved to the end of the bed slowly and sat down. "Hey, poppet."

Leo moaned or growled, I couldn't decide, he didn't trust her not to touch him and he didn't want it. He looked at me and I could see he was ready to run. It was the same look that he had when he didn't quite know what to feel about things or know how to make it better. I was starting to see that Leo had relied on me a lot to make him feel better. In the alley, Leo had just been…Leo. The boy that I had always known, the one who struggled with life on the street more than the next person.

Looking at him now though, made me see that it wasn't the street life he struggled with, it was just life. His world around him, the people in it, it all held a danger to him which he kind of knew but didn't understand. He felt no safer here, within these walls, than he did out in the open under the sky. Usually, with others out of sight he would slowly feel better with me and settle down, but Kendal wasn't and couldn't go away. He needed medical attention and although I wanted some breathing space for him and me, it couldn't wait. I was no doctor but just looking at his back, I knew. How did you make it better for someone, when the thing that was making them uneasy wasn't going to go away? I looked at Kendal and then back to Leo who was still looking at me.

I smiled at him. "It's just Kendal. I know you like her." Leo shook his head which made me smile again. I looked at Kendal. "He's very tired. He knows you've come to make his back better but he just doesn't have the strength to deal with it at the moment."

Kendal nodded at me. "It's okay, Joe. Hey, poppet, can I hold your hand?" She held out her hand to Leo and Leo turned his face away. Kendal smiled. "Mm, you're not even going to let me sweet talk you, are you?" Leo scowled and shook his head making Kendal smile.

She didn't seem put out by his behaviour but I had no idea of how to move forward here. The only option I could see was to just force the treatment on him and I wasn't liking that idea.

Kendal smiled at me and patted my knee sensing my worry. "It's okay, Joe." She looked at Leo. "Are you tired, Leo? Would you just like to go to sleep for a while? I don't mind if you want to sleep." Kendal looked at me. "Sleeping would be good, Joe, don't you think?" Why was she asking me? And then I got it as she continued. "I think if Leo wants to sleep then that would be okay, be good, better for him?" She wanted to give him something to make him sleep. He could sleep through his treatment and be none the wiser.

I nodded to Kendal and then looked at Leo. "I think you will feel much better Leo after sleeping." I could see Kendal turn her back to us and fiddle about in her bag. "Lie down with me, Leo." I patted the pillow and Leo turned and looked at Kendal.

One thing Leo wasn't, was stupid, he knew something was going on. Honesty. Kendal had said that Layton was always honest with Isaac.

I pulled his face back to mine. "Look at me, Leo." He looked sad, unsure about taking his eyes from Kendal. "Kendal needs to finish looking after your back, but I know it hurts when she touches it. If you go to sleep, she can do it without you even knowing and when you wake up it will feel so much better." He looked panicked again and shook his head. "Hey. Look at me." He already was but I could see that he was fighting his need to just get away and his thoughts were elsewhere. "Kendal will give you one little scratch on your arm and you will fall asleep here with me. I want you to be better, Leo, so we can sit outside tonight and look at the sky." I saw a flicker of something in his eyes. "You want to look at the sky tonight don't you? With me, like we always do?"

He nodded and I watched him waiting. "If I go to sleep, can I come, Joe?"

I nodded. "If you go to sleep now, I promise I will take you outside when it gets dark. You have to let Kendal look at your back though while you're sleeping."

"What if it hurts and I wake up?"

I smiled at him. "It won't hurt, I promise, not while you're sleeping. You can think about nice things, like the stars and the moon and then tell me all about them when you wake up."

"I don't like sleeping on my own."

He started to get agitated again. "Hey, you won't be on your own. I will be here with you. I will watch out for you like I always do when you sleep. You know you don't have to worry. I won't let anyone near you. Just Kendal and me, just so she can make your back feel better." I saw him flick a look to Kendal and he scrunched his shoulders.

He was struggling to say yes. He wanted the moon and the stars but he was scared and I didn't blame him. He had been taken from his home and his friend, been stripped and poked, and made to share his secret, which he had hidden for so long from everyone. Now he sat with me and a relative stranger, who we were telling him was going to touch him when he went to sleep. Can't say I would have agreed either.

I could see it was all a little too much. I touched his face and stroked it with my fingers. "I know you're scared, Leo, I know this day has been so busy and confusing but we're here together. I'm not leaving you and I don't want you to go away. I want you to be well, feel better, I know you want that too. It can't be nice to feel your back all the time."

He shook his head. "Nah, I don't like it, not all the time."

I smiled at him. "Then go to sleep for me so Kendal and I can make it better." He stared at me like I was letting him down in some way and shook his head. I was fast losing his trust. I sighed heavily and looked down and absently spoke to Kendal. "You're only going to get one chance at this so be ready and…excuse the language."

From the corner of my eye, I saw Kendal give a silent thumbs up and nodded. I hated what I was about to do, no matter which way it went. My only thought was that at least it was honest.

I looked up at Leo annoyed. "Right, I've fucking had enough, Leo! Stop being such a fucking baby! You give me your arm now or I'm going to fucking make you. You know I will. Whenever I need you to bloody do something, when I need you to take a fucking customer, when I need you to be quiet and hide so people don't take you away… every time I have to get fucking riled up… don't I always do what's best for you?" His bottom lip was trembling, his tears already threatening. "Don't be such a fucking scared kid all the time, it's just a scratch."

"Joe?" I hated myself. It wasn't the first time I'd had this sort of rant at Leo but it was usually in life or death circumstances when I had to be firm with him, when I needed him to do as he was told to live another day.

I shook my head as I held out my hand. "Do it, Leo, or I'm just gonna go."

Slowly Leo lifted his arm out to me, he was shaking and I knew he was so scared. I also knew that he could change his mind in a second because that had happened a few times too, so I grabbed his wrist while I had the moment and held it tight as Kendal leaned forward and stuck the needle in his arm. He cried out, looking at it and tried to pull away but I held him firmly and grabbed his other hand that he was just about to use to grab at Kendal.

I changed my words, trying to soothe his journey into sleep. "Good boy, good boy… it's okay, it's just sleeping, Leo…" He looked at me and cried out but I could tell he was already feeling the effects of the drug as his moans got weaker. He tried to kick out but the action was more of a wiggle and as his body became heavy I leaned forward so he could fall on me.

"J…Joe?" He was so frightened. I tipped my head to his and looked into his eyes.

"I'm right here, Leo, I'm going to watch over you." I could feel his head getting heavy and he shook his head against the feeling that was taking him. "It's okay, it's just sleep, you can go to sleep." His eyes closed and I moved his head onto my shoulder to support his body against mine and stroked his head. "Good boy, it's just sleeping, Leo, count the stars for me." It made me smile as he mumbled.

"One..." He never said any more.

Kendal moved immediately onto the bed.

"Hang on, Joe." I was taking all his weight and between us, we moved him onto the bed onto his side. I sat looking at him and stroked his face.

"How long will he be out for?"

Kendal was placing his arms in front of him and taking the pillow from his head so he was lying flat on the bed. "Just a few hours. You were amazing, Joe."

I shook my head. "Yeah, well I feel like a shit… he was so scared. He's going to hate me."

Kendal reached out and touched my face. "He was, I know, but he'll feel so much better and he'll know it was because of you. You have a lot of sway over him, you just need to learn how to use it." She looked at his back. "This is better. I can do a whole lot more. I can give him his full check over, take blood, check his hole and the rest of his body."

I looked at Kendal. "Don't hurt him." It was silly to say it but in my head, I had a little voice telling me these people liked this sort of thing, liked pain.

Kendal smiled. "Of course not. Come on, help me get him out of his shorts." I undid his button and zip and Kendal pulled them down his legs while I eased their journey over his body. I rolled him onto his stomach and made sure he was comfortable. It was the first time I had seen him naked in a long while and I sat looking at his body, a little stunned.

Kendal moved from the bed. "I just need to get some things." I nodded and she left the room.

I leaned over him and whispered in his ear. "When did you change? You look fucking hot, I had no idea you had grown into such a sweet thing."

The last time I had seen him naked, he had been a young boy, shapeless and skinny. He was still skinny but he now had some tone about his body and soft masculine curves that made me want to touch them and I couldn't have avoided seeing his full-sized manhood hanging between his legs. Christ! When had he grown that! I smiled and without thinking, I swept my hand over his small round arse. I kind of felt a little sneaky, looking at him without him knowing but I needed the head start. I needed to get to know him better and I needed to do it quickly and things couldn't always go quickly with Leo. I bent and kissed his arse cheek and smiled to myself as I registered the stirring of my cock between my legs.

I shook the thoughts from my mind and looked at his back. I had the urge to touch his wounds but I didn't want to make them worse so I traced my fingers around the outside. Kendal came back in carrying some stuff, I snatched my hand away and sat back, looking at her questioningly about the equipment.

"I need to check his hole and I need him to be clean so I can check properly. It's kind of like a mobile cleaning kit." I winced and she smiled. "It's not very pleasant but he won't know about it while he's asleep. How do you boys keep yourself clean on the street?"

I grimaced and shook my head against the thought of it. "Ginger managed to tap into this cold water pipe and attach a hose that someone had kindly left in the alley. We use it for pretty much everything. The force of the water is really strong so with good aim you can get yourself kinda clean...hurts though, it's bloody cold." I touched my fingers to my mouth, to stop and remind myself to cut the language and looked apologetically at Kendal but she was busy. "I'm not sure Leo ever did it properly, he hated the cold water. I know Ginger used to take him under there sometimes and make him wash."

I smiled at the memory but it had been tough listening to Leo's squeals of upset and cries of 'No, don't make me.' Ginger didn't care. "Ginger hated that Leo never washed every day. Considering where we were and the way we live, Ginger was a bit of a hygiene freak. We had a toilet but with no flush but we used the water from the pipe to flush it. It wasn't very nice but it beat digging a hole. Sorry...if that offends you."

Kendal was busy setting up the machine she had and she smiled at me. "Please, Joe, I've seen... and heard way more stuff than you could ever imagine. You can't offend me so stop worrying. The slaves here have their bodies used in all sorts of manners, for pleasure and pain but also to humiliate them and degrade them. It can make my life as a medic a little difficult and...interesting but I can usually find a way." She looked at Leo. "If not, then I knock them out." She smiled at me. "This will be a little less traumatising for him."

I nodded agreeing. "Do you have to knock the slaves out to treat them then? Do they have a lot of... do they need a lot of medical attention?"

Kendal shook her head. "Actually. no. Rarely am I needed after a visit to a client but they get sick here like any other adults. Bugs, viruses, muscle strains and appendicitis to name a few. Occasionally, though rarely, has it ever been through mistreatment, but those are still too many. Even if it's just a sickness bug or flu, it can be hard to examine a slave as they are kept very sheltered. I can usually gain their trust though but some things, like this, can't wait."

I nodded as she gestured to Leo's back. "Can you show me how to look after him?"

She smiled. "Of course, let me just finish getting this ready." She was setting up bags and I turned and stroked Leo's face. He had never had so much attention. It was a shame he was too scared to appreciate it. "You can take the lint off his back."

I looked at Kendal as she spoke and then back to his back. I took hold of the lint and tape, taking it slowly from his skin. The cut under it, on his left shoulder blade, was the worst of the lot and made me wince.

Kendal joined me. "That one's going to need a stitch or two, just to hold it together for a few days, while it heals." She sat on the other side of him. "First thing, always wash your hands, especially with open wounds like this."

I left the bed, went to the bathroom and washed my hands thoroughly under the warm water. Warm water. I looked around the bathroom space as I wondered whether Leo would like to shower now that it was warm. I was getting way ahead of myself, thoughts churning, trying to work out what was happening here. I dried my hands and headed back to the bed and sat again beside him.

"I want to touch but I don't want to hurt him."

Kendal nodded. "Well, looking after his wounds means you will have to hurt him a little. Don't think of it as hurting him, it kind of creates a barrier that is hard to move past for both you and him. Not on this occasion, as he's sleeping and we have the luxury of just doing it but when he's awake, the aim is to gauge his pain while you touch him. It sounds silly but by watching him when you clean them, you can get a better idea of which ones are the ones that are bothering him. Sometimes, a papercut wound can cause more upset than a more prominent wound. If you watch him carefully, you'll get to know which ones are sore for him and you might catch an infection before it becomes a concern.

"Watch though, they can be a little sneaky and plead agony over a graze if they are really needy for attention." She smiled. "Your best gauge is when they have finished playing and you do their first aftercare. Their emotions will be raw and you will get a true picture of what each wound feels like to them. From then on, you will know the very sore ones to the not so sore ones and it will be harder for them to fool you. Anyways, the first thing is to have everything clean and as sterile as possible. Always use a clean cloth to bathe them. Even wounds that haven't broken the skin can feel like they have to them, so dab gently rather than wipe. You are soothing them and lessening the risk of any infection. These here..." Kendal pointed to marks on his back. "These are older wounds, not quite healed but they won't feel so bad to him. The pink lines you see are very old ones."

"Are they scars?"

Kendal sort of nodded. "Yes and no. Some of those will disappear completely, others may stay and scar. He will have no pain from them now." She pointed to another lot. "These are recent. These are like paper cuts, just on the surface of his skin, these will be sore but with care, they will heal quickly in a day or so. The newest ones you can see. They are deeper, angrier and they will be causing him a lot of pain. Most of them have started to knit together apart from this one, which I'm going to put a stitch in just to hold it together so it can start healing. If ever he has wounds like this you should call me."

I looked up at her and shook my head. "I would never do this."

Kendal smiled. "No, I know, but he may do it to himself or something similar. Also, a wrong touch with a whip can have the skin peeling like a banana skin, it can happen to even the most skilled Dominant." Shit. A whip? Hell, I had a hard time just saying no to Leo and hurting him with that! Kendal half laughed at my confusion. "You'll be surprised what you will do for him when he wants it. Don't worry, Layton will help you." I gave a very false smile. "Right here, you clean these up and then you can dry his back and put this ointment on. It seals them off from getting dirty and helps soothe their soreness.

"We do have some numbing cream but we don't use it unless we have to. If there's an issue with the healing, then feeling it is going to be our first sign that something isn't right."

She handed me a cloth and I dabbed at his back avoiding the larger one on his shoulder. Kendal guided me, encouraging me to be firmer while I grimaced and winced. With Leo asleep, she was all I had to teach me about how firm I should be with them.

"He will feel these and he will moan, wriggle, and squirm and he may strop a little. He'll request that you don't touch but you have to remember this is for his own good. He will soon accept that this cleaning is part of his need, as he will accept that cleansing his hole before play is part of it too. No one here will punish him like this so don't be surprised in the future if he asks you to touch them and make him feel them. If the play was good and took him to good places, he will want to revisit it in his mind, remind himself.

"Likewise you can ask him to show you how they make him feel. Do not be afraid of his wounds, they mean something different to him and when you start to play with him, you will have a better understanding and they will mean something different to you too. The more accepting you are of them, the more open he will be to you. Encourage him to look at them in the mirror and touch them, if he wants to, and watch him while he does it. It is just encouraging him to explore and understand his need and not be afraid of it. Isaac loves his wounds, he likes feeling them and looking at them but he has been taught to embrace it and freely shows those who understand what they mean to him. With your help, Leo will learn that it is not a bad thing."

I took the towel and dabbed at his skin to dry it. "When you look at them, do you think they are a good thing?" She spoke like they were special…or something.

Kendal smiled. "I see a very strong and powerful need. I don't punish or play with slaves and have no need that makes me want to do that. I know that what Layton and Julian see when they look at them is different. They understand it and can admire it as something beautiful." She smiled at me. "Leo wanted these, not this pain he's in now with them but at the time he wanted to feel these, as they were given to him. This is what makes Leo who he is, the person you love wants to feel this. You need to look at it like that to see its beauty until you understand more.

"This has been part of Leo for a long time, you couldn't see them, you didn't know but you still loved him. Leo will eventually show you what it means to him, once he understands he doesn't have to hide it here. This desire and need is something natural, he doesn't think about it or rule it in any way and sometimes when he feels it, it's going to be more important than eating or drinking. The need for it is that strong. He's still there though, Leo the boy you love, it just sometimes gets harder to see him but he'll need you to catch him at the other end."

Catch him. Right.

I didn't have a chance to think about that further as Kendal offered me a tube of ointment.

"Squeeze a little on your fingers and rub each wound gently, don't rush, this is nice and soothing and a chance for you to get to know his wounds a little, feel the bumps and the scarring tissue so you get to know them. I'm going to start to clean this one."

I nodded and started to spread the ointment on his back. I kind of got lost in them, touching each one over and over, feeling it under my fingers, feeling his body under my touch. By the time I had worked my way up to the top of his back, Kendal had stitched him and was covering it with a new piece of gauze.

I held out the tube for her. "No, keep it here, you can put it on every day. It will be good bonding time for you both." Kendal slipped from the bed and started fiddling with tubes.

"Are they going where I think they are?"

She looked sorry. "Yes."

"Jesus, shit…"

"It's not pleasant, Joe, I know but I'm not sure when I will get this opportunity again to do his full arrival checks."

I stroked my hand over his head. "Arrival checks?"

She nodded. "Everyone in this world has to have a medical check done annually and upon arrival. I will need to do yours when I've finished his." Oh shit.

I looked at the tubes and then at Kendal. "Them?"

She shook her head. "No, you can cleanse. I'm sorry, Joe, it's a rule, it keeps this world safe. It has to be done."

I nodded and looked at Leo. "God, he would be mortified. Will he know?"

She shook her head. "No. He may have an urgent need to empty when he wakes but it will just be any water that is left over."

I nodded. "Then what happens when he's clean?"

"I will open him up a little, have a look, check his prostate, check his skin around his hole. I'll check his cock, get a sample of semen, check his testicles. They are just basic checks, oh and take blood."

"Do all slaves have these?" She nodded. "And you have to put them to sleep?"

She smiled and shook her head. "No, not unless it's absolutely necessary. The slaves do what their Keeper requests of them and although it's not very nice they will let me. Some take a little more patience and a little time… If you need a break, Joe? It's a lot to take in."

I shook my head. "I want to stay with him, be here for him." She nodded.

She climbed on the bed and lubricated the tubes and pipes. I turned away and stroked his face. Fuck, I was glad he was asleep, I wouldn't have been able to explain all this to him. I heard a machine and turned to look, watching the first lot of water being gently pumped into his body. I turned and looked at him suddenly, feeling completely overwhelmed. I wanted to stay for him but it was a little more than I was ready for. He still looked worried even though he was sleeping.

"Joe?" I looked at her. "Go and have a break, make a tea. This is a lot, it isn't nice, I know." I looked at him and felt upset. Is this what his life was going to be like now? I wiped my hand across my face. Kendal came and put her arm around me. "Joe?"

I shook my head. "I don't want this for him."

"Joe, no. It's not going to be like this. I didn't mean to scare you. This is just a one-time thing, I promise. Go and take a break. I'll watch him."

I nodded a little overcome with everything. I didn't want Kendal to see me crying.

I stepped from her and leaned down and kissed Leo's face. "I'm just going to make tea, Leo..." I turned and left as the machine started to change the tone. Whatever it had filled him with, it was now sucking from him; I didn't want to think about it.

CHAPTER FOUR

JOE

I sat in the kitchen for a while and cried quietly. I never cried. In six years, I couldn't remember when I had cried. There had been moments when I had to fight back tears, of course. When Leo had returned to the alley looking a beaten mess, when Ginger had saved Leo from near death at the hands of a customer, when Leo had got fucked the very first time by a customer and had cried out my name, and then today, stepping to get in the car to leave him. I'd won all those battles. I wasn't winning this one and gave up trying, crying harder, covering my face with my hands, to hide, to muffle the sound…both those reasons or not any of them. I didn't know.

Luckily, the kitchen had been empty when I got here and I was alone. By the time I had settled myself, I couldn't decide what I was crying about. Was it over Leo or me? Was it this moment we seemed to be in or the whole God damn life we had been dealt? Six years of street living or Leo's…need? So many things, I couldn't decide and then that made me smile at the whole crazy situation. I was wiping my face when Peter walked in.

"Hey, Joe, everything okay?"

I nodded trying to pull myself together. "Yeah, I…I just came for a break." Peter did a double look and if he knew I had been crying, he chose to ignore it, for which I was grateful.

He smiled, walked over to the counter and started to boil the kettle. "Mm, me too." A movement at the door caught my eye, and I turned and watched as Isaac stepped inside the door and then sank to the floor, curled up inside a blanket. He looked like he was naked and not very happy.

"You've been followed."

Peter turned around and looked at Isaac, who then dropped his face from him as if he didn't want Peter to look at him. Peter turned and continued to make the tea. I wasn't sure what was going on but Isaac was being very different from earlier and I continued to watch him.

He lifted his face and poked his tongue out at me. "Charming."

Peter turned around. "What?"

I turned to him and smiled. "Oh, nothing. I'll go and leave you both." I seemed to be intruding.

Peter looked at me. "No, stay. You said you came for a break. Ignore Isaac. He's unsure about his place with me at the moment, he doesn't much like me and he's trying to figure it all out. The fact that he wants to be in the same room is progress, despite how it may look. Stay and have tea with me, we actually have a lot in common."

I looked at him questioningly and he smiled, turned and collected the cups, giving one to me and then taking one to Isaac. He put the cup on the floor and then touched Isaac's head with his hand. "Behave and you can stay." Peter walked back and sat at the table with me.

"What do you mean?"

Peter sipped his tea before answering. "You and I are learning the same things. What it's like to love a submissive with a natural need for pain." He made it sound so normal but then he lived in this world. I supposed it was for him, normal.

"You already know, don't you? Know about this need? Understand it?"

Peter nodded. "I know about it. I have lived here for a while and have seen it, a lot, but I've never tried to understand it, I've never needed to understand it. I just accepted it. It's different though when you become involved with one that has this need. It means you can no longer stand on the outside and watch, emotionless, while it is given and taken. You have to start accepting not only what it means and feels like to them but what it feels like to you."

Yes, I was getting that. At the moment I couldn't decide what it felt like. "What does it feel like to you?"

Peter smiled. "I'm still working on that bit. I'm trying to learn what it means to him, to see the places it takes him, then I'm hoping my feelings will become a lot clearer to me."

Maybe he was right, maybe we were alike.

Thinking about them earlier, how Isaac had clung to him in the café, they had looked comfy. "You and Isaac are settled though, aren't you? You seemed settled."

Peter half laughed. "Isaac is my first male love, usually I go for the ladies...still do, they still do it for me, get my blood boiling, my heart beating, my cock hard. Isaac is the first man to ever give me those feelings, it's still a little new to me."

I nodded, although Kendal told me earlier, I was still a little shocked over that. "That must be a little strange? I mean not to me, I've always batted for the other team, always known. I don't think I could love a woman though, not like that."

Peter nodded. "The feelings came naturally, it was when I realised I had those feelings that it became a little strange. Isaac makes it very easy to love him though, it doesn't feel so strange when I'm with him, it feels right, he makes it feel right. I'm hoping that he is going to make me feel that way about everything, loving him while seeing to his need. Our relationship has become a little unbalanced and Isaac brought that to my attention today with the help of Layton."

"What do you mean?"

Peter smiled, briefly looking at Isaac, although the look was full of love. "I haven't been aware of Isaac's needs and it's made him uncomfortable and unsure about what he means to me. Being with him was so new to me that I forgot that he needs more than just love when he feels unsure or when he gets into trouble. He needs boundaries and rules to help make his place clear, and there have to be consequences to him breaking those or again, the place becomes unclear. It allows him to think too freely and he can't deal with the thoughts and feelings.

"They have to be kept in check so he is very sure of his place. With Isaac not being a slave though, Layton balances his needs and his wants with a little freedom so he can feel part of the world without actually trying too hard. I allowed him too much freedom and it made him unsure of his place with me. I'm trying to put it right quickly and it has come as a bit of a shock."

I frowned. "I don't suppose this has something to do with the sound of breaking plates I heard earlier?"

Peter smiled and nodded. "Mm, Isaac kicked out, well his version. He doesn't do it very often because he's been taught to verbalise his emotions but sometimes they get the better of him. Because we're new to each other, I just wanted to love him and I gave my love so easily. He stopped working for it and thought he could just have it, all of it without trying to earn it or giving anything back. It became a given to him, well, that's what he thought. When I tried to share it with another person, he threw a jealous tantrum. If I had loved him like he needs to be loved, he wouldn't have felt so threatened because he would have been sure of me, sure of his place, and so here we are." Peter looked over at Isaac and got up and went to him.

He crouched down in front of him, touched his legs and feet, then his hands and then got up, went to a tall cupboard in the room, and pulled out another blanket. He shook it out, went back to Isaac and wrapped it over him, on top of the other blanket and then came back to the table. He seemed so sure of what he was doing.

I would never have even noticed that Isaac was cold. "You seem to know a lot though, you seem like you know what you're doing. I haven't got a clue."

Peter smiled at me. "You'll learn. Layton will teach you a lot. He has taught me about Isaac, he's known him a long time so he understands so much about him, his mind. Isaac and I are still learning about each other. You've loved Leo a long time, you know him really well, it won't take you long to get to grips with the way his mind works."

I shook my head. "I thought I knew him, but I didn't, not really."

Peter nodded. "You do, you have been looking after all his needs, save one. He already has a place with you. You just have to make him more sure of it as you both learn about his need. You kind of have a head start on me." Peter smiled at me and I smiled back but I didn't feel as confident. "Leo will teach you too, if he sees a weakness, he'll snap at it. He'll try to get his way and cause you trouble as Isaac has done." He sort of chuckled. It was hard for me to see the…fun in what happened here.

"Isn't it wrong to keep their minds too tightly bound? Surely if they want to be free..."

Peter shook his head. "They want it, they want to be free like everyone else, they do, but it's kind of like they don't quite know what to do with it once they've got it. It's too much for them, opens up too many choices and becomes too big, the world is too hard for them." Well, that was true and not just for Leo. "Take Leo's back, you've only got to look at that and know it's not safe for them to have their way, to have too much freedom. They don't make very good decisions and certainly not safe ones when it comes to wanting things because they are led by this need in them to want to feel more.

"The people that come here to be slaves understand that, that's why they are willing to give up their lives to others because they know it's safer. It doesn't stop them from asking for their will to be done but they know that here, it will not be given to them, no matter what they do. They will always be safe and have their need seen to safely. Isaac may not like what's going on right now but he will be a lot happier and settled once his place is secure...I think." Peter half laughed "How is Leo doing anyway?"

I shrugged. I wasn't sure. "Kendal knocked him out, he wouldn't let her touch him and she said it would be better for him. She's just stitched one of his cuts, and now she's giving him a thorough check. Once he was asleep, she said to come and sit here for a minute to have a break. I was a bit... overwhelmed with the checks. She's nice and good with Leo, patient." She felt normal, out of everyone who I met here, almost out of place. I sort of skimmed the actual act that Leo was having inflicted on him, he would be mortified and I hadn't wanted Peter to know what was being done to him.

Peter nodded. "The checks are not the nicest welcome to our world. He'll be okay. You won't find a better doctor who understands as she does." Peter looked at Isaac. He had moved a little closer to the table, although I hadn't noticed him move at all. Peter smiled at him and then looked back at me. "What about you? How are you doing?"

I half smiled and shook my head. "Really, I don't know. I'm just trying to take it all in and process. Leo's pretty distraught about leaving Ginger and the alley and I'm not sure how to deal with that. Usually, when he gets upset I ignore it and try to make him forget but I promised him I wouldn't forget Ginger and the alley."

Peter nodded. "I think you should do the same thing. You're not asking him to leave the memory of them, just the feeling that he's in. Once he moves on from that feeling then you can talk about them without him becoming upset. If he gets upset then move the subject on, he will soon learn that if he wants to have them as a memory then he has to stay in the moment with you. Layton will be able to guide you better but try and watch him, so you can learn. They are pretty fascinating to watch because they show their feelings so openly. Once you begin to understand them, you will see that what they say doesn't always match what they're actually feeling. I think that's why a lot of Dominants forbid their subs to speak, they can get a clearer understanding of where their mind is and look after them better." Leo often didn't speak. I just thought that was Leo.

I looked at Isaac fleetingly then back to Peter. "Is that what you're doing?"

"Kind of. Isaac, as I said, is a little different. Slaves live in their own world, cocooned from things that have no bearing on their needs. Their world is their Keeper, who sees to their every need, beyond that they don't need anything else. Isaac's world is a little bigger and to live in it he has to learn a few life skills but he still needs the security of being restricted. If you put a slave in a cage they will feel safe and secure, it becomes their space, their world. When they are taken from it, they feel vulnerable. Isaac still needs the cage to feel secure, he just has a bigger one. The bigger space allows him to feel part of the world that Layton lives in but still with the security that he requires. He is allowed a certain amount of freedom within his space, which allows him to interact with Layton and others but sometimes even that can be too much for his mind to understand.

"Layton understands Isaac so well that he knows when to make his cage smaller or a little bigger depending on what Isaac is feeling. The street visit made Isaac's space very big and that's okay because he can deal with that for a while but then he starts to get lost in it. I, and Isaac, have always allowed Layton to control his space but today when we got back here, Layton was busy with Leo. Isaac needed it closed, he needed his world made smaller so he could breathe and feel safe but I didn't notice because I had never controlled it or Isaac like that.

"What I had been doing, was leaving the door open and letting Isaac lead while I followed. That was okay while we were very new but now I think we reached a point in our relationship where Isaac became unsure of where we were going and what we're doing. He showed his insecurities very clearly when he didn't have my undivided attention. Layton put him back in the 'cage' and closed the door immediately to stop him from getting lost. But it has shown me that I now have to start taking control of it. So that's what I'm doing. I have just squeezed his space very tight and he didn't like it because me controlling it is new to him. I have never asked anything of him before. I have released it a little to give him time to breathe and think about it before I squeeze it again."

"Wouldn't it be better just to keep him there, if it's confusing?"

Peter nodded. "If he was a slave he would be taught to stay in it and accept his boundaries but because Isaac lives more freely in our world, he has to learn to give up his control when asked but be allowed to come back from it to have the freedom he likes. Giving him time to breathe and think about it shows him that I don't want him to stay there, stay permanently submissive, I just want him to go there when I request it, when I want to see his subservience to me. His breathing space will be the time he can speak freely and ask for comfort and share his thoughts with me, but at the moment, he's unsure of what to think or feel about me, so he's not going to share. He's not as unsure as I thought he would be though, I didn't think he would follow me, I thought he was just going to sulk. It gives me some hope that this isn't going to take very long for him to understand that when he's with me, his world is just as secure as when he's with Layton. Something that I hadn't been showing him before."

"Is it acceptable for Isaac to love both you and Layton?"

Peter laughed. "It is to Isaac. Isaac's need and sexual drive demand a lot from him, physically and mentally. He fuels it with attention, love, and comfort, getting those things allows him to sleep peacefully and regain his strength. If he had to get all those things from one person alone, forever, he wouldn't be as fulfilled as he is and the person giving it would be extremely worn down. He has another love, too, his name is Marcus. He doesn't see him very often, not like he sees me because Marcus has to work away a lot." Blimey. A three-way relationship.

"Three of you? And you all control him? He's submissive to all of you?"

Peter smiled. "Isaac's main love and the one with the most control is Layton. Layton owns him."

Jesus, I couldn't believe I was talking about people being owned. It was so far from street life as you could possibly get. Isaac had called him Master…

"His Master? He called him that."

Peter nodded. "Isaac has had some problems here, traumas that he's struggled with and Layton was the one who cared for him while he was healing. Isaac would submit to him above anyone else, without question or thought. He has guided Isaac through some bad and difficult times and has earned Isaac's unconditional love and trust. Having him as a Master is a big thing to Isaac. It means he will never go back to the vanilla world, that he always has a place here wherever he is or whoever he's with. If Isaac has any worries or uncertainties then Layton, his Master, is his safe place until things are worked out." Isaac had now made his way completely over to him and was sitting, leaning against a chair beside him.

Peter reached out a hand and stroked his head. "Isaac and I are working towards that trust level. He needs to feel that sort of security with me or he will always demand Layton whenever he feels unsure. He has to learn that I'm no less important, that I can help him and he can trust me in the same way. I don't do things for him yet that Layton does, so it's going to take time but today is the beginning of that. Marcus...he doesn't control him and he doesn't request that Isaac is submissive. Their friendship is based on...hmm, I'm not sure what. Love, need, an understanding of each other? They were originally client and slave but formed a bond that neither of them was prepared to break. Marcus has a foot fetish and Isaac willingly gives him his feet to punish and worship but their relationship goes beyond that, deeper."

Foot fetish? Fucking hell. I felt like Alice in fucking wonderland! I had to contain a feeling of hysteria that was threatening to come out of my mouth.

I rubbed my hand over my mouth and pinched my bottom lip. "If Marcus doesn't control him or request his subservience isn't Isaac going to get into trouble with him at some point?"

Peter shook his head then swigged the last of his tea before answering. "Marcus understands that it's natural for Isaac to be submissive and while he doesn't request it of him other than when they play, he will ask it of him momentarily, to keep him safe. Isaac can have freedom for a while, like I said earlier, when he returns to Layton he has his peace again. We all love Isaac very much, nothing comes above his safety, not his needs or ours.

"I know that loving three people sounds strange to you but it's not strange to Isaac. Each relationship is different to him, special and that's how he makes you feel. You have to understand that if you love Isaac, because he likes to talk about his other loves. He will talk about Layton and Marcus as easily as he talks about the food he likes and he doesn't do it to cause any bad feeling, that sort of thought would never enter his mind. Isaac has helped me a lot with my understanding about loving him, loving a man. If it feels right, good, then Isaac sees no bad in it."

"What about the three of you though, your feelings about each other? Surely there must be some awkward feelings when you are all together?"

Peter shrugged. "The three of us are rarely together, maybe fleetingly. For Marcus and I, our paths rarely cross and when Marcus collects Isaac, he doesn't stay around very long. Since meeting Isaac though, Layton and I spend a lot of time together but I never feel jealous of him or awkward. When we are together with Isaac, Isaac will follow his feelings and slip from one to the other, enjoying the attention he gets from both of us but if he is unsure he will be drawn to Layton because to Isaac, Layton is the stronger Dominant. I'm not sure what will happen as I become more confident with my control of him. It will probably be agreed that Layton will take the lead control as that is what Isaac is most comfortable with. We all love him."

"Doesn't that make you feel...second best?"

Peter smiled. "Layton never makes me feel like that, kind of the opposite actually, he makes me feel very important to him." There was a knock at the front door which made me jump. Peter stood and put out his hand to me, gesturing me not to be agitated and then touched Isaac's head. "Stay here with Joe, I will be back in a moment."

I turned and watched him leave the kitchen, then, Isaac moved from where he had been sitting towards the door. I thought he was going to follow so I quickly stood and then stopped when he just sat next to the door. He looked worried, nothing like the Isaac I had met in the alley. Was it because Layton wasn't here? I walked over to him and crouched down and he held the blanket tighter to him. I didn't know much about Isaac but I remembered he liked to hold hands so I held my hand out to him.

"It's okay, Isaac, he's coming back. You can hold my hand?" He moaned, which made me a little confused and I was glad when Peter spoke.

"Don't try and be friends with him."

I took my hand back. "I thought...I thought I could help him."

Peter smiled and walked towards us and touched his hand over Isaac's head. "He's not ready to be...helped and he doesn't know you so he wouldn't ask you. When he met you in your world, you were sure of yourself and a little bolshie, he wouldn't have been afraid of you, more drawn to you, especially as Layton was giving you the okay. Now in his world, he knows you are unsure. He can feel it and knows that you can't keep him safe. He's a little confused at the moment, about what I want from him but when he stops fighting against me and accepts my control, he will feel more secure about asking me to have him." Peter looked at him. "Right Isaac, back to work. Your toybox has arrived." Peter turned and looked at me. "If you need me, knock on the door and go back to your room and wait, so Leo is not left alone. I will come as soon as I can.

"Hopefully, Isaac will be more settled and want to make friends with you tomorrow. Can you also tell Kendal that we will eat later?" I nodded as Peter turned back to Isaac, took hold under his arm, and pulled him. "Come on, back to your room."

They left and I stayed where I was, crouched by the door, then I just sat back on the floor. Toybox? I bit my lip and shook my head. This place was strange, but I felt safe here. Even sitting alone in this strange kitchen felt safe. I looked around. I couldn't remember the last time I had been in a kitchen and certainly not one as big as this. It suddenly felt very closed in and claustrophobic and I got up and headed outside.

I let the door shut behind me and took a deep breath, enjoying the fresh air. I had no idea what time it was but the sun was pretty high in the sky, so I guessed early afternoon. Time meant nothing on the street, there was nothing to do that was time-bound so who cared? It just mattered when the day ended and the night came, because that's when the vanillas stepped into our world looking for their escape, their pleasure, their fix, or whatever it was they wanted so badly that they were prepared to pay for it from the street trash.

I looked around. The porch was long and wide and had a couple of seats along the side of the house and a few steps down into the garden. I walked forward, sat on the top step and dug out my cigarettes from my jeans pocket. Two left. Not hours ago that would have bothered me, now it seemed unimportant. I took one out, lit it, and took a long hard drag on it. Fuck it felt good. I didn't want to think about Leo and what was being done to him but the image of him lying on the bed naked kept seeping into my thoughts. I shook my head trying to move it. Was this the right place to bring him? He was just a street boy, he knew nothing about living. He didn't even know how to interact with people. He just knew me and Ginger, and although he was comfortable with the other boys in the alley, he rarely spoke to them. The only other person I knew he spoke to was Mikey, Manni's son and that, I was sure, was only because Mikey fed him a lot.

Beyond those people, his life was just one struggle after another. Having customers, being hungry, running out of toothpaste, he hated it. He dreaded the night coming, I knew. Sitting with me and looking at the sky was the only good he found in the darkness and that's why he clung to it so much, why it was so important to him. Would it be better to take him back to the street? Not the alley, we couldn't go back there. My time there had come to an end and Leo couldn't be near Ginger. No, somewhere else, another street, somewhere we could find our own place. Where people didn't want to touch him and do things to him that he wouldn't understand. I shook my head. That I didn't understand.

Kendal was not a bad person, she would never willingly hurt him that I knew. She was trying to help him, trying to make him feel better. I had just never seen such things done to another person. She was caring for him, far better than I ever could. He had this thing, this need that they all seemed to understand, maybe he was in the right place, a place that understood him. Maybe he would be better off here without me? They could look after him, give him everything he needed, keep him safe from people and himself.

I nodded. I needed to walk away, now, while he was sleeping. He'd be upset but it seemed the most sensible thing for him and me. I knew nothing of this need he had, I couldn't help him. I dragged on the last of my cigarette, dropped it to the floor and then stood on it, stuffing the box back into my pocket. My head was right. It was the most sensible and easiest thing, walk away, walk away and leave him here. They could help him far more than I could.

The image of the boy I loved, lying naked and alone on the bed, flooded my thoughts. Fuck it! Hell. It was the sensible thing to do but I had never listened to my head where Leo was concerned. I turned and walked back into the house.

CHAPTER FIVE

JOE

I went straight in when I reached the bedroom door. I didn't know what to expect when I walked in but whatever Leo was having done, I would deal with it with him. My momentary thought of leaving him again had made my insides hurt. Nothing, I decided, was worse than that. I was a little surprised at what met me. Kendal was sitting cross-legged on the bed with Leo's head in her lap. She was stroking him with a cloth, bathing his face.

She looked up and smiled. "Are you feeling better?" I nodded and looked at Leo. "He's okay, Joe. I've just given him a good wash. I was just cleaning his face up and chatting to him. Are you okay? You looked...did you think I was going to hurt him?"

I shook my head then shrugged. "You're a doctor, I thought you were just going to do doctor things. When I left the room..."

"I'm sorry, Joe. I have learned to work quickly to do the things I need to do. Sometimes I have to put the doctor things first, but I never forget them, despite what it may have looked like. With Leo sleeping, it makes it easier on me but I never forget who they are." She looked at Leo, stroked her fingers over his face and smiled. "I think he looks a little more settled." I looked at Leo again and it was true, he didn't look so worried. How could someone show their feelings, even in sleep? Kendal looked at me. "While I was washing his feet, I found a small cut, it's okay but I thought I would let you know. I've cleaned it up."

I shook my head. I should have checked him after he had walked without his boots in that alley. "He never said...I didn't think to look. I should have done, I would have done had we been home. I always checked his feet when he didn't wear his boots." I shook my head again. I needed to get my shit together.

"It's okay, Joe. It's a big change for both of you. With what Leo's dealing with, I doubt the cut even registered. Washing him gave me a chance to soothe him and work at the same time." She smiled at me.

"Do you do that for the slaves? Be nice to them?"

She dried Leo's face with the towel and then just stroked him with her fingers. "I try to, with the time that I'm there but they just want to be with their Keepers. I'm a little in love with Leo." Well, this day just kept on giving.

I looked at Kendal wide-eyed. "You love him?"

Kendal half laughed. "Don't panic, Joe. I'm mean, I am a little taken with him." I moved into the room. "Can you pull the blanket over him, he's feeling chilly." I looked at the bottom of the bed and there was a folded blanket. I pulled it out and swept it across his body, laying it carefully over his back. Kendal patted the bed and I sat.

"Is Leo just like one of the others?"

Kendal smiled. "They're all different, they all feel different. They're all beautiful but I sometimes feel more connected to some." She sighed. "I'm a little tired and needy, so pay no attention."

"Needy?" I tried to keep the panic out of my voice but Kendal smiled so I guessed I failed.

"I'm not about to start falling at your feet and asking you to punish me." She laughed which lightened my worry a little. "I'm just feeling a little in need of some one-on-one attention. It makes me a little…vulnerable to feelings, theirs and mine."

I smiled in understanding, although I didn't understand at all. "You seem pretty...normal. I'm sorry if that's not the right word."

Kendal smiled. "Mm, probably best not to use that in front of the guys. They will have you sitting there all night demanding your opinion of 'normal'." Okay, that didn't sound fun, I would have to remember that. Kendal laughed. "Oh Joe, I'm kidding. They do like a good discussion though. By normal you mean balanced?" I nodded. I would have to remember that. Not normal, balanced. "I've lived with my need for a long time and have managed, with the help of friends, to find a way of living with it. It doesn't control me like Isaac's or clearly, Leo's does to him."

"So you control it?"

Kendal shook her head. "No, I don't think control is what I do. I live with it. I can feel it but it's not a strong feeling so I can move it from my thoughts, most times. Sometimes the balance sways a little to one side for a while and I can't ignore it. I think Leo has made it sway a little." She smiled at me. "I don't know why some make me feel it more than others. I see a lot of subs."

"So…do you have a Keeper then?"

Kendal smiled. "I suppose I do, of sorts. He's a friend, more than a friend. He's someone who's always allowed me to be honest about my feelings, good or bad and he's always straight and honest with me." Kendal smiled. "It's not always a quiet relationship. I'm very opinionated, as is he." I smiled back at her and then looked at Leo.

"So, can he hear you? You said you were chatting to him." Kendal looked down at him.

"I like to think so. You never know. I was just telling him how beautiful he was and how good he had been and that it was over. Touching them when they sleep is still unsettling for them, I just wanted to soothe his sleep." As if he knew we were talking about him, Leo turned onto his side and pulled his legs up. I was a little surprised. I thought he was fast asleep. I looked at Kendal. She shook her head. "Don't worry, he's just slowly drifting from drugged sleeping to more natural sleep. He'll wake when he's ready."

I reached out and pulled the blanket over his toes.

"Did you know today was the first time I have seen him naked in nearly two years? He's…changed."

Kendal looked confused. "No, I didn't...I thought you both...I'm sorry, Joe. I didn't realise and then you saw me pulling him about. I didn't realise how new this all was to you, how new he was to you. I thought it was just his need."

I shook my head and smiled. "I think I would have noticed it if he was sleeping with me. I thought he preferred Ginger but then he used to come to me so easily as if he had never slept with Ginger at night. It was a little confusing. He used to make me forget though, forget that he went to Ginger at night. He would look at me and make me feel...important, loved, I'm not sure but he made me feel something. Then every day it would hurt again to see him reach out to Ginger, follow him. Even when Ginger was mean to him. I hate that I thought this, but… sometimes I wanted Ginger to be mean to him so he would come and find me. I didn't mind being used; I just liked being with him."

Kendal smiled sympathetically. "He wasn't using you. If anything he was using Ginger. He shared nothing more with Ginger than his need, he shared everything else with you. I find it amusing that you have a little mean streak."

I looked at her and smiled. "Don't tell him."

Kendal tipped her head and looked at me. "I thought you were going down the road of honesty? You were honest about the needle and sleeping."

I nodded. "Yes, but I'm not sure where my honesty has got me yet."

"Meaning?"

I half-smiled. "I didn't like where my honesty took him. I couldn't stay in the room, stay with him. I kind of feel like it was false. I haven't had time to talk to Leo about anything yet. I'm not sure what he's prepared to tell me, how honest he's prepared to be with me. I want to know what the things that have happened today mean to him. I have never thought about whether I was being honest with him or not. I just said things to him to make him feel better or make him quiet. I don't want things to change between us, I know they will. Just knowing what I know now changes things but I still want us to be friends. If being honest spoils that then I don't want to be honest."

"If you lie, then isn't that making your relationship false?"

"I'm not ready to accept that everything we've shared was false. I've never thought about whether I was lying to him either. I don't intend to lie to him, I've just always moved him forward, however I could, now I'm having to think about it." I smiled at her. "I just want to say nothing and let him do all the talking but that's not going to happen. Leo can sit happily for hours without saying a word."

Kendal smiled. "That's his honesty." I looked at her, questioning her. "Subs are not very good at expressing themselves verbally and if you try and force them to, they will probably say things to make you quiet, say things they think you want to hear to please you."

I shook my head. "Isaac speaks perfectly well? He says honest things." I had seen and heard Isaac speak well. Did Leo say things to appease me? I wasn't sure Leo thought things through like that.

"Isaac speaks what's in his head, what he feels at that moment and to people he's sure of, he knows. You can't compare Leo and Isaac. Isaac has been made to feel very secure with his need, his submissive nature, and his life. He has been given the freedom of speech but Layton still watches him to gauge his true feelings. When Leo sits with you for a few hours and says nothing, he's actually telling you something very loud and clear."

"What? That I'm boring him?"

Kendal smiled. "That he's content in your company. Your honesty about the needle and sleeping will do exactly what you said it would. It will make him feel better. Soon you'll be able to make him feel better without him sleeping and he will let you do those things because he trusts you and your honesty with him. He will always be honest with you, it just may not always be in words." Kendal sighed. "You must find your own way of understanding him, I know that. I'm just trying to help."

"Thank you." I smiled at her. "I'm not trying to be difficult if that's how it seems. Don't stop helping." We sat for a moment in silence and then I remembered what Peter had said. "Peter was in the kitchen when I had my break. I think something is going on with him and Isaac. He says to tell you that they will eat later?"

Kendal nodded. "That means he doesn't want me knocking at the door." She smiled. "The stew will stay warm in the oven. You lot can help yourselves when you're ready." It sounded like she was going.

"Are you leaving?" Please say no.

She shook her head. "Not if you don't want me to? I was going to stay the night but feel a little exhausted so I thought I would go and see Julian and Jacob. I need to do your checks first but I will be back tomorrow, first thing. If you're still unsure, Joe, I can stay if you want to talk more?"

She looked tired, more than tired.

"I feel better when you're here but I think I'm just stalling. I'm scared Kendal, scared of being alone with him, which is so stupid because I've been alone with him for four years. Peter said that he and I were alike, on the same kind of journey, learning what it's like to love someone with a need like theirs but I watched him with Isaac, he seems to know what he's doing. Isaac looked worried, unsure and Peter seemed happy to let him be, let him have those feelings. I just wanted to make it better for him but when I tried Isaac looked even more traumatised." I smiled. "He poked his tongue out at me."

Kendal smirked. "Isaac and Peter are working out some issues. Despite how it may have looked, they are working them out together. They are at the very beginnings of their relationship and Isaac is still learning to trust him, which is sometimes going to be tough as he was let down by a few of his other Keepers before. Your presence probably felt like an intrusion so he was just showing you, although he would have been punished for it." I was so glad I never tattled on him. "Peter will be watching him closely until he learns to ask for help in a nice way, which Isaac knows, he just needs to trust Peter to share his insecurities with him, instead of lashing out when a feeling becomes overwhelming. Subs are highly emotional and an unsure feeling or thought can have the quietest and mildest natured person lashing out and being violent to whoever is near them. It's not acceptable behaviour, it's not an acceptable way to show their feelings."

"But if their Keeper is watching them all the time as you say, surely they can see these feelings building in them?"

Kendal nodded. "A lot of the time, a Keeper can know and understand where their slave's mind is, but their emotions are very susceptible to the slightest change. In a single moment, a slave can go from feeling secure and loved to being unsure and worried. It can be for the slightest thing too, a change in routine, maybe an unsure touch, something they heard or saw. They are taught to ask their Keeper to have them if they feel overwhelmed with emotion, not lash out because they are worried by it. Asking is done initially on action. The slave will hold their wrists out to their Keeper or will sit by them with their head bowed. It's kind of like a silent request. They are saying, I know my place with you but I'm feeling unsure of it. I'm trusting you to have me and make it right. If they are needy they will ask like this too."

"Ask to be given pain?"

Kendal nodded. "They are asking for help from their need. It's the slave's way of telling their Keeper that they are not settled."

"You said initially the asking is done by action?"

Kendal nodded again. "Once the keeper understands what is wrong and has made them feel secure with their relationship again, then they can talk about it. A slave that feels secure and safe with their Keeper can talk honestly with them without fear. Some things though cannot always be put into words. Being needy is not usually spoken about. Not because they are forbidden, but because their thoughts are usually consumed with it, and they can't sit and talk about it with any rational thought. The understanding must come purely through action to each other. It gets a little more confusing too, if the slave is awaiting a client and cannot have their need salved. The Keeper must work very hard to keep them feeling secure and comforted but also encouraging their need for it. It's a difficult time but if their relationship is strong, a slave will lay quietly with their Keeper, trusting them while their thoughts are consumed." I thought about what I had seen in the kitchen.

"Peter said that Isaac was unsure of him, yet Isaac moved to be close to him. Was he asking Peter to help him?"

Kendal pursed her lips and frowned a little. "Without knowing what has passed between them it's hard to tell. I know what started Isaac's unsure thoughts. It sounds like Isaac is unsure about asking Peter. Asking is a direct action, not a slow one that is thought about. Isaac needs to learn to earn Peter's love and Peter needs to earn Isaac's trust so that there is never any doubt between them. Then in future, when Isaac becomes unsure, he will be able to ask for reassurance in a more acceptable manner, not by throwing plates."

I half laughed and Kendal smiled back.

"See, I don't know these things. I don't know when it's okay for him to feel unsure or when I should make it better. How do you learn that?"

"By watching him and seeing the places it takes him and seeing what brings him back to you where he is content and feels secure. It's okay to make him feel different emotions. What you're showing him is that if he wants the good stuff, the good feelings, he has to work through the bad ones with you. In an acceptable manner of course. I understand that seeing Leo unsure and worried is not nice but if you just make that better without him sharing anything with you, then those unsure feelings will always be there because they have not been dealt with, merely swept aside. He doesn't have to share everything all at once, that would be too hard on him, just one small thing and then you can show him that it's good to share his thoughts and feelings.

"You can let him have his comfort and love to help him until you request a little more from him. He learns to share his thoughts and learns that it earns him your unconditional love, he learns to trust you, unconditionally too. Remember though, he may not know how to verbalise his thoughts or feelings. His sharing with you may not be a spoken thing, his actions may tell you more than what comes out of his mouth. He may say he loves you but wants to be away from you, he may say he hates you but wants to be with you, it can all get very confusing but you will soon know him and understand him better than he knows himself. Your care of him will go beyond what he thinks he needs. You'll know when he's cold even when he doesn't tell you."

I nodded. That I already knew. He had been freezing to touch sometimes and never said a word. I didn't know why he didn't say that though. "Why doesn't he say it? He likes to talk about random things but then I know sometimes he's been freezing and never said a word."

Kendal smiled. "Because other things are more important or more prominent to him that being cold just doesn't seem to register. I expect just being with you was enough to make the cold not feel so bad or that his back was so painful, it extinguished the cold feeling. They can't deal with too much at one time so they shut out a lot. That's why they need a Keeper to look after them and take care of them. I'm sure he would have happily sat and froze to death just to be with you. You can make him think about it by requesting that he gets a blanket if he wants to be with you or you can take the thought and just get the blanket for him.

"It depends where you want his mind to be at the time. If you want him to think about other things then your job is to care for him while he does that. If you want to teach him subservience to you, about earning things, then you request something of him so he can have what he wants. He wants to sit with you so he has to get the blanket. Do you understand? You can take his mind wherever you want but you must always care for his wellbeing first and foremost." I nodded.

Yes, I was beginning to see actually how much he had needed me on the street. "Joe?" I came back from my thoughts and looked at her and smiled.

"Sorry, I was thinking, just connecting the things you are saying with things that happened in the street. They make a lot of sense...I think."

Kendal smiled. "They are just basic examples and things I know you did for him many times over the years. You cared for him and you looked after him because you love him, that hasn't changed. I just want you to know you can still do that but also get Leo to give something back in return, something that he hasn't really had to do. Which is why you are unsure of his love for you." I nodded. "Don't be afraid of questioning his feelings for you. He may not like it because you never asked him. He shows you his love in different ways but sometimes you need him to make it clearer to you, there is nothing wrong in that, just start gently so it doesn't come as too much of a shock."

"Is that what Peter is doing with Isaac? Requesting that he shows him?"

Kendal nodded. "I think so but Peter can be a bit more forceful. Isaac accepts his place with Layton and he is very secure with it. He needs to find that security with Peter, it's not new, just new to him with Peter. Peter can push him a little harder because he knows that place. Leo has never been asked to show anything to anyone, he took and gave only what he wanted and you can see the trouble that got him." Kendal smiled. "Firm and gentle. It will take a few tries but Leo will soon understand what he has to do to get something he wants from you." I smiled. "Don't try and force too much of what you're learning onto him in one go. He won't understand it and it will make him too unsure. Just now and again when you see an opportunity to test it a little, don't be afraid to. If it doesn't work out well, then you can get him back and try again in another moment. When you become more sure of what you're asking of him and know where it's taking his mind then you can start to be more persistent in your requests. Always w..."

"Watch him." I smiled. "I get it. Watch him for things he's not telling me."

Kendal grinned at me. "Am I preaching?"

I shook my head. "No, not at all. Don't stop helping, I need all the help I can get."

"No one expects you to know it all. Or get it right every time."

"He will though won't he? If I get it wrong it will confuse him."

Kendal shook her head. "No, not at all. If you can see that what you're doing or asking him is confusing him then you can change it. He will follow wherever you take him. Just try not to be unsure, if he feels that from you then he won't want to follow you and that can lead him to get up to mischief." She smiled. "Then you're in trouble."

"Great." Kendal laughed and I smiled back.

"Right, let's get your checks done." I scowled at her and she laughed a little. "I'm sorry, they're a little invasive but needed I'm afraid. If you want to pop into the bathroom and get yourself undressed and cleaned up. They won't take long."

I blew my breath out slowly. "Is it okay to tell you that I'm worried?"

She frowned and looked at me sympathetically. "I know, Joe, I'm sorry. I've seen it all before, many, many times over, if that helps?"

Not really. I just nodded to her and got up and headed to the bathroom.

Twenty minutes later I left the bathroom feeling shamed and a little traumatised. I was so glad Leo had been asleep, although I wasn't sure he would always be given that luxury. I had had things poked in my cock, stuck in my hole, had bloods taken, and had my body groped by Kendal, it was all slightly mortifying. She had left me to sort myself out and give me a moment, which I had needed before I faced her again.

In the bedroom, she was sitting back on the bed with Leo again.

"You okay, Joe? I'm sorry, I know it's not nice." Still feeling slightly mortified I just nodded and avoided looking at her until she spoke again. "Are you ready to take over here?" She looked down at Leo.

"Are you going?"

She smiled at me. "Are you panicking again?"

Yes. I was surprised at how anxious I was to be left alone with him. Hell, I had been alone with him so many times. It was Leo, how hard could it be? I smiled at Kendal.

"A little. I know you have to go, it's okay. If I see Peter, I'll tell him about the stew in the oven." Stew in the oven seemed so unimportant right now. Kendal eased herself out from Leo, who squirmed a little at being disturbed then settled again against the pillow.

"No worries, I'll leave a note for him. If you need immediate help, Peter will help you, if you need me, he will call me. I can be here within ten minutes okay?" I nodded. Breathe. Kendal bent, kissed Leo's face, and stroked her hand over his cheek. "Mm, he is a little sweetheart." I sort of smiled and she looked at me. "You already know that though." She gathered her stuff together. "Don't forget to feed him, he will forget his hunger with everything."

I shook my head. "He always tells me that."

She smiled. "Just be wary. Things are a little different here for him. He didn't have a lot to think about on the street. He's going to have so much in his head right now, he'll forget to tell you things. Just like we spoke about." I nodded. Kendal came and stood in front of me and reached out her hand and touched my face. "I'll be back first thing in the morning, bring Leo to the kitchen for breakfast." I nodded. The morning seemed a long way off. "Are you going to be okay?"

I smiled. "Of course. Thank you for looking after him. I forgot to ask about the checks and everything. Was it all okay?"

She smiled. "Considering everything, he seems good, a little skinny but we can solve that. His hole is a little sore, use the ointment if he seems uncomfortable. Other than that all seems okay with both of you."

"Cream on his hole?"

She smiled and nodded. "You are now in sole charge of his body. Get to know it again, Joe." I nodded again. Kendal leaned forward and kissed me. "Call me, for anything. You are going to be just fine." I half smiled at her. She picked up her stuff and left the room.

I sat for a while looking at him and telling myself to breathe over and over until I felt silly. I stood up and looked down on him and then made a decision. I kicked off my shoes, stripped off my clothes, and slipped under the blanket with him. It felt good to feel him next to me. I edged closer so our bodies were touching and revelled in the feel of him for a moment. I leaned my head on my arm and lay my face close to his, stroked him and then kissed him. Then I lay back and did what seemed to be one of the most important things. I watched him.

CHAPTER SIX

JOE

I had no idea how long I had watched him before I fell asleep. It had been a while. I had watched him do nothing, just sleep, but it had me completely engrossed. The way his eyelashes lay touching his cheeks, I had no idea they were so long and the way his tongue snuck out every now and again to lick his dry mouth. His lips were quite full and feminine, surrounded by a soft dusting of facial downy hair that looked like it was struggling to grow. He had never shaved, he never had to. His ears stuck out a little but it was because he had no hair, at least that's what I thought, as when his hair had been longer, I hadn't noticed his ears. It had seemed ages ago I had taken him to Mikey to have his hair shaved. His hair had been a deep brown and had always seemed like it was trying to curl but not quite managing it. I couldn't wait for it to grow again, for him. I would make sure I looked after it this time.

I had laid listening to his breathing and that had been my last thoughts. I opened my eyes to see him again and was met with an empty bed. I sat up immediately, panicked. My heart was beating so loud, it was a moment before I heard the sound of running water over the thumping in my body. I moved quickly from the bed, headed to the bathroom and stopped when I saw him. I was so relieved. He was sitting, still naked, diagonally facing the bath so I stood still and watched him quietly.

He was looking at something in his lap, but I couldn't see what. He fiddled around and then put his fingers in his mouth. The bath tap was running, the hot tap, and steam was filling the air above it. He reached out his hand into the steam and waved his hand through it, then he put his hand under the water and snatched it back, making me smile. He went back to whatever was in his lap before repeating the whole thing. This time though, he put his hand in and out of the water and it made me quietly laugh. It had been a long time since he had felt hot water. I watched him repeat the whole thing again but this time he put his hand under the water and held it there until he moaned out.

"Leo!" He jumped, startled and turned to look at me as I walked towards him. "Are you trying to burn yourself?" I took hold of his wrist and looked at his hand. It was bright red. I turned the cold tap on and stuck his hand under it as I looked at him, scowling. He didn't like the cold water. "What were you doing?"

He scrunched his face up and looked away from me. "It's too cold, Joe." He pulled his hand from me and the water and put it in his lap.

I turned off both the taps, crouched down to him, and looked at the top of his head as he looked down, but I could see him smiling on the side of his face.

"Leo?"

"I had a hard cock too." It took a moment for me to realise that my cock was hanging semi-hard between my open legs. I covered it with my hand.

"Fuck off, Leo!" He looked up at me and smiled and then the smile disappeared.

"Are you missing the alley, Joe? I miss the alley."

I sighed and sat on the floor in front of him, crossing my legs in a mirror image of his pose.

"No, I'm not. Show me your hand." Leo lifted his hand and I noticed something in his lap by his feet. "What's that?" I moved his other hand. A mangled tube of toothpaste sat in his lap and I picked it up. "Leo, how much of this have you eaten?"

He shrugged. "It tastes nice, I like it and I'm hungry."

"Leo! Half the bloody tube has gone! You can't eat it like that, you'll give yourself a stomach ache." I put the tube on the floor and looked back in his lap. There was something else. I reached down, it was a bar of soap, it had teeth marks in it. Jesus.

Leo smiled. "It smells really nice."

"Did you try and eat it?"

He shook his head and then spoke. "No. I just wanted to see if it tasted like it smells…and I can tell you, Joe, don't try it, it's horrible."

I shook my head and put it with the toothpaste and looked at his hand. It was still bright red. I sighed. Great. I was doing a bang-up job watching him. He'd been with me for less than a day and he had eaten half their bathroom and burned his hand.

I looked around for a bowl or something but there was nothing so I took a small towel from a rail, ran the cold water on it, wrapped it around his hand and held it.

"Are you still mad about my back? Is that why I had to go to sleep? Are you mad because I woke up?"

I looked from his hand to his face. He had not a single clue what was going on or where we were and all he was asking was, if I was mad with him. I was just about to answer when he spoke again. "I think I already have a stomach ache because I went to the toilet and it was like water. Am I sick, Joe? Sick like before in the alley? Did that lady say I was sick?"

I smiled at him. "No, Kendal said you were perfectly healthy. Does your back feel better?" He shrugged. I had no clue what that meant. "Did you have a nice sleep?" He shook his head and I worried then that he had felt and known about everything that Kendal had done.

"I like my own bed."

"You didn't have a bed, Leo, you had a box on the floor."

"I liked it."

"You rarely slept in it, you slept with Ginger." I saw something fleetingly cross his face. Confusion? I wasn't sure, it was so quick.

He smiled at me. "You were snoring."

Okay, change of subject. Should I take him back to the subject of Ginger? This was normal for Leo though. He would often say things that bore no connection to what we were talking about. Had he purposefully been doing it all this time? Avoiding things he didn't want to think about? I hadn't taken any notice before, it had just been Leo, going off in his own little world, chit-chatting about nothing and everything. I decided to let him carry on. So far, I had tried the back subject and Ginger. Neither had got me anything so I wanted to see what were safe subjects for him.

I smiled at him. "Was I? I was really tired. Besides, it was nice and warm lying next to you."

He smiled. "I like being naked with you. Can we sleep naked forever?"

Well, this was progress. As far as I knew he had never slept naked, not even with me before...before Ginger's arrival. I unwrapped his hand and ran the towel under cold water again, squeezed out the extra and wrapped it back over his hand.

"We can, when we're indoors, where it's safe like this. Have you slept naked before?"

He shook his head. "My jeans hurt me when I sleep in them. They squeeze my cock too tight, look." He pulled his cock in his hand and showed me a red line that cut across the base of his cock down to his balls.

He seemed to have no hang-ups about being naked with me, or me looking at his body. I reached out my hand to touch him and he covered his cock with his hand. Okay, looking was acceptable, touching was not it seemed.

"I just wanted to see, Leo, make sure it was okay. I have some ointment that can make it better."

"Ointment that Isaac said about? He said that it makes it better, not hurt so much."

I nodded. "Yeah. Kendal gave it to me for your back but it makes lots of things better. Do you hurt anywhere else?" Would he tell me about his hole? He shrugged.

I was still unsure what his shrugging meant. I sat and watched him for a while and he just sat and looked around the bathroom like it was the most interesting place ever. I suppose when you hadn't seen one in four years it was. He looked at me watching him and then took his eyes from me without saying a word. What was going on in his head? I knew that leaving Ginger had hurt him, that leaving the alley had hurt but he wasn't saying a word. Surely he must wonder where we were? What we were doing here? And yet not a word about it.

"Why are you talking differently?"

I half-smiled. "Am I?"

He nodded and looked at me, waiting for an answer. I didn't know what to say, I wasn't quite sure what he meant. I tried to think of what I would have said to him in the alley if he'd asked me a question I couldn't answer.

"Fuck, Leo, I don't know, don't ask silly questions."

He smiled at me. "That's the same."

I smiled back at him. Was I so different here? I had been making an effort not to swear in front of Kendal, she never said but she probably wasn't used to such language. I never liked swearing so much but on the street, if it didn't have a swear word in it, no one listened and if no one heard you then you could easily disappear. Leo rarely swore and when he did it was usually to copy Ginger and always sounded so wrong.

"Do I swear at you a lot?" He smiled and nodded, he seemed quite happy with that fact. "Everybody swears on the street don't they? It's because we're all trying to be someone."

"Who? Who are you trying to be?"

I smiled. "Just someone that matters. I don't need to swear here, there's no one to listen to me."

"I'm listening to you."

I smiled at him and cocked my head in question. "Even if I don't swear?"

He nodded. "I don't mind if you don't swear, you always matter to me. I always listen to you."

I half laughed. "Mm, I'm not sure that's true but that's a nice thing to say. You matter to me too, a lot." I picked up his towel wrapped hand and kissed his fingers that stuck out of the end.

He looked at me seriously. "Can we go home now? I don't like it here."

Had he been playing with me? Being nice in the hope it would get him what he wanted?

"But I thought you liked it here. It has hot water and toothpaste."

He shook his head. "No, the hot water hurts like the cold water."

"Then why did you put your hand under it for so long?"

He shrugged and then answered. "Coz it didn't matter when it was cold so I thought it wouldn't matter if it was hot. You always said that it didn't matter when I said it was too cold."

I shook my head and closed my eyes fleetingly trying to hold back a smile. "Hot water burns, Leo, you know that don't you?" Surely he knew that?

He shrugged. "It feels the same…I wanna go home."

I unwrapped the towel and held his hand for him to see the red skin.

I shook my head. "It's not the same." His bottom lip quivered. "Cold water does hurt. It makes you shiver and it makes you feel cold inside but a few minutes won't damage you. A few minutes under a hot tap burns your skin, not just for a moment but forever. It might make you feel the same but it's not and you must promise me you will never do it again." He nodded and I could see he was trying not to cry, which made me feel bad. I sighed. "I just don't want you to hurt yourself." I felt bad.

"I wanna go home." Jesus.

"Stop…just…stop."

Nothing good was coming of this day for Leo but keeping him safe was my job wasn't it? Looking after his…wellness, had they called it? He was still staring at me with that desolate look in his eyes. Change his thoughts. Yes, change what he was thinking about.

"Let's get dressed and I will show you the house." He didn't move. "Come on." I stood and pulled him to stand and took him into the bedroom.

I got dressed in my jeans and t-shirt and Leo just sat on the bed. I looked around for his shorts and found them screwed up half under the bed. I pulled them out and shook them as I walked around the bed to him. "We'll have to be more careful where we leave your clothes." I bent down and put his feet in and then pulled them up. He didn't help much, at all actually and I had to drag him to his feet to do them up. He sat straight back down again. I sat back on my feet. "Come on, Leo, you're not helping."

"I wanna go home." For fuck's sake! I really needed him to stop saying that.

"The alley is not your home anymore, Leo! Saying it is not going to make it happen. I can't go back there, you can't go back there, we can't go back there! The alley is not a good place."

Leo let out a crying growl at me, like I had never heard from him before and he thumped his hands on the bed. I realised my words had hurt him and I reached out to apologise as I pushed myself up on my knees as Leo screamed out. "You're not to say that! I hate you!"

He shoved his hands out towards me, both of which caught me full force in the face in my upward motion. I was thrown off balance and fell to the side, my forehead caught the bottom handle of the chest of drawers that sat beside the bed. I stopped myself from falling completely to the floor and just rested my head against the drawer while I tried to regain my surroundings. Leo looked at me, he looked completely panicked and moved over to the other side of the bed and slipped to the floor out of my sight.

I pushed myself to sit, trying to catch my breath, touched my hand to my head and then licked my lip which Leo had caught when his hand had made contact with my face. I couldn't decide what hurt more. I felt my nose running and I wiped the back of my hand across my face only realising then that it was also bleeding.

I sat listening to Leo's crying. He sounded desolate and sad. We were both lost without our place in the alley. We were both alone in a strange world that meant nothing to either of us.

We had no home, not even a box that was ours. I had looked after Leo for four years and we had had some pretty hard times but he had never lashed out at me. He was hurting and I had hurt him more.

I shook my head. What was I doing? I had hurt the only thing I ever really cared about. I wiped my arm across my face and got up and walked around the bed to see Leo sitting, curled around his legs.

I sat down next to him and whispered his name. "Leo?"

He had his face buried in his knees. He didn't look up to speak to me. "You said...we could...talk about...the alley...you said...it wasn't...a bad place." His voice was broken with his upset.

"I know, Leo, I was wrong to say what I did, I'm sorry." His body shook as he tried to control his sobs.

I had no idea what to say to make it better for him. I sat for a moment watching him and then I thought of something. I had to take him to a place that wasn't strange to him. Somewhere he could breathe, where he'd always been able to breathe. I moved and grabbed the blanket off the bed and wrapped it around him.

I held out my hand to him. "Come on." Leo lifted his tear-soaked face. "I know how to make it better." He looked at me with his big sad eyes, unsure of me and I hated it. "I promise, Leo, come on." He slowly moved his hand to mine and I took it firmly. I stood and pulled him up.

"Is it home?" I half smiled and regretted it as I felt my lip split and pulled painfully.

I nodded. "Yes, kind of." I wrapped the blanket around him and he watched me before he slowly reached out and touched my face.

"I hurt you."

I shook my head. "No, it's nothing. Here, hold the blanket in this hand." I put Leo's hand over the pulled blanket closing it around the material and took his other and walked him through the house and outside.

I was kind of relieved it was dark. I had no idea how long we'd slept and had hoped it would be. I saw Leo take a deep breath as I sat down on the porch floor. I still held his hand but let him stand there a moment, while he caught his breath. He stepped forward to the edge of the steps so he could look at the night sky from under the porch covering.

I tugged at his hand. "Sit here with me and you can see it."

He turned and looked at me and then back at the sky as if he were weighing up whether his view would be enough. The night air was cold but the sky was clear of clouds and it was a full moon. Leo and I knew a lot about the night sky just from watching it. I remembered reading that at this time of year it was called a hunter's moon and it was supposedly when hunters gathered to find their prey. I wondered if that was apt for this place I'd bought Leo to. Leo didn't care, it was the sort of night sky that he enjoyed most. He felt like he could see the whole world.

Usually, by now he would be nattering about nonsense, a piece of shiny glass that he found or a sound he heard and I would be attentively listening. He was silent now, consumed with utter relief, I could tell. He took a stuttered breath as the night sky had the effect it always had on him, it calmed him. He was so far forward now, I was struggling to keep hold of his hand from my seated position and I released him. He immediately looked at me and stepped back and held out his hand again.

I took it back in mine. "Sit with me, Leo."

"But you're all broken and bloody?"

I swept my face against my shoulder trying to wipe away any blood. I felt lost and broken but Leo was calm again and I wanted him to stay that way.

"It's just a scratch."

Leo looked at the sky and stepped back and just sat in front of me. His hand was behind his back as he still held my hand. I leaned forward and stroked my other over his neck as he leant his head on his knees and looked at the sky. "Do you want to talk, Leo?"

He shook his head. It was so unlike him. When we were waiting for customers, Leo was always quiet and hardly spoke. He always looked withdrawn and shy, usually looking down at his feet, trying to ignore the eyes of asking men. But when he and I went off and sat and looked at the sky, he would change completely. It was like he was holding everything in and it would all come bursting out and not usually in any sensible order. Things were not right with him and because I had no clue how to make it right, I let him be in his silence.

We sat for ages and when I felt his hand slipping from mine, I knew he was fighting sleep again. I encouraged him to move back beside me, which he did and eventually, he was leaning on me. I watched him stare aimlessly out at the sky as I stroked my finger gently over his scalp. He fought for a long time to keep his eyes open and I watched, as each time his eyes shut, it became harder and harder for him to open them until, in the end, he lost his fight. His body lay heavy against mine and I listened to him breathing and knew from watching him earlier that he was asleep. I pulled the blanket over him further and laid my head back against the wall.

Now that he was safe, I let the tears fall.

CHAPTER SEVEN

JOE

I had never felt so alone, which was mad because I had been alone for as long as I could remember. Foster home after foster home, as I wasn't wanted by my drug-addicted parents…if I even had two parents. I got told they couldn't look after me, I was probably about five or six years old, I didn't really know, so I was put into care to find somewhere better…yeah, that had worked out great.

Every time I was welcomed with open arms and a smile. False people being false nice, being false friendly, as they tried to pretend to love me better. I never felt a connection to any of them, and the feeling had obviously been mutual because I always got moved on when other children stayed. Apparently, I was difficult to get on with, to connect to. The older I got, the quicker I seemed to move and because I moved so often, I never had any friends. I wasn't in the schools long enough to make any and as I grew older, I went out of my way to not make friends, knowing that I would probably be gone soon.

The one good thing about that was, I spent most of my time alone studying. I was a grade-A student…up until I walked out of their system. I looked down at Leo. It didn't matter, because Leo and I were as different as night and day and yet here we both sat, on some stranger's porch with nothing and nowhere to go. He was the closest I had ever got to having a friend. Him, and if I thought about it, Ginger too.

I couldn't remember my first day as a homeless street boy. It kind of happened gradually. My last foster home had been busy with many children and I soon realised that if I was late from school, no one seemed to notice or care. The realisation that I didn't matter came one night when I heard Kathy, my foster carer, calling the younger ones for their dinner. My name was never called. I waited, quite a long time, believing she would remember her eldest foster child and I would hear my name being shouted up the stairs but it never happened. I never left my room that night and no one came to see if I was in or out, if I was dead or alive.

After that, I didn't go home a lot. When I did happen to go home and was noticed, all I got was an earful of noise about how I treated them with no respect. I was about sixteen when I came in late one night after walking the streets and overheard Kathy and her husband talking about the social visitor coming the next day to speak to me. I knew what that meant. I had stood in the hallway for a while listening to them, then turned around and left the house for the last time. I couldn't do it again. I wasn't particularly sad, it had never been my home, not really.

I had spent so much of my time on the streets by then, that I already felt more at home there. I had already known then that I was gay, that I liked other boys more than girls. I had never been with another boy, touched or even kissed one but I knew just by walking the streets, it would be the male gender that made me look and feel things, that society told me I should feel for the female species. The street changed my hopes and dreams very quickly, if I even had any then, I barely remembered them if I did. Within the first week of being officially homeless, I became official street trash by sucking my first cock for money. It had actually been another street boy. I earned two pounds and a few belittling names because I was useless at it. It was the start of my street living.

I had moved around a lot in the beginning and got my skill of cock sucking down to a fine art before I found the alley where Leo and I had met. I quickly gained a place there after a fight with an older boy over a customer. After that, my place at the foot of the alley was rarely questioned or challenged, just the odd scuffle and the customers were many, so there I stayed, until yesterday. I felt another tear run down my face.

Alone didn't come close to the pain I felt inside. If I couldn't keep my friend safe here then what chance did we have on the street? I knew the answer to that. None. No chance. By taking Leo from the alley, I had given him a slow death sentence on the vanilla streets. I pulled him tighter to me and touched my broken lips to his shaved, bristled head. He wouldn't even understand if I said sorry. Just spending this time with him away from the alley had shown me that he needed so much more than I knew how to give. I breathed quickly while I struggled to keep the desolation from taking me again.

I was so lost in my misery, I wasn't even bothered when I saw a dark figure with a torch, walking through the woods towards us. The fear didn't touch the pain I was feeling. I pulled Leo closer to me as the figure came out of the trees and walked across the grass towards us. Then, through the night light, I saw it was Layton. I was so lost I didn't even feel relieved. He walked up the porch steps, crouched down beside me, and put his fingers under my chin, lifting my face to him. I felt dazed and lost.

"You forgot to breathe." I felt another tear run down my face and when it hit the corner of my mouth Layton wiped it away with his thumb. "You can breathe now." My body shook with a sob that I held inside. Layton looked at Leo and smiled.

I looked at Leo and then back to Layton, feeling like I had to say something. "I...I think...I think he's alright, he's not hurt."

Layton looked back at me. "I can see that." He looked back at Leo. "He's just a little stuck." Layton swept a hand over Leo's head. "I came for you." He looked back at me and leaned forward and kissed my forehead.

I didn't understand. Had I done such a bad job that he'd come to take me away from Leo? Was it time for me to move on again? The thought hurt but hadn't that been my thoughts too? That Leo would be better off without me? Safer?

Layton half-smiled. "Stop thinking, Joe, and just breathe. I'll get us some tea, ninja style, without Isaac knowing I'm here." He grinned at me before leaving to go into the house.

I took a deep breath to try and settle my thoughts and was doing okay for a while, then I heard Leo's stomach rumble loudly. Fuck! I hadn't fed him. I had known he was hungry when I had seen him with the toothpaste but I had forgotten and he hadn't reminded me like he always did. Kendal's words repeated in my head. "Don't forget to feed him as he'll have a lot going on and won't think to tell you." As if to condone my feeling of being useless as his carer or Keeper or whatever it was I was supposed to be, his stomach moaned again.

I covered my hand over my face and cried again, lost in such despair that I didn't hear Layton return until he spoke.

"That's not breathing."

I wiped my hand down my face and looked at him as he sat cross-legged beside me. He had brought a tray with tea, a first aid box, and more blankets. He shook one out and laid it over Leo and then shook out the other and gestured for me to lean forward. I did and he wrapped it around my shoulders.

I cried again as I spoke. "He's hungry, I didn't feed him, I forgot to feed him."

Layton smiled, seeming unbothered by my lack of care for Leo. "Leo's been hungry before, Joe, another night is not going to hurt him. It probably feels normal, helping his thoughts to quieten."

I looked at Leo and stroked my fingers across the back of his neck where my hand lay. The action disturbed him and he moved and lay his head on my lap so he was laying a little sprawled across the porch. Layton smiled at him and moved the blanket to cover him again.

"How can you smile at him? Aren't you worried for him? Concerned?" Layton looked at me and smiled and then turned and passed me the tea.

"Nope. He has you doing plenty of that for him. Despite what you feel and what he tells you, he's content to be with you. I smile because I like to watch them sleep. Their thoughts and feelings and actions are unconstrained in sleep. It's no different from watching them when they're awake. Being submissive and needy is hard work mentally and physically and takes a lot out of them. The slaves sleep a lot, you will find that Leo will too if allowed, especially as he has a lot going on." Layton opened the first aid box. "Now, let me look after you while you worry about him. He has your undivided attention which he's loving I'm sure, he's just not quite sure what to do with it.

"He has now become your main focus and he will have realised that which I know had something to do with this." He pointed to my face. "On the street, your attention towards him was patchy and uneven, given when he needed it and sometimes not. Because he never got it always when he wanted it, he would have learnt that you controlled it and tried very hard to work out what he had to do to get it. Making Ginger mad at him got it from you, as did standing quietly waiting for customers." Layton started to clean my face. I frowned as I thought over what he said. "Don't do that, it's making it worse."

I tried to stop frowning as I apologised. "Sorry. I don't think Leo thought like that. He was asking for attention from Ginger usually. And how did standing in the alley waiting for customers get my attention? We rarely spoke when we were looking for business."

Layton smiled as he wiped the blood from my forehead. "Don't underestimate their minds. He would have learnt very quickly that Ginger rarely gave him the attention that he sought. So why would he, two years on, still keep asking?"

I smiled a little understanding what Layton was telling me. "Because he knew I would make it better when Ginger got mad with him."

Layton nodded. "Exactly. The asking of Ginger became not about having his attention but having yours. It became a sure-fire way of getting it. Making Ginger mad gets Joe's attention, it rarely failed, didn't it?"

I smiled. "No, never. The street thing though?"

Layton smiled. "At the end of each night, you took him away and sat with him. To him, it was like praise for being good. Likewise, when he had customers, you came and sat with him and gave him praise. The more distraught he was the more attention you gave. I'm sure he worked that out as well."

"He was lying to me?" Layton scowled and shook his head as he put some cream over the cut on my forehead.

"No, not like you or I consider lying, he wasn't being deceitful, just working to get what he wanted. I'm sure in the beginning he was upset about what he had to do to get money. He would have learnt how to activate those feelings, actions, that then led you to give him attention. If you'd looked at him closer, I'm sure that you would have seen he wasn't as distressed as he made out. It's called being a sneaky little fuck and they are very good at it." Layton smiled as if amused.

"It's amusing?"

He half laughed. "Yes, mostly. Sometimes it's intriguing to watch them work. They go to a lot of effort to get what they want. As long as what they want is not harmful. I like sneaky little fucks." He smiled as he cleaned my lip, making me wince. "They are exciting and it's challenging to keep a step ahead of them."

"Is Isaac sneaky?"

Layton grinned. "Yes. Drink your tea before it gets cold and use this side of your mouth." I lifted the cup to my mouth and sipped it, then drank it quickly. Layton wiped my nose and face with a piece of cotton wool. "You're a bit of a mess but it looks worse than what it is. Are you going to tell me what happened?"

I frowned, confused. "What are you doing here? I thought you were coming tomorrow?"

Layton smiled and closed the box. "Would you tell me then?" I looked at Leo. "You don't have to protect him from me if that's what you worried about?"

I didn't look at him. "I don't know what happened. I mean I know how this happened." I pointed to my face. "I was getting up to try and calm Leo down at the same time he wanted me to go away. His hands met my face, then my head met the bedside table. He didn't mean it, when he saw the blood he panicked and hid."

I saw Layton smile and he reached out and swept his hand across Leo's head. His look was one of wonder, care and amusement?

"They are always sorry afterwards."

"Are you angry with him? Should I be?" I looked at Layton and he looked back at me seriously.

"You weren't? You never even, for a moment, thought about teaching him a lesson and giving him one back? That's the way things are sorted on the street, isn't it? Don't you fight for your places there?"

Slightly taken aback, I shook my head at Layton. "Yes...I mean, yes that's how you get your place but no, I never thought about hitting him back." I swung my head round to look at Leo. God no. Did he want me to hit him? Hit Leo? I shook my head. "I couldn't...I can't. It's Leo, I've never had to fight him for anything." I looked back at Layton and he smiled at me.

"It's okay, Joe, breathe." I looked at him, confused. "Your non-reaction is a good thing. For now anyway."

I frowned at him and then scowled as it dawned on me what he was doing. "Were you testing me?" Layton shook his head. "Fuck you!"

Layton held his hands up. "I just wanted you to see, Joe."

"See what? That he's better off without me!?" Leo stirred in my lap and Layton put his finger to his lips and slipped back from us, into the shadows of the porch.

"Joe?" Leo turned and looked at me, half asleep. "Did I touch the water again?" I stroked my hand over his head.

"Shh, Leo. No, go back to sleep."

"Can we sleep naked again?" I smiled at him.

Whatever had passed earlier between us, whatever I had made him feel earlier, I had clearly been forgiven for it. I looked into the darkness across the porch.

"I'm going to take him in."

Leo lay his head against my chest and closed his eyes. "Who are you talking to, Joe?"

I leaned forward and kissed the top of his head. "I'm just telling the stars that it's time to go inside now."

He repeated my words sleepily. "The...stars."

I pulled Leo onto my lap and then struggled to get up. Layton stepped back into the light and took hold of my arm and helped me up while I held him. I had never carried Leo anywhere. He was a lot shorter than me and a lot smaller in build and he was surprisingly light. I looked at Layton as he held the door open for me to go back into the house. Without a word to him, I took Leo back to the bedroom.

Leo was asleep again as I laid him on the bed. I took off his jeans and laid the blanket over him. He stirred on the bed and I put my face beside his and kissed him and stroked him until he slept again. I stripped off my clothes and sat cross-legged on the bed, watching him.

Layton had pissed me off and I felt agitated. How dare he think that I would ever hurt Leo. He didn't know us. He thought that popping by the street every now and again made him know me and Leo? He knew nothing of the struggle Leo and I had gone through just to survive each day. I looked down at my arms and hands that were covered in dried blood. Nothing on earth would ever make me hurt him, it didn't matter how many times he hit me.

How many times did he hit me? In the four years we had been friends, he had never even raised his hand to me. This world that was supposedly so good for them, people like Leo, had made things different between Leo and me and I didn't like that. Leo was different from the other street boys, I had always known that. From the minute I had met him, I had been drawn to him like no other boy. Even when I had taken him back home that first time, I had struggled to forget him, which I thought at the time, was stupid because boys came and went all the time and I never gave them another thought.

When he had turned up again a few weeks later I had been overwhelmed with the feelings I had for him. I had never shared those with him, I had never really acknowledged them to myself, they had been so new. It was only yesterday that I had let myself feel it and accept that it was love I felt for him. Four years was a long time to realise that, but when you had never felt it before, been given it or given it yourself, how were you supposed to know? I just knew, when the time had come to walk away from him, that I couldn't because of those feelings, they wouldn't let me go. Now it seemed, life was dealing me another barrier, another wall to climb, another blow to the chest. It was making it difficult for me to stay with him.

Was it selfish of me to want to stay with him? Was I holding him back from his true calling to be a slave or something here in this world? Would he be happier, more...balanced, without me? I didn't want to think about it. I reached out and stroked the back of Leo's still red hand. It was still warm to the touch, the skin still sensitive from the burning water. I wanted to lie with him and feel him next to me but I was too scared in case I fell asleep and he woke without me knowing.

Fuck Layton and this world. When I saw him next, I would tell him that I wanted to take Leo away, back...I wasn't sure but not here, not where he felt so lost. I needed to find somewhere Leo and I could call home, even if that was just a box somewhere. The door opened behind me and I jumped then relaxed a little as Layton walked in.

"Shouldn't you knock?" He walked into the room carrying a tray. Great, more fucking tea. They were obsessed like it was some magic cure.

"Yes but I'm not welcome, am I? So, you wouldn't have let me in. Besides I'm still lurking in this house ninja style so I can't stay in the hallway until you are ready to let me in."

I had to stop a smile from taking my mouth. "You don't need to be here. He's safe, I passed your test." Both of us were speaking in hushed tones.

"I said it wasn't a test, not from me anyway. I also told you I wasn't here for Leo. I have never doubted your ability to keep him safe, not on the streets and certainly not here." Layton sat on the floor next to the door. He wasn't level with me so I didn't feel the need to look at him. "I said what I said because I wanted you to see that your love will always keep him safe. Even without conscious thought. I wanted you not to doubt that, you will need to not doubt that. And just to add another point, I will never lie to you." Oh yes, honesty, he was big on honesty.

I flicked a look at him. He was sitting there quite casually drinking his tea, one leg bent and the other tucked under it. I became very aware that I was naked and took some of Leo's blanket and laid it over my lap.

"You weren't so honest with me when you told me about this world a few years ago."

"Everything that I told you was true. You concluded that it was sexual slavery and you weren't wrong, it is... and a whole lot more. I didn't lie about their other needs, I didn't tell you, it's different. If you had asked questions, I would have answered them honestly. You didn't ask." Jesus fucking Christ!

"I was too busy trying to survive, have you already forgotten where I've been for the last seven years?!" I was struggling not to raise my voice so I looked back to Leo, it was easier.

"No not at all, which is why I never told you more. You had enough to deal with. Being honest is very important to me, to this world. I surround myself with the most honest people I have ever met, it's important to me that I return that honesty. It doesn't always need to be verbalised. I'm not sure what you're angry about? That I didn't tell you everything? That you have been street trash for seven years? Or is it that you're struggling to be honest, Joe?"

I put my head in my hands as I tried to fight off the painful confusion. I had not shed a single tear in six years and even before that. Why was it that all I was doing now was crying? I could feel it again, the need to cry, and I wasn't even sure what it was for either.

"Being honest is hard. You have not had to be honest to anyone about anything, not even yourself. If it hurt, you told yourself it didn't. If it felt good, you told yourself it wasn't real. There was no one challenging those thoughts and feelings, no one wanted to know, no one particularly cared if what you said or showed them was true or not. Except for Leo.

"Yesterday you had to accept that you felt something for Leo because it was too painful not to. Having opened that door to him, you are now trying to shut it again. I can see what Leo thought of that. I know you are trying to protect yourself, Joe, but you don't have to protect yourself from Leo. He's desperately asking you to make sense of the things he's feeling and thinking but you have to give him something." I closed my eyes tight but it didn't stop the tears. When would these people understand? I didn't know how to help him. "Come and sit with me, Joe." I shook my head and Layton sighed.

I couldn't go crying on Layton every five minutes, showing him how fucking useless I was.

"Fine, if you won't come to the mountain…" I looked sideways at him and watched him kick off his shoes and socks. "Then this mountain doesn't mind coming to you." He pushed himself up and came and sat close behind me on the bed. He wrapped his arms around me and pulled me back to him, laying his head against mine. I cried harder.

I lifted my arms in a half-hearted attempt to move away but then just dropped them to the bed and I let him hold me while I cried.

"It's okay, Joe." He kissed the side of my face. "This is just the dam breaking, once it's down, it will be easier to get at what's inside. I know you feel low and alone but you're not."

Each time he spoke he seemed to spur another wave of crying. "Look at him lying there so beautiful and content, Joe. You have done an amazing job of looking after him, even today."

I shook my head. That wasn't true. I couldn't speak though, and just cried some more. When I tried to speak, I couldn't catch my breath and the loss of control seemed to have increased my feeling of being useless.

Layton kissed my face and held me. "There's no rush, let your body find its release first, then you can tell me." I lifted my hand to his arm and gripped it tightly and held onto him as the last of my tears fell until I lay exhausted. He stroked his hand over my hair, letting me rest with him. I took a deep breath and he kissed me. "That's it, Joe, it should be a little easier to breathe now." I turned my head sideways and leant it against him. "Are you feeling a little better?"

I raised my eyes to him. "Am I meant to?"

Layton smiled. "I did say a little."

I lay my face back against him. "I never cry. I feel stupid."

I felt Layton smile. "The fact that you can share that with me means it has done its job."

"If you came here to make me look and feel stupid then yes, job done. You can ninja back off now."

Layton half laughed and stroked his fingers through my hair. "Oh no. I haven't finished yet."

"Great."

Layton laughed a little at my sarcasm. "Besides, you don't seem in any hurry to move." I went to lean forward and he held me tight to him again. "Don't try and run away, stop fighting, Joe."

"Stop making me feel like I have to. I don't like feeling like this, feeling stupid."

Layton shook his head. "You're feeling vulnerable and I understand that that is not a good feeling for you, that it's new. It's not something that you could allow on the street but you have space here and time to work through these feelings." He kissed the top of my head then swept his hands over my body, leaning his chin on my shoulder.

"I'm feeling vulnerable because I'm naked."

Layton smiled. "You're quite beautiful...for street trash." I smiled and then winced which made Layton laugh. He kissed the side of my head and then took my hand. "Come on."

I turned and looked at him. "Where?" I looked at Leo. "Leo?"

"Is quite safe. You're a mess, your nose is bleeding again, let me look after you for a while." I shook my head. I wiped my hand across my face.

"I'm not leaving him."

"We're not leaving him, we're just going in there." Layton pointed to the bathroom." I looked back at Leo. Layton tugged at my hand. "My ninja status runs out by morning." I looked at him.

"I don't understand, you're coming back aren't you?"

Layton stood and smiled at me. "Of course but it may not be tomorrow like I said. I have to wait...until I'm told." He smiled at me and then looked at Leo. "If he stirs we will hear him. He's had a busy day, he'll sleep."

"He's been asleep most of the day, he never sleeps this much."

"He's never been allowed, which was right. The street is not a safe place to sleep, not the sort of sleep that he needs and wants." There were different types of sleep? Layton smiled. "Plus he's the got the residual of what Kendal gave him still inside his blood. Come on, Joe, I'm going to show you how it's done."

I looked from Leo to him confused. "What....sleeping?"

Layton laughed a little. "No, I'm hoping you already know how to do that. I meant sharing." I went to say something and he spoke, putting his fingers to my lips. "Wait...Not yet." I sighed as he pulled me from the bed and into the bathroom.

CHAPTER EIGHT

JOE

In the bathroom, he turned and shut the door and I looked at him, concerned.

"Okay, I will leave it open but promise me you won't start shouting and compromise my ninja status."

I smiled at him. "You can hide again."

Layton opened the door halfway and I nodded happier that I could hear Leo if he called out. Layton stripped off his clothes and I looked at him a little unsure and questioningly. What was he expecting?

"Now, I'm vulnerable to you. Isaac is extremely important to me. If he finds out I'm here, it will hurt and confuse him and damage the trust between us. I'm naked and have nowhere to hide."

He walked over to the bath and started to run the water then sat on the floor. I sat opposite him and then looked at the toothpaste and soap, which Leo and I had left on the floor earlier. I leaned forward, picked them up, and held them in my hands, looking at them. Layton put his hand in the water and sat watching me.

I didn't look at him as I spoke. "I don't have the energy to shout. I'm sorry I was angry with you."

"That's okay, I deserved it for what I said." I looked up at him and then at the bath.

"Did you sneak into my room to…have a bath?" He laughed at me and looked at the water.

"No, we are having one. Isaac is always telling me how beautiful his baths are with Marcus. I rarely have the time for them. I figured you and I could bathe together. It's the middle of the night and we could both do with something to relax us and... you're a mess." I looked down at my hands and arms that were streaked with blood. No wonder Leo had been scared. "What's that?" He nodded to the things in my hand.

I held them up, one in each hand and smiled at him. "Leo's dinner."

Layton was just watching me. I put them back into my lap and fiddled with them as he turned off the taps and stood. He took the toothpaste and soap from my hand and looked at them.

"Mm. I'm sure there's a story that goes with these." He moved across the bathroom and put them in the basin and then turned back and held out his hand. I took it and he pulled me to my feet. "Come on, we'll get the worst off with the shower then I'll wash you in the bath."

He walked me to the shower, took the shower head off its mount, turned it on and sprayed it over my arms. I half-heartedly rubbed at them and then looked at him, unsure.

He smiled at me and turned off the shower. "I can see you're still feeling a little awkward with me. For someone who earned their living by sucking cocks, you're a little self-conscious."

"Well, I rarely had to be naked, no one ever wanted to suck mine..." I looked at him suddenly realising how that sounded. "Shit…That wasn't a request or some sort of opener..." Layton laughed and I smiled at him.

He wasn't shy or conscious about his nakedness but then he had no need to be, he was gorgeous, toned and fit. He reached out and stroked my face. "When you smile, Joe, it changes your face."

He smiled at me as I felt even more awkward and looked away from his closeness. He kissed the side of my face, took my hand, and led me to the bath. Stepping in, he waited for me to join him and then sat down, letting my hand go. I sat down with my legs curled into me.

"Okay, you're starting to make me nervous now." I smiled at him shyly. "Right, that's it. I think it's time to break a little ice." He reached for me and took my hand and pulled me between his legs.

I was a little panicked and put my other hand out to him which he took in his. He leaned forward and kissed me on the mouth. I was a little taken aback by his gentle lips on mine. He took my face in his hands and kissed me again, this time asking with his tongue for entry into my mouth. A little stunned, I gave it to him and he kissed me deeper. I winced as his lips ground against my cut one and he pulled away and touched it with his finger.

He smiled at me. "So in need of attention and yet so unwilling to accept it. Is it so hard, Joe, to accept that someone just likes you without money paving the way?" I swallowed hard and just looked at him.

Was I so emotionless that he had noticed just from a kiss? Maybe that was why I was struggling to connect with Leo.

"Am I frigid?"

Layton laughed and looked at me, sweeping his fingers over my ear through my hair. "No, you're scared. You have no idea how beautiful you are."

I looked at him and shook my head a little. "I'm just a whore, there's no beauty in that."

"Really? Because Leo's a whore and I know that you see him differently. Isaac is a whore and I know he's beautiful. I have a house full of whores who all feel and look beautiful. Whore is just a word that the vanillas like to knock around when they have to pay to get the feelings that they want. You suck cock, I don't need to pay to know that that is beautiful." He smiled at me and I sort of smiled back. He made it sound hot. He smiled at me more. "Is that a little spark of something I see?" I turned my face from him and he gently pulled it back. "It's a good feeling. It's hot and sexy and beautiful. Let it burn, Joe."

He took my mouth again, gently at first, and with his words running through my mind I let him. He plunged his tongue deep into my mouth and I wanted it. I pushed my mouth against him a little harder and then he held my head while he searched my mouth. I felt warm inside me, and I leaned closer to him, then slowly touched my tongue to his. He did a little moaning sigh and the warmth inside me seemed to jump a few degrees. Now my body took on actions all of its own. I put my hand to his face and plunged my tongue into his mouth. Never had I felt the need to have something so badly.

It wasn't about his mouth, having his mouth, it was about the feeling inside me. I felt like my temperature had shot up and it was making me lightheaded. He swept his hands up the side of my body and I lifted my leg over his, drawn to be closer to him. My cock became hard and demanding between my legs and that knowledge made me break away from him. A little unsure of how I had gotten so close to him, I looked at him, worried and a little ashamed of my unconscious actions. He wasn't smiling, he was just looking at me, his eyes, which had been brown, were now bright with caramel flecks, almost sparkling. He lifted my other leg over him and pulled me towards him onto my knees so that I straddled him and took my mouth again.

He held my face and then moved his hands to my shoulders and pushed down on them and I sat back on him. His hard cock slipped between my arse cheeks and I could feel his length across my hole. I broke away from him and looked at him, breathing hard and fast. I was embarrassed and nervous. It had been ages since I had been fucked. I couldn't remember the last customer that had wanted to pay for my hole. I couldn't remember wanting it like I did now. It scared me. It scared me because I had never wanted it, not for the reasons I wanted it now, not for me. I had wanted it before to earn more money but it wasn't money driving this feeling I had.

I wanted to come and I hadn't done or wanted that in a long time either. The feeling, the want, was new to me and I didn't quite know what to do about it. The freedom of it burning inside me was addictive and I wanted more but it was also overwhelming. The speed that it had spread through me was too fast for me to deal with. I was no tease and having thrown myself at Layton I felt like I couldn't now deny him what he so clearly wanted. I looked down at my hard cock half in and half out of the water, trying to get my thoughts and feelings all in one place.

Layton tipped my face up to his again. "You can just breathe into the feelings, Joe. I know you haven't felt them in a long time."

I shook my head at him. "Not a long time...not ever." He reached his hand up and stroked my face questioningly.

"Have you never shared with anyone, Joe?" I shook my head.

I had never had a relationship with anyone. I gave my body because it was paid for, never because I wanted to. This was different, it felt different. I put my hand on his chest ready to…feel or push away. I didn't do either and it just lay there. I had no idea why I suddenly felt the need with Layton.

"Joe?" I looked from my hand, as it lay on a hard tattooed chest, to his face. I felt unsure of my own body and thoughts.

"I'm no tease…so if you want to come..."

Layton leaned forward and took my mouth gently this time, not asking for anything. He broke away and swept his hands up my body as I still sat on him.

He smiled as he spoke. "I always want to come and you are a tease." His look was full of lust. "Just looking at you makes me hard, and seeing as I'm not going to go blind any time soon, means I shall sit here and be wanting."

Fuck, was I so fucking needy for affection that I just threw myself at the first person who showed me any?

"I'm sorry."

He smiled at me again and pushed me back so I slid down his legs. Our cocks were touching in the water as we sat very close. My legs were spread over his and around his thighs. He picked up the sponge, lathered it up with some lotion, and started to wash me.

"You've had a long and difficult day, your emotions and feelings are very raw and very open. I didn't mean to take you places you had never been before. I thought I was just reopening a gate, I didn't know I was unlocking something new to you."

"Are you surprised? That I have never had a relationship with someone, I mean?"

Layton smiled. "Maybe a little. In all these years out on the street, you never met anyone that you wanted?"

I smiled and nodded. "Yeah, I did."

Layton looked at me questioningly.

"It was just never the right time and then..." I shrugged my shoulders. "I think I waited too long, he went with someone else and then we just seemed to slip into a kind of just good friends relationship. I didn't feel I could say anything then. I didn't want to hurt either of them."

Layton looked at me suspiciously. "Are we talking about a certain someone who's sleeping next door?" I smiled shyly and nodded. Layton smiled back then leaned forward and kissed me gently. "That is very beautiful."

"What? That I liked him and missed my chance? I'm not sure I did miss my chance, I think it was more I never knew what I felt, what to do with it."

He half laughed. "No, that you're shy about your feelings for him. What about before the street? Wasn't there anyone? Someone that made you realise you liked other boys?"

I shook my head. "No, I just knew. I used to walk the streets and find myself looking at other guys." I smiled. "I used to try and test it. I used to look at the girls and try and imagine getting it on with them, it just made me want to laugh but when I looked at the guys and imagined getting it on with them, it made me hard. It never failed."

Layton smiled at my memory. "Your first proper kiss with a man? Your first fuck?"

"A customer. He was an all-nighter and he was okay. He was gentle and patient. I don't think he was my first proper kiss though, I think that just happened...with you. I've never kissed like that, it was... hot."

Layton laughed and shook his head. "Fuck. It was hot…and explains a lot. Sharing a kiss like that with someone feeds your body. You should try it with Leo although don't be surprised if he gets a little confused like you did."

I felt shy again which made Layton smile. He picked up my hand and soaped it, scrubbing gently at my nails. I sat and watched him for a moment while a million questions and feelings and God knows what else swirled around in my head.

"How did you get here? I mean, why are you here, now? Where did you come from when you came out of the woods?"

Layton smiled. "I was at Julian's house, which is just through the woods. When Kendal arrived she kept on about you so I know she was concerned. She was worried that she had preached at you and confused you, overloaded you with too many things to think about. She's very smitten with Leo. It's a good job he never came to the house before today, I think she would have kept him."

I laughed and Layton smiled and kissed me. It was like a reward for smiling. I wasn't even sure he knew he did it every time I smiled.

"I thought you were going home?"

He rinsed off the soapy suds as he spoke. "I did. Seems apart from one thing, nothing else was in dire need of my attention and I was finding it a little distracting being home without Isaac. I was watching this house on camera when I saw you and Leo come outside to the porch. You both looked a little detached from each other. I couldn't sleep so I thought I would come over and watch you both sleep but you were still sitting there when I got here."

"Camera? Are we being watched?" Layton shook his head as I looked around the bathroom.

"No. They are just outside watching over Julian's land. Jacob is very important to him but more independent than Isaac. He's rarely alone but sometimes he stays here with a friend. Julian allows him the freedom to do that and can make sure he's secure while he's not with him."

"So, this is Julian's house?"

Layton shook his head. "No, it's Jacob's. Julian gave it to him. Jacob is not a slave and has never been, well, he was not brought to this world to be a slave. Julian's house is not far away, hence the reason I came on foot through the woods." Layton lifted the sponge to my face and wiped at my nose.

"Is it still bleeding?"

He smiled and shook his head. "No, just a little dried blood."

"Why were you going to watch us sleep? And why are you hiding from Isaac?"

Layton half laughed. "You have a lot of questions and I will answer them but understanding me and my relationship with Isaac is not going to help you understand Leo or your feelings for him." I looked away from him. "I came to watch you sleep because that's what I do when I know that a Keeper and his charge are struggling with each other or just generally finding it hard to breathe. I didn't expect you to be asleep but I thought if I sat with you, you would find a little comfort in having me there and you may have been able to find some peace. I can see now though, it is not just Leo's need that is stopping you from finding it with him."

I looked back at him and frowned but he just smiled. "I'm trying to avoid Isaac because he has to find his way with Peter for a while and he will be finding it a little confusing. If he sees me, he will want and expect me to make his feelings go away, make it right. I can, but it will only increase his insecurities with Peter.

"He has to see that Peter can make him feel safe and secure too but to learn that, he has to also know that Peter can make him feel other things, not such pleasant things. It teaches Isaac that Peter is and can be trusted to control him and keep him safe. They will swing back and forth between nice pleasant things and not such nice things until Isaac willingly accepts them from Peter and feels sure enough of him to show him how it makes him feel. What Peter is doing is asking Isaac to be honest with him, not hold his feelings inside him until I come along and make them better. Which is what he has been doing. Their relationship is new and I have let them be while Peter got used to his feelings for Isaac but today when Peter did something that felt threatening to Isaac, and because Isaac is unsure of his place with Peter, he reacted very badly."

"Oh, the breaking china." Isaac had a lot of people around him that…got him. "What did Peter do that was bad?"

Layton smiled. "He shared a passionate kiss with Kendal. Isaac has never had to share Peter's affection. It was Peter's love that made Isaac quiet because he gave it constantly and freely and never requested that Isaac earn it in any way. To then suddenly see Peter give that to someone else, hurt Isaac's feelings. When you only get one thing from someone and then they give that one thing to someone else, there is nothing else there to secure that relationship. Isaac will quite easily accept that I kiss other people and love them, even fuck them because our relationship is built on more than just those things.

"It is time for Peter to show Isaac that he can give him other things, take his mind where he wants when he wants and Isaac isn't going to like it much or be very sure about it at first. I have left him with Peter and it is Peter's decision when he'll be allowed to see me again.

"He'll hold on to his feelings for a while because that's what he does, he puts his unsure feelings aside and waits for me but he can't do that this time. Peter is going to make him feel all sorts of things until Isaac understands that he must be honest with him and trust him to guide him through them. It's a testing time for them both, while they both find their place with each other and become comfortable with it. If Isaac sees me, he'll doubt my trust in Peter to have him. And if he finds out I was here and didn't come for him when he felt low, it will damage some of the trust we share. Isaac mustn't know I'm here. For Isaac and me and for Isaac and Peter."

I shook my head. "I won't say anything. Isn't it hard for you? Knowing he's just there and that Peter is making him feel unsure?"

Layton smiled and stroked his fingers around my face. "Mm, more than you know. I always want to protect him from things that make him unsure, make things right for him and in return for that, he lets me have him and take him wherever I want. His relationship with Peter is different, new to both of them and me. I have been kind of protecting his feelings and thoughts about it. The relationship was not giving Isaac everything he needs, but Peter is new and wasn't ready to take control of it. Also, Isaac's faith in Keepers is very low. Letting Peter in completely will give him a Keeper he desires and needs, but he will find it hard to trust that Peter isn't just using him as the others did to him.

"What happened today shows me that Isaac needs more from Peter if their relationship is going to be as secure as they both want it to be. So, for the first time, I have handed complete control to Peter and taken myself away so I will not feel the need to step in. Usually, I would say when I return but I have left it up to Peter. Which is why I can't come back when I said I would." Layton smiled. "I did stand outside their door for a while. They were talking so I'm hoping that's progress."

I could see how hard it was for him to be away from Isaac. I didn't know how to make him feel better so I leaned forward and kissed the corner of his mouth to try and relay my understanding. Watching Leo with Ginger had been hard.

"Why do you want Peter to control him?" Layton kissed me back before I sat again in front of him.

"Because Isaac needs and wants that control and he wants Peter. If that relationship is ever going to last or fulfil their needs, then Peter needs to learn to control Isaac's world both physically and mentally. Sometimes when he's being 'independent' and mostly when Isaac has had enough of the world. I love Isaac, he is my heartbeat, my soul, and I want to always know that when he's away from me he is being given the best care and his needs are being catered for. Peter has to learn not only submissive needs, but he also has to learn Isaac.

"My Keepers don't like being away from their subs, but if you love someone, you want to make things right for them. Do you understand?" I did. I got it. If you loved someone you would do anything for them even if it felt difficult, so...

"Why don't the Keepers see to their slaves need then?"

"The Keeper's relationship with their slave is a little different. Looking after a twenty-four-hour submissive with pain needs is a difficult and tiring job. No one can do it forever, it would be damaging to both sides. The Keepers are mostly caregivers, so their desire to top or dominate might not be their most prominent desire, just something they want to dabble in now and again, so this gives them that opportunity. They get to care for the person they love without restricting their desires but when a Keeper does play with their sub, it then becomes something much more intimate, it's loving and strengthens their connection. It's kind of like our way of helping a relationship that would probably not last very long."

"But you see to Isaac's needs."

Layton smiled and nodded "Yes. I want to share everything with Isaac, I have shared everything with him. To continue to do that, I need Peter. It kind of brings us back to why Isaac must find his place with Peter. It's important for me so I know that Isaac is always getting the best care, always being loved, but at the same time having all his needs seen to. It's important for Isaac so he doesn't feel lost when he's not with me. Rather than him going to clients to have his need sated, he needs to get everything from Peter that he gets from me. Do you follow?" I nodded.

I was now very worried about where that left Leo and me. If he was saying it was impossible to be with someone like Leo all the time then where were Leo and I going?

"I don't want to send Leo to strangers. He hates customers, they scare him. How can I send him to strangers that are going to hurt him?"

Layton smiled. "Wow, you jumped. That's okay, I can catch up." I looked at him, confused, he ignored me and continued. "You haven't seen Leo when he's needy, I haven't seen Leo when he's needy. Looking at his back tells me that it's not a nice place to be for him and he will probably do anything to have it sated, regardless of how much it scares him. But, that is a few days off yet, I hope."

"Days!?"

Layton nodded. "Breathe, Joe. You're starting to get loud." I put my hand over my mouth and looked at the door. Layton laughed a little which made me look back at him. He took my hand from my mouth and kissed it. "You didn't wake him."

I sat quietly for a while, my head hurt trying to take in everything. Days? How many days? He was going to want pain. That was still new to me, still a little strange. If I thought about it too much it fucking scared the life out of me.

"Joe? I really need you to share some of your thoughts. I don't know you well enough yet to work out what's going on in your head."

I sort of laughed. Not from amusement but hysteria. "We're sitting here naked."

Layton smiled. "It's sitting without clothes, it doesn't help me work out what's going on in your head. It's a start. You need to help me a little more."

I felt panicked, worried. "Can you take him?"

Layton frowned at me. "Take him where?"

I shook my head. "Away, away from me. It would be better for him, wouldn't it? Now you know, you can just take him into your world and look after him and he'd be safe, won't he?"

"Yes, he'd be safe but not very happy. Don't you want to come, Joe? Don't you want to share this journey with him? He wants you to." I looked at Layton who was looking concerned at me. He had kind of gone out of focus for a minute but now he was clearer again.

"I'm not a good Keeper or friend. We've been here less than a day and I haven't done a good job. I know he's distraught about leaving the alley and Ginger and yet he's saying nothing to me. He just keeps asking, can we go home, over and over. I was meant to be watching him and I fell asleep and when I woke up he was gone from the bed. He was in here eating half the bathroom and trying to burn himself under the hot tap. Then on top of that, I forgot to feed him. It was the last thing Kendal said. She said, don't forget to feed him because he would forget to say. He never forgets that he's hungry, he always tells me and he didn't but I knew. He was eating toothpaste, he always eats toothpaste when he's hungry and all I did was be angry with him because of his hand.

"Then I tried to move him from his thoughts, I could see he was upset and I tried to forget about it and said I would take him to look at the house." I shook my head at Layton. "He said he wanted to go home and I said the alley was bad. I shouldn't have said it, I don't know the right things to say to him. If I did he wouldn't have hit out at me, he's never done that."

I felt like I was crying but I had no tears left. Completely lost now, I tried to say something else but I didn't know what else to say. Layton reached out his hand and cupped my face and I held his arms, clutching at him as if it would give me the answers I needed.

"It's okay, Joe, breathe and we will talk about it. None of those things are so bad." I looked at him dismayed.

"They're not?"

He shook his head and smiled. "No, they are all fixable. It wouldn't have been half as painful if you had just told me them one at a time." Layton was looking at me and I felt stupid again.

"See, I'm just not good at it." Layton scrambled around behind him and pulled the plug. "Are we getting out? I'm not ready." I was starting to sound like Leo. Layton brushed his hands up and down my arms.

"You are freezing and getting wrinkled. We'll bathe again, hopefully next time it will be more relaxing."

"It was relaxing...I thought." What did I know? It had been years since I'd had a bath.

Layton laughed. "That's because you are wound up tighter than a spring." He tapped my arm. "Come on, get out." I sighed and moved back to untangle my legs from his. He stood up, stepped out of the bath and started to dry himself while I sat and looked at him. "Are you going to get out? Or just watch me?"

Jesus, I was staring at his naked body like some wanton...whore.

"I'm not ready."

He smiled and picked up another towel and put it around my shoulders. I leant my chin on my hands on the edge of the bath and just...watched him.

CHAPTER NINE

JOE

I had suddenly become some sex starved wanton hussy. I couldn't take my eyes from him as he dried himself and I wasn't even being sneaky about it. He didn't seem to notice or if he did he was ignoring me. He wrapped the towel around his waist and leaned up against the wall with his arms folded, watching me a moment before speaking.

"Are you going to get out?"

I nodded but made no move. My mind was already on its own course, my body following close behind.

"You've got a good body." Fuck knows what I was doing. I shook my head trying to shake off the thoughts, the need, for…what? His touch? Attention?

Layton stepped towards me, crouched down in front of me, and stroked his hand through my hair. He touched his mouth to mine, gently, cautiously.

"Come on, time to get out." He took my hand in his, stood up. and gently pulled me up and out of the bath. "Let me dry you." I frowned at him. Dry me? Like, dry me dry? Like I was some kid or something?

"No, it's fine…"

"Let me look after you."

Right now I couldn't speak or even question him as he stood me up, took the edge of the towel that was around my shoulders, and started to dab and gently stroke at my face. As he watched what he was doing and worked his way down my body, I watched him. His chocolate brown eyes, which had flecks of yellow, seemed to flare with his concentration. His lip ring protruded further, the more he pushed his lips together. Now and again his tongue would pop out to wet his lips and I would see the flash of metal that was impaled through it. What would that feel like…shit, I needed to stop…but he wasn't. His hands were touching me…

I felt like a caged animal being prepared for…the game? A game? What was even more disturbing was, I wanted to play. It was like he was well out of my league, the sort of customer that pulled up in a car and offered me big bucks to get in the car and spend time with him. This time though, I had seen everything that was on offer and for the fucking life of me, I couldn't deny I was interested, my body was interested. When was the last time I had come? Even had an offer? Fuck. His hand drifted across my chest, drying the droplets of water and I closed my eyes as I felt my cock rise to get his attention. It was mortifying.

I could feel the heat in my face, my short breaths taking in the extra air my body was asking for. Jesus Christ he was definitely going to have me down as a tease but I just couldn't control it, either my thoughts or my body.

"I think…" A sweep of his hand over my cock made me gasp and open my eyes just as he took my mouth, then he swept his mouth across my cheek and whispered in my ear.

"Don't think…just feel." He took my mouth again and I met his asking tongue with my own.

I felt feverish and needy as fuck. I already wanted my orgasm even though it wasn't even asking yet. This wasn't going to be one of those all-nighters. This was going to be a quick pleasure fuck and I felt fucking desperate for it.

He was stroking my cock and I opened my eyes again, not realising I had closed them. "Fucking beautiful…" I couldn't take my eyes from him.

I tentatively lifted my hands and they shook, trembling against his shoulders.

"Shit…I'm sorry…" I wasn't sure what I was apologising for but I was losing any semblance of what was right and any control I thought I had. I pushed my back into the tiled wall behind me and pushed my hips forward, thrusting my cock further into his hand. Yeah, it was too late, there was no going back now so I threw myself into it. "You wanna fuck a needy street whore?"

I reached out and took his nipple in my fingers, drawn to the small metal ring impaled in it, and rubbed it gently making him lean forward and take my mouth.

I had this vague awareness that he was fumbling around on the basin beside us and then leaned into my ear and breathlessly spoke. "Turn around."

No hesitation from me, I turned like the fucking pro I was, pushing my face and chest into the cold wet tiled wall and then pushed out my arse to him, spreading my legs. I dropped my hand to my cock and stroked it in my fist as I heard the squelch of lube. I wasn't even fucking bothered about it being wet or dry, I just wanted.

"Give it to me, fuck, I want it hard." I felt his hand wrap around my middle, pull my arse out further to him, and then felt the film-coated cock slide between my cheeks.

Of course, he had wrapped it. Us street whores had all sorts of germs…the thought made me snarl just as he found my hole and forced himself straight in. The pain of being stretched open so fast made me drop my cock, brace myself against the tiles and give a grunting cry at the same time as he reminded me how long it had been.

"Jesus, you're fucking tight."

I whimpered as the burn subsided only to snatch another breath and moan as he thrust forcefully again, all the way out and back in. My face was pushed into the wall with his forceful thrust, his hand pushing me hard against the tiles and, every now and again, his fingers would try and soothe the hold. The pain and the pleasure of it was so raw, I felt overwhelmed with it and muffled a sob into the wall before I managed to reach down and take hold of my dick again.

I couldn't remember the last fuck I had but I knew it hadn't been anything like this. My feet were kicked further apart and then my hips were grabbed and dragged back, impaling me hard on his cock again. The thrusts were slow and forceful. Each time forcing me into the wall, dragging my face against the tiles as his heavy thrusts hit my prostate, sending zaps of pain and pleasure through me. They became so hard and fierce, I had to grunt my breaths to get my air and at one point, I put my hand behind me to stop his entry but the action was weak and shaky and ignored. I squeezed my cock hard in my fist, my strokes were not about creating any pleasure, just about holding my junk while the orgasm burned inside me.

I closed my eyes and lost myself in every hard pounding, lapping the pleasure up like a cat with cream. The searing pleasure came swift and quick, I couldn't form any words as one last heavy painful thrust from him across my prostate had me spiralling. My cum shot from my dick over and over, making me growl into the wall with each exploding wave. I gripped the wall with my spare hand to stop me from falling into an exhausted heap but then an arm swept around my chest and middle, holding me, while the thrusts became small and quick.

His face was next to mine, his breaths quick, his words whispered. "Fuck, Joe…Jesus…Joe…fucking gorgeous…" And then he forced himself hard into my arse and growled his pleasure as he mocked thrust against me with each wave of his orgasm.

I closed my eyes against the embarrassment and humiliation I felt as he pulled me tight to him and kissed the side of my face, as we both came back from our pleasure and panted heavily.

"Fuck…" I said.

"Fuck…" He said.

I turned my face towards him over my shoulder as he released his hold on me.

"Get your own fucking words…" I said, trying to lighten the situation. He slipped out of my hole before leaning over me and brushing his lips over the side of my face.

"Well…it was…fucking sweet. Did I hurt you?" It seemed a strange thing to be asked and I shook my head.

"I guess you can't take the whore out of the street boy." Unconsciously, I lifted my hand and covered my face. Talk about being fucking desperate and wanton.

"Stop, Joe." I watched under my lashes as he stepped to the side, slipped the condom from his dick and binned it. It seemed to condone my whore status even more and I was further humiliated.

"I didn't even think…of course you wrapped it…I guess you don't want any street disease…"

"Hey!" My face was grabbed and my whole body was turned to see a frowning Layton looking at me questioningly. "What the hell, Joe?"

I felt my lip wobble and I shook my head and covered my face with my hands.

"I'm sorry…I didn't mean…I didn't mean for any of that to happen…" I closed my eyes against his stare.

"Hey, hey look at me." I opened my eyes and he softly smiled at me. "It was fucking hot, you were fucking…hot and beautiful. I said not to tease." He looked at me amused. I was breathing heavily looking at him and he shrugged. "Yes, I used a condom because you've only just arrived here and, until you get the all-clear from your checks, I have a whole world to protect. I can't risk them, for anyone or anything. Do you understand, Joe?"

I bit my bottom lip and nodded. "I'm sorry…"

He smiled at me. "Stop fucking apologising, it was damn hot and I'm not sorry." He leaned forward and kissed me, softly at first, licking at the corner of my mouth until I kissed him back. "So fucking gorgeous, Joe." He lifted his thumb and stroked my lip which was sore again. "Come on, under the shower with me, let's get cleaned off."

He took me under the shower, washed me and himself, and then we ended up back in the towels drying ourselves as if it had all never happened. He went and checked on Leo through the open door, which made me feel bad because I had forgotten him in my lust.

"Shit, is he okay?"

Layton smiled at me. "He's still asleep."

I still felt like I owed him an explanation. "I haven't come for a really long time."

He walked back to me and took my hand, kissed it and then sat down on the floor by the sink and pulled me with him.

"My body has that effect on people all the time." He pulled me into his body and hugged me before kissing the side of my head. I could hear his amusement in his voice. "It's a cross I have to bear."

I gave him a quick look as I smiled at him. "Thank you, for easing my humiliation. I'm not usually so…needy."

"It was hot, Joe, you are…hot. Enjoying a moment of pleasure is not humiliating. It is something we do a lot here, you'll see." He pulled me against him again and kissed me again before pulling my face up to him. "You sure you're okay? It was pretty ferocious? You were pretty tight, when was the last time you were fucked?" I felt my cheeks flush as I pulled my face from his fingers.

"I'm fine…You just took me by surprise. It's been a while…they like…younger boys…"

"Hey, I'm not judging. Use some of the cream that Kendal left for Leo if it gets too sore." There was a moment of quiet where he just played his fingers over my shoulder and neck before he spoke again, moving the subject away from me, which I was grateful for. "Have you asked him about Ginger? About what Ginger said?" I nodded.

"Yeah. When I mentioned Ginger he just looked confused. He was saying he liked his own bed and I said he didn't have one, that he used to sleep with Ginger. He changed the subject then, told me I snored."

Layton smiled. "Because he would have liked listening to you sleeping. He doesn't want you to be negative about Ginger, if he got that from your tone he won't want to go there. What was he doing when you found him after waking?"

I shrugged. "I'm not entirely sure. He was sitting here, beside the bath, with the hot tap running. He had the soap and toothpaste in his lap, which I think he was eating now and again. Then he put his hand in the steam. It looked like he was trying to catch it and then he put his hand under the tap until it made him cry out. Why would he do that?" Layton stretched his feet out in front of him, crossing his ankles.

"Did you ask him?" Why did he never just answer me?

"Yes but he just said it felt like the cold water. He did ask me if I missed the alley."

"And?"

"I said I didn't. I didn't want to upset him."

Layton cocked his head sideways and looked at me. "You lied to him?"

"No. It's an alley full of shit and rubbish. What's to miss?" Layton rested his hand on his lap. He was so relaxed.

"It was your home. Leo will always think of it as home until he becomes settled somewhere else. You shouldn't lie to him. You can't expect him to be honest with you if you are going to put up barriers. I know you're hurting too." I stayed silent. "The hot water thing will be him trying to work out his feelings. He's trying to see if things are the same, feel the same. He's feeling alone, Joe, lost without his familiar surroundings. It will make him unsure of everything, even you."

"He said I mattered to him. He was asking why I spoke differently, why I wasn't swearing at him and I said that on the street you had to swear to be heard, to be someone that mattered, then he said I mattered to him."

Layton smiled. "That's beautiful. See what happens when you're honest with him, when you talk to him? He's desperately trying to tell you things."

"He hit me after that."

Layton laughed a little. "Well, you broke a promise to him. You said the street would never be a bad place, then you said it was. He's confused and frustrated because he doesn't understand and you just added to it. He didn't mean it, mean to hurt you. He was just showing you how he feels, it just came out as an action rather than words. Now your face feels like how Leo's feeling inside." Great, thanks.

"He wouldn't sit with me on the porch at first. He said I was broken."

Layton smiled. "Mm, they are very perceptive. You looked like he felt, it would make him feel a little unsafe. You did well to calm him down so quickly. Taking him outside was very quick thinking. It's good that you know how to do that."

I shrugged. It was Leo, I knew what Leo liked.

"He likes the stars. Not very handy though if he flips during the day...the day sky doesn't have quite the same effect."

Layton half laughed. "Mm, it is a glitch. I'll think about it, see what I can come up with."

I laughed and frowned at him. "You're going to find a way to bring the night sky into the day?"

Layton smiled and shrugged. "I've been known to work miracles before you know."

I turned into him, needing to feel his support. He pulled me into his body further and I lay my head on his chest. I had no idea what was wrong with me. I wanted to feel whatever it was he made me feel.

"Tell me what I should have done. I need to get it right for him."

Layton kissed the top of my head and ran his fingers through my hair. "I thought you wanted me to take him away?"

I thought about it again. Layton had offered me a place in this world before either of us had known about Leo. He must have seen something in me. I didn't feel very strong or much like a leader. I felt lost without the alley too. My home.

"It hurts to think about not seeing him again, not being with him. But his need scares me. I don't think I can be the person he needs me to be but the thought of sending him away to strangers to have it, doesn't feel right either. You asked me to come here before we knew about Leo, so you must have seen something in me that made you think that I could do this. I'm just not sure what it is. Honestly, I don't want you to take him from me but can you be honest with me and tell me if you think he would be better off?"

Layton sighed. "Taking Leo and putting him with an experienced Keeper would be the easier option. Taking you and putting you with an experienced slave, after some training, would also be easier on you. This world is not about doing the easy thing, it's about doing the right thing for both you and Leo. Leo doesn't understand his need either, Joe, he has a lot to learn about it, about sating it safely. I think that you and Leo can learn together and I'm not saying that is going to be easy on either of you but at the end of each day, you both get to be with each other under the stars. I know that is important to Leo…and you.

"He has had the most difficult time today, tonight, sharing his need with strangers, ripped from his home, now in a strange place but he accepted it all as he lay with you on the porch. Being with you is more important to him than anything he has or will endure. You have to ask yourself if it is the same for you? Regardless of what you and Leo share, good or bad, does it still feel right? If you're feeling angry with him or feel sorry for him then it's probably not right but if you are looking at him and loving him just the way you've always done, the way you've always felt, then surely it shows you that it doesn't matter about the places you go. As long as you can both come back and find that place together.

"Finding that place is not always easy, but are the feelings you have for him worth it? Only you can decide that. I can tell you that Leo thinks it is. He has shown you over the last four years that he will endure anything to share a moment under the stars with you."

I thought about him. Leo. I had watched him struggle every day on the street. He had endured a lot. He had been raped by his stepfather and then every day he did things that he didn't like, got pushed around by the other boys and customers but when he was with me, he was just the same, Leo. The Leo that I loved to watch and listen to. If he could find his way through those things, alone, to be with me, then surely together we could find our way back from anything?

There was nothing like that feeling of being with Leo, just me and him. Hadn't that been the reason I hadn't got in the car? Just for that moment with him? We hadn't come close to sharing ourselves with each other but if just sitting with Leo felt that good, then what would it be like to really know him? I wanted to know and even if all we ended up with was what we had now, those moments where we sat together, that moment was worth fighting for.

"I want that feeling. It's just a small thing but if Leo is prepared to fight to have it, then so am I." Decision made. "He stays with me." My heart started beating really fast. "Fuck, now I'm scared."

Layton kissed me and laughed a little. "There's nothing wrong with a little fear, it keeps you on your toes. Let's talk about Leo's needs. It will be back very soon. He's too new to go to clients so you can stop worrying about that for a moment. That may not even be the path he wants to take. He only knows one way of getting his fix, and razor blades really are not that safe or nice. I think it might be better if you both come and stay at my house as soon as you see it. It will give us a chance to watch him and get to see his need. He's never had to wait for it so it will be new to him and a little confusing, it might make him a little angry. It will be new to you too, to see Leo like that.

"I wouldn't want you to deal with that alone, it can be difficult to watch and tiring. Hopefully, Isaac and Peter would have worked out their issues by then. It would be nice to have Isaac around to ease his journey, especially in the beginning. Leo only knows the pain of having his need sated, he has never had it connected to his pleasure. That is something that they have to learn but it doesn't usually take long." Layton smiled. "They like both."

"So, you will do it for him?"

He nodded. "Yes, for now, if he's agreeable. Until you decide what you want to do. For now just do what you've always done."

"I tried, it's not working."

Layton smiled. "That's because you're trying to do it right. Everything that Peter and Kendal tell you is right, but not necessarily right for you. You know Leo, even though you think you don't, you do. There are some things he's kept from you but that doesn't change who he is. You didn't do anything wrong today...actually you lied to him and I wouldn't advise that but I understand why you did. You were right to be angry with him for burning his hand, he must know that that is not acceptable behaviour. You were right to move on from it but you have to move him with you. You just left some things out. Leo wants to make you happy. If he does something good then tell him.

"For instance, not leaving the room when you were sleeping was worthy of a bit of praise. He could have gone anywhere in the house or garden, or into the woods, he chose to stay near you. I know he still got into trouble, but imagine if he'd done that in the kitchen? You wouldn't have been close by. He got nothing nice from you so it's no wonder he didn't want to move on with you. Even in the alley when he messed around with customers the first thing you always did was comfort him, don't change that, he still needs it. Did Leo used to talk to you a lot in the alley?"

I nodded. "Yes, when we were alone. Mostly rubbish, silly things…but I liked listening to him, sometimes he made me laugh and he liked that."

"That's why he did it, told you crazy things in the hope that one of them would make you laugh. You need to get back to that."

Did Leo think that much about what he did? I wasn't sure.

"I tried. When we got onto the porch I asked him if he wanted to talk, that's when he would usually talk. He didn't want to. So I left it, left him. He just sort of drifted looking at the sky. I should have pushed a little harder shouldn't I?"

Layton tipped my face up to him. "No, Joe. This is what I mean about knowing Leo. Sharing is important, as is everything else that you've been told, that you're trying to learn. You did exactly what you should have done. You held out your hand to Leo and allowed him to share his thoughts but you also recognised he wasn't ready and just comforted him. He was extremely traumatised by his outburst and what he had done to you, he would have struggled to verbalise his thoughts. Pushing him to do so would have taken him right back to those unsure feelings. You have given him a chance to breathe. His thoughts haven't gone away and you should still try and share them with him, but you showed him that he's still safe with you even after what he'd done. He's already forgiven you for making him feel those things."

I smiled and nodded. "Yes, I know. I kind of got that when he asked to sleep naked with me. We slept naked together yesterday, it felt good to feel him next to me again. I guess he liked it too." I smiled. "He wasn't shy about his body. I mean when we woke and we were both naked. I thought he would be. I haven't seen him naked for a long time...his body has changed."

Layton smiled. "The boy you took under your wing is now a young man. He has no reason to be shy about his body, all he knows is the customers wanted it. Isaac said he understood very little about himself, his self-awareness." Layton half laughed. "Isaac gave him a quick lesson, one that I'm sure he will share with you once he feels he can. Isaac likes to share...especially orgasms."

I smiled. "Leo hasn't shared what happened but it was only really yesterday wasn't it? Do you mind that Isaac shares?"

"I am particular about who I share Isaac with, but now and again he will meet someone who he's very drawn to. Isaac understood Leo from the moment he met him. He knew about his need even before Leo shared it with him, which is probably why he felt drawn to him. He wanted to share something beautiful with Leo. No harm could come of it, nothing that would come between our relationship so I saw no need to forbid him the pleasure he sought. I was not aware that you would be following us back into this world though. Now they've tasted each other a little, they will have strong feelings of wanting to return there again with each other.

"I would advise that they are not left alone for too long. Isaac's need to share his orgasms can be a little insatiable. Forbidden or not, sometimes he can't help himself." Layton was smiling as he spoke about his love.

He seemed to know Isaac inside out and accept his behaviour as part and parcel of who Isaac was. He even seemed to love it and find it amusing. It was clear that their relationship was very strong, that they didn't doubt each other's feelings, even if they took a little side path for a while. I could only wish for mine and Leo's relationship to be like that, to be that secure. It seemed a long way off, if not impossible at this moment. Even snuggled against Layton now, felt a little underhand but I just needed it.

Layton kissed the top of my head and stroked his fingers over my arm. "Are you tired, Joe?" I was, desperately so, but I still need this time with Layton.

"Is it time for you to go?"

He shook his head. "No, I have a few hours if you still need me."

I smiled against him. "I bet your Keepers don't need you, do they? I expect they just get on with it."

"Actually they do. Being a Keeper is a very difficult job. I often sit with my Keepers and do exactly this, talk to them about their worries and their fears and love them a little. Everyone needs to feel comforted and appreciated, everyone gets a little lost now and again, it's not a bad thing, Joe, to need help." That made me feel better, knowing I wasn't the only one who felt like this. I yawned and closed my eyes. "You're exhausted."

"No, I'm good. I'm just resting my eyes."

Layton pulled me onto his lap, which was embarrassing and a bit mortifying, but it felt so good so I just closed my eyes and tried to enjoy it. He wrapped the towel around me tighter and held me close to him and stroked his fingers through my hair.

"Leo might wake up so I can't sleep." I heard Layton's smile on his breath. I sat there fighting the urge to just let it take me. "It will be better...tomorrow...won't...it?" I didn't hear his answer.

I was being moved and couldn't decide whether to take any notice, then I remembered Leo and I opened my eyes. I was on the bed with him and Layton was pulling a blanket over me. He bent and kissed me.

"I will stay as long as I can, to watch you both. Go back to sleep." I followed him as he sat on the floor by the door and then I turned and looked at Leo. I kissed his lips gently and closed my eyes. If Layton was still here then it was safe to sleep for a while.

I woke with a start. He was gone again. I sat up quickly and looked at the bathroom and listened. The door was shut. Fuck! I scrambled from the bed and lunged at the bathroom door but just as I got there a movement at the bottom of the bed caught my eye. Layton? No, the head I could see was not Layton's spiked hair, it was a shaved head. I let my breath go, relieved and then panicked again. What was he doing sitting on the floor at the end of the bed? I walked slowly towards him and he turned his head to look at me and smiled.

I saw the toothpaste in his hand and then panicked again. He had been in the bathroom. I quickly dropped to my knees and grabbed his hands and looked at them. No, he wasn't burnt. His hand was still a little rosy from yesterday but other than that, he was fine, unhurt, safe. I breathed a sigh of relief again and then sat and looked at him. He was looking back at me like I was mad, slightly unsure of my manic actions. I smiled at him.

"I was just checking something." Leo held out his hands to me to show me again and I smiled and took one of his hands and kissed it. "It's okay, I've checked them now." I looked at the toothpaste. "Did you get that from the bathroom?"

He shook his head. "No, the door was closed. Isaac gave it to me."

I looked at his shorts laying by his feet. It must have been in his shorts all this time. I smiled. He was now stocking up with emergency supplies of toothpaste, it was kind of amusing. I took the toothpaste and put the lid on. He was hungry, starving probably. At least he seemed to have only just started on the tube, it was still quite full. I put the tube on the floor. He hadn't left the room and that was a good thing. Layton had said that he should know when he did good things. He was looking at the toothpaste.

"Leo?" He looked at me. "I'm glad you stayed here with me, that you didn't go anywhere."

"I don't know where to go. I needed to pee and I didn't know where to do that either." Oh God.

"Leo, did you take a piss somewhere?"

He smiled at me like I was crazy. "No. Not indoors you idiot. I'm not stupid!"

Relief again. I looked at the bathroom door. Leo knew how to open doors, he knew the bathroom was right there. I had no clue what had stopped him from going in there. It was just a door. I stood.

"Come on, I need to take a leak."

He took my hand that I held out for him and I pulled him to his feet. I was still finding his naked body…new and it was hard not to stare and linger on it longer than was polite. He didn't seem to notice or care. In the bathroom we shared the toilet and Leo flushed it…and flushed it and flushed it, and flushed it some more.

"Okay that's enough, there's no more water, you need to wait until it fills up again. It's just a toilet, Leo, I know we didn't have one that flushed but nor will they here if you keep doing it, you'll break it." I turned to wash my hands in the basin and heard it flush again. "Leo!" I turned to look at him and he was still standing over the toilet looking in the pan. It made me smile. I wished I could look at the world through Leo's eyes sometimes. "Come and brush your teeth. Are you hungry?"

He looked at me then and walked over. "I'm so hungry, Joe, my stomach hurts, can we go to Manni's?"

Oh shit. I gave him a toothbrush from the two new ones that had been left on the sink, and he set about brushing his teeth, giving me a moment to think. He had no idea where we were. Did he think Manni's was just around the corner like it had always been? I looked at the towels that still lay on the floor from my time with Layton last night. Honesty. I looked back at Leo as he washed out his mouth with water, well, he mostly drank it but it was close enough, and then he looked at me expectantly.

"No, we can't go to Manni's. Kendal wants us to have breakfast with her. We are really far away from Manni's, too far to go there for breakfast. We need to come back here after breakfast and talk about some things. Besides, I don't have any money and we don't have to pay for food here."

These were things I knew he would understand, we'd get to the other stuff…later. When he looked at me it was with wide eyes and a little excitement. He had nice eyes…beautiful eyes.

"It's free? Like where Isaac took me?"

I smiled and nodded. "Yep, it's free." I bent, picked up the towels and shook them out before hanging them over the rail.

I wasn't ready for his next question. "Who were you talking to in here?" I shot my head round to look at him.

Fuck, had he heard us? I had no idea what to say. The honesty thing popped into my head but if I told him and Isaac found out, it would cause trouble for Layton. I decided to keep it as honest as I could and see what happened from there.

"I was having a bath, it was nice, relaxing. When your back is better, we can have a bath together." I had made that up to throw him off the questions but actually, I realised I wanted to share a bath with him.

"Who were you talking to when you were having a bath?" Bloody hell, was he always this annoying?

"I thought you were sleeping?"

"I was asleep but I heard you talking." Shit…how did that work?

"Just a friend." He was still looking at me. Fuck. I was going to have to lie. This wasn't a good start. "A friend of Isaac's…err, Kendal, it was Kendal. She was asking what we wanted for breakfast. She just popped in… for a minute." I realised then that if he heard Layton talking he would know it wasn't Kendal. "She wanted to know how your back was."

"Did she fix your face?"

I smiled and nodded as I answered, grateful he'd accepted the answer. "Yes, that's why she came, for that too. How's your back feeling?"

"I like it again now." I smiled. It was feeling better, not so sore, at least I hoped that's what that meant. I would put some cream on it again after breakfast. "Does your face hurt?" I touched my tongue to my lip.

"A little but it feels better." Better than my hole did, that was for sure. This was good though. We were talking. Not about anything much but it had progressed from yesterday. "Shall we go and get some food?" Leo's face lit up and he nodded. I was not going to forget to feed him today, no matter what.

I took his hand and walked back into the bedroom. Leo sat cross-legged on the bed while I found our clothes. My shirt was covered in blood and Leo's didn't look too pretty either. I remembered then that Kendal had said there were clothes in here we could use so I went to have a look. I found the linen trousers. I wasn't sure what Leo would think about them.

"Look, Leo, new clothes!" I tried to sound as excited as I could about them. I held them up to Leo and he just sat there and looked at them. "You like new clothes, don't you?"

"I like my clothes."

I sat on the bed. Leo had a stubborn streak, that wasn't new.

"I know you do but they are all messed up. You can wear these to breakfast and I will ask Kendal to wash our clothes. These won't rub you as your jeans do."

"Can't we eat breakfast here? You can get it and bring me some, like you used to do sometimes."

"Don't you like these, Leo?" He shrugged. "Come on, put them on and see how they feel."

I held them out to him and he took them slowly. I went back to the drawer and found black ones and I put them on. When I turned back to Leo he was still sitting there holding his. I remembered what happened yesterday when I had dressed him, I had tried to move him forward too quickly. I went and sat on the bed next to him. I was just about to say something when I realised that, had we been in the alley now, I wouldn't be expecting him to say or do anything. I often went and just sat with him at the back of the alley, usually after he had had a customer. I reached out my hand and took his, linking our fingers and just sat with him. We sat for so long in silence that I thought we had probably missed breakfast.

I wished he would just tell me what was going on in his head. I turned his hand over and stroked his palm with my fingers. Leo just liked to sit sometimes but it was usually after talking for a long time. Not talking like we had done this morning, that was different, that was a conversation between us. When Leo talked to me about things, it didn't usually require me to reply or speak very often. Which was good because sometimes I didn't understand where the things he spoke about came from.

Once he spent an hour talking about a birthday cake he'd seen a random person carrying in the street. I smiled at the memory. When he had left a gap for me to get a word in and I had asked him about the cake and why it was important, he'd changed the subject. It was usually after bouts of talking like that, that he fell silent like he was now and kind of drifted.

I looked from his hand to his face and he was smiling. He stretched his hand out in mine. It was tickling him but he didn't want to move his hand, he didn't want it to stop. I smiled at him then lifted his palm to my mouth and kissed it.

He looked at me. "Do you think Kendal makes nice breakfasts?" Yes! He was back and not a single bit of blood spilt to get there. I felt a little proud of myself.

I smiled at him. "Well, she makes nice dinners doesn't she?" He nodded. "If you get dressed we can go and see if she's still doing breakfast, I think we might have missed it but we can have something else, I'm sure." Leo looked at the linen trousers. "There're just trousers, Leo. Look, like mine." He still looked unsure. "If you want to have anything to eat, you have to put them on."

I thought he was going to be really stubborn because he just sat there for a moment, then he slowly dropped his legs over the side of the bed and started to put them on. I was going to help him but then decided while he was moving I would leave him.

"Good boy, Leo." He stood up and pulled them over his arse. They looked really good sitting on his hips and more as an excuse to touch his skin, I put my finger in the waistband before I tied them for him. "Are they too tight?" He shook his head and said nothing more.

I stood then, went into the bathroom, and looked in the mirror. I looked at my bruised face and then rubbed my hand through my hair. I had enjoyed my time out with Layton last night and I did feel a little better this morning. I wondered what time he had left? Had he been able to protect his ninja status? I remembered the kiss and touched my fingers to my sore lip. It had been crazy what that kiss had made me feel and I blamed it for what happened after too. Leo appeared in the reflection next to mine and I smiled at him. He looked beautiful, lost but still beautiful. I shook my head a little. I had never allowed myself to think about him too much, now I was using words like beautiful to describe him.

"Does your lip hurt?" I turned and leaned against the basin. Fuck, he looked hot in the white linens.

I smiled at him and held out my hand. "No, not hurt." He walked towards me and I took his hand. "I'll show you, later maybe. You look nice in white. Are you ready?" Leo took a deep breath. "Are you worried?" He nodded. "It's just breakfast with Kendal, you like Kendal."

"I don't like it here." Of course. Strange customers, strange houses, strange clothes, it all made him feel uneasy.

"I know it's different and I'm not sure how long we will be here but I promise though, that wherever we go, we'll be together."

He frowned at me. "I don't want you to leave me here, I don't know where we are. Can we look at the stars when we go?"

I smiled and leaned forward and kissed his cheek. "Only if we leave at night."

Leo smiled, liking that idea. "I want to leave at night."

I smiled back at him. "I'll bear that in mind. Now, come on, let's go and get some food." I took Leo through the bedroom and he stopped to pick up the toothpaste. "You don't need that."

"I want to take it."

I was a little uneasy about breakfast this morning too, so if Leo wanted to take something that brought him comfort when he was finding things difficult then surely that was okay? I smiled at him.

"Okay but you're not to eat it." I turned and put my hand on the door and paused a moment while I took a few clearing breaths.

If getting breakfast was this hard and took this long, what did the rest of the day hold? I turned and looked at Leo. He was just standing there looking at me, waiting. I smiled at him and his stomach growled loudly. I smiled and opened the door.

CHAPTER TEN

JOE

We could smell the food as we entered the hallway. I looked back at Leo and he was looking around. Being inside was new to both of us but Leo became unsure when new things happened. New boys on the street, new dumped rubbish which hadn't been there before, all unsettled Leo and he would seek me out for a while to either just wait with me or talk to me about it. When he spoke about the things that were worrying him, they were never the actual topic he spoke about. The bag of newly left rubbish would be a side story that slipped in as he told me about something familiar. I used to think he just liked the sound of his own voice until I started realising the story was just a way of him getting to the point or issue. I tried to give him something to ease his anxiousness and pointed to the door on the other side of the hallway.

"That's Isaac's room," I remembered Kendal showing me yesterday. His room was neat, tidy, and plain, with a wooden floor and white walls. She had said Isaac liked it like that.

"Does Isaac stay here all the time?"

I shook my head. "No, Isaac just stays here sometimes. He has a place with Layton too."

We walked to the end and turned the corner slightly. I could hear Kendal humming in the kitchen and I pulled Leo with me and stopped at the door. Kendal had her back to us and I felt unsure about just walking in, this wasn't our place. "Hey."

Kendal swung around and smiled. "Hello, boys. I thought you were never going to come out." Her smile was replaced by concern. "Oh, Joe, your face?" Shit, I had to say something quick after I had lied to Leo.

"Is much better since you looked at it... last night... in the bathroom..." I saw confusion cross her face and then she seemed to get it.

"Oh, yes, of course...come in, come in." She waved us in and when she saw Leo, she walked around the table and reached out her hand. "Leo, good morning, poppet. How are you feeling this morning?" Kendal kissed the side of his face.

"I have new clothes." He did like them.

Kendal looked at his linens and smiled. "Oh, and they look so good. Are they comfortable?"

Leo nodded and held out his hand with the toothpaste. "I have toothpaste."

Kendal took his hand and looked at the squashed tube. "Oh, wow, so you do. Do you want me to take it?"

Leo snatched his hand back and shook his head. "No, it's mine, Isaac gave it to me." That was a little rude.

"Leo!"

Kendal put her hand up to me. "It's okay, Joe."

I looked at Leo. "That was rude, Leo." Leo dropped his face down. "I'm sorry, he's a little unsure of what's going on. It's why it took us a while to leave the room, he had issues with the linens, although he seems to have got over them now. Are we too late for breakfast, I can make something else for us if we missed it?" Not that I knew how to cook.

Kendal smiled and took my hand. "Aw, sweetie of course not. Breakfast is whenever anyone gets up, there are no set times. Come on, relax, take a seat. It's all ready. I'll just do the eggs and tea." She looked at Leo. "Would you like tea, honey?"

Leo didn't say anything so I answered. "Yes, he would thank you and thank you for breakfast. I haven't cooked... ever, I'm not sure where I would start. I will have to learn."

Something else on my to-do list. Kendal gestured to the table and I walked Leo over and got him seated before I sat down next to him. She set about busying herself while she spoke and I sat holding Leo's hand.

"Oh, honey, you don't need to thank me. I always cook for the guys if they're here. If you ever get hungry and I'm not here just come and help yourself to anything. Maybe I could teach you a little basic cooking? I don't mind?"

Food started to arrive on the table and it smelt and looked so fucking glorious! Hot rolls, sausages, bacon, mushrooms, beans and toast.

"Erm, I'm not sure where we'll be, but thank you. Can I help?" Kendal put some plates on the table.

"Nope, just grab a plate, the eggs are just coming."

Tea was delivered and I gave Leo and myself a plate. I watched Kendal in awe of her organisational skills, as she seemed to have everything under control before I realised Leo had undone the toothpaste and was just about to suck the tube dry.

"Leo!" I had never known him to be so rude. "The food is coming, you don't need the paste. Put the lid back on." He waited for a moment as he stared at me and then put the lid back on. "If you are rude again in company, I will take the toothpaste away." He gripped it tight in his hand and put it on his lap. I felt a little embarrassed but Kendal seemed to ignore it all.

"Here we go, eggs. Now help yourself, Joe, I'll sort out Leo's." Kendal took a seat next to Leo on the other side. She turned and looked at him and reached out and rubbed his arm. "This is just like being at Manni's but a little smaller. You must be so hungry, poppet. Shall we start with tea? How many sugars do you like in your tea?"

Leo immediately looked at her, he seemed a little excited and I could feel him fidgeting. "Lots... can I have lots? Joe and Ginger never give me lots in but I like it."

Kendal smiled and got the sugar bowl and a spoon. She put three in and stirred it and then gave it to Leo. I picked up mine and started to drink it. I never knew he didn't like the tea I brought him, I only put one sugar in it, he always just drank it without saying anything.

Leo sipped it and then held it out to Kendal. "Can I have more sugar?" Jesus, four!

Kendal smiled. "Well, four is too many to have always but you can have four just today, okay?" Leo smiled and nodded thoroughly enjoying this extra attention he was getting. Kendal put another sugar in and stirred it and gave it back to him. "Right what would you like from the table, honey? A roll?" Leo nodded. "Sausages?" Leo nodded. "Bacon?" Leo nodded. Kendal smiled. "Would you like a bit of everything?" Leo nodded which made Kendal laugh. She leaned forward and kissed him, which Leo soaked up.

Kendal piled his plate with food and Leo seemed happy to sit with Kendal and eat. He even let go of my hand so he could hold his fork. The toothpaste never left him though, even though he struggled to hold both. I helped myself to food and started to eat.

"This is amazing, Kendal, thank you. I... we had a few issues and we didn't get dinner."

Kendal smiled at me while stroking Leo's arm. "Yes, I know. It was a busy day yesterday. Have the issues been resolved?"

I looked at Leo and then back to Kendal. "For now. Is his back okay?" Leo quickly turned and scowled at me.

Kendal patted his arm smiling. "He's eating so I would say that's a good sign." She looked at Leo and took his attention again. "It's okay, honey, no one's going to touch you while you're eating. It feels better though, doesn't it?" Leo nodded and went back to his food. Kendal looked at me. "Did the...bathroom talk help?" She knew Layton had been here. At least I hoped she did and didn't think I had been talking to myself.

I smiled and nodded. "Yes, a lot. Would it be possible to wash our clothes today? My shirt is covered in blood and Leo's is mucky from his back with the ointment."

"Yes, of course..."

Kendal's words were cut off by Peter. "Good morning everyone."

I turned to see Peter and Isaac entering. Peter was walking behind him with his arms wrapped around him protectively yet propelling him forward. He seemed reluctant to come in which I thought was strange since he sometimes lived here. Isaac was wearing white linens the same as Leo's and Peter was wearing black, the same as mine but he also had a linen top on. Isaac was looking down, he looked a little unsure but not as much as yesterday. They stopped just inside the kitchen and Peter kissed Isaac's face.

Kendal spoke. "Morning guys, you hungry? Seeing as you didn't eat yesterday either, I assume you are?"

Peter smiled. "We are starving, aren't we, Isaac?"

Isaac never lifted his face as he whispered his answer. "Yes."

Peter stroked his hand over Isaac's hair. "He's feeling a little bad about breaking the plate and cup yesterday."

When he saw Kendal and Peter kissing, I guessed. Seemed it wasn't just Leo then with a temper when things were not as they wanted. I smiled and looked back at Leo. He seemed unaware of their arrival and was trying to make a sandwich out of his food. Kendal smiled at Isaac and held out her hand.

"Come here, sweetie." Isaac looked at Peter who nodded to him and he left him to walk to Kendal. She got up and took his hand. "I don't care about the plate, I care that we are still friends?" I looked at Leo as they stood beside him talking. I was a little worried that their conversation would upset him. He turned to watch them and I looked from him to them as they spoke. "You know Peter and I always love you but sometimes you have to wait, Isaac, you have to be patient."

Leo turned back and picked up his roll with his left hand and then I noticed the toothpaste was on the table. I leaned forward to see what was so important that it had made him put down the toothpaste and found he was holding Isaac's hand. I looked at Isaac who was standing listening to Kendal and then looked at Leo who was eating his roll. Both behaving impeccably. I turned a little to look at Peter, he was watching Isaac and then moved across the room to make him and Isaac tea. He didn't seem to notice so I thought I would stay quiet.

Isaac spoke and I looked back at him. "I didn't mean to make you feel bad."

185

Peter spoke across the table. "Isaac and I have spoken about what happened." I looked at Peter and then back to Leo who raised his eyes to look at him suspiciously. Peter turned a little and smiled at Isaac. "You can sit with Leo, seeing as you've already said hello." Ahh, he had noticed.

Kendal looked at Isaac and Leo and noticed their hands, she smiled at them. "Aw, you two are a little sneaky." She leaned in and kissed Isaac. "He's a little sweetie, isn't he, Isaac?"

Isaac smiled at her as she gestured to the chair at the end of the table, where she had sat. Peter sat next to Isaac opposite Leo and gave Isaac his tea, while Kendal did for Isaac what she had done for Leo, she made up his breakfast plate.

Leo seemed unmoved about the room full of people, which I was a little surprised about but when he and Isaac looked at each other and smiled I realised that Isaac's arrival had a lot to do with his calmness. I sat drinking my tea, watching them until Peter spoke. Kendal was standing behind him and put her hand on his shoulder.

He took her hand in his and looked up at her. "How was your night? Did you get some rest at Julian's?"

She nodded and kissed Peter's face. "Yes, a little. How was yours?"

"A little busy. Isaac and I are going to spend the day having some quiet time and catching up on some sleep." Peter looked at me. "Seems as though yours was a little busy too? You didn't knock, I would have come to help."

I smiled and shook my head. "It's not as bad as it looks. I was taken by surprise." I half smiled. "Then help arrived." I looked at Leo as he took Isaac's tea and started to drink it. "Leo! That's Isaac's."

Kendal and Peter laughed and Isaac spoke. "He's thirsty, I don't mind if he drinks it."

I looked at Peter. "I'm sorry. Leo's not used to…" I gestured my hand at the table, "…sitting at a table, or so much food…or sharing it with anyone."

Peter smiled at me. "Stop worrying, Joe, he's fine. He's very comfortable with Isaac." I sat back in my chair still feeling on edge.

"I can see that. He wouldn't even let Kendal have the toothpaste, it got forgotten when Isaac came in."

Peter nodded. "It was a little sneaky but they were just saying hello, on the quiet."

Kendal stood up from leaning on Peter. "I'll make some more tea." More tea? I was still clutching my last one.

I looked at Leo and Isaac who seemed to be having some sort of silent conversation. Isaac was smiling at Leo and stroking his fingers over his hand and up his arm. Leo had laid his arm out on the table to him so Isaac could have it.

Peter spoke. "Isaac, leave Leo a moment and eat your breakfast." Isaac sort of sneered and then reluctantly did as he was told.

I sat watching them for a while as Leo constantly asked for Isaac's attention by reaching out and touching his hand or his arm. In the end, I took Leo's hand and held it and he leaned into me and watched Isaac. I could tell he was a little peeved at not being able to just have Isaac's attention and touch but I didn't want Isaac to get into trouble because of Leo.

I was just about to suggest I take Leo away when another man walked into the kitchen making me jump. He looked like one of the suits that frequented the alley, dressed in a shirt and freshly pressed trousers with shiny shoes, and a matching jacket. Even under all that, I could tell he was buff. He had a shaved head and a shade of a goatee on his chin. My heart skipped a beat as he entered the room and I put it down to him being a stranger but there was something about the way the room changed with his presence. It made me uneasy. His deep voice rolled around in my head, making me look away for a moment before being drawn back to him.

"Well, this is very cosy." Leo immediately clamped closer to me and I held him tight trying to reassure him. I had no idea who it was but Kendal and Peter smiled at him and even Isaac seemed pleased to see him. He walked straight round to Kendal and kissed her. "And you're playing den mother." He stroked his hand over her hair and looked lovingly at her as she smiled back. "Mm, and enjoying every minute." He kissed her again on the lips before moving away and bending to kiss Peter on the side of the face.

They were big on kissing here I was noticing. "I was beginning to think you'd run off with Isaac. Jacob is missing you desperately. He's whining that you've forgotten him." Ooh, was this Julian?

My mind worked overtime trying to remember everything I had been told. Jacob's house…with Julian…shit, I couldn't quite remember and Leo's slight moaning breath took my thoughts. I gave him a squeeze to reassure him as Peter spoke.

Peter laughed. "Where is he?"

The guy half-smiled. "With a friend. Keeping him company while he pines for a certain someone."

He looked at Isaac and smiled. Isaac got up and the guy opened his arms in welcome and Isaac walked into him, wrapping his arms around his middle. The guy kissed him and then scooped him up and turned him to sit on the counter behind him, much to Kendal's mocked disgust.

"J!"

He smiled not taking his eyes from Isaac or any notice of Kendal's wrath. "I can't help it, he's beautiful." He kissed Isaac's smiling mouth, who was loving the uninhibited attention. "Mm, sugar." He smiled at Isaac.

Leo had loosened his grip and was watching the interaction, almost straining from me to see it. He'd never seen a suit act so outwardly flamboyant with their touch or manner. I released my hold a little which made him lean back against me so I tightened it again, pulling his hips closer to me and holding him to me. Feeling secure again he wanted to watch more.

The guy, possibly Julian, rubbed his nose over Isaac's before brushing his hands up his arms. "So, Isaac, have you and Peter played yet?" Peter laughed and Kendal again gave mocked disgust. She was clearly smitten with the guy so I knew she didn't mean it.

"J! You can't ask him things like that!"

He smiled and kissed Isaac again, seeming amused. I was sure then who this was, it was Julian, the guy Kendal had spoken about. The guy who owned this house…or owned…Jacob? Who owned this house? I was going to have to pay attention more.

"Why?" He looked back at Isaac for an answer. "We all know it's only a matter of time, even Isaac does. He knows he's beautiful."

Isaac sort of giggled his answer. "No, I have to wait."

Julian laughed. "He's holding out on you, Isaac," Julian cupped Isaac's face in his hands and kissed him on the lips again and then whispered in his ear.

He pulled Isaac from the counter and Isaac went straight to Peter who pulled him onto his lap wrapping his arms around him. He was kissed again.

Isaac, I realised, was constantly lavished with love and attention, from everyone, it seemed. If he wasn't being kissed, he was being touched in some way. It made me see how difficult yesterday had been for him when he had sat quietly wrapped in a blanket, getting the barest of attention from Peter. I wondered if that was where Leo was? Sitting and waiting for attention like Isaac received? Leo had certainly been intrigued by it all. I had always held Leo's hand or hugged him when he was upset but the touches were very distant compared to what we were seeing. Kisses had been few, but street boys just didn't do that, couldn't show that sort of emotion or attachment.

Isaac's touches and kisses were given completely openly and freely and they were all full of emotion and feeling. Even just as an onlooker there was no doubt that they all loved Isaac to some degree. Is that why Isaac seemed so balanced? So able to cope with his life, his need?

I was broken from my thoughts when Julian turned and looked at us. "Mm, and who do we have here?" He studied us for a moment, looking us up and down and then shook his head. "Is Layton opening a new nursery wing at his?" Fuck him. What did that mean?

Isaac, ignoring him, spoke. "It's Leo." Julian looked at Isaac and smiled. He lifted his hand and touched his face, amused by Isaac.

"I know who he is, Isaac." How did he know? He looked at Kendal. "I came to see what all the fuss was about." Kendal tutted. "Well, you can't talk about someone for hours on end and expect me not to want to know more." Mm, okay. I felt edgy, my fight sense on high alert.

Kendal smiled. "It wasn't hours...well, maybe one or two. You have to behave around him, J, he's not just new, he's really new."

Julian smiled at her as he walked around the table to us. He stopped and looked at Leo's back. "Ahh hell, now what the fuck is mother nature up to? That's...very shiny." He reached out and touched Leo's cheek with the back of his fingers and Leo seemed drawn to his touch, leaning into it, which made Julian smile. "Mm, that's nice, Leo, hello to you too." He caught the bottom of Leo's chin and pulled his face around to his. "Well, you're...different, aren't you? Mother nature has a sense of humour it seems." What the fuck did that mean?!

I tightened my hold around Leo and Julian looked at me, then moved his hand to my arm and took it from around Leo. I was just about to say something when Julian looked at me and shook his head. "Be quiet." He held his hand up to me in a gesture to back off.

I felt uncomfortable; I didn't want him saying, doing bad things in front of Leo, to Leo. I didn't want to scare Leo.

I looked at Peter for help, guidance and he smiled at me. "It's okay, Joe."

I was a little agitated about letting this stranger touch and talk to him and watched Leo for any signs of distress. Julian had gone back to looking at Leo and smiled as he continued to stroke his fingers over Leo's face.

He spoke to him. "Of course it's okay. You already know that though, don't you." Leo, who had slipped forward with his touch and was nearly laying on the table, just looked at him which made Julian smile. "With your huge eyes and sticking out ears." Julian gently touched each part he spoke about and then brushed his hand over Leo's hair. "And, dear lord, what has someone done to your hair to make you look so… odd?" Okay, that was it, he was upsetting him.

I reached out to take Leo back but again Julian lifted his hand and blocked mine. I looked at Leo and was just about to say something when Leo edged closer to him on his seat and whispered in answer.

"I got fleas."

Julian raised his brows slightly amused. "Fleas eh?" I frowned as Julian smiled at him and ran his thumb across Leo's lip. "Oh so eager to share too, even though you're a little scared. You can show me." Julian gently pushed his face down to the table and seemed to hold him there but he was still stroking him so I knew his hold was not forceful. Leo didn't struggle or put up even a little resistance.

I put my foot up on my chair, leaned my arm on my knee, and covered my mouth with my hand. I was a little unsure about watching this, it seemed dominating but intimate, forceful yet, caring? Even loving.

Julian leaned down and put his forehead against Leo's as he lay on the table and whispered to him. "Be a good boy."

Then I watched as he stroked his hand firmly down Leo's back, pressing each wound with the pad of his fingers and then dragged it back again. I saw Leo's body tense and strain against the soreness and it made me wince. Leo lifted his hands a little as if he didn't know how to move from him and then laid them on the table on either side of his face.

Julian whispered again. "Oh, clever boy, Leo. That's right, you can breathe in it…"

I wasn't happy. Leo wasn't moaning or making a sound but I could see he was experiencing pain from his touch. My attempts to take him back had been ignored but I couldn't watch it any longer.

I'd try polite first. "Enough…Please... can you not hurt him?"

Kendal spoke. "J, that's enough, you're making Joe worry."

Julian took his hand from Leo's back and put it to his head and stroked his fingers over his hair.

He kissed him and smiled against his face. "Good boy, that was beautiful, wasn't it?" He watched him for a minute before whispering to him again. "Just keep breathing, it will go away in a minute." Julian lifted his face from him but kept his touch on his neck, just stroking, not holding. Leo never moved as Julian looked at me silently.

I had the bottom part of my face leaning, hiding across my arm. Leo shook a little and I fleetingly looked at him and then back to Julian, holding his stare. He wasn't one to be ignored. He had piercing blue eyes, different from Leo's, brighter, lighter blue.

Kendal broke the silence. "Do you want tea, J?"

Fuck's sake, what was it with them and their motherfucking tea? I found myself panting slightly as Julian answered without taking his eyes from me.

"Yes, please and make one for the boy here, make it sweet, he's a little shaken." I wasn't sure if he was talking about me or Leo. He smiled at me amused as if he had heard my thoughts. "I was talking about Leo but I think you should also have one." In the corner of my eye I saw Kendal smile and turn to make the tea. I dragged my eyes from his amused gaze and looked at Leo again. He still hadn't moved.

Julian spoke, bringing my attention back to him. "I wasn't hurting him, I was sharing with him, he'll be back in a minute. He's just remembering and wants to hold onto it. How, actually, did you manage to keep him safe for so long?" He reached out a hand towards me and I flinched a little which made him smile. He pushed his fingers against my forehead and tipped my face up from behind my arm, scrutinising my sore lip. "You need to learn to move quicker." Then he did something that went completely against what I was feeling from him. His fingers turned gentle against my face and he brushed them across my skin a few times before bending and kissing my forehead. "Hello, Joe, I'm Julian." *Pompous fucking twat*. And then he was gone.

Unfortunately, not completely gone, although I felt like I could breathe easier without him in my immediate space. He went and sat where Isaac had been sitting at the end of the table next to Leo. He cocked his head to look at Leo for a moment, who was still laying against the table, staring into space it seemed. Isaac was still on Peter's lap looking completely taken with Julian and had obviously understood everything that had just taken place, between Julian and Leo, whereas my heart was still beating really fast from confusion.

Kendal turned and tutted at him. "You could have introduced yourself first, I said they were new."

Julian smiled still looking at me. "Forgive me, Joe, I thought she was talking about Leo." Whatever. "Seems he's way ahead of you in the understanding stakes. Which makes me want to ask again, how did you keep him safe for so long?" Without waiting for an answer he spoke again, looking at me but the question was clearly not for me. "I can't believe he seriously thinks this is going to work?" Julian looked at Peter and Kendal and then back to me.

Who was he talking about? Who was *he*? Layton? And what work? Leo and I? I was very aware that we were in his house and I wasn't sure what power that gave him but I was sure about Leo.

"He stays with me. If you want us to leave, then just say." Julian smiled as I reached out and touched my hand over Leo's.

Kendal spoke as she turned and passed the tea. "Take no notice of him, Joe. Of course, he doesn't want you to leave." She looked at Julian. "Can you try and be nice, they're already struggling."

Julian just seemed amused and ignored her. "So, where would you go, Joe?" I felt unsure and hoped I didn't look it.

It was clear he didn't want us here, well not me anyway, but having decided that leaving Leo was not an option for either of us, we would both have to go. I felt a little panicked about that but I had lived with worse feelings. I didn't know what the answer was to his question and felt a little agitated that I couldn't come back with something solid. Leo turned his face on the table and looked at me and it hurt my insides. I couldn't learn all I needed to know to keep him safe on my own, not quickly enough.

"Mm, I thought so." Fuck him!

My mind was working hard trying to find an answer. Leo had been doing this a long time and I had managed. If I left here, I would need to enlist the help of Ginger again. We had managed between us before, I could learn, learn from him. It meant I would have to fight though, to get my place back and possibly fight Ginger. He wasn't going to welcome us back, I would have to earn that privilege again. It wasn't going to be a one-time thing either, I would constantly have to earn my place there with my fists. Leo opened his fingers and mine dropped between them and he held them. I was willing to fight for him. So my answer was simple.

"Back, I'll take him back."

Peter spoke. "Joe, there's no need." He looked at Julian who was sitting staring at me and gave his name in a warning and questioning tone. "Julian?"

Julian smiled. He clearly wasn't finished with his games. I hated him already. "Haven't you lost your place?"

Leo sat up and moved back to me, leaning on my leg that was still up on the chair. I looked at him and kissed him. I didn't want to talk about leaving or the alley around him, not until I was sure of my plans. I watched him for a moment and realised he was off, staring into space again or whatever it was that Layton had called it.

I looked back at Julian. "I can get it back." He seemed to know about the street, about having a place. If he did, then he would know how it worked.

"Isn't that a little risky?"

Kendal joined in. "Joe, no. Julian, can you stop it…"

Julian ignored her as he continued to hit me with the futility of our situation. "I mean if you lose...who's going to take care of Leo? If you're injured..." Fuck him!

"If I lose, then I know I lose everything." Leo would have nothing and no one, I knew what that meant for him. Did he think I didn't? Then he reached out and pushed my tea towards me.

"Drink your tea, you look drained." What the hell?!

"Julian, that's enough!" I looked down at Leo and kissed his forehead as Peter spoke.

I knew I had a lot to learn, my to-do list was growing every hour. My head hurt if I thought about things too much but I couldn't just leave him here. The same way I couldn't leave him when I first met him or leave him when he'd turned up bloodied and battered. I hadn't been able to leave him ever since. I had tried, I had tried to get in the car but four years was too long to spend with someone, watching them grow, feeding them, loving them.

He had changed, he had gone from being a kid to an adult and I had stood back and allowed him to go in any direction he wanted. I hadn't realised at the time what that direction was. Was it time to step back again? I had taken him from the place he felt safe to somewhere I wasn't equipped to look after him. I couldn't now abandon him.

I tried to ignore Julian as he spoke again. "I just want Joe to think about what he's doing and who he's doing it for. He knows nothing."

Peter spoke again. "Neither do I, but you're not suggesting that I forget Isaac and never see him?"

"That's different, Peter. You know this world and understand what brings people here. He has no understanding of that boy's needs, he can barely look at his wounds."

I didn't want to listen to them anymore. They were talking like I didn't exist, wasn't sitting right here but I couldn't move Leo as he was. No wonder Isaac had thrown the plate if this is how they spoke to each other. Using my upset and anger, I manhandled Leo onto my lap and then scooped him up in my arms, giving him an extra jump to make sure he was secure, before I stood and walked towards the door.

Kendal called after me. "Joe, don't go. It's always like this when we get together."

I turned and looked at them all. I didn't belong here, we didn't belong here. "It's okay. I promised Leo we would leave at night, he understands the night better than the day. We'll be gone by morning." I turned and walked Leo back to the room listening to Kendal's raised voice as she spoke to Julian.

I walked in the bedroom and kicked the door shut.

CHAPTER ELEVEN

JOE

I had felt so confident when Layton was here. Even this morning I had woken with a new sense of worth and purpose. Now though, it seemed to be failing me. I sat back on the bed with Leo and opened my legs so he sat on the bed between them. He was clinging to me like a monkey, his arms wrapped around my middle holding so tight, although he still seemed out of it. I pushed pillows behind me and just sat loosely holding him in silence, quietly seething.

Now, even more, Leo needed to tell me what was in his head but I needed to think. We had to leave tonight. The plan I had spurted off to Julian about going back to the alley had been a spur of the moment thought but now I had to think about it as an option. I shook my head. Option? Who the fuck was I trying to kid, I didn't have any options. Layton had said Leo's need would be back in a matter of days. I had to find somewhere safe for him, for us, before then.

I had no idea what he was going to be like but Layton hadn't made it sound easy. If I left here, would Layton's offer of help still be available? I needed it to be because if it wasn't, I really was in deep shit. I ran through what Julian had said. He was confusing. He had been a little aloof with me at first, choosing to talk to Leo and keeping me distant, then he had seemed to notice me, then been aggressive, then showing me something that boarded on kindness. Then it had changed again.

He was questioning Layton's idea that Leo and I could stay in this world together. He was right in what he said, I didn't understand. I hadn't seen anything apart from marks and wounds and only heard about this need that Leo and Isaac seemed to share, but he wasn't giving me a chance.

Wasn't that how it worked on the street though? When new boys turned up, no one gave them a chance, they were ignored and pushed out before anyone got to know them. Fearing that they would… what? Break some secret code of street conduct? There was none. No. It was because no one wanted to see another boy be condemned to the life that we already lived. No one wanted to see another boy fail, fall sick…die. That's why the strongest got to stay and the weaker ones got moved on.

Is that what Julian was doing? Moving me on to save me from...what? He was wrong about something though. I could look at Leo. Nothing would ever make me not want to look at Leo. Not when he was covered in dirt, had some suit's cum drooling from his lip, or twenty-odd cuts across his back. He was still Leo and no one knew him as I did. Yeah, okay, Ginger had fed this pain thing he had, but having someone lie in front of you quietly while you cut them to pieces, didn't tell you everything about a person. It showed you he was different, weird...I smiled. That's what Ginger had seen, weirdness. He wasn't weird to me, yeah, okay, he was different, but I already knew that. From the moment I met him, I knew he was a little different.

I smiled again and stroked my fingers over his ear. Now, I knew he was a *lot* different but I had also found out what made him different, well, some of it. I had been a little taken aback, I mean who wouldn't be? Your best friend, your love, was a fucking pain addict...who liked four fucking sugars in his tea! I mean, who wouldn't be a little shocked? It didn't matter, sitting here with him now, I knew that it made no difference to my feelings for him.

When I looked at him today, I felt the same churning inside that I felt a week ago when he was sulking because he didn't want to wear his boots anymore. Or two weeks ago when he had got the giggles because the clouds in the night sky had looked like an erect cock and the stars had looked like they were ejaculating. I kissed the top of his head and smiled. I still loved him and I loved that I could just...touch him.

I had no idea what he thought of me but I knew he had relied on me to get him through each day on the street and, having brought him here, he was relying on me to get him through this. The thing he had kept secret from everyone had exploded out into the open and the consequences of that were, so far, not good. Had he known things would change so drastically? Is that why he had kept it so quiet? Of course, it was. The alley, the street, was the only place Leo had ever felt safe, which was a crazy thing to say. Why would he want to jeopardise that by changing anything?

This world and these people may not want me, but Leo needed me. He also needed the understanding that this place could give him. I wasn't so stupid not to realise that but it left me with a difficult choice. Again, I thought about what Julian had said. *Think about what I was doing and who I was doing it for*. He was absolutely right. Taking Leo back to the street was not the best thing for Leo, I would be doing it for me so I could be with him.

Even if I did manage to win back my place, I would have to watch Leo even more carefully than I had before. I couldn't do that and earn money and if Leo was a pain junkie like everyone was saying, I knew that there were going to be some pretty rough times. If being a pain junkie was anything like being a street drug junkie, then I knew it, I had seen it so many times.

No, he needed me, even if it was just to get him through until he had what *he* needed. Wasn't that Layton's explanation of a Keeper? They could all challenge the decisions I was making, that was okay, I was kind of making them blind and if someone made me see a wrong decision before Leo got hurt, then that was a good thing. But there was no way on this earth they could challenge the fact that I loved him and tell me he would be better off without me. The only person I would ever take note of, regarding us being together, was Leo. If he ever told me or showed me that I wasn't needed or wanted, then I would step back. I didn't want to think about that now.

Leo lifted his head and smiled weakly at me and I smiled back. He just kept coming back from the places people took him. I was going to work so hard to understand where he went, to understand this need and what it felt like to him. I kissed the corner of his mouth.

"You came back...on your own, without me dragging you."

"I'm tired, Joe." I half laughed. He was still the same old Leo. He shivered and I wrapped my arms around him.

"That's okay, you don't have to move for a moment." Now I had worked a few things out, I had to try and find a way he could have me and this world.

He wasn't ready to be a slave, he wouldn't understand it, not going off to strangers. I double-checked that thought, to make sure it wasn't me who wasn't ready. I definitely wasn't but I knew in my heart he wasn't either. Even Layton had said it. That made me feel better about that decision but it didn't help me.

Leo needed a permanent home, somewhere he felt safe, regardless of what was going on and whatever else he was feeling. It didn't need to be grand, like this house. The alley had been far from grand, it was a dump but Leo had felt so safe there. He knew it inside and out, every brick, every bit of junk. He even noticed when another bag of rubbish was left on top of a million other bags of rubbish.

Yes, we needed somewhere permanent, somewhere where things were the same, constant. I wondered what Julian would think of us living in a box in his garden? It made me smile. That fucker, that would screw up his well-ordered life.

Maybe Layton could help us? There must be jobs in this world? But, then where would Leo go when I was working? Did they have street boys here? No, of course not, they had slaves, they didn't need the streets to get what they wanted. Fuck, why was everything so fucking hard? I didn't know enough about this world to know what my options were. I would have to go back in there and ask them. If they threw the idea back in my face, then the only option left to me was to take him back to the streets of the vanilla world, and hope that Layton would take us in when the time came that we needed his knowledge.

Right, a plan. If the plan didn't work then it all became a bit sketchy again but I would deal with that when I knew that there was nowhere here for us. Here was better for Leo, so I had to give it every chance to try and make that happen. I looked down at him. He was playing his fingers over mine, quite happy to just sit with me as always. This world gave us more freedom, even Leo was aware of it. We had sat with each other so many times but never with such intimate touches. We needed this, needed to be able to find each other, get to know each other. Even if we weren't here, I would have to find moments where we could do this.

I looked at his back. It looked so much better but I needed to wash it and put the ointment back on after the night's sleep. I needed to speak with them quickly so I knew where Leo and I stood but his well…ness must always come first. I remembered that from Kendal. Take him wherever but always look after his health first. I reached out for the ointment on the side of the bed.

"Leo?" He turned and looked up at me. "It's time to do your back again." He scowled at me. I shook my head at him. "No, no scowling. It's important. If you want to sleep naked with me tonight then you have to have your back cleaned." I could see him thinking about it, so I waited. He sighed and laid his head back on me.

"Okay but not bad touching, just cleaning." I smiled. He wanted to sleep naked with me so much that he was willing to earn it. Both pleased me a lot. I leaned forward and kissed his head.

"Good boy, sit up while I get some water." Leo sat up and crossed his legs and I quickly went to the bathroom.

I didn't want him to change his mind. I washed my hands and grabbed a small bowl of warm water and two towels, trying to remember everything Kendal had shown me. Leo was still sitting waiting and he was anxious, I could tell by the way he was pulling at his fingers and shaking his knee.

I would need to get better prepared, so when he agreed in future, I didn't leave him waiting. "I'm back." I climbed back on the bed and put the water down. I touched his arm. "Schooch back to me, I want you to be close." Leo pushed himself back in between my legs and I wrapped them around his. I rinsed one of the ends of the towels in the water and then squeezed it out. "What's bad touching, Leo? What Julian did? That man in the kitchen?" Leo nodded. "Take a breath." I touched it to his back avoiding the lint covering his stitches. "Is this bad touching?"

"No." Good.

"If I hurt you too much, you can squeeze my foot really hard, okay?" Leo put his hands on my feet so I took that as agreement and continued to clean his back. "I thought you liked Julian's touching?" He shrugged his shoulders. "You can say if you liked it, I'm not mad or anything."

"He scared me. I wasn't ready, I thought he was a customer. You took me away." Okay, that was a lot of things but he didn't actually answer my question.

"I took you away because you were resting and they were talking loudly. After you knew he wasn't a customer, were you still scared?" Leo nodded and I waited.

My patience paid off, he spoke. "It hurt and scared me and then I remembered," I recalled Leo's hands waving agitated in the air, that must have been when it hurt when it scared him.

"Remembered what?"

"Ginger from the alley." Did he think I had forgotten him?

"Then you liked it?" He shrugged. I waited again but he never spoke. "You liked it when Ginger did it to you?" He nodded. Okay, the shrugging was getting easier to understand. He shrugged when he was unsure how to answer or unsure of his answer. "So, Julian touching you, made you remember the time with Ginger? When you liked it?" He nodded. Right okay.

It hurt, a lot, but it hurt like it had hurt when Ginger had given it to him and he had wanted it to hurt then. The sharing had been a little one-sided, I decided. Julian had kind of made him remember when he wasn't ready or sure about him. I would have to be so much more aware when these people asked stuff of Leo. They might understand his need but Leo didn't and they didn't know Leo.

He wasn't a slave and understood little of being under someone's command. He wasn't a leader by any standards but Leo had lived independently with a little help, for the last four years. To thrust him into subservience and demand it, scared him, especially with strangers. To him, they were no different to having customers and Leo was well aware that customers couldn't be trusted.

I dried his back, dabbing it with a towel and a few times he tightened his grip on my feet. If Leo was ever going to trust me to share with him, I would have to show him that I was able to keep him safe from people like Julian, who thought they could just touch.

"Leo, if you are ever unsure of something or someone then just reach out to me, okay? You don't have to say anything, just show me, like you used to in the alley." He didn't answer. "We're done here."

He immediately turned and laid out across the bed laying his head on my leg. Leo would stand at the end of the alley, leaning against the wall looking down at his feet, trying to ignore the customers who looked his way. If one approached him he would reach out and touch me if I was close, which I usually was. If I wasn't close, he would walk over and stand by me. He would only ever go with a customer if I told him it was okay and even then, he didn't like it.

I picked up the tube of ointment. "I need to put this on, Leo, then we need to go back to the kitchen for a while." Leo shook his head. "What are you saying no to? The ointment or going back to the kitchen?"

"Both."

I smiled. "This ointment is like toothpaste." Leo lifted his head and looked at it and then me. "You can't eat it because it doesn't taste nice but it does the same thing. The toothpaste takes away the bad tastes and the ointment takes away the bad feeling your wounds give you."

He gave me a big goofy smile. "That's no way the same."

I laughed back. "Mm, okay maybe not. You can stay there, you don't have to move. I can do it like this."

Leo laid his head back on my leg and just lay there. I wasn't sure if that was acceptance or not but I squeezed some out onto my fingers. I stroked my other hand over his head. "It won't be so sore now, it's getting better okay?" He nodded and I saw this as his acceptance of having his back touched again.

As I covered the first cut, he tensed his body. "Leo?" He didn't say anything or move but I knew he was listening. "I do miss the alley. I said I didn't because it hurts sometimes when I think about it." Leo moved his eyes to look at me and I saw his understanding. He turned his face into my leg and kissed it but never said anything until I had finished his back.

"Can I have tea again in the kitchen?"

I smiled at him. "Yes, of course, but only with two sugars. You have had way more sugar than you're used to, I don't want you to be sick." I wanted to warn him about what might happen in the kitchen. "Hey listen, you know how boys sometimes had fights about who was staying in the alley or not?" He nodded. "Well, I might have to fight in the kitchen."

He frowned at me. "What, like hit someone?" I smiled. I hoped not. I was quite strong and used to fighting but I didn't like my chances against Julian or Peter.

"No, not hitting. I need to fight for us to stay here, so I may have to say things that you don't understand or you're not sure of and say them loudly."

"Are we the strangers?"

I nodded. "Yeah, we are, and they're not sure about me, about us but you need this place."

"Coz we don't have the alley anymore?"

"Yep and because I can't keep you safe on the streets, not on my own. I need to fight for a place here with them, so we can stay together."

"Are they trying to take you away, like Ginger?"

I lifted his face to me so I could see him. "I'm not going anywhere. If we can't stay here then we will find somewhere else, together. It might not have a proper bed or hot water..."

"Will it have toothpaste?"

I laughed. "I'm sure we can manage toothpaste, yes."

He sat up suddenly realising something. "I left my toothpaste in the kitchen, can we go now and get tea and get it?"

He didn't seem at all concerned about what I had just told him. I smiled at him. His back was forgotten, he was kind of amazing. I wanted to kiss him like Layton had kissed me last night but it would have to wait. With any luck, Julian would have gone now and I could just speak to Kendal or Peter. They would be able to tell me if there was any way of staying here in this world with Leo.

I leaned forward and kissed his forehead. "Yes, but I need you to wear a top, okay? It will stop people from thinking they can just touch you."

"Like before? When I always had to wear my clothes?"

I nodded. "Yes, like before but not for always, just for now and only when I say. Okay?" He nodded.

I moved off the bed and went back to the drawers. I had seen the linen tunic in there earlier but had left it off to let his back breathe a little. What I was doing now was not about Leo's need, it was just about Leo. I took it out and shook it and walked over to Leo. I waited for him to complain but he moved forward on the bed towards me and I helped him put it on. It was a little big because he was so slim but it did its job.

I stood up and held out my hand. "Come on, I want tea too." I couldn't believe I said that.

As we walked towards the kitchen I could hear Peter's voice. I hoped he was speaking to Kendal or Isaac...or Layton. I could really do with speaking to Layton right now, seeing him. When I heard the voice that replied I knew he was still there. My heart jumped a few beats. I took a deep breath and kissed Leo's hand and then smiled at him.

"It doesn't matter if we lose because I love you." If I needed evidence that the word meant not a lot to him then, his blank stare back at me showed me very clearly.

It made me smile and that's how we entered the kitchen, with me smiling at Leo. They all went silent before I even took my eyes from him. I walked straight over to where Leo had sat before and picked up the toothpaste and gave it to him. Whatever comfort he got from it, he was going to probably need it.

Kendal was the first to speak and I could hear the unsure surprise in her voice. "Joe?"

I looked at her, then Peter, who still had Isaac on his lap. Isaac was just staring at Leo and I looked fleetingly at Leo to see if he was taking any notice. He was staring back and there was warmth in his eyes. He liked Isaac. Sometimes it wasn't always clear when Leo liked someone but it was very clear he liked Isaac. Peter and Kendal were surprised that I had come back. I looked at Julian who was looking at me with…interest, I couldn't tell what he was thinking and didn't care…well, I tried not to.

I sat Leo in the chair I had been sitting in, resting my hands on his shoulders and looked at Kendal. "Is it okay if I make us tea?"

Kendal smiled softly but then Julian stood and I stepped slightly between him and Leo. I wanted to make it clear from the off that he wasn't to just touch Leo. Julian smiled at me and went to the kitchen counter and flicked on the kettle.

I wasn't quite sure where to start but then Leo spoke and completely took everyone by surprise. "Kendal had a bath with Joe."

Peter shot his head round to look at Kendal questioningly. Julian turned and leaned against the counter, smiling amusedly. I looked at Kendal as she half smiled and bit her bottom lip.

"I'm sorry." I felt bad. My lie to Leo had put her in an uncomfortable position as the room all looked at her.

Somewhere, I could hear Isaac asking why Kendal never had a bath with him, which made me bite my lip and regret it when it hurt. She smiled more and shook her head and then looked at Peter as he looked at her questioningly.

"Really?" I could see Peter's confusion. He was obviously not party to Layton's late-night ninja visit, whereas Kendal and Julian obviously were.

Kendal did an awkward grin and nodded. "Apparently so."

I looked at Leo and was going to say something but he wasn't looking around the room telling everyone, he was just looking at Isaac, telling him.

Isaac replied. "Was it like ours?"

Leo shrugged. "I don't know, I was sleeping." Leo smiled at him.

They were sharing...something, I wasn't quite sure what but Isaac seemed to accept that Leo didn't know everything because he had been 'sleeping'. I smiled and looked at Peter who was still looking at Kendal. He seemed to be waiting for the explanation for the impromptu bath time visit.

Kendal smiled at him. "It was just a… short visit to check on Joe, I was not really…feeling myself... if you understand?" Peter looked at me.

I wasn't sure if he understood, then he spoke. "You should have knocked if you needed help."

I shook my head. "It was fine really, it kind of happened unexpectedly... then help arrived." I fleetingly looked at Isaac to see if he was taking any notice but he didn't seem to be.

Peter, following my glance, kissed Isaac. "Don't be fooled, he's all ears. I understand."

I nodded. Thank God.

Kendal smiled. "Right well, I'm glad that's out in the open. I'll make the tea." Julian put a hand on her shoulder to still her from getting up.

"It's okay, I'll make it." He looked at me. "Take a seat, Joe."

I looked down and pulled out the chair which Leo had previously sat in. I was still holding his hand and I put it to my mouth and kissed it. It drew his attention back to me from Isaac. His eyes then skipped around the room looking at everyone except Isaac and stopped on Julian for a long moment before looking back at me.

"It's okay." He was waiting for the fight to break out. I didn't want him to be uneasy. I looked up at Kendal, Peter and Julian, although he had his back to me. "I have something to say…to ask."

Peter spoke. "Ask away, Joe."

I took a deep breath. Mine and Leo's fate was in their hands. "I've been doing some thinking. You were right to challenge my decision to take Leo back to the streets. I know it's not a good place for him to be but you are making it impossible for him to stay here."

Julian turned and gave everyone their mug of tea.

"No, we're not." I fleetingly looked at Julian before taking Leo's tea and putting in the sugar. I smiled at him as I gave it to him and he smiled back.

"You want me to leave him because you think you understand him better than me, I get that. You do understand his need but none of you knows Leo like I know him. You are all strangers to him and he understands that he is a stranger to you. It's difficult for him to understand how you are friends and how you can help him when all he feels is fear in your company. To Leo, you are all customers, just waiting to have him and you condoned that thought, by touching him without making any attempt to make friends with him first or giving him a chance to know you.

"Leo is not one of your slaves, he may have the same need, the same characteristics, but he has lived independently with me for the last four years. I thought, when this need of Leo's came to light, that I didn't know him as well as I thought I did, I thought that Ginger knew him better but having someone lie quietly for you while you give them what they crave doesn't tell you anything about the person. You think by touching Leo's back and reminding him of the moment when he wanted it and craved it makes you understand him, but it doesn't. It makes you understand his need, I get that but Leo is more than that and he needs to be able to come back from it.

"Whether you like it or not, Leo needs me to help him, the way I've always helped him when things have been difficult for him. I've never let him down before and I didn't even know I loved him then. Leo needs somewhere he can call home, home is important to him, it doesn't need to be four walls so for him it doesn't actually matter where he is, as long as he's with me, he will accept it. I know the best place for him is here with people that understand his need, he needs this world but he needs me too. Nothing you say or do will change that, nothing will make me doubt it.

"I am prepared to work for our place here. I'll do any job but I must be able to keep Leo with me. I need to know if there is somewhere here for us? If there is anything I can do to earn some money so we can stay in this world for Leo's sake? If having me here is too difficult then Leo and I will leave." I looked at Julian to make a point, suddenly wishing I wasn't half-naked and had also put on a linen top.

"That decision is not based on my selfish need to be with him but because I know, whatever help you can give him won't mean anything to him without me." I looked from Julian to Kendal and then to Peter. "So, is there? I don't know much and what I do know you already have an abundance of but I can read and write."

"Are you begging, Joe?" I looked at Julian. I fucking hated him and had to control my middle finger which was itching to cut the air.

"No, I never beg for anything, I work for it... do you want me to? Will it appease you in some way?" Julian grinned at me, enjoying my angst. *Fuck you!*

Kendal jumped in scowling at Julian. "Enough! We will find a place, Joe, somewhere you and Leo can stay."

I shook my head at her. "I don't want us to stay somewhere, we have to have a place here. It has to be somewhere Leo can feel safe, where he can return to after he's had his…fix. Somewhere he doesn't have to earn, not ever. If he never becomes a slave, I want his place here to still be safe, for him to still be safe. I don't want him to feel like you're all waiting for him, like customers. If there is a job I can do, maybe I can rent somewhere in this world?" Julian smiled. It pissed me off that I was amusing him. I turned and looked at Peter and Kendal. "Is there anything? I don't know how things work here but there must be something?"

Peter shook his head. "It's not that simple here, Joe. No one works here, not for money, not directly anyway."

I looked at Julian as he spoke. "Everybody earns their place here."

"So, what? Leave Leo here to slavery and he gets a place? It's bullshit! You know, this world is no fucking different from the vanillas, if your face doesn't fit then what? Forget them, leave them on the street…well that's fine. Leo and I have survived there a long time…"

Kendal spoke out. "Joe, we'll speak to the council. Julian is just trying to protect this world, he's not against you. None of us are against you. It's just, no one comes to this world without a need for it, it's just difficult."

Peter spoke, looking at Julian. "That's not entirely true, is it? You took me in. If it goes to the council Julian will you fight for Joe and Leo to stay?" Julian didn't answer.

I looked at Peter. "What's the council?" I was shaking. I was mad and a little upset at Julian's treatment of me.

I picked up my tea to try and calm my nerves and looked at Leo. He was laying on his arm. He was doing what he always did when things got difficult in the alley, he was shutting it out. I leant down and stroked his neck and looked at him. He looked back at me, so I knew he wasn't off on one of his trips. I smiled at him, trying to reassure him. He lifted his head, leaning his chin on his arm and looked at Julian and then stretched his hand out to him. He wanted Julian to tickle his palm, he was trying to make friends with him, he was trying to help.

I took his hand in mine and held it. "It's okay, Leo."

Julian looked at me frowning. "What does the boy want?"

Like I was going to tell him. I ignored his question. "What is the council?"

He smiled at me. It wasn't a friendly smile, it was smug. He believed I didn't know Leo at all. I didn't want him to touch Leo again. I didn't want Leo to feel he had to make friends with him just to stay with me or stay here.

Peter answered. "The council is run by people who run slave houses here. It was set up a few years ago to make important decisions about this world and to create rules to keep the slaves safe. Both Layton and Julian sit on the council and have a strong influence over decisions that are made. The council will not be pleased about Layton bringing you here without asking their permission first but if Julian and Layton both support the decision then it could sway their decision to let you stay."

"Can I speak at this meeting?"

Peter shook his head. "No, only Council members are permitted." He looked at Julian. "What do you think Julian?"

He shook his head as he spoke. "I think involving the council will be asking for trouble."

I ignored him and looked at Peter. "But you, they let you stay?"

Peter half-smiled. "I'm not really sure. Julian? Did you ever tell them about me?"

Julian smiled at Peter. "It was none of their business."

Peter half smiled again. "What about telling them about Joe and Leo?"

Julian shook his head. "They'll want Leo, and they'll stop at nothing to get him. The only safe place for him then would be slavery. It's asking for trouble." Julian looked at me. "If you want to stay with him, then you can but not here. If they find you, they will take Leo. If we ask for you to stay and they refuse, they will seek you out on the vanilla streets…for Leo. Leo's need is… extreme, once we tell them about Leo, and they see him, they will be eager to have him. Layton was wrong to bring you here together."

Kendal spoke again looking at Julian. "We can't put them back on the streets, J. How will Joe keep Leo safe when he's needy?"

"Exactly my point. Without putting Leo into slavery, there is no safe place for him here or there." Julian looked at me. "You are welcome to stay here while you make a decision."

Kendal spoke again. "You're exaggerating, J."

Julian looked at her, raising his brow to make his point while he spoke. "Really? Have you forgotten what Kellen did to Jacob when he took him? Have you seen Leo's need? It's really…pretty. They will want him and they will find a way to have him. Without the protection of slave status or a slave house, he will be no safer here than on the vanilla streets."

I looked at Kendal and could see the truth of what he said in her eyes. I looked at Leo who was watching me. I couldn't work Julian out, couldn't decide if he disliked me or not, as I had first thought, but he did seem to be concerned for Leo's safety. It seemed my idea of Leo and I staying here was not so safe after all. At least on the streets, I was on familiar territory, I knew the rules, knew how to get by. I just had to somehow figure Leo into it all.

Peter spoke again. "Joe?" I looked at him. "We'll figure something out. You are both safe here for now."

I nodded and looked at Leo again, he was looking at Julian again. My animosity towards Julian had waned a little since I realised he was just trying to do the right thing for Leo and what he had said had little to do with me. He hadn't been trying to keep me out, just trying to keep Leo safe. I let go of Leo's hand and looked at Julian.

"Leo would like to make friends but he's unsure of you." Julian turned his attention to Leo who looked at me in question. I nodded to him, letting him know it was okay and he reached his hand across in front of me to Julian, palm up. I looked at Julian. "He likes his palm touched gently, so it tickles."

Julian slid his hand over Leo's and played his fingers across Leo's wrist first, he didn't seem to need any guidance from me. Leo smiled back at him shyly and it made me smile at Leo.

"Hello." I was taken aback that Leo had even spoken to him, even though it was whispered. If I didn't know any better I would think he was flirting with Julian.

"Hello, Leo, did I scare you?" Leo shrugged.

Isaac, who had been quiet this whole time, was obviously feeling left out and a little jealous of Julian's new friend. "You scare me."

Julian looked at him and smiled. "I scare you when you want to be scared, Isaac, when you want to be friends we are friends. Do you like Leo?"

Isaac smiled and nodded.

Peter spoke. "He and Leo spent some time together in the house by the street."

Julian smiled and looked from one to the other. "Mm, I bet that was beautiful."

Isaac smiled and Leo again surprised me by answering. "Like the moon and the stars."

Julian looked at him, a smile playing on his lips. He was still rubbing his fingers over his wrist.

"Really? As beautiful as that? Oh my, Leo, what an amazing journey you have ahead of you."

I laid my hand on Leo's neck possessively and he looked around at me.

"You're coming, Joe, aren't you?"

I smiled at him. "Of course, but I think there are some places I can't come, like when you stare into space but I will just wait for you like I did today."

Leo suddenly took his hand from Julian and gave it to me and I kissed it.

Peter laughed. "Ouch, you were shafted."

Julian sat up, smiling. "I can take it." Julian looked at me. "Do you understand what he's doing Joe?"

Oh God, here we go again. He was about to tell me that I was useless and knew nothing about Leo. I kissed Leo's hand before holding it in mine and rubbing my thumb over his skin. They could say what they liked, I didn't need to know everything about Leo to know him or love him. I looked at Julian and shook my head.

"I don't need to. Nothing you say will make me change my mind about leaving him. I know him, I know Leo. He needs me and I will stay with him until he shows me he doesn't need me anymore and until then, you and your…hungry junkie friends can't have him." Shit, that was meant to stay in my head!

Julian laughed. "I was merely going to say that he was showing you as the most important person in the room. It's unusual, especially after I showed him that I understand him, I'm not usually snubbed." Both Peter and Kendal laughed, amused.

I looked at Leo again who was now leaning his chin on his arm looking at Isaac. He was holding my hand tightly.

He was doing amazingly well considering we were in a roomful of strangers and I wondered what was going through his head. I was not the most dominant person in the room, I knew that and so did the others. In fact, I felt so unsure, I wondered if Isaac was above me in the domineering stakes. If we were on the street now, it would probably change things but then I doubted it. Even if Julian did find himself out on the pavement, I doubted that it would change the air of command and control he seemed to emanate. Leo was just used to me and I felt bad for my outburst. I had called Julian a junkie!... He had seemed to find it amusing, but all the same, I felt like I should apologise, after all, I was in his house.

I looked back at him. "I'm sorry, I didn't mean to be rude and call you a…erm…names."

Julian laughed a little again. "I like honesty."

Kendal stood up. "That's enough now guys." She looked at Leo and then at me. "You are safe here, Joe. No one knows you're here for now. Layton will come up with something, somewhere that is safe for you both." It didn't sound like there was a place.

Isaac turned and looked at Kendal. "Is Layton coming?"

Peter said his name in a warning tone. "Isaac!"

Isaac turned and looked at Peter and then bowed his head. "Sorry."

I guessed they were still working on things. I felt for Isaac. I wouldn't want anyone to keep Leo from me but Layton's explanation about having someone who loved him as much as he did, did make sense. No one knew Leo like I knew him. Not even Ginger knew his soft and gentle nature, he never had time for it. The only person I could think of who Leo was more open with, was Mikey, Manni's son. He would sometimes sit with Mikey while I waited for business or if Ginger left him stranded at the cafe. He would wait for me to collect him.

The times he had walked back to the alley alone he had been propositioned by customers who thought they could just touch him without his permission. It was even more upsetting for him in daylight than it was at night, so Leo rarely ventured anywhere alone.

The alley. It was only yesterday morning but already it seemed like we had been away for ages. Leo and I still had to talk about it, about Ginger, about not seeing him again and about his need he had for him. I looked back at him and he was staring at me.

"I think it's time to go back to the room, Leo."

"Did you win?" I smiled at him. He had lost track of what had gone on.

"Of course." He smiled at me.

Kendal spoke. "Would you like more tea? Food?" Christ, no more tea! These people were obsessed!

I shook my head but Leo spoke. "I'm still hungry."

Kendal smiled at him. "I can bring you in something when I check his back."

I shook my head and felt like looking at Julian when I answered her. "I've already checked and cleaned his back and put on the ointment but can I ask, will he be able to shower?"

Kendal shook her head. "No honey, the stitches have to stay dry. He can have a shallow bath. I can bring in some food in a while if you like?"

He would need to eat again today because I didn't know when we would eat again after tonight if we left.

I smiled. "Thank you, yes please." I stood up and pulled Leo with me and then started to move towards the door.

I turned back and looked at them and they were all looking at us. I felt like the poor relation, the outcast of the group. It didn't matter anymore. I looked at Julian. "Thank you for letting us stay here." He nodded his head and I looked at Kendal and then Peter. "Thank you for your help." I looked at Isaac and then Leo. "Say goodbye to Isaac, Leo."

Leo looked at Isaac who had looked up and was looking at Leo. "Bye, Isaac."

Isaac smiled at him. "Bye, Leo."

I turned and left the room and could almost hear their sighs of relief. I was trouble that they just didn't need. I turned and looked at Leo and smiled at him. I had never been so sure about anything before.

CHAPTER TWELVE

JOE

Once in the bedroom, I took off Leo's linen tunic to give his back a rest. He sat on the bed cross-legged and looked at me as I folded it up and put it on the side. I had failed to gain a place here for us but it didn't matter. I hadn't lied to Leo. We were staying together and I felt like I'd won something. I planned to leave tonight still, but I couldn't tell them, they didn't understand. I couldn't keep Leo safe here, I didn't know it, not like I knew the streets. I turned and looked at him. He smiled at me and I smiled back.

"Kendal is going to bring you in something to eat in a minute then you and I are going to talk."

"What are we talking about?"

I walked back to the bed and half sat on it in front of him. "Lots of things, whatever you want to tell me."

I wanted to tell him that we weren't staying but there was a chance that he may tell Kendal so I would wait until after her visit or maybe even later. I reached for his hand and turned it to stroke his palm but he was still holding the toothpaste.

I smiled and took it. "Why do you like toothpaste so much, Leo?"

"Coz I do."

I laughed. "I know that but why?"

"It makes me feel better."

"I know you liked it after customers but you never used to carry it with you."

"It's a nice thing when things are not nice."

"What's not nice?"

"Here, the people, you."

That took me by surprise. "Me?" He looked down, away from me. "Hey? You don't have to hide from me, you can be honest, Leo. If I have worried you or scared you then you should tell me." I waited. Nothing. "Have I worried you? Made you scared?" He nodded. "Leo?"

"I'm hungry."

I took his other hand, he had to tell me. "Leo, look at me."

He slowly looked up. "Am I bad?"

I frowned at him. "No, you're not bad. Why would you think that? Did I make you think that?" He shrugged. "You're not bad, you could never be bad."

He looked away, down, again. He was talking in riddles and I wasn't following. I sighed and he looked at me. It gave me an idea. I dropped his hands and laid back on the bed.

"Fucking hell, Leo, you're talking in riddles again." I put my hands behind my head. Leo edged closer but never said anything for a while.

When he did speak I could hear the uncertainty in his voice. "Joe?"

I didn't look at him. "What?"

"I don't want it to come back. Are you going to leave me here with them when it comes back?"

I turned and looked at him. "Do you want me to?" He shook his head worriedly. "Then no. Have I ever left you?" He shook his head again. I turned on my side and leaned my head on my hand, facing him.

"But it's all different now, you're different."

"Me?" He nodded. "Mm, okay, I can see why you would think that. I'm still Joe, I'm still the Joe that sits with you under the stars and gets you food and listens to you when you speak. Are you scared about it coming back?"

He nodded. "It makes me angry." He reached out and touched the cut on my lip, poking it with his finger. "And sad."

I refrained from making any face to show of the soreness he had created with his pocking, I didn't want him to feel worse.

"I'm not going anywhere, Leo, I don't care how you feel or what you do. I know who you are like you know who I am. Why am I not nice?" Leo smiled at me which made me smile back. "Were you just worried that I was going to leave you here?"

He nodded. "It's what they want, isn't it? They want me because of what I do, what I want."

He understood more than I realised. Honesty. I wasn't sure about it but he was talking to me and I didn't want him to stop.

"Yes, but they also want to help you understand it better. They are just a bit undecided about me. This place is secret, Leo, and we can never tell anyone about it."

Leo nodded. "I know. Layton brings other boys here, doesn't he? He brought Orion here?" Fuck, how did he know these things?

"Maybe, did Layton tell you?"

Leo shook his head. "I know, I watched Orion...I know Noah, too."

I sat up, completely taken by surprise. "How?" He bit the inside of his mouth. "Did you meet him?" He nodded. "Is he like you, Leo?"

Leo shrugged. "Maybe."

I frowned at him. "Leo, did you know Layton took boys...like you?"

"Maybe. Didn't you?" I was taken aback by how much he knew.

I shook my head. "No, not really. I mean I knew he took boys that were…different but I was never quite sure what it was about them that made them different. I thought, I hoped, he was helping them find their way…home or something." Had I thought that? I realised I hadn't really thought about what happened to them. I'd avoided thinking about it. "Why did you keep so quiet? Layton could have helped you a long time ago."

He shook his head. "I didn't want help. He took the boys on their own and we never saw them again, they never came back. I didn't wanna never see you or the alley again, I wanted to stay. I wasn't sure if I was like them. Orion was like Ginger, he liked the customers, he went in cars and everything but I used to watch him under the wa'er and he was all marked."

"When did you see all these things?"

He half shrugged. "When Ginger was sleeping and you were watching the alley."

"And Noah? When did you see him?"

"When Ginger was sleeping and you were having business. I came to sit with you because I couldn't sleep and he was at the back of the alley, I think he was hungry. You were with a customer and I sat with him. We both watched you. I like watching you with the customers. I think he's like me but he doesn't know what it's called." What the hell?

I smiled at him, ignoring his side-tracked memory of me. "Pain junkie?" He smiled back. "What did he say?"

"Nothing much. He was hurting though, I could tell."

"In pain?"

He shook his head. "No, maybe."

"I don't understand then, Leo. Hurting?"

"He was jumpy, like the boys with the drugs." I shook my head, still not following. The boys with the drugs…addicts?... wanting a fix? Okay, maybe I understood. Noah was wanting a fix, he was jittery, needy.

"Is that what it's like, Leo, when you want it?" He shrugged. "Does it hurt?"

He nodded and pointed to his head. "Here and here." He pushed at his stomach.

"Stomach ache?"

He smiled amused. "No, not like being hungry, like further inside...it hurts my dick too."

I smiled now. "Your cock?"

Leo looked unsure. "Yes, can we eat now? I don't wanna talk anymore."

I had made him feel unsure. I reached out and took his hand. "Yes, Kendal said she would bring it. Can you tell me about your cock? Does it want...pain?"

Leo shrugged again. "I don't know what it wants but it wants to come and when it comes it hurts again so I never let it come anymore." What?!

I was gobsmacked. "What…not ever?"

Leo smiled. "Isaac made me come...in his mouth!" I smiled.

That had obviously been extremely likeable for his cock. I was about to ask more but there was a knock at the door and Kendal came in carrying a tray. Leo moved back on the bed excitedly. I was a little annoyed that I had said for Kendal to bring the food now. Leo had been talking a lot and told me things I wasn't aware of. Apart from his nonsense ramblings, he was quiet on the street, I never realised just how much he knew about the comings and goings there. I looked from Leo to Kendal and smiled at her.

She smiled back and looked at Leo. "There we go, poppet." She put the tray down in front of him. "I made you some soup and some buttered rolls."

Leo looked at me. "Can I have it?"

I smiled at him and nodded. "Of course."

Leo immediately picked up a roll and stuck it in his soup.

Kendal smiled at him and then looked at me. "You okay, Joe? It got a bit heated this morning, it's all a little confusing. Julian can be..." I moved back on the bed allowing Kendal to perch on the edge and nodded at her.

"Difficult?" She smiled and bit her lip. I sighed. "Yes, I'm fine and yes it's all confusing. I'm not sure why Layton brought us here if it's so impossible. Did he think I would just part company with Leo? He didn't give me that impression last nig...when I spoke to him, he said Leo wanted me to share it with him. Now I'm told it's not safe here for him with me."

Kendal nodded as I looked at Leo to see if he was listening. He seemed like he was engrossed in his food but having learnt a few things about what he knew, I wasn't so sure that he wasn't looking at one thing and listening to us.

"Layton understands new slaves better than anyone I know. Julian is always wary of new additions here. He's not as mean as he makes out and I've told him that he was out of line."

"Was he telling the truth? Are there people here that would just try and take him, who would want him?"

Kendal looked uncomfortable, which already gave me my answer before she spoke. "Yes, maybe. There are rules here, but it's not like we can go to the police if they are broken. There are some Dominant house owners that would want to have Leo and his need working for them. It would earn them a lot of money. Which is why it is not wise to inform the council of your arrival here, not yet."

"Would it be safe for Leo to be in a slave house then?"

Kendal nodded. "It would be better. The slaves are very precious and within a slave house, under a Dominant's protection, they are extremely safe. They are with a Keeper for most of the time and the premises are guarded. There are very strict rules about entering a slave house uninvited or forcefully, the punishment is usually severe, given by the council." I looked at her questioningly and she continued. "Physical punishment."

"Like what? Beaten?"

Kendal looked unsure about sharing. "Not quite but similar."

I shook my head. "Tell me, I want to know."

She sighed. "Like being caned or whipped...maybe tortured...depending on the rule that was broken." My mouth dropped open. Fucking hell! What the hell was this place!?

"Isn't that a little...ancient?"

Kendal smiled back. "It's what this world is about. It's to teach a lesson. We don't lock people up, there are no prisons here, no police. There are no concessions given. If you fall unconscious the punishment continues until it has been administered. It's a harsh lesson but some don't care and will still break the rules. Need like Leo's is...it's like a drug to some and money to others."

I shook my head in disbelief. "You have to understand, Joe. People like Isaac and Leo are very precious here. There are people in the vanilla world that would rob a bank for money, or steal diamonds from another, people are no different here, they just want different things. A Dominant with a strong need will do anything to have it salved. The slave is always treated with respect though, they are the valuable item. A slave that is traumatised is of no use to anyone."

I sort of pushed out a hysterical laugh. An item? When did being a human become an item?

"Surely being...slave...knapped is somewhat traumatising? Jesus, these are people we're talking about!"

Kendal shook her head. "The slave will go where they are told." Kendal smiled. "Slave knapping is very rare but not unheard of. It is usually the council that decides the punishment of rule breakers. That can also be taking away a slave from an owner so most slave knapping as you call it, is usually agreed and, the fact that these are people is not forgotten or taken lightly. These people gave up their will to be used and treated as a commodity, it's not like they were kidnapped and brought here. What Julian was trying to convey was that Leo has no house to keep him secure. Once the council finds out you're here there will be a lot of interest in Leo, without slave status or some sort of pass by the council, he is protected by no one, he has no ownership."

"And Isaac and…what's his name, Julian's friend?"

"Jacob?" I nodded. "Well, Isaac has been released from slavery by the council and they authorised his ownership to Layton. The council had little choice really because of the circumstances behind his withdrawal from slavery. Jacob is a little different. Julian does not own a slave house personally but owns a lot of the land that this world is part of. He holds great sway with the council but Jacob's place here is not as secure.

"He has been ordered once, by the council, to join the slaves because Julian broke a rule and removed some slaves from another house. Julian managed to get him back and took ownership of him but by keeping him separate from the slaves, he puts him at great risk. The council could decide to remove him from Julian at any point or this world but for the moment they are quiet about it. As I said, Julian has a lot of say in the council."

"Remove him? Send him back to the vanillas?"

Kendal nodded. "Yes, if they chose to. He's Julian's private play partner, it's not heard of here for Dominants to have private play partners, there's not much call for it and it's deemed inappropriate." Kendal smiled at me. "I don't think the council are sure what to do about it and they're wary of making waves with Julian…for now."

Kendal smiled. "What would Julian do if they banished him?"

Kendal shrugged. "It's not likely to happen because Julian would make it difficult for everyone by taking back his land."

"So, like everywhere else on this planet, money talks."

Kendal smiled. "Yes, I suppose, although none of this is about money, not really. It's about people and their different needs. Money does swap hands but it is used to secure the slave's health and wellbeing and that of their Keepers, the rest is put away as payment to the slave should they choose to leave. This is not a prison to keep people in, it's a world where people can come to be themselves and the rules are there to protect them."

"And keep people out."

"No, Joe, not like you're saying. People are welcome, but when it is not clear why they want to be here, then the council gets suspicious. You have no understanding of this world or the slaves and Dominants and their different needs, it makes people uneasy. Not because they don't like you but because they want to protect what is here. It is not a hideaway for vanillas. The people here need this place, they need its safety and security so they can live their lives freely and be accepted for who they are, not what society says they should be. Leo can be who he wants to be here, the boy he wants to be."

Kendal looked at me sympathetically. "Layton was going to bring you here and train you as a Keeper. He saw qualities in you that he believed would fit this life and I think he was right. I think that over time you would have learned, will learn, to understand the needs of the slaves. Now that has changed and you have no time. Loving Leo has put you both at a disadvantage. Neither of you understands his need very well and neither of you has any guide. It makes it difficult for you both but that has never stopped Layton before. The council would probably request you were separated but Layton has his own ideas on what works." She smiled again. "He loves new things, new challenges and has a total understanding of both new subs and Keepers, more so than Julian."

I shook my head feeling so overwhelmed and confused. "I thought Julian didn't like me, then I thought he did, then I thought he didn't again, and now...he just confuses me."

Kendal sort of laughed. "Yes, well, that's Julian for you. He has the poorest people skills of anyone I know, but there is nothing he wouldn't do to keep you and Leo safe." I wasn't sure I believed that. Leo maybe, I wasn't so sure about me though. "He wouldn't have let you stay here if he wasn't concerned about you both and I know he wouldn't want you to leave."

Something occurred to me. "If the council finds out that we are here, will he be in trouble?"

Kendal smiled and nodded. "Possibly but that would never worry him." She looked at Leo and smiled. "I made you some food too, Joe, don't let Leo have it."

I looked at Leo as he slurped his soup from the spoon then put the spoon down, picked up the bowl, and started to drink from it. I laughed and then realised how rude he must seem.

I looked at Kendal who was just smiling at him. "I'm sorry, the whole knife, fork, spoon thing is…well, it'll probably seem like a waste of time."

Kendal laughed. "Really, Joe, you should stop worrying. He's eating, it's always a good sign, I don't care how it goes in." I half smiled. Kendal reached out and patted my leg. "It must have been a struggle for you to watch him in the street. When you used to come to the house and tell me about him, I never realised how hard it actually was for you. You never said anything."

I shrugged. "Leo didn't make it hard, he made it easier, he was a reason to keep going."

Leo put down the bowl which made both Kendal and I look at him. Kendal smiled, put her hand in her pocket and pulled out a tissue. She unwrapped it and held it out to Leo. Leo tipped his head to look at it but didn't take the biscuits that she held. He moved back away from her and the tray.

"I don't want my back touched." He looked at me. "Do I have to?"

I shook my head. "No. I've already seen to your back, Kendal is just being nice."

Kendal took the biscuits back and wrapped them again. "It's okay, Leo, you can have them when I'm gone. I had to sneak them out because Isaac would have wanted them and I'm not sure Peter would have allowed it."

I looked at her. "Why?"

Kendal smiled. "Isaac can be easily led to do things for food. Peter wants him to do things for him just because he asks, not for any prize he might gain from doing it."

Leo had let me do his back with just a promise of sleeping with me. I decided to test something.

"Leo turn around and show me your back. No one is going to touch." Leo looked suspiciously at Kendal. "Leo." He looked at me. "Just showing, no touching, I promise." He sighed and turned around. "It looks alright, doesn't it? I did it like you showed me this morning."

Kendal smiled at me and nodded. "It looks great, Joe. I'll take the stitches out in a day or so, there were only two just to hold it together."

"Good boy, Leo, you can turn around now."

Leo turned around and picked up the toothpaste that I had left on the bed. He played with it in his hands and watched it. I had made him anxious and I reached my hand out to him. Without looking up, he took it in his. It made me aware of what Leo was prepared to do for me. I squeezed his hand to reassure him.

I looked back at Kendal. "Thanks for the biscuits, I'm sure Leo will have them. He's a little anxious after the kitchen incident with Julian, he scared him."

Kendal passed me the biscuits. "Well, he's gone now. I'm heading off too, I have some errands to run. Would you like me to pop back later?"

I shook my head. "No, really we're fine."

Kendal smiled. "Well, help yourself in the kitchen and call Peter if you need anything. I'll see you tomorrow, for breakfast?" I smiled at her. "Eat your soup, Joe." She leaned forward and kissed my cheek before standing and leaving the room.

I looked at Leo, thinking. Even Kendal seemed a little off with me.

I sighed and Leo looked up at me. "Are you angry?"

I smiled at him. "What? No. I'm just trying to work this place and these people out."

"Do you like them?" I smiled at him again and held out the biscuits.

"I think they are good people but they don't understand us. Here, eat these while I eat my soup before it gets too cold."

"Can I have some?"

I laughed at him. "No, you've just eaten yours, here." I offered him to take the biscuits which meant he either had to let go of my hand or the toothpaste. I watched him trying to decide and then to help him, I slipped my hand from his and pulled the tray to me. He took the biscuits and just sat watching me eat and I let him sit for a minute before I spoke again between mouthfuls. "Do you like them?"

He shrugged. "I don't know them. They don't seem to want to be friends, they just talk a lot." I smiled at him. "Why are we waiting here?" It was the first time Leo had questioned what was going on. "I don't like waiting."

It was a good question and one I didn't really know how to answer. We did seem to be waiting and I wasn't sure what for. I wished Layton was here. He always seemed to know the answers.

My resolve to leave tonight was still strong. Being here was trouble for them and I didn't want to stay anywhere we were not wanted. It seemed like having brought us here, they now didn't know what to do with us. I was in a strange place and couldn't make decisions here for Leo and me, so I had to get back to where I could. I needed to speak to Layton about Leo's need returning but I needed to find somewhere for us to stay first then I would swing by Manni's to see if he could contact Layton for me.

"We're waiting for it to get dark so we can walk under the stars."

"Are we going back to the alley?"

I shook my head. "No, somewhere new, Leo. Just somewhere you and I can be together and I can look after you okay? You know we are never going back to the alley, we can't go back there. We don't have a place there anymore, we have to go and find a new one."

"Ginger was mean to take it away."

I finished the last of my soup and pushed the tray away. "He wasn't being mean. I didn't have a place there anymore, the customers didn't want me anymore, you know that. They wanted you because you are younger and sweeter than me but you don't like them. Ginger has to look after the alley and make sure the other boys have customers so they can eat. You and I were just taking up space. If you and I find somewhere else with different customers, I can earn enough money to feed us, well, keep you in toothpaste anyway." I smiled at him but he wasn't happy. "Does talking about Ginger make you feel sad?" He nodded. "I know you liked him and he liked you too, a lot."

I could see Leo's tears in his eyes waiting to spill over. "Then why did he take my place and put another boy in it? Do you think he sleeps with him?"

Being replaced had hurt him. I guess he had kind of loved Ginger.

"I don't think Ginger will sleep with anyone else. He just liked you a lot. Ginger is not like you and me, he doesn't need anyone…people. He likes to be free to do his own thing and sometimes, he needed something more. You were special and it made him do things for you, things he will never do for anyone else. You and Ginger will always be friends, you just can't be together and I know that hurts."

Leo shook his head. "We did things for each other… I don't like him anymore." A tear spilled over and ran down his cheek.

Layton had said that Ginger had made it easy for Leo to leave, for me. He had taken his place from him because that is what Leo understood. He knew that when Ginger did that, that he couldn't stay there and had to go with Layton. Ginger had had to hurt him to move him on and Leo didn't understand why his friend, who had slept with him for so long, suddenly didn't want him anymore.

"I know that's not true. You are just hurting and it's making you say things you don't mean. Tell me about Ginger, tell me the things you liked about him."

Leo just sat and I could see thinking about him was hurting him. His tears were streaming down his face and dripping off the end of his chin. He was squeezing the toothpaste in his hand over and over. I moved the tray on the floor and sat beside him, holding my hand out to him. He gave me the biscuits and I put them on the side and held my hand out again.

"Come and lay with me, Leo." Leo immediately moved towards me and I moved my leg around him so he sat between mine. I pulled him against me and stroked the back of his neck.

I didn't have an understanding of what he had shared with Ginger and always believed that their friendship had been one-sided. I had watched them from a distance and had always felt shut out. Knowing what Ginger had been doing for him made me realise that the friendship wasn't as one-sided as I had thought.

"Did you and Ginger used to talk?" Leo shook his head against me. "What not at all?" He shook his head but didn't speak so I left him while he cried quietly against me. I guess he wasn't just crying over Ginger but for the whole life he had had there which was now gone.

Leo and I used to talk a lot but we never spoke about Ginger, not really. I always tried to forget about him when Leo was with me and apart from knowing when Ginger had upset him, I never asked about his time with Ginger and Leo never shared. Now I knew why and being away from him made it easier for me to talk, now I didn't have to share Leo with him anymore. I wanted to make Leo's thoughts right about Ginger. Ginger could have so easily kept Leo with him, instead, he had turned his back on him so Leo would turn to me and I owed it to Ginger to make things right.

I kissed the top of Leo's head. "Ginger took your place away, Leo, because he knew you wouldn't be safe there with him. He knew he couldn't watch you or keep you safe. He didn't do it to be mean to you, he did it because he liked you and wanted you to be okay."

Leo tipped his face up to me and I wiped his wet cheeks. "Why can't Ginger come here with us and we can all be together?"

I smiled. "Because Ginger can't sit still for more than a minute, not like you and I sit. He likes to be free to do his own thing and not worry about anyone else. He likes the street life and the alley, not just because it gives him somewhere to stay but because he likes the life and freedom it gives him. He likes the customers, he likes sucking and fucking strangers for money, he finds it exciting." Leo made a face and it made me smile. "Did you and Ginger fuck?" I wanted to know what they had shared. I wasn't sure he would tell me but he answered straight away.

"Yeah, sometimes, after."

"After what?" Even as I asked, I realised what he meant, after Ginger had given him what he wanted. "After Ginger had made you quiet?" Leo nodded. "Did you like it when he fucked you?"

Leo shrugged. "Sometimes I wanted it and sometimes I didn't, but I let him because when he fucked me, he let me stay with him all night if I didn't make a sound while he did it, and I liked that. I liked sleeping with him, it was warm and I felt safe. Sometimes though, he just wanted me to go away...I made him angry." So their fucking hadn't been about sharing anything intimate, just about taking, just about their need. "Are you mad that we did that?"

I smiled at him and kissed his forehead. "No, not at all, why would you think that?"

Leo shrugged. "Because sometimes you were like mad when he made me go away and I would come and sit with you."

I had been, a little. I had been jealous of their time together.

"I was mad with Ginger, I thought he was using you but I think you both used each other when it suited you both. Why did you stop sleeping with me, Leo, when Ginger came to the alley? Was it because of what he did for you?" Leo shook his head and laid it back on my chest.

I had believed then it was because he had grown up a little and didn't need me anymore, then when he had started to sleep with Ginger I thought it was because he liked him more. Since yesterday I had thought it was because of what Ginger had been doing for him, now though, I wasn't sure about any of those. "Leo? Why then? Did you like Ginger more?" He shook his head. "Because I missed you when you didn't sleep with me."

"I missed you too."

I tipped his face up to look at him. "Then why? I don't understand? Is it something to do with Ginger?"

Leo shrugged. "If I tell you, you gotta promise to not be angry with me?"

I frowned at him. "I don't know where this angry thing comes from. I have never really been angry with you, have I?"

"Not what you say but I know you are sometimes. I like it that you never say angry things."

I smiled at him. "You know too much. I promise I won't be angry."

"You made me feel like a kid and I wanted to be...different. I felt different when I was next to you."

I frowned at him. "I don't understand. Because of your need for pain?"

Leo shook his head. "No, maybe, I dunno. Ginger was different when he came, I was like the other boys, he spoke to me the same. So I tried to be like them, I know I wasn't good at it. I didn't know about this thing then, not in the start, I think that was an accident, it just happened."

He had lost me. So many things that I didn't understand and he obviously didn't either. Had I treated him like a child? He had been, when he had arrived at the alley, he had been a child. When Ginger arrived, Leo had been about sixteen, it was a confusing time for any adolescent but I hadn't thought about it. Leo was just Leo and it was only now that I saw him differently, saw his body was different to what I remembered.

Had he grown into a man before I had realised? I knew that he struggled mentally with being a street boy but I was realising he actually understood as an adult, then it all seemed to get hazy, lost in his head. Maybe he shut it out on purpose? Who could bloody blame him for that?

"What was different, Leo? When you laid next to me, what felt different?"

Leo scrunched his shoulders and I knew he was struggling to say, or find the words. "I wanted to feel you... I wanted you to touch me... differently. You touch me differently now, I like it."

"So, why did you go away from me?"

"Because you didn't and I didn't wanna wait anymore."

I smiled at him. "Did Ginger touch you differently? Is that why you slept with him?"

Leo shook his head. "Nah, Ginger never touched me, he didn't wanna. He watched me sometimes but he never touched me."

"Watched you?" How had I missed all this?

He nodded. "Watched me come when I touched myself. Why didn't you touch me? Didn't you like me?"

Bloody hell! I shook my head slightly embarrassed by his openness and my thoughts.

"God, no, I do like you, I've always liked you. You were just a boy and I couldn't see that you were changing into a young man. I didn't see it, see that your needs were changing. I should have, I should have talked to you."

Ginger had never seen Leo as a child, only as a street boy, a little different but a street boy nonetheless. In Leo's eagerness to grow and be like the others, he had been drawn to Ginger because of how he had treated him. Ginger had put expectations on Leo, which I never did, and Leo had tried to live up to them. He rarely did and that's when he would turn to me when Ginger had got pissed with him.

This whole thing had been going on right in front of me and I had been blinded by jealousy it seemed. I hadn't even known then that it was jealousy, I had just been pissed off, mainly with Ginger. Guess there wasn't room in the street for feelings or, maybe it was me? I wasn't great with people. Maybe now Leo was an adult, that now included him? That thought just made me sad.

CHAPTER THIRTEEN

JOE

This thing he'd had with Ginger had been about him growing into an adult. The pain thing, that had been an entirely separate thing that had happened around the same time it seemed. It all must have seemed very confusing, to have adolescent hormones raging through his body and then this need for pain too, all of it coming at him at once. Him leaving my bed had been kind of like him leaving the nest, breaking free of his childhood and it had just coincided with Ginger's arrival. I stroked my fingers around his ear.

"I liked sleeping with you, Leo, I liked looking after you and I missed you when you stopped coming to me. Things are different now, your body is different...your thoughts are different. When I look at you, I feel differently too, you make me feel... hot." Leo whipped his head up to look at me and I smiled at him. "I think we need to get to know each other again but not like before. Things are different between us, aren't they? When I touch you like this..." I stroked my fingers around his ear lobe. "It means something different now, doesn't it?" Leo nodded.

My touches before had been touches of comfort, like a parent would give to their child, soothing and endearing and never given in sight of anyone. They had not felt like the touches given by a lover because I had never thought of him like that and Leo had picked up on that.

"Can you still look after me though? I like it when you do that."

I laughed at him. He wanted more from me but he didn't want to lose what we already shared.

"I'll always look after you, that will never change. We don't have to change what we have or do now, we just need to add to it."

"Now? Can we do it now?"

I laughed again. "If by 'it', you mean what I think you mean, the answer is no. This is not something you and I are going to take from each other, it's something we are going to share because we both feel it. It's not going to be the same thing you had with Ginger, I'm not sure what you and Ginger were doing. Do you know, understand what you and Ginger were doing?" Leo shrugged.

I was sure that even Ginger wouldn't have been able to answer it either, I don't think either of them knew. Maybe it had just been something different in what was a mundane life.

It was my hormones that seemed to be raging now though. Since seeing him naked on the bed, I hadn't been able to shift the image or the thought of being naked with him, touching him intimately as I had never touched him before. What I had shared with Layton last night had just seemed to fuel those feelings, which was a little strange. A touch given by one person had fuelled my feelings for another. I was sure some head doctor would be able to explain it, have some fancy name for it, I just found it a bit weird.

Leo and I had both grown up on the street, our knowledge of love and what it made you feel, was virtually zilch. Trying to leave him yesterday had hurt and the pain of it had made me realise that Leo was not just another street boy, he meant far more to me. Knowing now that Leo also wanted more from me too was a little exciting but we couldn't just fuck, that wasn't what I wanted for us. I had to take into account his need and be very sure that what Leo and I shared had nothing to do with him wanting a fix.

I didn't want to be his fix, I wanted to be his love, something that was always, not just when he craved it. I wasn't sure how that worked but Layton and Isaac seemed to have it. Maybe next time I saw him I would ask him, he was the closest thing I had to a friend here.

Leo was still looking at me like he was waiting for something. I leant forward and kissed his lips gently and held them there for a moment. Leo parted his lips and touched his tongue to my lip and I pulled away from him startled and stared at him. Did he know how to kiss like Layton had kissed me? Had he and Ginger kissed like that?

"Who taught you to kiss like that?" Leo dropped his face away from me and he became agitated. I felt bad but Leo and I had never kissed like that and I certainly knew customers didn't. "Did Ginger?" He shook his head. "Leo?"

"It's not a bad thing, I know it's not. Why're you making it a bad thing?"

This was not going well and to prove that point, Leo moved away from me. I made a half-hearted attempt to keep him with me but he threw himself forward on the bed and hid his face in the cover before I could stop him. This love thing was proving a lot harder than I had thought it would be.

I had wanted to move slowly forward, give us both a chance to get used to it but Leo seemed to want to just throw himself into it and I had been taken aback by him. His emotional outbursts were changing so quickly and I was struggling to keep up. He had gone from crying and being upset about Ginger to talking calmly, then seemingly wanting, and now stropping. Was this part of his need causing this? Was it me? I moved and laid on my side beside him.

"I didn't mean to make it a bad thing. You took me by surprise, I didn't know you knew how to kiss like that. I liked it. I liked kissing you." He turned his face a little so I could see one eye and I smiled at him. "You can't throw a strop every time you don't get what you want. I know I said things were going to be different between us but it can't just happen just like that. We need to get to know things about each other. We both need to learn about this need you have, I don't want what we share to be confused with that. I want to know that when we are together that it's mutual, equal, that we both want it for the same reasons."

He turned his face and lay it on his hands to look at me. "I don't know how to kiss, not really, not with tongues. Isaac showed me and I liked it, it made me feel hot and I wanted to feel it with you, I thought that's what you wanted. You said you wanted to get to know each other but not like before, we never kissed with tongues, so ain't that different? I don't understand you, I waited but you can't say it's going to be different if it's not because I can't wait anymore, I don't like it."

I laid my head on my arm still facing him. He had lost me. Was he giving me an ultimatum? Surely he didn't understand something like that?

"Waiting, when? Just now? You were waiting for me to kiss you?"

"No...yes, not just now, waiting for ages before, in the alley, not for a kiss..." He thought about it. "Maybe for a kiss, for things to be different, like kissing with tongues, I think, different like that. I waited for you. You kissed me now, so I thought things were different but then you didn't want it so now I'm... pissed off." O-kay.

"You've been waiting for things to be different between us, even while we were in the alley?" He nodded his head against the hand he lay on. "Since you stopped sleeping with me?" He nodded again. Christ. Had I been blind? How had I not seen? It was a long time to wait for something, someone. I smiled at him. "Okay, sit up." I sat up and looked at him and he looked back unsure. "Come on." I leaned forward and pulled at his hand.

Leo slowly sat up in front of me and I stretched his legs around me and put mine over his, so we were sitting groin to groin, our bodies close.

"Are you gonna to hit me?" For God's sake! This boy!

I laughed at him which made him frown at me. "Leo, you say the strangest things, have I ever hit you?"

"No."

"Then why would you say such a thing, or think it?"

He shrugged. "I dunno what you're doing." I smiled at him and reached up and held his face in my hand, stroking my thumb over his cheek.

"I thought that seeing as you had waited so long and so patiently without getting…pissed off, that it deserved something…nice. Close your eyes."

He stared back at me. "Why?"

I smiled at him. "Do you trust me?" He paused a moment before nodding. "Then don't ask questions, close your eyes."

He closed his eyes then spoke again. "Can I ask a question now they're closed?"

I laughed quietly. "What Leo?"

"Don't you like my eyes?"

I rubbed my fingers gently across his closed lids and watched as the corners of his mouth turned up slightly. He liked it, he liked the touching.

"I love your eyes, they are like deep pools of water."

He smiled as I traced my fingers around his face. "I like water pools."

"Mm, me too. You have the longest lashes and a small nose…"

I traced my fingers to his mouth. He had quite full lips for a guy. A guy. He was a guy now, not the kid who I had found me all those years ago. I could feel the down of facial hair across his skin, it was so soft under my fingers and so light it didn't cast a shadow across his face at all, which was surprising, as his hair was so dark. I wondered how long it had been trying to grow, or if it ever would. I had never noticed it before, or even thought about his lack of facial hair.

I swept my fingers gently over his lips and the sharp indent v below his nose and he parted them as it tickled. "Keep your eyes closed." I did it again and his lips quivered and I leaned forward and touched mine to his and kissed them.

I felt Leo's breath against my mouth as the air sighed out of him and I kissed him again, as I held his face. I felt the first unsure movement of his lips against mine as if he wasn't sure whether to join in or carry on waiting. This was as new to me as it was to him, but it felt so right, so good to feel his mouth against mine. I unconsciously closed my eyes and kissed him again and this time I touched my tongue to his lips, stroking across his top lip, asking him to open them further to me.

His lips parted a little and I pushed my tongue into his mouth and touched it to his, asking him to play. His tongue was hesitant at first and then his face leant into my hand and he met my asking tongue with his. The feeling inside me seemed to shoot all through my body, making my heart beat faster, my stomach roll and my cock throb to life. Leo lifted his hand and touched it to my body and then as if burned he took it away again before touching again.

He moaned quietly into my mouth and I felt his thighs flex under mine, as he tried to thrust his hips forward. I had never felt so wanting and I moved my hands down his neck and around his body, pulling him to me.

He moaned again as our mouths and tongues devoured each other hungrily. This was ten times more powerful than what I had felt with Layton and I pulled at him hard, making him whimper and quiver. I never knew a kiss could feel so good, so powerful. The moaning, whimpering sounds he was making were making me feel so hot. I swept my hands up his back and felt the gauze covering, under my fingers. Shit. His back. In the heat of the moment I had completely forgotten and now realised why he was moaning and quivering so much.

I swept my hands gently around his shoulders and up to his face again and slowly took my mouth from his. I opened my eyes and looked at him. His eyes were still closed, his lips parted, waiting still. "Open your eyes, Leo."

As if dazed, he took a moment to follow the request and then he started to breathe heavily.

"I can't breathe." Fuck, had I hurt him?

I looked at him concerned. "I'm sorry, did I hurt you?"

He smiled at me and shook his head. There was something different about his smile and in my concern for him, I couldn't quite fathom what it was. He lifted his hand to my face and touched his fingers to my lips and as I looked at him, I realised what was different. The sad dark child eyes that had always looked back at me were gone. The blue was now laced with flecks of green? Silver? I wasn't sure but it made his eyes brighter and for a moment, I was lost in them, until he spoke.

"I want more." His words were breathless, wanton and I knew then that what I had felt had been the same for him. I kissed his fingers and stroked mine around his face.

"Was it worth waiting for?"

He nodded and I smiled at him. "I want more." His words became more demanding and less breathless. I leaned forward and kissed his lips gently and then sat and looked at him. He shook his head. "I want more." He repeated.

I had thought that he wanted more kissing but now looking at him, I knew he was asking for more than that. His eyes were alive, dancing with vibrant different blue/green colours, his body tense and quivering. I understood what he wanted because the feelings were burning inside me too.

It would be just so easy to lay him back and take him, take my pleasure from him, but I didn't want it to be like that. This was new to both of us, these feelings, this fire that was burning in my stomach...and groin. I needed time to get used to these feelings because I had never felt them with anyone, not like this.

I shook my head before speaking. "I understand, Leo. I feel it too but we need to just…just get used to these feelings..."

He frowned at me "I want it. Why can't I have it?" Have it? I had become an 'it' and I wasn't sure I liked that.

"Enough, Leo. This is why you can't have 'it'. I want us to share something beautiful, not 'it'. You will have to wait a little longer. Let's just get used to the way we make each other feel for a while."

Leo sneered at me. He dropped his hand from my face and pushed it at my body, pushing me away and I fell back on my hands. He was agitated and I wondered if I should just give him what he so badly wanted?

The kiss had been hot and beautiful. This wasn't and I wasn't sure what to do about it. He moved his hand to my leg and pushed it off of his, so he could free himself from under me. I watched him. His movements were jerky, agitated and it was clear he was having trouble dealing with the need and the feelings that were inside him. They were certainly new.

He sat back from me, then moved again a little further, rubbing his hand over his cock through his linens. He wanted to come, that was clear but I didn't want this to be like the moments with Ginger, where Ginger made him needy and then watched him as he pleasured himself. My cock had been semi-hard too but I had just revelled in the feeling, knowing there was more to come. This was enough for now, these new feelings that Leo and I had shared, we needed to get used to them, not throw ourselves at them.

What if this had been about his need for pain and not about his need to be with me? Me touching his back had seemed to send him into a wanton frenzy and I was unsure of that. I hadn't purposely done it, I had forgotten in the heat of the moment, lost in the kiss.

I didn't want him to think I had made him needy and then left him to get on with it. "Leave it, Leo, it will go away."

He sort of snarled at me and then slipped off the edge of the bed to the floor.

This wasn't how I wanted it to be, how it was meant to have played out. I had wanted to spend the day loving him, being together, enjoying the new feelings we had for each other. He was still touching himself, I could tell by the way he was looking down.

"Leo, if you make yourself come I will be very angry with you. This wasn't about that, it was about sharing feelings." Leo looked up over the bed at me defiantly and I could see he was still stroking his cock. "Fine." I moved off the bed towards the bathroom. "I'm not watching you, I'm going to have a bath, you can join me when you've finished."

I walked into the bathroom and sat beside the bath on the floor. How had that all gone so wrong? How had something so good turned into this, us sitting in separate rooms? Was I being selfish? I had felt the same want too, my cock had grown hard with the need for more. Was I moving too slowly? Should I just let him have what he wanted and love him after? I got up and walked back to the door to see him. I expected him to be in the throes of his orgasm but he wasn't, he wasn't even touching his cock. He was sat back on his knees and his upper body was turned into the bed, his hands clutching at the covers, his face buried into the side of the bed.

I stood for a moment and watched him, again undecided about what to do. If I went to him, he would think I hadn't meant what I said and I had meant it. I didn't want him to sit alone and pleasure himself as he had done with Ginger. I had to show him that what we were sharing was different and he had to understand the difference of what we were now. I turned back into the bathroom and walked to the bath. I would do as I had said, I would run a bath for us and wait for him. I turned on the taps and sat on the floor.

I felt awful like we had had a row, although nothing had been said. I thought about the kiss and it made me smile. It had been a little awkward, clumsy, full-on. We definitely needed to practice more, we couldn't get in this state every time I wanted to kiss him. He had to learn that a kiss didn't mean more than a show of our affection, of our love...and my body had to learn that too. I put my fingers to my lips. God, his mouth had felt good against mine. Hot, wet...fuck, enough. I got up and turned off the taps and tested the water. Not too deep so his back wouldn't get too wet and not too hot. I sat back on the floor and waited.

I didn't have to wait as long as I expected. Leo walked slowly in and sat, sort of half beside me and half in front of me. He wrapped his arms around his legs and laid his head on his knees sideways, looking at me. I had avoided his eyes while he settled but I looked at him now.

"I didn't come...are you mad?" He had switched back to talking, which was good. This side of Leo I understood and it gave me time to think.

I reached out my hand and stroked my fingers over his head. "Maybe a little, not with you though. The kiss was too much, wasn't it? I felt it too, it should have been slower. It took us both by surprise. It was our first proper kiss, I forgot about your back, I'm sorry if I hurt you."

"I liked the kiss."

I smiled at him. "So I saw. I never meant to make your feelings difficult."

Leo shook his head against his knees then raised his fingers and tapped his head three times. Something I had seen him do in the past when he had struggled with his thoughts. "I think they were already difficult...from the waiting."

I smiled again at him. "Mm, it was a long time to wait."

"Are you gonna make me wait again because I was bad?"

"You weren't bad. Wanting those feelings isn't bad, you were just a little too eager...it was too fast. I don't want our relationship to be about just fucking or coming or even your need for pain, do you understand that?"

He shook his head. "No, not really. Isn't that why people stay together because they like the way they fuck together?" Oh, dear. Leo's life knowledge was poor.

"We've been together a long time and we've never fucked. People stay together for other reasons, not just sex, Leo. Where did you get that idea from?"

He huffed like he knew better. "The street. That's why people come, isn't it? For sex, to fuck. That's why those ladies came to the house with Steve. I heard them. That's why people are together...except us. I think it's because we're...best friends aren't we?"

I smiled at him. "Yeah, we're friends and that's what makes it different between people. I want us to be friends first, always. The street was not real. I know it felt real to you because you were there when you were very young but there are other things in life, other things more important than sex and fucking and wanting to come." He looked at me suspiciously, like he didn't agree.

"Then if you know that, why didn't you do them?" I had no idea where this Leo had come from but he had a point.

I had shown him no difference over the last four years. My life had been no different to his. Every day was about the same thing. Get the customer, suck the customer, make them come, take the money. No wonder his view of the world and the people was so tainted. He knew no other way to be with people. A hot kiss made him feel excited and wanting and he had never had to stop those feelings, in fact, he had to try very hard to even have them with customers.

His first life lesson had come from his home and that had shown him no difference either. People came to his house and fucked and then they left. It was sad. His life had been one alley after the other and they were not the sort of places to learn about real-life or real relationships, people or love.

I could only answer what I knew. "Because there is no room for those things on the street. The other things don't put food in your stomach or money in your hand and when you have to think about those things every day, the other things get forgotten. I forgot them...but you made me remember." It was time to be a little honest with him. "I have never had a relationship with anyone."

He squinted his eyes at me. "Then how do you know these things?"

"I've seen them. I remember my mum and dad even though I was young, I remember them. They used to sit on the sofa together and watch television, they loved each other. They used to kiss and hold hands and smile together and I never once heard them fucking."

God, it had been ages since I had thought about them. I could hardly remember their faces but I remembered how it had felt to be with them, safe. All that had changed one day when I never got picked up from school. They had been killed in a motorway accident from what I remember. That day was a bit hazy, I couldn't even remember how old I was, six? Maybe five? Maybe older, who knew. I just remember being taken by strangers and being handed over to more strangers and so on and so on.

Then he told me something that he'd never shared with me. "I don't really remember my mum. She was soft, like a blanket, I think."

I smiled at him. "I think that sounds like a nice memory of her, Leo. Not everyone is like Steve or the suits from the streets. Not everyone thinks like them or wants what they wanted from you. I want you because you're Leo, my friend, and I like it when we do things like this, talking and sitting together. I liked kissing you but if it confuses you too much then maybe we shouldn't kiss with tongues." I smiled at him and he sighed.

"I don't wanna wait again, I won't be bad." I held out my hand to him and he took it and moved closer to me.

"It's not bad to want more, I want more too but we have a lot going on. I don't want either of us to be confused about what we are sharing. I thought kissing like that would be a small step but it turned into a big step and I was taken by surprise too. I didn't want the first time you and I shared those feelings for it to end with you pleasuring yourself alone. I want to share that with you."

"When?"

I laughed a little at his eagerness. "When it feels right for both of us, when we understand things better. Not just each other but your need, too. We both have a lot to learn. You will just have to wait a little longer, but this time, I'm waiting with you."

"Can we kiss while we wait?"

I laughed again and leaned over and kissed his lips. "I think we can practice so we can get used to the feelings that kissing causes us, what do you think?" He nodded and I smiled.

We seemed to have come to an understanding, for now. I wasn't sure how long it was going to last but it gave me hope that Leo had not come at my request. If he could control that need when it had been so close then surely controlling it when kissing was going to be a little easier?

"I ran the bath, do you want to get in with me?"

"Is it cold?"

"No."

"Is it hot?" I smiled. He had learnt a lesson at least about hot water.

"No, it's just warm. I thought after, we could look at your back together?"

"Why?"

Layton had said it would be good for Leo to look at his wounds. He said it would help him understand his need a little better and I needed his help to understand it.

"Why do you ask so many questions? You never used to."

"Because I knew everything in the alley. When you asked me to do things I knew the reasons, now I don't and I wanna know. Is it bad?"

He had certainly proved to me that he had known more of what had been going on in the alley than I did, so I couldn't argue with him on that.

"Is what bad? The reason? Or wanting to know?"

"Both, I s'pose."

"Why are things bad here? You never said anything was bad in the alley?"

He shrugged. "Nothing was bad in the alley, I wanna go back...please?" Oh God. Was this going to turn into another fight?

I shook my head. "We've spoken about this, Leo. We can't go back, we don't have a place there." He sighed heavily.

Nothing was bad in the alley because no one questioned anything he did or requested anything of him, other than the customers and I knew he thought they were bad. My questioning of him was making him doubt everything that was going on. His security, the alley, was gone. The familiar street boy faces had now been replaced with strangers and everyone seemed to have an interest in him, whereas before no one cared. I suppose it was enough to put anyone on edge.

"If something is bad, I will tell you okay? If something is going to hurt or feel bad, I promise I will tell you. I want us both to look at your back so we can understand what your need is about, the way it makes you feel."

Leo shook his head. "No thanks, I don't want to." The please and thank you were a bit unsettling. Leo had never been so well mannered.

No one demanded manners on the street, they didn't get you respect, a place. I watched him for a moment. He was sad again. His eyes had returned to pools of darker blue and he was lost in it. It wasn't new, this look. He had come to the alley with it and it rarely left him. Sometimes when we sat under the stars, I would see it disappear a little and sometimes food made them sparkle. I knew from today that feeling hot and horny made them change but I wondered if the sadness would ever leave him permanently.

I didn't know much about his life before he had found his way to the alley. Only what his stepfather had done to him and today he had shared a little more. I wanted to talk more but Leo had drifted into silent mode and I knew pushing him now would serve no useful purpose. When Leo was done talking, he was done, I never challenged him before and doing so now would just make him more unsettled. I picked up his hand and kissed it.

"Come on. Let's have a bath and I'll wash you." Leo seemed happy to let me do that and we undressed and got in.

CHAPTER FOURTEEN

JOE

I spent some time washing him, his face, his hair. Careful not to get his stitches wet. He let me lead, tipping his head forward when I requested so I could rinse off the bubbles, lifting arms and legs so I could clean him all over. It had probably been the best wash he had had in a while and lack of speech from him, I decided, was that he was enjoying the attention. I washed quickly before returning my attention to him. This had been much more enjoyable than the bath I had shared with Layton and I understood now, why he thought ours had not been relaxing, I had been too upset and too needy to relax with him.

I looked at Leo looking so serious at me. I splashed water at his face and because he didn't quite understand that I was playing, I smiled at him and did it again. He turned his face away and looked hurt, still not seeing the fun in it and I sighed. "I'm just playing, it's meant to be fun." I turned his face towards me and wiped the droplets of water away. "I'm sorry, I was just playing." He, like me last night, was not relaxed at all, he was tense and uneasy. "Do you like the bath?" He nodded. "But you don't like being splashed with water?" He shook his head. Okay, I gave up. I had no idea about these quiet moments. "What are you thinking, Leo?"

"Why d'you wanna look at my back? You don't like it." His back was worrying him.

"I didn't like it before when I thought someone had been hurting you but now I know you like it, it's different. When someone touches it, does it make you think of Ginger?" He nodded then became agitated, pulling at his fingers and looking around the room, anywhere but at me. "Leo?" He didn't turn. "Leo!" He turned and looked at me.

"Why d'you shout my name when I don't wanna answer, I was ignoring you." Well, that was honest.

I smiled at him. "Because I don't want to be ignored, I want to look at you. Don't you want to think about Ginger?"

He shook his head. "No, not anymore, I don't wanna think about any of it. I want my back to go away and all the people. I thought it would go away now that Ginger is gone but it's not."

I frowned at him. "But you said, you knew it was going to come back? You said you could feel it."

He shook his head. "I don't want it to, not now."

Was he trying to will it away? Convince himself that it wasn't what he wanted? That it never happened? Even Kendal said that it controlled her when it got bad.

"Are you scared? Can you feel it now? Do you want it?" He shrugged. I could see that he was scared of it. The answer to the other two, I wasn't sure of. "What are you scared of?" He struggled to answer so I tried to make it easier. "Is it the pain?" He nodded. That was too easy, there must be something else. "What else? Is it other things?"

He nodded again. "I don't like it on my own, being alone with it. It takes me away and I can't get back. Who's gonna get me back now? I don't wanna stay in it, not forever, it's too much. I don't wanna stay here with strangers, with people I don't know. I need Ginger and now I don't know what to do to make it go away." He looked at me, his eyes full of tears again. "How'm I gonna make it go away?"

It hurt to see him so upset about something he clearly had no control over. I had no doubt now that it was starting to eat away a little inside him and it was causing him to panic because he knew Ginger wasn't around to salve it for him.

If he was a pain junkie and he had just lost his supplier, of course, it was going to make him agitated. I took his face in my hands and pulled it towards me. I needed to think but I needed to calm him down first before he got caught up in his panic. I kissed his forehead and stroked him.

"Hey, take a few breaths. You are here with me and I'm not going to leave you with any strangers. I don't understand this need you have but I want to, I want to be here for you. Layton said he would help us through it, I know he can. I see him and Isaac and I know he understands it. I know he can help you Leo, and me."

"I need to go back to alley, Joe...please, I need Ginger."

He wanted to be around the person that had always made it go away, made it better. Being away from Ginger was making him uneasy about what he knew was coming.

"Look at me, Leo." He lifted his head and looked at me. He was breathing heavily. "Do you want it now?" He shook his head. I felt relieved at his answer. "Then stop, you can breathe through this panic, this is all it is, you're just worrying about it and making yourself panic and there is no need. Ginger doesn't want to do it anymore so we are going to find you another way. Layton will help us, help you and while he helps you deal with it, I will be there with you. You won't be on your own, not at any time, even if it feels like it, I will be there."

"But I'm not nice, Joe. Ginger said I'm not a nice person when I want it. I don't wanna be bad. I don't want you not to like me." Fuck's sake.

"Is that what Ginger told you? Because he was wrong. I know you and I know that you are never a bad person. This need you have is just a small thing that we both have to learn to accept. You need to know where your fix is going to come from, I get that. Layton said he would give it to you and we both have to trust him. He's not a stranger, we both know him. You have seen what he does for Isaac, so you know he understands it."

I could see Leo was thinking about it. He had met Layton many times over the years on the street when he had visited. He liked him, I knew. He had always been happy to sit with him but would never leave the alley with him, never go to the house because it was out of his comfort zone.

Yesterday had been the first time he had left the alley with him but that had a lot to do with Isaac being there. He was already away from his home, we both were, and we would have to put our trust in Layton. My plan of leaving tonight was looking shakier and shakier. I had wanted to find a safe place for Leo before we needed Layton but I could see that that wasn't going to happen. Leo needed to feel secure now. He needed Layton to be around, we both did, to ease the fear of what was coming. We would have to stay...for now and that irked me a little to be reliant on these people, in this world, that clearly didn't want us.

Taking Leo away from the person that was going to help him would only confuse him more. Once we were on the street, Layton was going to be hard to contact and he would struggle to find us.

I looked at Leo, who was still struggling with his panic and smiled at him. "We'll stay here okay, Leo? Close to Layton."

"But you said we were gonna find a new place?"

I nodded. "I did and we will but now isn't a good time. The street is not a good place to be when you need a fix. We both need Layton to guide us through this and if we leave here now, it will be difficult to find him when we need him. We'll stay here, okay?"

Leo nodded. "What if that man comes and tries to take me? He wants me."

I frowned at him. "What man? Julian?" He nodded. "What do you mean he wants you?"

"I know what he wants, I felt it when he touched me."

"But you asked to be touched, you wanted to be friends?" Had I missed something else?

"Because if he takes me, I don't want him to be mean. So I wanted to show him I knew." Knew what?

"Knew what?" This was one of those talks where Leo's thoughts made no sense when they left his mouth.

"Knew him. That I knew him." I didn't understand. How could you know someone after meeting them for five minutes?

"He's not going to take you." Even as I said it, I wasn't sure about it.

He had spoken of people in this world that wanted something so badly they would just try and take it. Was he included in that? Had I been right when I said they were just hungry junkies? Unable to control themselves, their need, like Leo? No. Kendal was friends with him, more than friends...well, I wasn't sure. They all seemed to kiss each other so it was a little confusing, who liked who and who was having a relationship with who, but she wouldn't allow him to take Leo. Would she?

I shook my head and realised Leo was watching me intently. "He's not going to take you, Leo. I wouldn't let him for a start, and really, I'm not sure he would like sitting outside at night to watch the stars." I smiled at him hoping to draw his thoughts and it worked.

Leo smiled back. I definitely had to get us away from here as soon as possible. There were too many things that made Leo unsure, that I was unsure of.

"I think we have spent enough time in the water. You're going all wrinkly." I looked at his hand and his fingers were all white and waterlogged.

I wanted the night to come. I wanted Leo to sleep so I could get Peter to contact Layton. There were so many questions I had, I needed him. I just...needed him.

Leo and I stepped from the bath and I dried him and then wrapped a towel around him while I dried myself. When I looked at him he was staring at my body, my cock to be precise and I quelled the urge to cover myself from his eyes. He was curious about my body as I had been about his when he had been lying naked and asleep on the bed. Since being here, we had slept naked together but we hadn't really explored each other. After the kissing saga today, exploring bodies was the last thing we needed but just looking was a start to getting to know each other.

I finished drying slowly, more so Leo could watch me than to actually dry my skin. I was enjoying his eyes on my body and found myself moving so my muscles flexed a little more. I smiled to myself when I realised I was flirting with him and then felt bad after denying him earlier. It was a little teasing. I held out my hand to him for the towel.

"Finished?" There was a little sparkle in his eye when he looked at me.

"No."

I smiled at him and took the towel. "What do you want to do now? Are you tired?" Leo adamantly shook his head.

No, it was a silly question really, I could see what he wanted. He had stopped his orgasm earlier and now that need was going to be high on his to-do list.

"If we look at my back, can I come?"

Should he be asking that? I wasn't sure whether he should be allowed his orgasm when he could feel his need starting to ask. I didn't want to encourage anything that I wasn't sure of. This had been my doing, flaunting my body at him but I didn't want him to get upset again.

"No, Leo. I want you to ignore your feelings where your cock and your need is concerned. You can lie naked on the bed with me for a while until it gets dark. Then I'll take you outside."

He turned and walked out of the bathroom, leaving me standing there. I sighed, put away the towels, emptied the bath, and walked into the bedroom. Leo was lying face down on the bed. I walked around and sat next to him, stroking my fingers over his head.

He was a little pissed with me and rightly so, I deserved it. I hadn't been able to help myself, no one had ever looked at me with such want in their eyes. Had he been looking at me like that for the last two years? I was sure I would have noticed if he had, which then made me wonder again if this whole wanting me was just the beginning of his need. How did you know what was real and what was the need part? Having never shared intimately with Leo, I didn't know...but it made me hot seeing the desire in his eyes. I looked down at him. His face was turned away from me so I knew he was still sulking, still pissed at me.

We sat for ages before he spoke, even then he didn't look at me. "Do you think Isaac gets scared?"

I wished I knew the answer to his question so I could ease his fears.

"I don't know, Leo. Maybe we can ask him tomorrow? I know that he trusts Layton."

Leo turned his face on the bed. "Do you?"

"Yes."

Layton had been my friend since I came to the alley six or seven years ago. He had never been anything but nice and he was honest, about everything. He spoke openly about sucking cocks and anything else that went on in the street and never in a degrading way. He never made me feel I was trash. Before Leo had come along he would spend a lot of time with me, sometimes the whole day, even waiting while I had customers, before bringing me tea or something to eat. Sometimes he brought me clothes and not second-hand ones either, brand new ones with tags on.

When Leo had arrived and I had asked Layton to see if he would take him, he had spent the whole day with us both, getting to know him a little. He had been concerned about how young he was and had tried to get Leo to go somewhere safer but Leo had been still reeling from his stepfather's attack and just wanted to stay where he was. I had told Layton that I would watch out for him, I hadn't known then how much Leo would need looking after. I had thought that he hadn't grown emotionally, just stayed as the kid that had arrived but talking to him here, listening to the things he knew, that wasn't the case. He had knowledge of things I didn't even know, understood things better than I gave him credit for, he just chose not to share them, for whatever reason.

"I know you are worried about sharing your need with someone else, someone new but Layton isn't worried about the things you want. I think he understands your need to have it, the way it feels to want it. I think he is going to show us ways to make it go away without using razors."

"What ways? What's he going to do?"

Again I couldn't answer him. "I'm not sure."

"Will I have to lie quietly to have it? Like I did for Ginger?"

Oh God, question after question that I didn't know the answers to.

"Maybe, I think that's up to him. I think Layton will tell you what he wants like Ginger told you. Was it hard to lay quiet for Ginger?"

Leo nodded. "But he wouldn't do it if I made a noise. If I was really quiet and didn't move, he'd fuck me. I had to be quiet for that, I had to stay still until he came."

"Did you like him fucking you?" he shrugged.

"It hurt…a bit."

"Did you tell him it was hurting?" He shook his head.

"No. I had to stay quiet. Are you listening?" I smiled down at him and he smiled back.

"I am listening, I'm just trying to understand why he fucked you and why you let him if it wasn't nice." He sort of shrugged.

"I think he just liked fucking, I think he just wanted to come. If I laid still and let him come he let me stay with him the whole time, he never made me go away." Ah, yes, he got to stay with him.

"Is that when he watched you come?"

"No, I had to go away if I wanted to come, to my bed. He didn't want anyone to know what we did."

His actions earlier were starting to make sense now. He wanted to come so he had moved away from me like Ginger had taught him to. It was all pretty messed up really. Leo had been a hole to fuck when the urge had taken Ginger. Each gave the other what they wanted and took something else in return. It was a strange kind of relationship, two completely different people with different needs, both using each other.

I had been trying so hard to make our relationship different from what he had with Ginger but it already was. We didn't use each other, we were together because we liked each other's company. I liked looking after him and he liked being looked after, we wanted the same things from each other...so far. Leo's need for pain was going to take him places that I had never been, I wanted to go with him, share it with him but I was scared too. I knew that I loved him, I didn't know if he loved me. What if his need took him from me? What if I couldn't travel his path with him?

He spoke, drawing me from my thoughts. "I know when you're thinking things, you don't talk to me for ages."

I smiled at him. "You know too much, Leo, you're too clever." He smiled at me. He liked that. I leaned down and kissed his head. "I think you're amazing and...I think it's time to put ointment on your back again."

He scowled at me. "I don't like it when you think those things, only the amazing bit, I like that, not the other stuff." I turned and picked up the tube from the bedside and then turned back to him.

"I do it because I love you and I know it makes your back feel better. Do you want to sit up, or stay there?"

"Stay here and it only feels better afterwards, not when you do it. Can we go outside afterwards? I can't breathe." I sat cross-legged beside him and undid the tube.

"Feeling a little stir crazy?" I touched the first bit of ointment to his skin and he sucked his breath in.

"I'm not crazy." He moved his hands under his face and laid on them as I continued. "I just want to feel free. I used to feel like part of the night, like a star, now I feel like I fell out of the sky and I'm stuck."

I laughed a little. Now that sounded more like the Leo I was used to. Crazy talk.

"Well, that sounds a little crazy but beautiful too."

He wasn't used to being kept in between four walls for so long. He jolted a little as I touched one of his cuts and then settled again.

"It's too quiet here, don't you think it's quiet?"

I hadn't thought about it. There had been too much going on but he was right. There was no traffic noise, no sirens, no hustle that was always a continuous hum in the background when we were in the alley.

"I've been busy...thinking but now you mention it, it is a little quiet." He was noticing so much more than me. "Are you missing things from the alley?" He nodded. "What else are you missing?"

"The trains that go past every day...and the other boys, not just Ginger, the others. I miss the sound of the customers when they come and the smell of them and the alley. I miss my clothes and Manni's food and the tea that you used to bring me and trying to get warm."

I looked down and around at him. He had his eyes closed.

"You didn't like my tea, you said earlier it didn't have enough sugar in it? And you never liked being cold and never spoke to the other boys...and you certainly didn't like the customers!" I smiled as I spoke.

"I still miss it all. I could breathe when it was cold and your tea made me warm, even though it never tasted of sugar. The other boys never spoke to me but I liked them, I liked their faces, I liked watching them with customers, I've always watched them and...sometimes they spoke to me."

Well, that was news to me. I shook my head. Did I even know him at all?

"Why did you watch them?" It seemed strange that he would watch them when he didn't like being with the customers himself.

"Because I never knew how to do things so I watched them to see what they did, then I just watched them because it made me hot." I stopped touching him and looked at him.

"You never knew how to do what?"

"You know, be with the customer. No one showed me, you never showed me so I thought I should just know but I didn't. I tried to see what they did...I don't think I did it properly because the customers were angry with me. I made Isaac come though, he said I didn't suck like a girl."

Oh dear God! He had been fourteen, of course, he had never... "How did you know? Coz I watched you too and you made them come really quickly? Did you just know?"

I wanted to take him in my arms and hold him so tightly. How scared he must have been. By the time Leo had arrived on the street I had been serving customers for well over a year, four or five times a night, sometimes more. It never occurred to me that he wouldn't know, it was just cock. When I had started, I just wrapped my lips around their cocks and let them lead, let them fuck my mouth, then as time went on I learnt to take control from them. They did it my way or they didn't get my mouth, it was as simple as that...He had watched me?

"Leo? Your first time with a customer, was it your first time?"

He opened his eyes and sort of smiled at me. "No, Steve, remember?"

I felt sick. "He was scum."

Leo's smile disappeared as he spoke. "Yeah, I know I shouldn't have done what I did, but he was my first though. I'd never seen a hard cock before that, just pictures in a book."

He spoke so matter of fact about it, so calmly. We'd never spoken about what had happened to him. When I had found him in the rubbish he had been hurting and I hadn't really known him. As time went by, he seemed to forget and so did I. You never looked back living on the street, it was never worth it.

Leo had closed his eyes again. "Leo?"

"What?"

"Do you want to talk about that night? What he did?" Leo shook his head against the pillows.

"No, thank you." He never wanted to speak about it and we were back to good manners again.

"Do you want to talk about sucking cocks?" He never opened his eyes but smiled.

"Okay." Finding something he did want to talk about I turned my attention back to his back.

I had finished but it seemed the more he thought about what he had to say the more anxious and agitated he became. With his back being touched it seemed to divide his attention, so he couldn't think too much about one or the other. I traced my fingers over his cuts gently. Most of them didn't pain him, but now and again I would touch a sore one and he would flinch a little. I went back and forth to good ones and then bad ones just to keep his thoughts occupied.

I spoke. "I didn't know about sucking cocks, not when I did my first customer. I kind of just held my mouth open and let him fuck it. I did that a lot, for a while. I suppose I kind of taught myself, realising that sucking cock actually meant sucking and not just sitting there with my mouth open. Different customers like different things, some like just their cock head sucked, some like to feel your mouth down their whole shaft and some like to feel your tongue working over their sensitive tip. You just have to listen to them and feel their body under your hands to know what is floating their boat."

Leo opened his eyes and looked at me, smiling. "Floating their boat?"

I smiled back. "Making them want to come." He closed his eyes again. "Were you scared, when you took your first customer?"

He opened his eyes and pushed himself up slightly to look at me again. "Do you remember it?"

I did but I wanted him to tell me. He had been so distraught after, I had had to take him inside and sit with him. He had been shaking and retching and thinking about it now, I had given him toothpaste to take away the bad taste.

"No."

He closed his eyes again. "I remember. I got slapped for putting my teeth on him. Then he shoved his fingers into my throat and told me that's how deep he wanted to go and how wide he wanted my mouth. I tried really hard but my jaw ached and he put his fingers into my mouth and pulled it open while he fucked it. It made me choke and when I tried to push him away so he didn't push his cock in so far, he kicked me. He came in my throat and I had to swallow but as soon as he took it out, I sicked it out again. He paid me lots but I never wanted to do it again." He paused a moment, and then a half-smile took his lips. "You gave me toothpaste to take away the sick."

It wasn't a nice memory or a nice experience for his first time. No wonder he had struggled after that. His first two experiences with men and their dicks, were just plain rape scenes. One had hurt him physically, the other mentally. He had asked me if it was always like that and I had said yes, I hadn't known what had taken place. After that, he had avoided the customer's eyes and it had been a month or so until he took his next customer and that had been reluctantly, with a little bit of persuasion from me.

He worked up to two or three a week and then a customer had fucked his hole and he had become withdrawn again after that. A few weeks passed before he would even come down to the mouth of the alley again, he stayed in the back, watching, waiting for me. Things never really improved but it was hard to be annoyed with him.

Then Ginger arrived and things all changed again. Not immediately but within a few months of Ginger arriving, Leo seemed to make more of an effort to go to the front of the alley. Sometimes he would take a customer, sometimes he wouldn't, that's when he started letting me choose them for him. If they were rough with him, he was usually a little distraught and some got away without paying. Ginger would be so mad with him and he would turn to me for support.

I always thought it was more from the customer than Ginger's anger, that never seemed to worry him. He would come and sit with me at the end of the night and it was almost as if the whole night had never happened, not the customers or Ginger's angry words. He never spoke about it.

His voice pulled me from the memories. "You remember now, don't you? You're thinking."

I smiled. "Yes, I remember now." I carried on tracing the marks on his back.

What a shit life he had had. He had relied on me to get him through but really, I hadn't helped him at all. He had dealt with so much himself, on his own. He had so much strength that I had never seen. I swept my hand over his linens across his arse and he opened his eyes and lifted his head to look at me. I turned my head a little to meet his look.

"Sorry, I wasn't teasing...I got carried away...touching, thinking. You've dealt with so much, been so strong and you're lying here looking...like the night sky when it's clear and full of stars. Lie back down."

He looked at me confused. "Haven't you finished?"

I shook my head. It wasn't lying, I hadn't finished looking and talking. "No, lie back down."

He sighed and put his face back on his hands. "It's taking a long time. I'm not strong, not like you or Ginger or the others. I tried to be, I tried hard but sometimes it was too much. You know the cold water pipe that everyone showered under?"

"Yeah."

"Well, you know that moment just before you get under it when you know what it's going to feel like?"

I nodded. "Yeah." It was fucking cold.

"That's what it felt like."

I frowned at him as I stroked my fingers over his back and sides. "That's what, what felt like?"

"Waking up in the alley. I knew what I had to do...sometimes, I just couldn't do it. You and Ginger and the other boys you always went under the water, every day. I just stood and watched. I wanted to do what you all did, but I couldn't. It was easier if you made me."

I couldn't decide if he was talking about the shower now, the customers, or both. I guess it was everything. I knew from the moment I saw him he didn't belong on the street. That he wasn't going to make it, which is why I took him back home. He hadn't run off or complained and just gone back. When he'd turned up again, his options were limited. It was with me in the alley or alone on the streets or the vanilla system. He only allowed me to make him do things if he wanted it, and he had wanted to stay in the alley.

I don't know why I took him in. I had been a lot like Ginger before he came, I enjoyed being alone and doing my own thing...well, I thought I did. Leo had filled my life with something. Layton had been against it, he wanted him to go to the social services but having travelled that path myself, I couldn't see any good in it for him. Had I made his life hard? Had I let him struggle for my own selfish need of him?

"Do you wish, Leo, that you had gone somewhere else? Maybe into the system, a foster home or somewhere nice, warm?"

He smiled and opened his eyes and looked at me. He suddenly seemed so grown up. "Of course not, I wanted to be with you. I thought when you took me back that you didn't want me, like me but then when I came to find you after I had sex, you looked after me. I didn't know where to go after that night, I couldn't go back, he said not to. I didn't know anyone; I just knew you."

I smiled at him. "You hardly knew me."

"I knew enough. You were nice to me, you sat with me when I was sad and when I was quiet and when I was...noisy. Was I noisy?"

I laughed a little. "Maybe in moments. Mainly talkative, when the moment takes you."

He occasionally growled if he wasn't happy or got frustrated and I had heard him screeching when Ginger put him under the cold water pipe to get clean.

"That's what I meant, you never told me to shush or shut up."

"Probably because I couldn't get a word in."

He smiled and closed his eyes again and yawned. "I know you're making that up." I smiled. "You do...like me...don't you?" Had he not heard me tell him that I loved him?

"Leo, I love you. Have you not heard me tell you? I know I didn't say it before but I didn't know, I mean, I felt it but didn't know it was love."

His voice was quiet, his words slurred with sleep. "Then...how do you...know now?"

"Because it hurts when I'm not with you..."

As if he hadn't heard me he continued. "Is it...like holding...your hand?"

"Leo?" I leaned over towards his face. "Leo?" He dragged his eyes open to look at me and then they closed again.

I leaned forward and kissed his cheek and whispered in his ear. "That's exactly what it feels like. Sleep tight, Leo."

I sat back and watched him. I wasn't touching him but it felt like he was sleeping in my arms. I stayed with him for a long time before covering him with a blanket and then taking myself off to the bathroom.

CHAPTER FIFTEEN

JOE

I sat on the floor where Layton and I had sat and curled my arms around my legs. I felt like Leo and I had moved forward a little today but it didn't stop the feeling of being lost. He had and was, dealing with a lot of things, things that I was only just beginning to understand. He took in so much of what was happening around him and kept it to himself. It was like he didn't want to think about it and not thinking about it made it go away, at least in his head.

He was certainly confused about his craving for pain. He had said that it had gone now that he wasn't with Ginger and then panicked about it returning, saying he could feel it coming. It made me a little confused too. Was this what it was like for him to want it? Confusion? Uncertainty? Layton said it was going to get worse, bad. Was this it? What had he been like with Ginger when he wanted it?

Ginger. Another thing that I knew he still wasn't completely sure of his feelings on. He had swayed from liking him to hating him, to not wanting to think about him then wanting to talk about him. He wasn't over the trauma of being separated from him. He had cried today about it but I still felt he was suppressing his feelings for Ginger and the hurt it had caused him, having Ginger tell him he didn't want him anymore. The alley was his home and Ginger was his friend and Ginger had removed both so Leo would have to move on. No, I knew Leo, that had hurt him, I don't think he had shown me yet just how much or even if he would ever show me.

I heard Leo moan out and I quickly got up and went to the doorway. He was still sleeping but his body was twitching and he was moving on the bed like he wasn't comfortable. I wondered if his back was paining him, then he rolled over onto his back and settled again. No, it wasn't his back, something else was seeping into his sleep, taking his peace, not letting him settle. I watched him again for a while and when he didn't move, I went and sat back on the bathroom floor. I could think better in here...ah, who was I kidding? I was hiding and I knew it.

I wasn't feeling strong and I knew Leo needed me to be. I wished I could take him away from here, to be on the street. I knew that in the alley we were going to struggle but I understood that struggle. I understood the hardships of street living, who was my friend and who was my foe. It wasn't completely clear here, who was friend, who I should be protecting him from and who I should just let have him. I didn't want anyone to have him. I laid my head back against the wall feeling distraught with the same questions going around and around, and having no answers. The bathroom door slowly opened wider and Layton stepped in and stood there.

"Hey, Joe." Oh my God. I lifted my head and looked at him. My whole body seemed to breathe a sigh of relief.

"Hey." I bit my lip trying to hold in the overwhelming feelings at seeing him but they wouldn't be halted.

My tears ran down my cheeks and I got up and walked a couple of steps before throwing myself at him. I wrapped my arms around his neck and buried my face in his chest. I had never felt the need for someone so badly in my entire life. I was drowning in my thoughts and I needed him to pull me from the waves that just kept lapping at me, trying to consume me.

He wrapped his arms around my naked body and kissed the top of my head. "It's okay. I'm glad you're still here."

I lifted my face to him, confused by his words. "Here?"

Layton put his hand to my face and stroked it. "I was worried you would be gone."

Ah, okay. He had spoken to someone.

I tipped my head back into him. "I was going to take him, I wanted to...but he needs you close by and I didn't know if I could find you if we left."

Layton kissed me again and rubbed his hands over my arms and shoulders. "Fuck, Joe, you're freezing. Come on."

With his arm around me, he took me back into the bedroom. Leo stirred again on the bed and I stopped and watched him. Layton looked at me, touching my face with his fingers to draw my attention. "It's okay he's sleeping, it's not very restful sleep but he's managing to keep whatever's bugging him away."

I looked back at Leo. "Is it his need?"

Layton smiled. "I've been known to read minds but I don't know Leo well enough to read him yet. You probably know more than me." He picked up another blanket from the bed and wrapped it around my shoulders. "Come sit and talk to me." He sat on the floor by the bed.

"Here? Not the bathroom?"

He smiled. "He'll be more settled if he knows you're close by." He held his hand out for me to join him.

He wasn't whispering, just speaking normally and I was concerned that Leo would wake and see him. I didn't want him to leave. I needed him, his confidence, his air of normality that he seemed to have, even though this was not normal...I wasn't sure what was normal but this is not the sort of thing that happened to vanillas, I knew that. I took his hand and he sat me between his legs, wrapped the blanket further around me and began to rub my arms.

"I don't want to wake him, I don't want you to leave."

He smiled at me. "I won't leave. Just don't get too excited and our voices won't disturb him." As he spoke Leo's hand draped across his shoulder from the bed. Layton smiled at it and kissed it. He looked at me. "He smells good."

"I washed him properly." I looked at Leo on the bed. "I think he looks kind of shiny now." I heard Layton's laugh and looked back at him. "Sorry, that's Leo talk for beautiful." Layton nodded his understanding.

I tipped my head against him, needing his comfort and he kissed my head and ran his hand over my neck and down my back.

"I understand it's been a little fraught today?" Just for a moment, I wanted to forget and just lay with him. "Julian can make things harder than they need to be."

I lay there a moment just listening to his heart beating under my ear. Was this how Leo felt when he didn't want to speak? I sighed heavily and rolled my head a little so my face wasn't lying completely against him.

"He doesn't want me here, he wants Leo... without me." Layton went to speak and I interrupted. "It's okay, I understand, he made it clear... the reasons. I can't keep Leo safe here. I need to find somewhere for him, somewhere he can feel secure, with me." I looked up at him. "Are you still hiding from Isaac?"

He smiled and nodded. "Yes. I took a bit of a chance coming here so early but I didn't want you to disappear. Kendal told me about the conversations you and Julian had, she wasn't sure if you were still thinking about leaving. Were you? Is that why you were alone in the bathroom?" I laid my head against him again.

"I was thinking. I was going to take him tonight but then Leo and I spoke and... he's afraid, scared. He's not sure where his fix is going to come from and he was asking to go back to the alley, for me to take him to Ginger. Not demanding... kind of asking politely. He said please a lot, Leo's never polite. I think he can feel it and it's making him panic. I told him that you would give it to him, that you would help him... I couldn't then take him away from here, it wouldn't have made sense to him.

"He's already worried about what you're going to do, whether he's going to have to lie quietly for you. I couldn't answer his questions, his fears. I'm telling him that you understand, and I think he knows that because of Isaac, but, if I took him from here, he would know that you're not close by and I don't think it would have made sense to him. It would have made him panic again."

Layton nodded. "Do you think his need is starting?"

I shook my head. "I don't know. Maybe. He sways between telling me it's okay now and gone, to saying he knows it's coming. I think he can feel it again and he's trying to deny it, not think about it, hoping it will not come. Why does it frighten him so much? He asked me if Isaac got scared. I couldn't answer him, does he? Isaac doesn't look like he's scared. He seemed to like his marks on his back, I can't even get Leo to look at his." I got kissed and pulled tighter to his body, which I needed so badly.

"Isaac gets scared. He understands that he wants pain, that feeling it will give him some peace. Pain hurts. Just because they want it does make it hurt any less to them. It's where you take their mind when you give it to them that's important. Isaac's fear is lessened because he knows I can make him feel beautiful while he has his fix. He knows I will give him what he needs, keep him safe, love him, make the pain a little easier to bear and help him deal with it when it's overwhelming."

"How? How do you do that?"

Layton smiled. "You make them feel hot. You make their pleasure important to you and them. You mix their need to orgasm with their need for pain until both needs feed off each other and they become one thing. That one thing, that feeling, is an extremely intense overwhelming feeling. It's when they are at their most vulnerable because what you have done is caused confusion in their mind and body. It's referred to as subspace, their mind is not capable of sane or sensible thoughts. They will do anything, take anything to have their pleasure but because of their confusion that you have caused them, pain given to them can seem intensely pleasurable to them.

"It can make them come if given in the right doses. This is where the Dominant becomes important to them. The Dominant becomes their world, the giver of their needs and they learn to become extremely submissive to that person so they can have what they want. For Isaac and me, this is a permanent state of mind for him. I request that he always sees me as important, that this feeling of wanting to please me never leaves him. For people who come together to just play, that feeling of Dom and sub is just a temporary feeling and when play is over they can both revert to being equals again."

"But Isaac doesn't seem like you have confused him? He doesn't seem needy all the time?"

Layton smiled. "Because he has his needs controlled and seen to when they ask. Not immediately, he has to wait for a little as it teaches him who has the control. I have given him clear expectations of his place. He behaves, he serves me, because he knows I can give him what he wants so he works hard to be a good… sub. His need, when it asks, still scares him because it is intense and overwhelming. It takes their thoughts and consumes them until all they can think of is having it.

"They can seem like a different person, almost possessed by their need but even though he craves it, he still knows what he will have to endure to make it go away. If you show them that you are still controlling them then it takes a little of the fear away, not all of it but the feeling of them being lost in it alone. If they see that you are in control then they will look to you to ease it for them, be that giving them what they want or suffering the need while you watch them."

"But that's not giving it to them though, watching them? That's not making it go away."

"No, but what you are showing them is that you control it, even while they feel nothing but just the want of it. By asking them to suffer it for a while, makes it not a bad thing. It makes it something they are doing for you, it changes their thought process of it. Rather than them being taken by it, it becomes something they are working for, for you. If they see that you have control of it and them, then they are not alone with it, it makes it easier for them to deal with."

I nodded thinking about what Leo had said. "I don't think Leo understands control. He said he didn't like being alone, that it scared him. He said that he's a bad person when it comes. Ginger told him that. It upsets him, he's scared of being bad with you…and me." Layton brushed his hand over my back.

"Leo has a lot to learn, Joe. No one has ever shown him how to share his need. When he wanted it he got angry with Ginger and to keep him quiet Ginger gave it to him. I doubt Ginger understood where Leo's temper was coming from. I'm sure it would have pissed Ginger off a little to have someone angrily demanding that he did it, so it's no wonder that Leo thinks he becomes a bad person when he wants it.

"He knows that's what got him what he wanted but he'll be shown a different way. If he wants it he will have to be submissive from the start, not just when he is given it. It will take him a few times to learn, but he will. It is just a bad habit he's been shown...I like breaking bad habits, it's challenging." I looked up at Layton and he was smiling. He looked at me and smiled more. "What you're seeing is my need, Joe. I am a little excited about playing with Leo, guiding him, teaching him." Oh God. Was Layton one of those hungry junkies too? Had I misread his motives for bringing Leo here? "Joe?" My uncertainty must have shown in my face.

"Julian said that there are people here who want him, if they knew he was here, they would just take him if they could. Is that what you've done? You've taken us from the street so you can have him?"

Layton looked concerned. "No. If you ever believe that what I do is not for Leo's wellbeing, then you can put a stop to it at any time. He's not mine, I know that and I would never harm him by taking him from you. Julian is right in what he says. It is clear that Leo's need is very powerful and strong, and that would make him extremely attractive to Dominants with stronger desires.

"He could earn a slave owner a lot of money and raise the status of their house among the council. They wouldn't want you though, Joe. They would see you as emotional baggage for Leo. They would like to have him and train him their way, not yours. Their way is not a bad way and they would never harm such a prized possession such as Leo, they would make sure all his needs were catered for...but it is very strict.

"They have a very narrow view of what a slave should and shouldn't do and they find it hard to see beyond those old fashioned, limited views. Leo would be expected to follow those rules from the start and his training would be guided by punishment, given to him by a Keeper with many years of experience. I run my house a little differently. It irks the council a little, but many new slaves come from my house and go on to other houses to earn their owners a lot of money so I'm kind of popular among the other slave owners." He smiled. "It means that while they are happy, the council will leave me alone to a certain extent and let me run my house as I see fit."

Questions, I had so many questions. "What's your need then? Like Leo's?"

Layton shook his head. "No, not really. It's a little of Leo's. It's more the reverse of their need. Where they like to be submissive and be led, I like to control and lead. I want to see a slave completely submit to me and do whatever I request, which includes suffering for me. I like to watch them moan and squirm while they have their fix.

"For me, there is nothing hotter and sexier than having another human give you themselves so you can play with them. Make them cry out in pain and willingly show you what it is you are making them feel. That works for pleasure as well, to hold a person on the edge of their orgasm and not allow them to take it, it's like having the ultimate control, it's painful pleasure for them and very addictive to watch."

I could hear his need, not only his words but his voice. He looked at me and smiled. "I never let my need come above the wellbeing of the person that submits to me. Always their safety and sanity come first. I would never take them somewhere I couldn't bring them back from, safe and sane and somewhere they wouldn't be willing to go again with me." Layton smiled at me. "I can see you have more questions."

I half smiled back at him. "I'm sorry, if it bugs you, I can stop?"

"I want you to be happy and secure with Leo's time with me. If he senses you have doubts about it, then he will too. You are the most important person to him right now. You are all he has left from a life he felt safe and secure in. He will be very attuned to your thoughts and feelings, taking his lead from you. It's no different to what he has done on the street, he was guided by you but was secure enough with his surroundings that if he didn't particularly like something, he felt safe enough to do his own thing."

"Like go with Ginger?"

Layton nodded. "Yes, possibly. He didn't know how to show you or tell you about his need. He felt more comfortable with his place in the alley because of you, it allowed him the freedom to be with others and that, by accident, turned into asking someone else to ease it, knowing he could come back to you if things weren't right. You were his safety and you are more so now. He will be looking to you for everything, control, comfort, love."

"Punishment? Because he's not asking. He's asking me to fuck him...after we shared a kiss."

Layton laughed a little. "I said it would confuse him. The feelings that the kiss evoked in him would have been the same as yours when we kissed. He won't ask you to punish him yet, when he gets needy, he will. He'll ask you because he knows you, at the moment he's trying to avoid it because you are unsure and he knows that. That is probably why he won't look at his back too, he's avoiding the whole thing. When his need gathers peace, he'll be different, feel different and you will be the first person he turns to. We'll move you to mine tomorrow night, so he can have a bit of time to get used to the place where he will play."

"And after? I need to find somewhere safe."

Layton nodded. "You will stay with me until he's back, recovered and I'm working on something, somewhere for you both, in this world Joe, not the street."

"But Julian said..."

"Yes, I know what Julian said. It is difficult for you to be here but it's not impossible. There are places you and Leo can be, that are safe. Here is one, mine, and... a few others. You did well to stand up to Julian, he likes you." Jesus, I hated to see how he treated people he wasn't keen on.

I shook my head. "I think he likes Leo. Leo said he wants him, he said he knows him. He scared Leo but then Leo attempted to be friends with him. I think he's worried that Julian is going to take him away. I don't know, I don't understand what went on in the kitchen. Would he? Would he try and take him?"

Layton smiled and shook his head. "Julian has very strong desires and would have understood Leo's. He's not a bad person, in fact, he's probably one of my closest friends. I trust him and Isaac is learning to trust him." Isaac had seemed completely at ease with him.

"Learning?"

"Julian and Isaac have a history from when Isaac was a slave. He ended up with Julian for a while. Julian's view of slaves is like I said before, it's old school. He punished Isaac harshly when Isaac was feeling unsettled and Isaac has struggled to move on from it. He has to quell the need to fall at Julian's feet every time he sees him. Julian has been working very hard to regain Isaac's trust and I think they are just about there. Julian will never lose his Dominant status where Isaac is concerned though but I kind of like watching them together. I like to watch Isaac squirm a little in his company."

I smiled a little at him. "Isn't that...evil?"

Layton laughed quietly. "Mm, a little but it makes me a little turned on to see Isaac try so hard and I know he's completely safe with Julian. Julian loves him. He's a little different from the subs and slaves Julian knows and actually, Isaac has Julian wrapped around his fingers but I would never tell him that. Julian's view of the slaves is that they should not be allowed any contact with others, that they should stay in their room until called upon to play and that you shouldn't make friends with them...I think I break all of those rules." A rule breaker? Was that a good thing here?

"When you find somewhere...will Julian know where we are?"

Layton frowned at me. "Why has he worried you so much? He would never harm you or Leo. I know how Julian comes across sometimes, he speaks his mind and likes nothing better than a good heated discussion but I promise you, Joe, he's not a bad person."

"He made it very clear there was no place for me here and that without Leo taking a slave position in a house, that we were not safe, Leo was not safe. Leo knows he has a need, I don't know how but he knows. What if he can't control it?"

Layton smiled. "Julian is extremely strong-minded and yes, his need is very strong. Leo would have been attracted to his dominance and the way others acted around him, with him. I assure you that Julian never loses control of his need, if he did then his play partners would not be around to tell the tale, I would not be around." I shot my head round to look at him.

"You play with Julian?"

Layton smiled. "I have been known to, now and again. It's not something I do often and not for a while but if I felt the need to, then Julian would be the person I went to. He plays very hard, which is why I know he never loses control of his need."

"He has a...friend though, doesn't he? Someone he plays with? This is his house, isn't it?"

Layton nodded. "Yes, Jacob. An amazingly sweet and beautiful man, extremely smitten with Julian. He's very submissive with Julian and so unlike Isaac. He's quiet and undemanding and never gives Julian any trouble, they love each other very much."

"And he plays with him?"

Layton nodded again. "Yes, often. Jacob is extremely strong-minded and takes a lot of Julian's punishments. When and if you meet him, you'll be surprised. He's not like Isaac and Leo, he doesn't seek attention like they do, not from others anyway. He's forbidden to play with others, not that he would want to and others are forbidden to play with him unless they have Julian's express permission. He's branded which means no one can fuck or use him except Julian."

"Branded? Like, branded…with a hot iron?"

Layton nodded. "In this world, it means that he is privately owned. If anyone breaks the rule, then Julian can decide their punishment."

"He did that to him?" Fuck, fuck…

Layton smiled nonchalantly like it was nothing. "It is the highest devotion a Dominant and submissive can show each other, to give and take that pain for them. Julian gave it to him to protect him when he was taken from him for a while. Branding a submissive is not taken lightly here, everyone understands the meaning of it. It's extremely rare as most Dominants and subs rarely play with just one partner because of their needs."

"Would you brand Isaac?"

Layton shook his head. "No, not to keep him. Isaac needs to play with others. When he's needy he doesn't suffer it well. He's used to having it sated by clients, strangers, so sharing his need with others is not new to him. He's not too keen on the idea of strangers anymore but he will happily play with people he knows. Jacob has never been taught to share with anyone but Julian and although it's difficult for him, he will wait for Julian's return, if he's away.

"As I said, Jacob doesn't require people and their attention like Isaac and Leo do. He's used to being alone. When he's needy, he withdraws into himself and just waits quietly for Julian, something that Isaac and most probably, Leo, could never do. They are just different; they have been taught different things. Isaac has been taught to show his need. Leo, well I'm not certain but I think he taught himself that if he created enough upset and noise, then Ginger would sate it."

"But he has to learn differently?"

Layton nodded. "Yes, not like Jacob, we will probably go for something more like Isaac's way. Jacob doesn't show his need, not outwardly. Isaac has been taught to show his need but to be very submissive. He'll openly offer himself. It's how he's been taught to show he's needy and how he's been taught to ask. He has learnt that demanding attention to his need does not get him what he wants, he has to show his need, his suffering of it. When it is decided he has behaved and suffered it enough, then it will be sated. If he wants it sated then he has to show his Dominant that he will submit, he has to earn his play. Leo has to learn to submit if he wants it sated, not create havoc or fight. He can show his need but in a more subdued manner, when he finds his place then he will have what he wants."

"Will it hurt him?"

"No, it will feel hard but only because he's never had to work for it. He wanted it, he got it, no one controlled it or him before. Once he realises that it is out of his control, he'll find it easier to wait. It is a much nicer place for him to be, knowing that he doesn't have to work at controlling it, knowing someone else has the control. It takes the edge off it, takes away the urgency. I will teach you both as we play but I want to take you to my house tomorrow so you can see some of my slaves. Will you come?"

I looked up at him. "With you?"

Layton nodded. "Yes, just you, just so you can see some of them. It will give you an idea of what it means to be a slave. Leo will have to remain here though, he doesn't understand and his presence would upset him and them. When we return, we will pick Leo up and bring him back, so he can settle in his new surroundings and get used to me a little before he plays."

I was a little intrigued to see Layton's house and his slaves but could I leave Leo? Was this a ploy to separate us? I was so mentally exhausted trying to figure things out and from all the new information. Out of all of them, I trusted Layton, I had to. I needed someone in my corner, I just hoped he didn't suddenly switch sides.

CHAPTER SIXTEEN

JOE

After deciding that I did trust Layton, I needed a way of getting the knowledge I would need for Leo. Going to Layton's was definitely a step in the right direction and at least it would get us away from that Julian guy, who I wasn't sure I trusted. I bit my lip trying to think of a way of working it all.

"I want to, but Leo will think I'm leaving him. Like you said, he just has me now, if he sees me walking away from him, he'll just think the worst because that's what everyone has done. He'll panic and won't believe that I'm coming back for him, he'll think I'm leaving him here with Julian or something."

Layton nodded. "If he's sleeping he won't know. Kendal has said she will come and sit with him. She can make him a nice warm drink with a little something in to help him sleep."

I shook my head. "I don't want to keep drugging him, is that what you do here?"

Layton shook his head. "Hey! No, never. I don't like it either but Leo has not learnt trust yet, or to behave himself when you ask. This is important for you and him, it will give you valuable insight into my world and Leo's needs. This will be kinder to him than the upset of separation from you for now. Once he has gained trust and understands that you control him, he will not need this sort of intervention.

"It is just a temporary measure to ensure his wellbeing while he is still feeling so raw from his departure from his home, the alley."

If it was going to help me understand Leo a little more, then I needed to go. I needed all the help I could get right now and it would be silly to turn down such an opportunity to learn more about this world that Leo and I now found ourselves in. I nodded slowly to him and he kissed the side of my forehead.

"I don't mean to be difficult, I just want to make sure he's alright. Should I tell him that we are leaving here?"

"What do you think? Will he be upset?"

I shook my head. "No, I don't think so. He'll be happier being closer to you I think, although another new place might be a bit unsettling."

"Mm, it will be better when you are living somewhere permanently, then he won't have so much to think about. And you're not being difficult, Joe, you're looking out for Leo's wellbeing, I understand that. You know Leo better than anyone, if you ever feel something is not right then you must always say. Leo is depending on you to see things in him that he may not understand. Now that we have agreed on our little visit, tell me about your time with him today."

I smiled at him. "We had a better day today, more settled, I think. Well apart from when I kissed him. I learnt a lot about him, things that he knew, that I didn't even realise. He knows that other boy you were looking for, Noah?" Layton didn't look surprised. "He knows a lot of things, things that he never shared with me or even spoke about. He knew exactly what was going on in the kitchen, what Julian was asking, saying. I thought he didn't understand...know. I'll have to be more aware of what I say in front of him."

Layton nodded. "They are not stupid. Isaac thinks and knows the same as I do but his thoughts work a lot slower, which makes him seem very childlike and he embraces that side of himself, which I like. Like Leo, he can sometimes have a perfectly good adult conversation and sometimes he even perceives things quicker than me, but they are rare moments when his head is empty and he's not needy or tired... or hungry.

"Isaac is who he wants to be, he doesn't work at being submissive, it's not something he has to think about, it's who he is and he just follows that feeling naturally." Layton smiled. "Leo would have been ignored on the street by the other boys so it kind of gave him a free pass to sneak around and see things that others did not. Because a lot of the time they seem like they are in their own world, quiet, withdrawn and maybe shy, people forget to be guarded around them.

"It's a little sneaky on their part and can, if not picked up by a Keeper or someone close, cause some issues, especially if they hear something that confuses them or upsets them. It's good that Leo is telling you though. Was he upset by the conversation in the kitchen?"

I shrugged. "I'm not sure. He said he knows that they want me to leave him here, that Julian wants that, I think that's why Julian made him feel uneasy. When I asked why he made friends with him though, he said he didn't want Julian to be mean to him. I didn't really understand."

Layton nodded. "It's what I said before. He recognises Julian's dominant status and was laying down his place with him, almost preparing it, in case. He was showing Julian that he understood and that, if they were ever together, asking Julian to keep him safe. It's very respectful and proof that Leo can ask nicely when he wants something."

"Then he took his hand away and gave it to me. Julian said he was showing me he thinks I'm more capable of keeping him safe than he is. I'm not sure that's what he was doing."

Layton smiled, amused. "He was in that moment showing both you and Julian who he wants to be with. He was deciding in his own way. What he feels and what he knows. I'm sure it all felt very confusing to him. He chose you though, it means he trusts you above others around him. It's not often that Julian is overseen as the most dominant, it will have a lot to do with his trust in you, it's a good thing, for you. When you become more sure of him as a submissive you will have a lot of control, he's already showing you that he will accept it from you." I bit my lip pondering his answers before more questions came to me.

"How do you love Isaac? I mean, how do you separate loving him from his need? I feel things from him, like I know he's been wanting me to touch him for a while. He said he'd been waiting but how do I know that's not his need talking, that it's his true feelings?"

Layton smiled. "The need they feel is never a separate thing, Joe. It is part of who they are all the time. I don't love Isaac differently when he is needy, I just choose how I will show that love. Is this confusion coming from the kiss?"

I nodded. "The kiss made us both...hot and wanting. He didn't seem to understand it. He demanded that I continue and when I refused he took himself away from me and started to pleasure himself. I get the wanting to come bit, and I get the moving away bit. He told me Ginger always made him go away if he wanted to come so I understand that's what he was doing.

"I didn't want us to be together because he needs to come, I wanted us to be together because we both wanted to share that with each other. Loving him is new to me, making a relationship with him, I'm not sure of the reasons he wants to be with me, whether they're the same...whether he loves me. Does that make sense?"

Layton nodded. "I understand what you want, Joe, you want Leo to tell you and show you how much he loves you. It's not that simple with them. I think he understood the kiss perfectly well and openly showed you how you made him feel. You chose to see that as him being needy, it may have been, it may have been that you just made him horny." Layton smiled. "Either way you made those feelings in him. It's what you choose to do about them that makes it either about you both or about his need."

I shook my head a little. "I didn't do anything, I didn't want to. I was a little overwhelmed. I didn't want him to come, not on his own after we shared the kiss. Should I have let him come? I asked him to stop, which he didn't seem like he was going to. I went away, into the bathroom and said I would wait for him there when he had finished. I did go back and watch him because I felt bad. I didn't want him to be alone but when I saw him he was just buried into the bed covers, not coming like I thought he would be. I left him and waited and he did join me after a little while. He said he didn't come and asked if I was mad. I don't know why he asks that, I've never been mad or angry with him."

"He's looking for clear guidance from you. He wants to know what makes you happy and what makes you…not so happy, he's trying to please you. Not coming at your request should have earned him huge praise. That is no small feat on his part, not following through with his feelings. Have you ever been on the brink of an orgasm and denied yourself?" I smiled and shook my head and Layton smiled back. "Then I suggest that you try it and see how difficult it is, it will give you some idea as to what he gave up for you. Then maybe next time he will get the praise he deserved. He's a step ahead of you, he knows what he wants from you and is trying to get from you.

"As for whether you should have let him come? That's your decision. My slaves, as long as their Keeper allows and they are permitted, are allowed to come pretty much every day, it keeps the feeling fresh in their minds but when they are due to go on a visit they will be forbidden for a few days, maybe more, it depends on the slave. Being forbidden makes them needy for it, which makes them needy to play so by the time they are with their client, they are quite willing to do what is requested of them, to endure the play so they can have their pleasure.

"Slaves are forbidden to pleasure themselves so that they are always ready to play when requested. It would be no good if a slave had just had their orgasm and then half an hour later they were asked to play, it takes their need to earn it away and then the pain they are given becomes just plain painful. The slaves are kept wanting and needy unless their Keeper or slave owner decides they can come. In my house it is the Keeper that decides, it gives the Keeper control and keeps the slave submissive to them because they know that they have to earn it from them."

"What stops them from pleasuring themselves then? Not just the control thing surely?"

Layton nodded. "Yes, most of the time. It is forbidden for slaves to touch themselves in any way, even washing could lead to touching that is not permitted. All sanitary and toilet needs are seen to by their Keepers. They want to please their Keeper or their client or whomever they are with so most of the time they will refrain, they get a lot of attention and praise for being good, remember. There are occasions where the slave has to be restrained, usually if they are being kept needy for a pending visit to a client. They will be edge played by their Keeper to keep the need fresh, to keep them wanting. It's very frustrating for them and they cannot always refrain from taking what they want so they are restrained so they can't...help themselves."

"Edge played?"

Layton smiled. "Pretty much what you did to Leo. You made him horny and then you forbade him the orgasm. Edge play is more controlled than that though, they will be taken right to the edge of their orgasm and then refused its release. The more they are refused, the more needy and wanting they become. It's pleasurably unpleasant for them but then their playtime will be more enjoyable when they finally get it. A slave that has been forbidden and edged for a few days will work very hard to have it when they play, it can increase their pain limits and make them a more challenging sub to the client."

I shook my head. "I didn't mean to edge him."

Layton laughed a little. "Don't feel bad, Joe. I think he quite liked the challenge of the control. He didn't quite get the praise he deserved but he did what you asked and that would have made him feel good."

"So I'm still not sure, should I have given him what he wanted? He wanted me to fuck him. I didn't want Leo's and my first time together to be like that. I wanted it to be more equal about giving and taking, sharing the moment."

"He wanted you to take control of him and let him come. He's only ever known fucking as a release. He doesn't know any other way. What you wanted was to make love, and you can do that but you have to show him. Making love is about you giving, it's slow and sensual and about you taking his feelings and wants into account. Fucking is about you taking what you want whether he wants it or not. Fucking is about your need, be it getting pleasure from his mouth or his hole and him learning that he has no say how deep you thrust, how quick or hard you want it. Fucking him is you taking complete control and him letting you have his body to do with as you want without him fighting against you.

"Isaac and I do both, I choose depending on my need. Isaac accepts either. He likes the pleasure of making love, he likens it to chocolate cake and he is very beautiful to watch but he likes to be fucked too. Fucking is about showing them their place, using them and them accepting that is what you want at that moment. Sometimes he fights a little against the control but they soon learn that the more they relax and just let you have them, the less painful it is for them.

"They find their place a lot quicker too, which makes it more acceptable to be used in such a manner. Fucking Isaac is when I can let my need of him have free rein, it's hot and powerful and consumes me a little which is why he must just let me have him. I could hurt him to have it. They get no pleasure from being fucked, it is not about their pleasure it is about yours and taking it. They do get sort of empowered by it though, it's being completely dominated, physically and mentally and that's a place that they want."

"And he accepts it?"

Layton nodded. "Isaac accepts my need as I do his. He will tell you that he likes fucking. He likes the control I have and not having control himself. He likes the place he finds, it's like being restrained very tightly but this is like mental restraint. He feels secure with his place, like taking punishment, it empowers him." I looked at him questioningly. Layton smiled. "If someone wants you so badly that they just take you, it is kind of empowering don't you think? Like being irresistible?" I nodded. That was a reverse way of looking at it I suppose. "There is an emotional low that comes with that place too but it can be managed, with praise and balanced with love.

"You can take Leo wherever you want. He may not understand the making love part at first but you can teach him. He understands fucking, the feeling of being used, the giving of himself, he did it with customers, probably not as willingly as he would give it to you. It's kind of empowering you, that he wants you to take him."

"Ginger fucked him...sometimes. He said he didn't always like it but that he let him. Was that like payment do you think? Ginger gave him something and he gave Ginger that in return?"

Layton nodded. "Yes, it sounds like it. Leo has learnt that he can earn things. He wouldn't see it like that, but that's what he was doing. He made a fuss, created a noise, he got his fix. He allowed Ginger to fuck him so Ginger would give it to him again next time he asked. He has lost the control that Ginger had over him and he's feeling lost without it. Asking for him is not so much about his need but more about the control Ginger had.

"Even Ginger sending him away would have been like him controlling Leo. The asking if you're angry or mad, the polite manners, are all about Leo giving you control, well, he's trying to feel like you control him. On our visit tomorrow, you will have a better understanding. You feel uncomfortable controlling Leo but it's what he wants and you have been doing it while you were in the alley, you just didn't see it like that. You saw it as looking after him and that's what it is but now that he has lost the safety and security of the alley, he needs the control to be more… intense."

"So...should I have let him come?" Layton laughed and kissed me. I felt stupid but I didn't know. "I mean, I get what you say, it's up to me but what if it's his need and I'm taking something...or giving him something and I shouldn't be, I should be making him wait?"

"That's the point, Joe. It doesn't matter. If you want to make love or fuck him, or just see him come then you should. If you want to make him wait then you can. It's your way, it's always been your way, you just didn't know it. You have made him wait and he is but it's eating at him. Even while he sleeps he's quivering, that's not his need for pain that is causing that, that is his need to come. You can make him wait, it would be intriguing to see how long he would suffer it before he felt compelled to do something about it." He was smiling.

"Is that you being evil again?" He smiled more.

"Yes. Not evil, curious. He followed your request, I was wondering how long he would do that for before his need to come got the better of him."

"Have you ever made Isaac wait?"

Layton smiled and nodded. "Yes. He hates it. He hates being edged which is why it's so addictive to watch. To keep him in the ecstasy of the feeling and then watch the painful torture as it is forbidden to him. Really, Joe, you need to try it, it is seriously painful, to be so close to that feeling and then have it taken away. It's even more painful when someone else is controlling it. Isaac would probably wait once on asking but if I did it to him again he wouldn't be able to stop himself from pleasuring himself, I would have to restrain him.

"It makes them suffer with pleasure, it's nice to watch because it's not paining them physically, just mentally. It's a good lesson to teach them, the connection between pain and pleasure. Pleasure can be painful and pain can be pleasurable, it just depends on how you give it to them. Now back to Leo. You are worried that if you let him come, it will take away from his need when it asks?" I nodded. "It is difficult to judge with Leo because I have not played with him before and do not know what he's like when he plays. You said Ginger never let him come?"

I shook my head. "No, he said if he wanted that, he had to go away, leave Ginger's bed."

Layton nodded. "I don't think he's ever been pleasured while playing. He's felt the connection obviously, wanting to come after playing means it does make him turned on, but he's never been allowed to have them both. To him, they are separate needs. We will teach him differently, it will make his play more enjoyable and less fraught but for now, until he learns that connection, I think you have free say over whether he comes or not.

"Letting him come will probably ease his confusion, and yours, over which need is asking. It will settle him better for the move to my place, too, he won't be dealing with too many things. Then when his craving for pain comes, we will have a clearer picture of how it affects him."

I nodded. Finally, I had some guidance.

"You could have just said that a while ago."

Layton stroked his fingers over my head and I lay against him, enjoying the affection. I couldn't remember a time in the years on the street I craved this touch, this closeness. It made me feel weak.

"I'm sorry, Joe, I wanted you to have the confidence to find your own way."

"I'm sorry, I'm trying."

He kissed me. "It's okay. Your confidence will come."

"I didn't want to get it wrong, make it bad for him."

"It doesn't matter if you get it wrong, that's how you learn. If you make a decision and Leo suffers needlessly because of that then you know never to do that again. Leo is so new that he will not know a wrong or right decision, a good way or a bad way, it's all new to him. If something you do pains him so much that he becomes uncertain, then you can promise never to do it again. Never apologise to him though, about his suffering, it will make his view of you tainted and uncertain. He must always believe that you wanted it from him, wanted to see it."

"I should never apologise? Because I have been. I've been saying sorry a lot to him lately since we've been here."

"You should refrain from it. There are times when you do things that maybe do need an apology but try and make those times when Leo is coherent and not suffering from any want or need. Being sorry because he is suffering from his need will not make it easier to bear, it will make him feel like you have lost your control of it and he must always feel like you are together, that he is not alone when he's needy. You are to help him deal with his feelings openly, share them with you, then he won't feel so alone."

"He has been sharing, talking to me quite a lot. To be honest, I've felt like it's a different person because he's never been so clear and coherent. He lets me see to his back without too much fuss now, that's progress right?"

Layton smiled. "You know it is. They are very complex people and each one is different, has different needs. He may not be feeling as safe as he's felt in the alley so he'll be fighting his sub feelings. You are doing a superb job of looking after him, you shouldn't doubt yourself so much, you've been doing it a long time and Leo is quite healthy."

"He's not happy though. I want to make him happy."

"Was he happy on the street?"

I thought about it. He wasn't. He was more settled than he was now but I would never have said that he was happy. I wasn't even sure if Leo knew what happiness was. I sat up and looked at Layton just as Leo moaned and did another shuffle around the bed. I watched him as he tried to get comfortable and he pushed himself up on his hand. I quickly turned, stood, and then knelt beside him. I stroked his face with my fingers and he lay back down. He shuddered and jolted a little and I pulled the blanket around him.

"I'm right here, Leo." He mumbled something in his sleep and settled again. I watched him for a moment before turning to look at Layton. "No, he wasn't happy on the street."

I looked back at Leo, leaned down and kissed him, then turned back to Layton, slipping off the bed. He held out the blanket which had slipped from me when I moved. He wanted me to join him and I did so, stepping back beside him, I sat down and he wrapped the blanket around me again.

"I thought he was going to wake and see you."

Layton shrugged. "No matter, we would have dealt with it. It's very difficult to decipher happiness in subs. Sometimes Isaac is happier just sitting with me, being quiet and just feeling me next to him. Other times he is happier when he is surrounded by the people he knows, like Julian, Peter, and Kendal. His happiness and what he wants changes from moment to moment."

"Does his need affect his happiness?"

"Of course. He has to do things that are uncomfortable and that maybe he's not too keen on, but the end result is a happier Isaac. I'm not sure Isaac thinks about happiness when he's needy though." Layton smiled at me.

"I'm not sure Leo even knows what it is to feel happy. Like love, he doesn't know what that is. I don't think he understands it when I tell him I love him, does Isaac?"

Layton nodded. "He does but I had to teach him and it took a long while. Isaac loves a lot of people and a lot of people love him, but the love we feel for each other is different to what he shares with others. If you want to teach Leo then you have to choose your moments to tell him. Telling him when he's anxious or needy or upset will not give him an understanding of it. Telling him now after he's just been taken from his home will not help him understand.

"Your moments have to be quiet times or when he is just about to take his orgasm, an orgasm given to him out of love, not out of play. They will mean different things to him. You can still love him at those other times but that is better conveyed with touches, rather than words that will be lost in his head with his other thoughts. He's never been loved so it will take a while."

"He asked me if it was like holding my hand."

"Well, that will be because you are making a big thing out of it and he wants to know. He wants to join you in the space that you call love and share it with you. Did you hold hands in the alley?"

I shook my head. "Not in the alley working, when we were alone, usually sky watching."

"Well, those times were obviously special to him, looking at the stars, holding your hand, feeling your touch. It's a good place to start to make him understand, building on those feelings."

"When...before we kissed, Leo said he'd been waiting for me...to touch him, he said he'd been waiting a long time."

Layton sort of laughed. "It sounds like he's had the hots for you for a while."

"Yes, that's what I got but he left me...stopped sleeping with me. I get that he grew into a man, that his feelings changed, I mean I never noticed, not then but now, I see it. I don't see how sleeping with Ginger was meant to make me see it."

"Leo was a kid when he came to the street. When he started to feel things for you it was the beginning of him changing into a young adult, a confusing time for any boy, even more so for someone like Leo. He had this rush of feelings he didn't quite understand and then Ginger turned up and Ginger saw him as a man, not the boy you'd known."

I nodded. "He said that, he said Ginger treated him differently."

"Then he had another rush of feelings he didn't understand, his need. You couldn't see what was happening to the boy you knew and in his confusion of everything, he couldn't tell you. Maybe staying with you was too difficult, being that close and not getting anything more from you than he had been getting as a kid. It's kind of like him having a teenage strop. He left your bed in a huff, not particularly to sleep with Ginger, you've said yourself he wasn't always allowed to stay there, but just to be away from you and the child view you had of him.

"He left you so he could grow but his feelings for you never left him, hence the feeling he has, that he's been waiting a long time. He's been waiting for you to see the adult that he's become even though it may not seem like it sometimes, his needs are definitely adult. I don't think the sleeping with Ginger thing had anything to do with you, it was just a coincidence, with his need and his new feelings of wanting to be treated differently. In the years away from you, he grew; in body and mind, his needs grew too. For both of you, your feelings have changed about each other and this has brought you together again."

Yes, it had. Things could have been so different, I could have lost my place long ago and he would have been lost to me, I could have gone with Layton and left him behind and never known his feelings about me. That made me smile. All I knew was he wanted me to fuck him, it wasn't very romantic or loving but it was a start.

"What's funny?"

"Oh nothing, I was just thinking about him. I went from not knowing how he felt about me to him wanting me to fuck him, it's a big jump and not very...romantic."

Layton quietly sniggered. "He'll realise, Joe, soon. He'll realise that his feelings for you are not just sexual. You might have to rethink your definition of romantic...but there can still be candles."

He smiled amused. "He knew you took boys like him, you know. He knew about Orion's need. He said he watched him under the shower and saw marks on his body. He said he wasn't sure if it was the same thing because Orion was different. I asked him why he never said anything to you and he said, he didn't want you to take him away. I think he was worried too about where you took them, he was concerned that they never came back, that he never saw them again."

"Wow, he is a little sneaky isn't he?"

I nodded. "I told you, he knows a lot, stuff I never even realised. I feel like he was creeping around the alley spying on people, I never even noticed him watching people. He said he used to watch me too, with customers."

"He's very clever. He used his submissive air to be invisible. No one worried when they saw him around, to them he was just a little slow and quiet and when he wasn't around no one missed him."

"He never spoke about the things he saw though, never said a word."

"There would be no reason to share it with anyone. What he saw didn't affect him. He didn't need to ask Orion about his marks, he already knew where they came from. He didn't need to tell you about Noah. He wasn't sharing his need with anyone; why would he share Noah's? He knew everything that was going on around him but it didn't affect him, he didn't need to think about it. The fact that he knew would have made him more secure with his place in the alley.

"Orion confused him about his need. Orion is not scared of his need, he wanted it, he went out and found customers that were willing to give it to him. He's not a natural submissive, he's unruly and arrogant and tries to control everything. His Keeper has to work very hard and be very firm with him. I will take you to see him tomorrow but I'm not sure how he will react to you being there."

"I don't want to cause trouble, I think Leo and I are doing enough of that."

Layton frowned at me. "You are not any trouble, Joe. Yours and Leo's presence is exciting and challenges my day."

"Well, I think you only say that now because you're away from Isaac but I know the others think it, even Kendal was different towards me."

Layton nodded. "Kendal is concerned for you and Leo. She was so worried that you were going to leave, I think she would have had us all out in the streets searching for you, had you gone. Julian did not get off lightly either, he got an earful at the way he spoke to you and about the way he made you feel."

"I didn't mean to cause arguments between them."

Layton smiled. "They are always arguing about something, if not you then it would be something else. They love each other really and their disagreements never last very long. When I left they were snuggled up on the sofa together, drinking tea, so you don't need to panic, you haven't caused any rift."

"Are they together? As partners I mean?"

Layton looked at me questioningly. "No. Julian's with Jacob, remember?"

I nodded. "Yeah I get that but...everybody seems to kiss everybody else so I lost track of who goes with who. I mean, Isaac's with you but sleeps with Peter and Peter loves Kendal...from what you told me. You play with Julian, sometimes and so I wondered if Kendal slept with Julian."

Layton laughed. "Mm, we do like to share. That's the point of our world, if we love someone, we show it. Kendal does sleep with Julian sometimes but not in a sexual way. He looks after her when she allows him to, when she wants it."

"When she's needy?"

He smiled and looked at me. "She told you?"

I nodded. "Kind of, she was explaining Leo's need in the car on the way here. He's her Keeper then, she said she had one, she didn't say it was Julian."

"Mm, I suppose he is. This world is different from the vanillas and the place that you know, Joe. Here we openly show affection to each other and no one thinks anything wrong in doing that. It is something that is not acceptable in your world, vanilla or street. If someone needs emotional support it is given freely, if someone needs to be loved or punished that is also given freely. It doesn't matter if it's man or woman or however they identify themselves.

"Tomorrow you will see a lot of kissing and touching, given freely as a welcome and as a sign of affection and friendship. A lot of what happens here is about touch and not so much about the words. Slaves do not always hear spoken words, they do not always understand them. They do understand touch, be that with fingertips across their skin, lips touching their lips, or a cane across their body."

"Like Leo wanting his palms touched, tickled?"

Layton nodded. "Yes, exactly like that. It means something to him, something different to words in his head, it's uncomplicated. I kiss all my Keepers and slaves as a sign of affection, as a sign of my love for them. I don't want you to think I sleep with all of them...I would be worn out." He smiled and I smiled back.

"Do you love all of them?"

He nodded. "Yes, my Keepers and slaves all hold a special place with me. Before Isaac came along they were my whole life and I spent a lot of time with them, so they all know me pretty well. Isaac keeps me pretty busy but I still try to see them all every day or every other day, depending on Isaac's needs. He sometimes visits with me but he hasn't been there for a while...I will probably take him up there when I get him back as a reward for being away for so long.

"He has some slave friends who he doesn't get to see very often and one in particular that he likes to spend time with. Elan. I will definitely take you to see Elan. He and his Keeper have a very special relationship, very close and it's recently evolved into something deeper. You will see that it is possible to be loving and controlling at the same time, that one does not take away the other." I could hear his affection for them in his voice, it was clear that he did love them.

"You must be very busy, how many slaves do you have?"

"Twenty-two at the moment, soon to be twenty-one. One of the slaves is going back to the vanilla world in a few days. There were more but a few have moved to other houses recently."

"Is it sad when they leave?"

He nodded. "Yes, especially if they have been with us a while, it's like losing a friend. The ones that have moved house I will see from time to time, the one who is going back to the vanilla world, I may not ever see again. I have Isaac now, he makes these things easier to bear." He looked at me and smiled. "Are you excited about coming to see them?" He was, I could tell.

"I'm nervous and a little excited." I looked up at Leo. "He'll be safe, won't he? While I'm gone?"

Layton nodded. "I promise you, Joe, he'll be fine. Isaac is in this house too, I wouldn't let anyone come within a mile...ten miles of it and no one in this world knows he's here. Now you should get some sleep. I'll stay and I'll wake you before I leave, you can take Leo outside and watch the sunrise together. He will be sleeping much of tomorrow so it will be good to wake him early. Kendal will have breakfast ready for you when you come back in and then you can spend a little time with him before I come for you."

I wasn't ready to be away from him yet. Things felt better when he was here. I leaned my head against him and he wrapped his arms around me and kissed me.

"I know at the moment things feel unbalanced between you and Leo, you are giving him a lot and not getting much back in return. That will change, Joe, once he's settled and he becomes more accepting of his need, he won't feel so anxious about things. Tomorrow, I will heap lots of love on you, to keep you going while yours is so sparse."

I smiled and he kissed me again. "Can you...kiss me again?"

Layton touched my face and I looked at him. He leaned forward and touched his lips to mine, gently at first and then with more urgency but no tongues. When he parted from me he looked at me and smiled.

"Better?"

I smiled and nodded at him. "Good night."

"Night, Joe."

I stood and climbed on the bed with Leo and Layton pulled the heavy blanket over us both. He bent, kissed Leo, and swept his hand across my head before leaving, turning the lights off and sitting by the door like he had done the night before. I watched him for a while and then I watched Leo, then I fell asleep.

CHAPTER SEVENTEEN

JOE

I was woken by a hand sweeping over my head. I opened my eyes and Layton smiled down at me, leaned in, kissed my cheek, and whispered in my ear.

"Time to wake Leo up."

I nodded groggily and stretched on the bed. Layton moved away and I turned quickly. "Are you going?"

He smiled and nodded. "I'll see you soon. Take blankets with you when you go outside, it's chilly. I'm looking forward to spending the day with you and to you and Leo coming to stay for a while."

I smiled at him. I was too, I was looking forward to being away from here and being close to him. He turned and picked up a cup off the floor and then opened the door carefully. He looked back at me, smiled and then left the room.

I turned back to Leo and pushed myself up on my hand and watched him. I used to watch him sleep when he slept with me before but now watching him, I knew my feelings had changed about him. Maybe Layton was right. Leo taking himself away had allowed him to grow. The distance had allowed our feelings space to change gradually without me feeling like I was taking advantage of him. It wouldn't have felt right, feeling the things I did, not then.

It felt right now though, now I felt free to love him. His hand lay open against the pillow and I touched my fingers to his palm and stroked them gently. His hand squirmed under my touch and jolted little, it made me smile. I continued and he started to stir, eventually opening his eyes to look at me. He stretched his hand out under my fingers and smiled.

Still half asleep he spoke. "I like that."

I smiled at him. "I know you do. I want to do something else I know you like." He looked at me expectantly and I shook my head and laughed a little. "No, not that, something that doesn't get you so excited. Do you want to go outside for a while?"

He sat up excitedly. "Now, are we leaving now? Are we going home?"

I sighed and shook my head. I didn't like making him disappointed but I had set him straight immediately before his excitement turned to be upset or stropping.

"No, you know we can't go back there, Leo. I told you we weren't leaving, that I'd changed my mind." He laid back down, unhappy again. I understood a little now why the slaves were not told too much. It raised their expectations of things to come. I would remember in future to keep my plans to myself until I was sure of them. "If you stop sulking, I will take you outside to see the stars before the day takes them."

He lay for a moment thinking then took a deep breath as if to clear his mood and nodded at me. "I want to see them, I miss them."

I smiled at him. "Yeah me too, well, actually, I miss sitting with you. The stars aren't that important without you." The comment seemed to pass him by, with no reaction from him at all.

It was true. I doubted that I would even think about day or night, the stars and the moon if it wasn't for Leo. Leo had needed something beautiful in his life when he lived on the street and that wasn't an easy thing to find. The night time meant bad things for him, gave him bad feelings, the stars let him find something nice in a bad thing. I had never understood it but I don't think I had ever really understood what was going on in his mind. It was becoming clearer to me now though, the more time I spent with him, the more he told me things.

I could see the connection to what Layton told me about submissive needs. Bad feelings were acceptable, not particularly liked but accepted. When I picked a customer for him, he would go with them, not particularly willingly but he would go. He knew that I would come for him after and sit with him. It was like he was earning that time with me and the stars.

I leaned forward and brushed my lips over his, careful not to make it any more than a show of affection. I didn't want to set off his need for more. "Come on, get up. Use the bathroom and brush your teeth, I will sort out your clothes."

I pulled at his hand and he begrudgingly moved himself up and off the bed. I watched him leave the room and I sat and listened to him pee and flush the toilet a million times before I had to shout at him to stop.

I moved myself to find his linen trousers and top. Layton had said it was cold out, although how he knew I wasn't sure. Had he left the room? He had, he had made himself tea, the cup hadn't been there before. What was he doing now? Sleeping? He must have been, he had been here all night. He was missing Isaac, I could tell when he spoke about him, how much love he had for him, even when he was telling me bad things about him, he loved those bad things.

It was strange. When he was with me he kind of made me feel special, like he loved me, I wasn't sure how he did that. He knew me, even though our meetings had been infrequent over the years, he still knew me better than anyone else. He had watched me with customers often, seen me when I was starving hungry, and had seen me desperately waiting at the alley, offering myself to them. I suppose when you lived on the street, there wasn't much to know about someone, or much to hide.

I was looking forward to staying with him. I felt more confident with Leo when he was around and at least he would be there to explain things when I didn't understand. I got dressed and sat on the edge of the bed, listening for Leo. It was silent. I tried to stay and wait for him but then thought about the hot tap incident. I couldn't hear water running but my need to know what he was doing got the better of me.

I wanted to rush in there but quelled the need to panic and casually walked in and used the toilet before looking up at him. He was standing sideways in front of the long mirror that was on the wall, looking at his back. It was the first time that I had seen him take any interest in what was causing his soreness.

I refrained from speaking and let him be. He wasn't taking any notice of me as I pissed and I wasn't sure he was even aware that I was there until he spoke.

"When I saw Isaac's marks on his back, he wasn't hiding them like I did." I wasn't sure if that required me to speak so I just stood and waited. "He forgot about them. I never forgot mine. I tried to." Again I wasn't sure whether to speak and detract him from his thoughts. He hadn't looked at me yet so I stayed quiet.

It was like I wasn't there, that he wasn't actually talking to me but just thinking out loud. "He didn't like them, mine, but he wasn't afraid of them. He had other marks on him, different marks, on his nipples." He turned then and walked over to me. "I can't find the toothpaste."

I smiled and looked at the basin. The toothpaste was right there. I picked it up and gave it to him. "There you go." He took it and brushed his teeth and I did mine.

That had been strange. I rinsed my mouth out and wiped my face as Leo went for a second helping of paste on his brush and then sucked at it. Was he comparing wounds? Did they do things like that? It was another thing that I would have to ask Layton. I waited for ages while he chewed on his brush.

"Leo, you're taking a long time, the stars will be gone if you don't hurry. Are you hungry?" He looked at me and nodded. "Why don't you tell me anymore? You were always telling me about your hungry stomach before."

He shrugged. "I forget to say the words when I'm busy." It made me smile.

Busy. He had been doing not a lot of anything since we had been here, I wasn't sure where the busy bit came from. He washed his mouth out with water and then sucked his brush again before putting it down on top of mine.

"I don't want to miss them." I took that as my hurry up as I stood watching him. I took him to the bedroom and helped him dress, then took two blankets off the bed and we went outside.

It was still completely dark out and I wondered what time Layton had woken us. He had given us plenty of time and I knew it was because he understood that things took a little longer with subs like Leo. It was never simple, not even just waking up and coming outside. He knew those things without even knowing Leo. I was holding Leo's hand and he was already looking skyward, pulling me further from under the porch covering. We had sat under the porch before but I knew that that wouldn't appease his need for the sky.

"We'll sit on the steps, Leo, then you can see." We walked down the porch steps and I wrapped the blanket around him before sitting and pulling him down with me. The other blanket I wrapped around me and him as he sat between my legs a step lower. I kissed the top of his head and he turned and smiled at me before looking back.

The night was cold but the sky was clear apart from the odd wandering cloud. Leo was almost smiling looking at it. I was glad now that Layton had suggested this. To see Leo peaceful and almost on the brink of what looked like happiness made me not feel so bad about making him sleep later and me leaving him. I hugged him tighter and looked up.

"There's no moon." Leo didn't look at me when he spoke. "Where is it?"

"Probably it knows that the day is coming so it already went away."

"Like we used to?"

I smiled. "Yes, like we used to."

The vanilla's day was our night, our time to sleep. As soon as the sun started to rise the customers would make themselves scarce and our business time would be over or reduced to a small trickle. If Ginger was around or just returning from some customer and had earned good money he would sometimes take Leo to Manni's for breakfast. Only if he was in a good mood though. I would take myself off to sleep until they returned.

I would watch Leo ask him to join him in his bed, pleading with him sometimes until either Ginger relented or got seriously pissed with him. I would take myself outside and wait, knowing if Ginger refused him he would be upset and come and find me. If he never came out, then I knew he was with Ginger and I would then take myself off down the alley to get any stray customer that was brave enough to venture there during the daylight.

Sometimes I would wake and they hadn't returned and I would head down to Manni's to find Leo sitting with Mikey. Usually because Ginger had seen a customer that he knew and wanted to earn the extra money. Leo usually looked bored and upset at being dumped and stranded but he would always smile when he saw me. I would sit with him while Mikey made me a tea and then I would take him back to the alley, put him to bed and sit with him until Ginger returned.

Ginger never apologised to Leo for leaving him and Leo never held it against him. When he returned it was like it always was between them, I would be the outsider again. I would always take myself away from them and try not to think about it. I looked down at Leo.

"Okay?"

He nodded. "It's coming."

"What is?"

"The new day."

I looked at the sky and it was changing colour but you could still see the stars.

"It is. It's clever isn't it, the way it changes? The stars don't fight it because they know they will be coming back."

Leo was looking up wistfully, his eyes reflecting the night sky, making them dance with expectation as he watched the new beginning. "Where do they go?"

"I don't think they go anywhere, I think they are always there. The daylight is so bright that they can't shine through it so they just wait until the daylight doesn't shine so brightly."

"Are they lost? Do you think it scares them?" There was a double conversation going on here and I wasn't sure what he was relating it to.

"Maybe they are a little worried because the night sky seems so far away but I don't think they're lost. They know the night always comes back for them."

"Isaac said I'm a star."

I smiled. "That's a nice thing to say."

He looked up at me. "I think you're my night sky." His words were so full of feeling that they sent a shiver down inside me.

It was the nicest thing he'd ever said to me. I stroked my fingers gently over his face and kissed him gently on the lips.

"That's very beautiful, Leo. Thank you."

He looked pleased with himself and continued. "Isaac is the moon, he knows things and Ginger is the daylight. When I was with him I still felt the same, like a star but he couldn't see me..." Then uncertain of his thoughts he added. "...don't you think?" I was quite taken aback by his thought process and the complexity of it. I had to catch up, quickly.

I nodded in agreement with him. "That's very clever, Leo. The daylight never means to harm the stars, Ginger never meant to ignore you, he was so busy himself that he couldn't see you properly."

He looked pleased again and looked back up at the ever-changing sky. Ginger was the sun, the daylight, warm when it touched but it also hurt sometimes. I closed my eyes and smiled as I was drawn into his crazy thoughts.

"He's coming." I looked at him at his breathless words. He was staring at the sky, his mouth open a little.

"Are you worried, Leo?" I couldn't decide. The daylight had now turned into 'he', it was a little bizarre.

He shook his head, still looking skyward. "No, not now. Not now, I know you're here. You always see me, even when it's light."

He had lost me a little but his look of awe as he watched the daylight consume the sky and the stars made me stay quiet and watch him. I wrapped my arms around him tighter as if to convey to him that it didn't matter whether it was dark or light, I still loved him, I still saw Leo the star, shining.

It wasn't long before the night sky turned purple and red and then finally blue. The garden and the porch were now lit up around us and Leo was breathing heavily and fast as if he was feeling something inside. I had decided not to share things with Leo, plans, but I wanted to tell him that we were leaving here later and going with Layton. I was sure that Layton wouldn't let me down so I felt safe about telling him. I wasn't sure what his reaction would be. I waited a while for him to relax and his breathing to settle before I spoke.

"Do you feel better being out here?" He nodded. He was relaxed, I could feel his body against mine. He was still looking at the sky and I smiled at him. "Leo?" He didn't answer or look at me. "Leo, are you ignoring me again?"

He leaned his head back against me and smiled. "No." He had been. He had been caught up in his beautiful thoughts and had tried to shut me out.

"Good because I don't like it when you ignore me."

He looked at me now. "Does it make you angry?" What had Layton said about this? He was testing, testing to see what pleased me and what didn't.

"Maybe a little, it makes me worry and if you make me worry for no reason that makes me a little angry."

"Okay." I took that as his understanding, not that he wasn't going to do it again.

"You know how we were talking about your need yesterday?" He looked away and nodded. He didn't want to talk about it. "Well, tonight, when it gets dark, we are going to stay with Layton for a while, so we can be close to him when it comes again."

He looked up at the sky. "I want to stay here, I like it here."

"But there's no one here to help you, Leo."

"There's you and that suit man...J."

"His name is Julian."

"Kendal calls him J, I like J better than Julian." We were off track.

"Well, you don't know him well enough to call him J and I don't think he can help you, not like Layton can. Layton's going to help both of us, I don't think Julian would like to help me."

"I don't need help, I just need Ginger then it won't matter where we are, then we can forget about it." Like he had been trying to do since it started.

"Leo, look at me." He turned his face towards me. "You can't forget about it anymore, you have to think about it, we have to think about it now."

"Isaac forgets about his."

I nodded. "I think that's because Layton has taught him about his need. He's shown him that it's not a bad thing so it doesn't worry him when it's not asking. When it does ask, he knows Layton will look after him and keep him safe while he has it. I want Layton to teach you and me, Leo, so you can have some peace and not worry about it all the time. I know Ginger made it go away but Ginger is not here and he's not coming. I can't help you, I don't know how. I want to, I want to learn but I need you to help me do that, I need you to show Layton what it feels like and I need you to let Layton make it go away."

"What if I'm scared?"

"Well, you're scared now, aren't you? Thinking about it, worrying about it all the time? I don't think being with Layton can make that worse. I understand that you're nervous. It's someone different who you're not used to, but Layton knows so much. I think it will be different but better different, I think he can give you what you want and make it feel not so…bad."

Leo sat quietly.

He willingly gave his body to Ginger but he knew him, he knew what he did, how it would feel. I felt for him, felt sorry for him but I couldn't show him that. He had gone from a life where he didn't answer to anyone, to being very contained and restricted, with people, including me, asking things of him. If I thought about everything that had changed for him, it was huge and all he had done was strop a few times.

He turned sideways and snuggled against me. "I want it to go away."

I kissed the top of his head and pulled him to me tightly, trying to instil confidence in him. "I know you do but I don't think that's going to happen so we need to find a way that you can live with it, without it hurting your mind all the time. I know it's possible because Isaac has that peace. I think we need to give Layton a chance. I trust him, Leo, and spending some time with him will help you see that you can trust him."

"Are you gonna leave me there?"

I leaned forward and nuzzled my face into his head. "No. I'm going to stay there too, with you. He's teaching both of us, remember?"

"I don't need lessons, I know what it feels like."

I smiled. I supposed that was true.

"Then you need to show me but because I don't know what it feels like, I'm going to need Layton to help me understand." I thought about the conversation earlier about the day and night sky. "I think Layton can teach me how to be the daylight, Leo, but teach me so I can still see you shine like you do at night. Would you like that? Would you like me to be the day and night sky?"

I could see he was thinking about it, understanding that I was offering to take Ginger's place, or try to at least.

"Are you gonna let me come?" I half laughed.

I knew I had to be careful when I answered but it amused me that that was what he wanted to know.

"I think that depends on whether you've been good or not but if I do let you, then I won't send you away to do it."

"I am good, I was always good...I think...I don't know. Will Layton know if I'm good? Then he can tell you."

I smiled against his head and kissed him. "Yes, I think that might be one of the things that he can teach me."

Leo turned and looked at me.

Now deciding it was the right thing, he didn't want to wait. "Can we go now?"

I smiled at his sudden eagerness. "No, and I want you to be quiet about it until we are in our room."

"Why? Is it a secret?"

"Yes."

He screwed his face up. "I'm not good with secrets."

I sought of hysterically laughed in silence. Everything he knew, everything he'd been doing for his time in the alley, did he not consider keeping them to himself, a secret?

"I think you are very good at keeping secrets." I was about to say more when the back door opened and Kendal came out smiling and carrying two mugs.

"Morning guys. It's chilly out here so I brought you some hot tea. Leo, yours has sugar in it. I'll start breakfast." For once, hot tea was very welcomed.

353

I looked at her and smiled. "Morning Kendal. I didn't hear you, I would have come and collected them."

She stepped down a step and crouched down and gave Leo his tea. He smiled at her as he took it and she smiled back and kissed his forehead.

"There are three sugars in it, poppet." He smiled more as she turned and looked at me. She held out my tea and I took it. "There's no worry, honey, I like looking after you and Leo."

I felt a little uncomfortable, which was silly. I had known Kendal for a while. She was always at the house when I went there and sometimes she would come and sit with me when I ate. Once the house had been so busy, I helped her with the washing up. She was quite pretty but her prettiness was hidden by something I couldn't quite understand.

"Did you watch the sunrise?"

I smiled and stroked my hand over Leo's arm. "We did. Leo was quite taken with it. He's never watched the stars fade away with such awe."

Leo interrupted. "They didn't fade away, they're still there."

Kendal smiled at him. "That's right, they are still there."

Leo was looking at the sky again and without looking at her he spoke again. "Joe told me." Kendal looked at me and smiled. "Joe told me something else too but I'm not allowed to say, it's a secret."

I sipped my tea and smiled into my cup as Kendal laughed a little. "Then I won't ask what it is, Leo, not if it's between you and Joe." Leo drank his tea and Kendal looked at me. "Are you okay Joe? Julian was tough on you yesterday."

I leant forward and wrapped my arm around Leo. "He was just saying it how it is. Leo and I are not part of your world, we are strangers. Everybody is wary of strangers, I don't think it matters what world you're in. I know you all think that it would be better for Leo if he had a Keeper that knows stuff." Kendal sat down on the step as I continued. "I know you think it too and I get it. You all understand the one part of Leo that I don't. Leo and I are friends, we were from the moment we met and that friendship has seen us through some rough times. Neither of us has ever doubted it, no matter what, we didn't even need to question each other, it just was.

"We believed in it and trusted it, sometimes it was so invisible, Leo and I couldn't see it, especially in the last year or so. I think I realised how powerful it was when I tried to leave... leave him behind. For Leo, I think he's realised as soon as his safe and secure world, the place he'd always known, started to crumble around him and disappear. I didn't know about Leo's need, what he's been doing with Ginger but that's the thing, it didn't matter and it doesn't matter now." Leo tipped his head back and looked up at me and I smiled at him. "Knowing about this need, doesn't change our friendship, does it?" Leo shook his head, still looking at me.

I kissed his forehead. "Leo needs someone to guide him, to teach him about his need and how to live with it. I've been doing that, I just didn't know it. I know one thing about Julian as does Leo. He has this need too. It kind of taints your outlook if you only know and understand that one thing about a person. I'm sure Julian is more than that.

"It doesn't make sense to give Leo to anyone because I don't understand that one thing, it makes more sense to learn about it because I already know the rest. Having a friend like Leo is rare, someone who doesn't care about what you wear, how many times you washed, how many cocks you sucked or even that you didn't suck any. Leo and I don't have to prove anything to each other, we just like each other.

"I was bothered a little by Julian...all of you, yesterday, then I realised the only thing that matters is Leo and me. I don't want to be away from him and he doesn't want me to be away, so, until that changes, Leo is staying with me and really, it doesn't matter where we go or where we end up. I was going to go, you were right, Lay...he told me you were worried. I didn't mean to worry you."

Kendal shook her head. "Oh Joe, I'm sorry. No one wants to take Leo from you. I do not doubt that he's better off with you. Just to look at him I see that he is settled and secure with you." Leo turned and smiled at Kendal which made her smile while she spoke. "I didn't mean to put distance between us. I'm glad you stayed and I'm glad you're going with him toda...tonight. There is no better teacher for you and Leo.

"You're right about Julian, there is so much more to him. He controls his feelings, his need without thought…I think you both took him by surprise yesterday. You're coming for breakfast this morning aren't you?" Leo turned and looked at me, waiting for my answer.

I smiled at him. "Yes, we're coming. Leo's starving. I'm concerned about...later. He's mine, if there's any doubt on that, then I can't go." I wondered if Kendal was understanding my cryptic words but she leaned forward and kissed the side of my face.

"No, there's no doubt. I promise it's safe for you to go and I know you don't like it but you need this time with him. Maybe it will help you understand Julian a little more."

I smiled. "Maybe." I wasn't sure I believed anything would help me understand him.

Kendal pushed herself up. "Right, well, I better get cooking. Eggs and bacon." Leo turned and looked at her.

"And tea and sausage?"

She laughed a little. "And tea and sausage just for you, Leo, because you are so good."

Leo looked a little excited when he looked at me and then I got the connection.

"No, not that good Leo, she means a different good."

He looked disappointed. "Oh, I didn't know there were different ones, will Layton know?"

I smiled and nodded. "Yes." I looked at Kendal who was looking confused. I shook my head smiling. "He wants to earn...something."

She smiled and nodded. "Come in soon boys, it's too cold to stay out here." She walked back into the house rubbing her arms and I wrapped both my arms around Leo and kissed the side of his face.

"Are you cold?"

"No." I touched his hands to check. He would say that to stay here I knew but his hands were warm. We sat in silence.

CHAPTER EIGHTEEN

JOE

We didn't stay out much longer. The breeze that was blowing got colder as the morning hazy sun rose. It started to seep through the blanket and when I saw Leo's bottom lip shiver a little, I knew that it was time to go inside. I carried the cups and held Leo's hand as we entered the kitchen and I was glad to see it was just Kendal there. She made us another fresh warm tea and within ten minutes there was hot food in front of us. Leo was helped by Kendal and he tucked into his quickly as I chatted to Kendal.

"Have you been to Layton's house?"

She joined us at the table. "Yes, many times. He has the nicest house, it's more relaxed, casual, the slaves are much more accepting of visitors. He takes more of a hands-on part with his slaves and Keepers. A lot of slave owners keep their distance from their slaves and Keepers, rarely visiting them unless there's an issue, they leave a lot of the care to their Keepers. Layton likes to get to know his slaves and see them in their different emotional states, from being needy to being content. He can usually spot an issue before it arrives, with the help of his Keepers. They all have the greatest respect for him and the way he runs his house. Are you looking forward to going?"

I was. Now that Kendal and I were back on track with our friendship, I felt a little easier about leaving Leo. I still felt guilty that he would have to be forced to sleep but I needed this time to learn as much as I could.

"Yes and a little apprehensive, I've never seen a slave."

Kendal smiled. "Well, Layton will look after you and he has a lovely lady there called Bea who makes lovely food, Leo will be spoilt." I smiled as Leo finished his plateful of food and looked at Kendal. Kendal laughed and took his plate. "You can have a little more, Leo, but I have to leave some for Isaac and Peter." She served him up some more bacon and toast and then sat again as I spoke.

"Where are they?"

"Oh, they will probably be out later, you two were up early today. Isaac is not always a good sleeper so they may have been up in the night. The dark is not a good place for him, he had to sleep with the light on for ages after..." She looked at Leo. "Well, when he came here. He would consider Leo very brave to be outside when it's dark. He feels safer in his room."

"Doesn't that Jacob person mind that we've all taken over his house?"

Kendal shook her head smiling. "No. Jacob has two homes, this one and Julian's house, he's comfortable in both. If Julian requests he stays there, it would not require a reason. He would never challenge a request given to him by Julian. Jacob is different to Isaac and Leo, he doesn't require so much attention from others, only Julian and he's not used to sharing Julian either."

"So how does he feel when you need Julian then? Does he get jealous?"

Kendal smiled. "No, he's very gracious. I am quite demanding when I'm needy so Julian makes arrangements for Jacob to be with a friend. Her name is Eden and they are very close. Julian allows them time to be together without supervision, it's kind of Jacobs time to be a little free of restraint and restriction for a while." Yet another person into the mix.

"And they sleep together?"

"Yes, not play though, their relationship is built on friendship. Eden was a slave for a short while and by chance, they met and have been friends ever since. Eden is a little submissive with Jacob, she likes the attention he gives her and Jacob gets to give it freely without having restraints put on him."

I smiled. So many relationships, I was going to need a notebook soon.

"Your lives are a little hard to keep track of. So many relationships intertwined with each other."

Kendal smiled. "Well, it's kind of what this world is based on, being allowed to show the feelings you feel for another. If you want to sleep naked with someone, then it doesn't have to go beyond that, mean more than that, it's acceptable to just do that even if you love another.

"Submissive people have strong emotions, even a friendship with someone becomes very important to them with intense feelings. If a relationship grows beyond friendship then the emotions become even more intense, which is where the submissive person will then want to submit to their stronger, more dominant partner.

"There are different levels, different emotions for every relationship, the strongest being the sort of relationship that Julian and Jacob have and Layton and Isaac, where the subservience becomes a twenty-four-seven thing and not just in play. This world is about accepting people's feelings for each other and allowing that to go wherever they wish."

I smiled at Kendal. "Or not, in Isaac's case?"

Kendal sort of laughed. "Isaac loves attention and knows that there is a place where he gets it. That all became a little confused after his trip to the street. Layton was giving his attention to Leo and so Isaac looked to Peter, who is always someone Isaac could rely on for it when Layton's attention was elsewhere. For one moment Peter gave his attention to...someone else, me, and Isaac felt a little lost and left out. Peter had never shared his attention with someone else when Isaac was around, so it was new to him. He had an intense rush of emotion that he didn't know what to do with, or how to deal with it. Peter's and Isaac's relationship is still new and they haven't quite worked out the rules and boundaries of it, which is why Isaac was so unsure. They're working on it."

"Doesn't that make you a little jealous?"

Kendal smiled and shook her head. "Peter and I haven't worked out our relationship either, we're still at the friendship stage and I'm happy with that. Peter loves Isaac and I accept that Isaac is an important part of his life. Peter has lived here a long time and has not really been involved with anyone. Isaac has changed that, he's ignited feelings that Peter has been ignoring for a while.

"If things were to move forward for Peter and me, then it would be because we both feel it, regardless of what his relationship is with Isaac. Each relationship is different. I haven't been very supportive of Peter and Isaac but not because of jealousy towards Isaac. I love him." That was clear to see. "I know the path that he is taking and I worried for him. But, if that is what he feels is right, then I can't deny him those feelings."

"I don't understand? What path?"

"Being Dominant, being Dominant with Isaac. Being Dominant is not just about controlling someone, it's about learning everything that goes with that. If he wants to play with Isaac then he will have to learn what that means for him, it means that at some point he will have to be...the bottom. A Dominant should never give something to a submissive without knowing what it feels like to receive it, it's kind of an unwritten rule. Peter has always just been...just Peter so when he started on this path, I wasn't very supportive. I have been shown the error of my ways." She laughed. "Now I see what Isaac means to him, I understand his need to be the best he can be for Isaac."

"You mean that Peter will have to play as a submissive?"

Kendal nodded. "At some point yes, possibly not as a sub though, just a bottom. That depends on how much he gets it, the place he would take in the play. If he wants to understand Isaac, which I know he does. If you love someone, you want the best for them, you want to give them things that make their lives full."

"How does one Dominant submit to another? Surely that causes conflict?"

Kendal nodded. "It can but as long as the understanding is there between them, it can be worked through. Layton has been teaching him and they have built a good trust between each other and I know they have talked about it. Nothing will happen until Peter is completely sure though, it's Layton's job to make him feel sure."

I smiled and looked at Leo, who was now drinking his tea. "He's good at that, making people feel sure."

Kendal smiled. "Yes, he is. Layton is all about understanding people's feelings and going with them rather than changing them to suit his own needs. It's why he's so good with the slaves. If they feel something then Layton wants to know about it, he wants to understand what made them feel that rather than telling them it's not acceptable. He understands people very well."

Peter had said that we were on the same journey, learning what it was like to love a submissive with a need. I was a little taken aback by the Dominants bottoming or submitting to understand their submissive, but I could see the sense of it.

If I was ever going to get an understanding of what Leo endured when he played, I knew at some point I would have to go there. Not yet though, I was nowhere near ready to take that step. I still needed to understand this control, dominant thing. Leo put down his cup and looked at me expectantly. I wasn't sure if he had listened and understood everything that had been said, and had come to the same conclusion as me. I wouldn't have put it past him to have understood. So I wasn't sure what the expectant look was.

I smiled at him and leaned forward and kissed him. "I'm not sure what that look is for, Leo, but we will go when I'm ready." That seemed to cover it and he sighed and rested back in his chair. I looked at Kendal. "I'm going to take Leo for a bath, do I have time?" I had no idea when Layton would be coming for me.

She nodded. "Yes, of course. I'll bring some nice hot chocolate in for you later, Leo."

Leo looked excited at the prospect. "I like chocolate."

Kendal smiled at him. "Then you will like this, it makes you feel warm and cosy inside. Maybe you and I can have a cuddle while you drink it." Leo smiled and nodded.

Kendal had cleverly paved his way to the sleep she would induce and I smiled at Leo's acceptance of Kendal, now that she was bringing him chocolate.

"I like them too, Joe only gives them when I'm cold."

I frowned at him and was about to protest, then thought about it and couldn't think of a time I had held him close just because I wanted to.

Kendal smiled at him. "Well, I'm sure he will when things settle down. You've been feeling pretty bad since you got here, so it's going to seem like that. I think you are starting to feel better now though, aren't you?"

Leo shook his head. "Nah, I still think about home."

Kendal reached out her hand and held Leo's. "Aw, sweetheart, it's okay to think about it. It was a nice place wasn't it?" Leo nodded. "If it makes you sad then you should try not to think about it."

"I like thinking about it, I liked it, it doesn't make me sad. I just miss it."

Kendal smiled. "Oh, okay. The memories are good, the feeling is not good?"

Leo nodded, pleased that Kendal understood. Now though, he seemed like he wanted Kendal to do something about it. He seemed like he was waiting for an answer to his problem. I looked at Kendal too. Kendal looked from me to Leo and repeated it.

She smiled. "It's a tricky one, Leo, but I think if you try hard you can make the memories make you feel other things. Is there something you remember about the alley that made you smile when you were there?"

I looked at Leo who was thinking about it. It was a tough one, there wasn't much to smile about there. I was about to try and move the conversation away when Leo smiled and laughed a little. Just the sound of it made me smile with him. He had found something, although I had no idea what he was thinking of.

He looked at Kendal. "It's funny."

Kendal smiled at him. "See. It's okay to miss the alley, Leo, but it's not nice to get stuck in the bad feelings. It's much better to think of the good things about it and remember the nice times. If sometimes that's too hard, then you can tell Joe and he will understand."

I reached out and stroked the back of my fingers over his cheek. Now that was something I did understand, I missed it too. Leo touched his hand to mine and linked his fingers through mine. He knew it too.

He looked at me. "I feel better now. Can we have a bath now? I want hot chocolate."

I smiled at him and kissed his hand as Isaac and Peter entered the room.

"Morning everyone." I turned and looked at Peter, still smiling.

"Morning." Peter was holding Isaac's hand and he gestured that he should take the seat next to Leo, which he did.

I wanted to take Leo away before he said anything about going to Layton's but Leo seemed happy to see Isaac, so I resisted the urge to whisk him away quickly.

Peter walked around and bent and kissed Kendal as Isaac and Leo shared a kiss across the corner of the table. It was strange how easy kissing came to Leo because he really hadn't done a lot of it in the alley. He had never kissed me, not until yesterday and I had never given him more than a touch on his cheek or forehead until we came here.

Kendal held out her hand to Isaac. "Morning, sweetie." Isaac held Leo's hand and looked at Kendal and smiled. Kendal smiled back. "Aw, you prefer to hold Leo's hand?"

"I didn't sleep well, I had the shivers."

Kendal looked concerned and turned that look to Peter. He was making tea and he turned a little to look at Kendal. "He had an unsettled night, something along the lines of overwhelming needs, feelings, and acceptance of his place, I think."

Kendal's look changed to one of understanding. "Oh, I see."

I understood too and was a little worried that someone would mention his name and remind Leo of our secret.

I smiled at Isaac. "Morning, Isaac."

He looked at me. "Can Leo have more tea? I don't want him to have mine."

Leo turned and looked at me, waiting.

I shook my head. "No, he can't." I looked at Leo. "You're having hot chocolate, remember? After your bath."

Isaac smiled. "I'm not allowed hot chocolate, it gives me erotic thoughts." Both Kendal and Peter laughed and I smiled.

Leo looked confused. "What are they?"

Isaac answered. "It's thoughts about having orgasms."

Leo looked worried. "Oh, I don't want that, I'm not allowed to come, not until I'm good."

Again the conversation was getting too close for comfort. Peter gave Isaac his tea and I took the interruption as an opportunity to draw him away.

"I don't think Kendal's hot chocolate will make you think about that. Say goodbye to Isaac, it's time for us to bathe and sort out your back."

Leo sighed. "Bye, Isaac. I'm leaving tonight so I don't know when I will see you." Leo looked at me as I started to panic a little. "Will I see him again? I want to."

Before I had time to answer, Isaac spoke. "Where are you going?"

Leo looked at me fleetingly before turning to Isaac. I couldn't think what to say so in my panic I ended up not saying anything before Leo answered. "I don't know but I'm going with Joe."

Isaac looked at me and then back to Leo. "Try and be good then."

Leo nodded and that was the end of that. No fuss or bother, just acceptance. Leo got out of his chair and I took his hand.

I looked at Kendal. "Later?" She smiled and nodded.

As I left the room with Leo, Isaac was speaking. "Peter…can I have a hot chocolate later?"

I smiled and took Leo back to our room.

We had a quick bath, mainly because Leo constantly asked to get out, so I washed him quickly and then myself. I washed his back, it was so much better now, the cuts were just pink little marks although he still wore the gauze over his stitches. We were sitting on the bed and I reached for the ointment that had now become part of his daily life and I wondered if there would ever be a day when I didn't need to see to his wounds. Even Leo had quickly become used to it and he lay his body over my legs ready. He was facing me and I smiled at him at the lack of fuss he now made.

"Do you mind having this done now, Leo?"

He shrugged. "I like you touching me, it makes it better."

I sort of laughed. There was a reason why he didn't fuss. "Well, I like doing it, looking after you. You were very good not to tell Isaac our secret." I touched the first lot of ointment to his skin gently but he didn't flinch so I continued.

"I did tell him, I wanted to. I like Isaac, it doesn't hurt when he's around, I don't have to think. Why are they keeping him from Layton?"

I wasn't sure how he had picked that up. "Who said they were keeping him from Layton?"

He shrugged. "No one, but they are. If I'm not good, will they keep me from you?"

I touched my fingers to his forehead and stroked them across his hair. "No. Isaac has not been bad, well not bad enough that they are keeping him from Layton. Peter loves Isaac and I think it's more a case of he wants to keep Isaac with him for the moment, not so much about keeping Layton away."

Leo didn't look convinced. "He feels bad though, I don't think he wants to stay with Peter."

How did you explain that Isaac was feeling bad so he could find a good place? Leo wouldn't understand it. He had been able to pick and choose where he went.

"He does like being with Peter. It's a bit like you and I, Leo. They are learning to live with each other. Isaac lives differently from you, if he wants to have peace and a quiet mind, he has to think about only the person he's with and what they want. He has to trust Peter to look after him when Layton's not around and trust that Peter will keep him safe. When he understands that, then Peter's love will feel better to him and he won't worry so much."

"And he gets kisses and hugs from everyone, like he did in the kitchen?"

I smiled and nodded. "Yes, when he accepts his place, he gets all the attention he wants and needs."

Leo fiddled with the blanket in his fingers and then spoke. "I would stay with Peter for that."

I was surprised. "Really?"

He nodded. "Not for a long time, just for a little while."

He had watched everyone as they had touched, kissed and caressed Isaac, without Isaac seemingly having to do anything to earn such adoration. It was the attention that kind of kept him in his place, it made him feel secure with them and his surroundings. Isaac hadn't been thinking about Layton when Julian had spoken to him and had even become a little jealous of Julian's attention on Leo. He had tried to get it back.

Was Leo so free that it made him anxious? Was having a place with a stranger more inviting than being with me?

"But Leo, you couldn't decide when you wanted to come back. Only Peter can decide that."

"You could get me." He hadn't understood. I barely understood the life that Isaac led.

I shook my head. "No, I don't think it works like that. If you stay with Peter and have his attention then you have to stay until he says you can leave. That would be your place, to do as he wanted."

I could see Leo thinking about it and I continued to brush my fingers over his head. I didn't want him to become unsettled and I could see that thinking about it was troubling him. "You don't have to think about it, Leo, it's not a choice that you have to make, for now anyway. You are with me and I'm not leaving you."

He nodded then frowned. "But you said I have to be good." I smiled.

He really didn't get it. He thought they just loved Isaac, which they did and I had no doubt that they wouldn't ever hurt him, he was a prized possession, but he had to earn that attention.

I had seen Isaac follow Peter and get nothing. I hoped today I would learn more because I had very little to tell Leo really.

"Isaac has to be good too, Leo." I waited and when he didn't answer I continued. "What does being good mean?"

He shrugged. "That I don't hit out or spit and lay quietly and let you do my back, don't come and go where you say. I think it means I have to not piss you off." I half laughed. "Does it?"

I had asked him to be good and yet he had no idea what that meant. For me, it did mean all those things that he said but I knew when Isaac said 'be good' there was more to it.

I nodded. "Yes, it means those things but I think there is more to it."

"Like what?"

I didn't want to bring up his need again but it had something to do with it...it had a lot to do with it. "I'm not sure. I think it's one of the things that we are going to learn. For now, though, I think not hitting me is a good thing...and letting me do your back. I don't think you've ever pissed me off so that's good."

I smiled at him and he smiled back and then lay more relaxed with his head on the bed. "I think I'll stay with you then, until I know."

I kind of felt second best. It showed me that he wasn't completely satisfied with me but he didn't know any different. I wondered if once he learnt more about his need, about this world, whether he would quite happily slope off with Peter or someone like him?

I rubbed the last of the ointment into his back in silence. I always looked out for Leo, even when I wasn't particularly thinking about it, I ended up doing things for him. If I only had the money for one tea, I always put a sugar in it because I knew he would end up sharing it with me and he liked tea with sugar, although finding out he liked four was news to me.

In the end, it was never a conscious thought, I just did it. If I was just here to pave his way to a better and easier life, one that made him happy, that maybe didn't include me, then maybe that was just my job. It made me feel a bit sick.

"Joe?"

"Yes?"

"It still doesn't matter does it?"

"What doesn't matter?"

"Any of it. Everything that's happening. We're still friends aren't we?"

God, he confused me. "Always, Leo. You're done now, you can get up."

He moved back a bit and laid his head on my lap. "I don't wanna. You're doing that thing you do when you're angry."

I wasn't angry, at least I didn't think so. I certainly wasn't angry with him but he had obviously picked up on my unrest.

"I'm not angry...it's not anger, and certainly not with you. We need to get dressed. Kendal will be in soon."

Leo was doing that thing where he only heard what he wanted and ignored the rest. "What is it then? It feels like anger or somethin' like it."

I sighed. "Leo, I am not angry with you...I have never been angry with you. Where does this angry thing come from? It's not from me but you seem to tar me with it all the time."

Leo pushed himself up on his hand and looked at me. He looked confused and then went to move away. I caught hold of his hand and he looked at mine holding his. "I'm going to get dressed, you want me to get dressed."

I couldn't argue with that, I had said it. I let go of his hand and he left the bed and went off to the bathroom. I put my head in my hands. Whatever had just happened I knew it had been my fault. Something between us had got confused or lost. I wiped my hands down my face and looked at the bathroom door, then moved off the bed towards the bathroom.

When I got there Leo was sitting on the floor putting on his trousers. Things weren't right between us, I felt it and so did he. I walked in front of him, crouched down and helped him with his linens.

"Leo, do you want to talk? Do you want to tell me something?"

Leo shook his head. "No, thank you...can I still have chocolate with Kendal?"

I nodded. "Of course. I want you to know that I'm not angry with you."

"Okay."

I stood up and held out my hand to him and he took it and I pulled him up. He kept his eyes from me and I knew it was not okay, but I didn't know how to make it right. I didn't know where it had gone wrong. I turned and picked up my linens as Leo pulled his trousers up.

I started to dress and then Kendal called out. "Boys? Are you still in the bath?"

It was kind of a relief to hear her and that also showed on Leo's face. He stepped towards the door and then looked at me as I called out. "No, we're just dressing."

I smiled at Leo. He wanted a hot chocolate with Kendal, he wanted to be away from me. I felt guilty again about leaving him when things weren't right between us but at this moment, being together didn't seem to be helping us. I held out my hand again to him and he stepped towards me.

"What?" It was said a little impatiently.

"I want you to know something else." I stepped towards him and touched my fingers to his face and then leaned forward and kissed his lips. "Always friends, Leo, okay?" He nodded at me and I smiled at him. "Go on, go and have chocolate with Kendal, I'll finish getting dressed." I saw a small smile as he turned and headed off to the bedroom.

By the time I got out there, Leo and Kendal were sitting on the bed together. Leo was holding her hand and leaning closer and closer to her. He wanted her attention, the attention he hadn't got from me. Kendal must have realised too because she put her arm around him and pulled him closer. Seeing him content with her made me feel bad but I couldn't forbid him it. I couldn't want him to stay with her and want me. Kendal kissed Leo's head and Leo made himself more comfortable against her.

She smiled at him as he got comfortable and then looked at me. "Everything okay?"

I half smiled at her and nodded. "Yeah."

I looked at the three cups on the tray. Kendal turned and picked one up and gave it to Leo.

"Here you go, honey, nice warm chocolate."

I became a little nervous and climbed on the bed next to him. He was about to have sleep forced on him and as he took his first sip, I reached out my hand and stroked my fingers around his ear. Leo looked at me and then went back to drinking his chocolate.

"Nice?" He nodded and I smiled.

Kendal held out a cup for me and I took it and looked at it and then her.

She smiled. "It's just hot chocolate."

We sat drinking and I watched Leo. He was so enjoying his drink, he was completely unaware of the effect it was having on his body. Some twenty minutes later he was leaning heavily against Kendal and she was brushing her fingers over his forehead, soothing his journey.

"It feels warm." Was this normal? I looked at Kendal as she spoke to him.

"Mm, nice isn't it? Hot chocolate always makes me feel warm and sleepy." Leo nodded slowly and I could see that it was taking an effort to drink the last from the mug.

"I feel...sleepy too." Kendal put a hand under his mug to support it. "Joe?" I leant forward so he could see me and I took his other hand.

"It's okay, Leo, if you're tired, you can have a sleep."

He nodded and tried to lift his cup to drink the last drop of chocolate as his eyes fluttered closed and Kendal took the weight of the mug in her hand. His hand slipped from the handle and fell against Kendal and she took the mug and put it on the tray.

I leant forward and kissed him. "Have a nice sleep, Leo." I watched his face for any sign of movement but there was none. He was fast asleep. Kendal made him more comfortable as I put my cup back on the tray. "If he gets a bit jumpy in his sleep, just stroke him."

Kendal smiled at me. "He'll be fine, Joe, I promise. I will take a look at his stitches while he's sleeping, clean them up and then, I brought a book." She laughed a little. "Quiet reading time...I don't get much." Her light-hearted chatter meant nothing.

I was feeling too guilty. "Don't leave him, not for a minute. I know he's sleeping but..."

"Joe. I promise. Layton will be outside waiting, use the front door." I nodded and looked at Leo peacefully unaware.

I slipped from the bed, put on my boots, and looked at him one last time before leaving the room.

CHAPTER NINETEEN

JOE

I stepped out of the front door, closed it and looked for Layton. There was no sign of him or a car so I waited. It was freezing and I had no jacket, dressed in just the linen clothes I had borrowed. It seemed ages ago that I had entered this house with Kendal, wondering if I was going to see Leo again, now he was changing my whole life and filled my thoughts every moment of the day.

Our mundane day to day street life had turned into some kind of rollercoaster ride, with ups and downs in extremes. One moment I was so sure Leo wanted to be with me, that he would do anything to stay with me and the next, I felt like I was clinging to him, that he was my lifeline, that I was tagging along where I didn't belong.

I had felt a little hurt today when he had said he wanted to go to stay with Peter. I did sort of understand, he had liked what he saw, he had liked the attention that Isaac had got from each of them. To Leo, Isaac hadn't seemed to earn it either, he had just walked into the kitchen and been touched and kissed and praised by all of them at some point.

Wasn't that what I gave him though? Unearned attention? I'd admit that on the street my attention to him had been few and far between and touches only given when we were alone, like holding hands. The street was a difficult place to show feelings and emotions though. Leo already struggled there and if it had been seen that he needed such attention all the time he would have been hounded by the other boys more than he already had been.

It was a show of weakness to need or show such things and yet here, it was more a show of strength. The other boys already knew he was an easy target, like when one of them took his sleeping box and Leo didn't even fight for it. He found a broken smaller one and laid on it until I came and sorted it out and got it back for him. He had asked Ginger that night to sleep with him after they had taken his box and Ginger had told him it was his own fault and he would have to get on with it.

That had been in the earlier days of Ginger's arrival, their friendship or relationship grew a little more as time went on and because of that, the other boys didn't bother Leo so much. No, I couldn't have given him more there, it would have made his and my life more difficult than it had been. I had been trying here though. Watching them and seeing their unrestricted, unrestrained feelings for each other, I had been trying to let go of my own built-in restraints and go with my feelings of wanting to touch and kiss and be near him. I was learning too but he didn't understand that, I knew.

I shivered and wrapped my hands around my arms and stepped back against the door. Was he coming? A thought occurred to me and I had a moment of panic. Had this been a ploy to get me away from Leo? I stood with that feeling for a moment. Was it so bad for Leo? I was alone out here but he wasn't. He was in there, warm and secure. He could learn their ways, learn what they wanted free of me.

I felt my eyes fill with tears at the sadness of not seeing my friend again. He would be frightened and scared for a while and he would wonder where I had gone but he would get over it...wouldn't he? I shook my head. No, he would think I had left him, deserted him, run off.

As much as he had hurt me today, I hadn't been angry with him because he had been telling me what he had wanted, it was his choice. This was not his choice and I knew, regardless of what he had said, that he wasn't ready to be without me yet. He still needed me to keep him safe while he found his way and even though his feelings for me may not be the same as what I felt for him, our friendship was no different.

I would not break the silent binds of that friendship until he showed me that it wasn't needed anymore. I wiped the tears from my eyes and was just about to turn and bang on the door with my fists when a large car came into sight and pulled to a stop in front of me. The door opened and Layton got out, with a blanket in his hands and walked towards me.

"Fuck, Joe, I'm sorry." He wrapped the blanket around me and looked at me. "Did you think I wasn't coming?"

I tried to hold back a shiver. "Of…course not."

Layton scowled. "Come on, get in." He pulled me away from the door and I headed for the passenger seat and got in as did he. He fiddled with some switches. "You should feel warmer in a moment, the chair is heated." He sat looking at me for a moment then repeated his question. "Did you think I wasn't coming?"

Upset, I nodded slowly. "I thought...for a moment, that it had been a ploy to get me away from him."

Layton reached out and stroked his hand over my hair and then leaned forward and kissed me. "It was my fault. I rang Kendal to say I was on my way and then I had a thought as I passed one of those natural earth shops on my way here." He picked up a brown paper bag. "I picked up a present for Leo, for you to give to Leo."

He held out the bag and, still a little shivery, I took it and looked in it. There were three crystals about the size of my finger. I looked at him. I wasn't sure Leo would appreciate three...what would be to him, stones.

"I'm not sure he'll..."

Layton smiled and interrupted. "They are light catchers, stars in the daytime. At least I'm hoping that's what he will see. He likes...shiny things, pretty things...doesn't he?"

I smiled, my mood thawing a bit and nodded looking back at them. He did. "Thank you...I do trust you...I'm trying, I had a moment's panic."

Layton smiled. "I understand. Us junkies are a little unpredictable but we're not mean, Joe, we wouldn't leave you out in the cold, I for one, know that wouldn't keep you from him."

I closed the bag and put it on my lap as the heat from the seat finally started to seep through to my skin. I looked down away from him, a little uncomfortable. "I may have been a little pissed off when I said that junkie comment..."

Layton laughed and did up his belt. "I'm teasing you. Hungry junkie is a good simile to how it feels, on both sides. Belt up, Joe."

I put my belt on and Layton set the car in motion.

I spent the journey staring out the window in silence, watching the world that I was so used to pass by. He and Julian had obviously spoken, for him to know the phrase I had used to describe the people in his world. I wondered what else they had spoken about. Outside got busy as we passed through a city or busy town and then we left the busy street people and traffic and headed down quieter roads.

"You are very quiet, I thought you would be full of questions."

I looked at him fleetingly before looking back out the window. "I think Leo and I had a...disagreement, argument, I'm not sure, there weren't any words said really but things went a bit wrong between us and I'm not sure I put it right." I paused a moment before adding. "I think it was my fault."

Layton questioned. "It's upset you?" I shrugged. "He upset you, he said something to hurt you." It wasn't a question so I didn't answer. "Whatever he said, Joe, he never said it to hurt you. Leo would never mean to do that, you mean too much to him."

I nodded. He was right, I knew. Leo never meant to make me feel second best but it still hurt.

"I know you are giving him a lot at the moment and getting very little back, it's a tough time for you. The well-ordered life that he more or less controlled has been taken away and he's trying to sort out his thoughts and feelings on the new things around him. That may mean that sometimes he forgets you, not because you're not important to him but because his place with you is so secure, he feels safe enough not to think about it." I nodded.

Layton continued. "You've always been there for him, Joe, when he needed you, from the minute he hit the street and needed something, someone, there you were, no questions asked, no demands. You held out your hand and he took it and whenever he needed it, there you were again, regardless of what he'd done. He still expects that hand from you, he knows that you are always there, so he's not always going to be guarded in what he says to you."

I looked at Layton. "He said he wanted to stay with Peter. He's been watching Isaac and Peter and...well, Isaac and everyone around him actually, he's seen the way they are with him, constantly attentive to him, touching him, kissing him, talking to him. He wants it, he wants that attention and I'm obviously not giving him enough. I think that's why he wanted to make friends with Julian."

Layton nodded. "It was definitely part of it but there is more to it with Julian. The making friends was more of a request. Julian took him to a place that he's never had to go without wanting it and controlling it. It scared him because it was done without thought from him but at the same time, that lack of choice and confusion about it made it a little inviting. He wanted to see what else Julian would give him. I'm glad to hear that Isaac is being lavished with attention and I can see why that would seem very appealing to Leo. It doesn't mean you're not giving him enough though. It means that you have found something he likes and wants and you can teach him to earn such adoration."

I nodded. "I did try to explain that Isaac earns it, but I didn't want to scare him."

Layton smiled. "So you tiptoed around the submitting his body part, and told him...what?"

I half-smiled. "That he had to do what Peter wanted if he stayed with him and he couldn't leave until Peter said he could. That's the bit that scared him off. After I said that, he wasn't sure about it all and said he would stay with me...for now."

Layton laughed. "Oh, ouch, I can see why that hurt a little. I think Leo understands a lot more than you give him credit for. You forget what he willingly went to Ginger for and laid quietly to have. It was a good thought. He's accepting that he's going to have to get his fix from somewhere else and seeing how loved Isaac was, he's thinking being with Peter is not a bad place to be. This has nothing to do with wanting Peter over you. He's...window shopping." I laughed and Layton smiled. "Well, not quite as blatant as that, but something along those lines.

"What is scaring him, is the lack of control because he's always had it. He said when it started and he said when it stopped. Ginger didn't particularly like doing what he did, he did it to keep him quiet, it wouldn't have stopped until Leo had had his fill of pain and suffering, until he didn't need any more to keep that feeling going inside him. When his need is asking, he'll be more ready to accept giving up that control, it will still scare him but his need will override the fear, eventually.

"This sort of fear is considered a good thing, it's hot to watch...for someone like me. I want to see that fear of what I'm going to do but not fear of me, that's not the same thing. Fear of what is coming, what might be coming, can be soothed and overridden if I choose. Fear of me, of the Dominant, cannot be overridden and is not fun. Julian didn't scare him, despite what he told you, what Julian made him feel, scared him a little, it's different and to affirm that, he requested something else from him to see if he would be given it, which he was. If Julian had scared him, he wouldn't have asked anything else from him, he would have tried to stay quiet and out of his attention.

"Kendal tells me his back is getting better so he can probably feel his need starting to niggle a little. The pain of his time with Ginger is coming to end and so a new craving is beginning. It will be good to spend a little time with him before it consumes him, I can get to know him a little better, see how his mind works."

"Don't you know him already? You seem to know?"

Layton smiled. "I know the basics of submissive need but each person is different. They think differently about things, like and dislike different things. Leo is not a slave and has had no slave training. His wants and needs will be a little different and erratic. You will see the difference between him and the slaves today when you see them and understand a little more about the place, I believe, Leo is looking for. The issue for him is getting there, to that place. It's the complete opposite of what he's been asked to do for most of his life, so the transition, this transition stage is difficult for him to understand.

"You are right, he does want more, he's just not sure what that more is. If sometimes there are moments when more isn't you, you have to have a little faith in Leo and trust your friendship, trust him. He trusts you, or he wouldn't tell you." I nodded.

I knew things were difficult for him, knew there had been many changes for him. He was seeing new things, different things, things that he never knew existed, like kissing with tongues, loving and caring touches, given just because they wanted to be felt. If he liked what he saw, I couldn't hold that against him just because it wasn't focused around me. The fact, as Layton said, that he was telling me openly that he wanted those things, surely showed me that he felt sure and secure with me. I hadn't appreciated his honesty, I hadn't seen it, I had just felt hurt.

"I think I need to apologise to him. Is this one of those times when I can do that?"

Layton smiled as he watched the road. "You can apologise to him whenever you want if you want him to know you are sorry for something. Do you want him to know?"

I smiled. "I want him to know. I want him to know how special he is to me and it blinded me a little to what he was telling me."

Layton half laughed as he turned the car into a drive. "Don't spoil him."

I smiled more. Not too much and not too little...balance. I looked out at the house.

"Here we are." I fleetingly looked at him and then back at the house again.

It looked like a house, nothing special, well a big house with a turret kind of thing but a big house. The car had come to stand still and I looked back at Layton.

"It's...nice."

"Really?" Layton looked out the window at it and then screwed his face up. "Inside is nicer, much more beautiful." He looked at me and smiled. "Ready to meet the rest of my family?"

"I'm nervous. What if they don't like me, like Julian? What if they know I don't belong here? What if they know I'm...from the street?"

Layton laughed. "The street is where my family were born, Joe. This is where you would have come, where I would have brought you, before Leo decided to tag along." He smiled amused. "We are just doing things slightly different to how I first thought. A slight shift in arrangements but nothing that can't be sorted. They already know about you and Leo and they are always excited to welcome new people. They trust me, trust my decisions, no one is going to challenge your place here, if they do they will have me to deal with. Julian is...different, I'm teaching him a new way of looking at things but he's a slow learner...don't tell him I said that." He grinned at me. "Actually, Isaac is teaching him to look at things differently."

I half-smiled. "He likes him, doesn't he? I can see the way he is with him."

Layton nodded. "Julian is a little taken with Isaac. He's different from Jacob, he's more demanding, needs more interaction to keep him balanced. I'm not sure Isaac is someone Julian could be around all the time...having said that, he's changed a lot and Isaac has a lot to do with that. Julian is starting to understand him a lot more and finds him entertaining to say the least.

"Julian is not the person I would have introduced to you—yet. I think I would have left him until last." Layton sort of laughed. "But he is close to Kendal and because she was interested in Leo, he wanted to see what had interested his friend so much. Try and forget about him for a while, if you want to talk about him later, then we will, but try, for the moment, to see this world for the first time as I would have shared it with you, a little more gently." He smiled at me.

"Okay. Can I ask something though? Would you leave Isaac with Julian?"

Layton smiled again. "Without thought."

I nodded. I don't know why but it made me feel better. I looked back at the house. I was still nervous about meeting Layton's family as he put it, but if this was where Leo was going to get his fix in the next few days, then I had to learn all I could. I couldn't ease Leo's fears if I had my own, and he would feel just as nervous as me, probably more so. It made me see and understand how anxious he was about where his fix was going to come from.

Layton spoke again and took my attention from my thoughts. "I know you're worried about this, about Leo and about what's to come for you both. I brought you both here because I believe this is the right place for both of you, regardless of whether Leo becomes a slave or not. I'm not about to just drop you here and forget about you both and leave you to fend for yourselves. Whatever you and Leo decide, I will find a safe place for you both.

"Not everyone sees things the way I do, but that has never stopped me before. Isaac has taught me that just because it's different, it doesn't make it wrong, or right. It just makes it different. Isaac's pretty smart, you know." Layton smiled and I smiled back.

"Well, this is certainly different to what I'm used to." I looked down at my linens. "It's okay that I wore these right? I wasn't sure whether to wear my own clothes or not, they're a bit shabby, so I went with these."

Layton smiled again. "What you wear is unimportant, half the people in my family don't even like clothes." He laughed. "Come on, no more stalling, they'll think we're not coming." He got out of the car and I followed slowly.

As I shut the door and shivered at the cold, Layton joined me. He stood behind me and wrapped his arm around me and kissed the side of my face and I closed my eyes fleetingly and tried to draw in the warmth from the touch.

"I'll show you around first and we'll sort out where you and Leo will stay. It will give you a chance to meet some people and settle your nerves before we meet the really important people."

I looked at him questioningly. "Who's that?"

He smiled. "The slaves. They don't run or rule this world but they are the most important people in it. No one forgets that, especially here." He kissed me again and released me and took my hand. "Let's get in, it's freezing out here."

HUNTERS MOON

CHAPTER TWENTY

JOE

I followed him to a large single door, through it into a small cloak room maybe and then another door and down some steps to another single door. It took us into a basement. A huge basement, I realised as we walked around the corner.

"This is home. Well, this is where Isaac and I live and call home. I need to change into my linens. You can have a look around or follow me, the choice is yours?"

I wasn't confident enough to be away from him just yet. *Would he think it weird if I followed him?*

"Err…I'll follow you if that's okay? I'll try not to cling all day but I need to for now." I smiled at him and he smiled back before leaning in and kissing me.

"Cling for as long as you need to." I followed him, looking around.

There was a bright yellow sofa and opposite it was a metal…animal cage? Beyond that in the corner, was a mattress on the floor. All of which looked strange and not your usual run of the mill furniture.

I looked at Layton and he was looking at me already. "Ask away, Joe. This is your day to learn anything you want to know."

"I'm…I'm not sure about your furniture choices."

Layton laughed out loud. "Yes, it's a little strange. The sofa was brought here when Isaac came to stay. He was in a very bad way and needed twenty-four-hour medical attention. There were a lot of people here at that time, all coming and going and they needed somewhere to rest. The sofa was a quick addition but I've grown to love it. Before that time, it was just me down here and I was rarely here long enough to sit so I did not need one.

"Since Isaac has joined me, we seem to have many visitors so the sofa has stayed. The cage has always been part of the room. It was used in my playtimes with slaves or play partners. It helps subs find their place. Really, now, it's just Isaac's, well, I know he considers it his but he doesn't mind sharing." Breathe.

"People…They stay in there?" Shit. *Caged humans! I wasn't sure how I felt about that.*

Layton nodded. "A few hours in the cage can focus minds, it can make a feeling more intense or calm, depending on what I want. It's usually a place where they get to rest so it becomes a safe place for them. It also becomes a restraint, so for example if a submissive is not behaving, following instructions, they would be put in there for some time out, to refocus their minds. They are still controlled but it gives them time to think about their place while still seeing you. They are contained in a small space with no attention, except when I see fit to give it. It's a safe and secure place where they can stay and still see their Dominant, so they still feel safe and also a place where they learn to deal with their needs.

"Isaac likes the cage most times and will sometimes take himself there if he feels a little insecure with his surroundings. It is also a place I put him if he feels a little lost and needs reminding of his place. The mattress is just somewhere more comfortable to sit with them, maybe after play, or if I feel I need to just spend some quiet time with them. If I'm training them then I would get them to sleep there. This place is geared for the submissive mind. No frilly decorations or furniture that can distract them from their purpose, which is, of course, to serve me."

"Will you put Leo in the cage?" Shit. *Say no. Please say no, I'm not ready.*

Layton sighed. "Possibly, it depends on where his mind takes him when he's needy. It's more a place to close down their thoughts, their space becomes just that of the cage, it makes their thoughts more manageable. The first time in there can be a little scary for them, it's like being restrained mentally rather than physically but they soon quickly understand that no harm comes to them. It's a good way of teaching them good behaviour, teaching them that you control them, it makes them feel safer if they know that, know their boundaries.

"I'm not going to put him in there as soon as he gets here, Joe. The cage, as you put it, is part of the furniture and though he will probably ignore it at first, he will want to know about it, as you do. He just won't ask so blatantly as you did. I want to help Leo understand his need, to be able to deal with it, to find a place where he can deal with it with your help, and mine for now. Finding that place for him will very much depend on him. If the cage turns out to be too restrictive for him then we will find something else, another place. We control it, but never to the point where his wellbeing is at risk of being permanently damaged.

"I have no doubt that being put in the cage will upset him at first, possibly make him angry but they are just initial reactions, you have to watch and be aware of whether those reactions are taking him in the right direction. If they continue for a length of time that I find unacceptable, then I will do something about it, try something else. The goal is to help him find a place he can live with his need, for most slaves, they find that place being completely submissive to others. Even though they still feel it, submitting their body and mind to others takes it away from them, they don't control it so they don't have to think about it so much, it allows them to still breathe.

"Of course, as the controller of them, you have a lot of responsibility. If they give you that control, you have to keep them safe and secure while they're needy and when you say, they can have it sated. If being in the cage is safer for them than being free, regardless of whether they like it or not, then I will put them in there. Once they are safe, I can then turn my attention to their emotional state and try and ease their fear. Do you follow?"

I wasn't sure. I certainly wasn't sure about putting Leo in a cage but I had to bow to Layton's knowledge of these things.

I was still looking at it when I answered him. "Maybe, I'm not sure. I want Leo to be safe. He's never needed a cage though."

"He's never had a choice in how he dealt with his need, he doesn't know any other way. He wanted it, he created enough fuss with Ginger until he got it or he served himself, cutting himself with a knife or letting the customer have him, neither of which is better or safer than the restriction of a cage."

I nodded. That was true. If I had to choose for him out of those, then I would choose the cage, even if it made him angry, he would be safe.

"Okay, yes, I understand a little more."

Layton smiled. "I want you to see that, although I like to see a submissive working hard to please me, their wellbeing is always first and foremost the most important thing, whether they like it or not. Finding their place is not about salving needs, either mine or theirs, it's about dealing with that need they have until I decide to scratch their itch. When Leo comes here tonight, I will start immediately with controlling him.

"That has to be backed up by you because you are the one that he will question. It means I may take him from you from time to time, not away as in separate you, but just take control of him from you. Ask him to sit with me, that sort of thing. You have to be sure of me, Joe, so he can feel free to be sure of me too. If he thinks you doubt me or things I ask of him, then, when it comes time to help him, he will have trust issues with me. I need to gain his trust very quickly and I need you to help me with that."

I nodded. That I did understand. "I trust you. I'm worried but I'm going to let you lead and try and follow, for Leo's sake." Layton smiled and reached out and touched my face. "You will be gentle with him though, won't you?"

Layton laughed. "I will make it as easy as I can, although I have to say, I'm sure he won't afford me the same." I smiled at him. Layton looked around the basement. "Is there anything else here that you're not sure of?"

I looked around the room. There were hooks and rings in the ceiling with rope and on the walls and the floor.

"The hooks and…things?"

"For play times, for binding or restraining the sub as I wish. It could be just their hands or I may want to see them completely restrained, it depends on what I want. Sometimes it's appealing to watch them squirm and move around, sometimes I want to see them completely immobilised and not be able to move from what I give them. Bondage can be intricate or basic, it depends on what I want to see and how experienced the sub is. Suspension bondage, where the sub is off the ground completely, is extremely mentally and physically taxing for them.

"It has to be taught slowly, their reactions gauged carefully. Once they have trust and overcome their fear of it, then many different poses can be introduced, with some more intense body contortions. I could watch a submissive in bondage for ages, it's quite beautiful to see them in such a submissive pose, waiting. It takes a lot of preparation for such a play though and it would usually mean a long play session, so the sub does have to be experienced, used to waiting patiently. Their rewards are usually good though. They get fucked and usually allowed to come depending on whether they have fulfilled my expectation." Erm… okay, breathe.

"Does Isaac play like that? I mean suspended from the floor?"

Layton nodded. "He does. He's extremely strong mentally and physically, even though to look at him, you may not think so. When Isaac is needy, it can make him pretty powerful and he can hold a pose for a long time to please me to have what he wants. Those are extreme playtimes though and there is a backwash from playing like that. It can take two to three days to recover from such play, mainly sleeping but it also takes a huge amount of love and attention to bring them back from that place that they went to mentally.

"It's not the place I would take Leo, it's not for new subs, that sort of endurance has to be learned." I nodded. He was very passionate about his life, his need and his slaves. "If I get a chance over the next few days, I will bring down a slave to show you some different bondage positions, maybe play a little. Maybe Leo would like to watch. It would be good to see his reaction to things such as being restrained, maybe some toys."

Toys. Peter had said Isaac's toy box had arrived.

"What sort of toys?"

"Well, we call everything a toy. From ropes to canes to butt plugs and dildos. There are also pegs and floggers. The list of play items is quite long and some more pleasurable than others but that's why they are fun to play with. If they want to have their hole filled with a dildo and feel that pleasure, then they have to take and endure the cane for a while. It's about them earning their pleasure but at the same time satiating their need for pain but it's all controlled depending on what the Dominant wants to see.

"A lot of what happens is mind games, telling their sub they are forbidden to come and then milking them until they lose that control or until they are begging the pleasure to stop. If the Dom wants to punish them for coming then the pleasure will continue until the sub loses control. They will then accept their punishment for coming against their Dom's wishes. It's sexual games with a means to the end, both players get their need sated."

"Just a little one-sided though?"

Layton smiled. "Well of course, the submissive cannot have any control or the relationship and play wouldn't work. Some slave trainers do give safewords but I prefer to get to know my slaves through play. This world is geared towards the safety of the slave so it's rare for them to have a safeword to keep themselves safe. If a slave has expressly asked for one though, it is written into their contract, but it would be reviewed frequently as trust is built.

"These are not games we play here, these are people who know about their needs and have decided they want to live and breathe them, not slip in and out of that place, but have it as a permanent feeling. Having a safety word kind of negates the life and feeling they are after but, as I said, it can be given." He sort of half laughed. "There's a slave owner here called Kellen, he runs a slave house with particularly sadistic clients, if it was down to me, I would give all the slaves that go there a safeword, just because of the clients and what the slaves endure…actually, his Keepers and staff too.

"For me, I prefer to watch them and bring them back from it, that way I become more empowered to them, I am the one who can stop their suffering, make it easier to bear, make it better. Leo will not be given a safeword before you ask." I bit my lip and nodded. Layton smiled. "He is well accustomed to being sneaky and getting his way, we need to take that away from him completely. He will be unsure of the new things he is given and will stop the play before he's even tasted it just because it is new and different, not because he's being pushed to his limits."

"Then how will you know his limits?"

"I'll watch him. From the moment he's here I will be watching him, getting to know his feelings on things, everything, getting to know him. Honestly, though, I don't think, seeing his back, he would recognise his limits anyway but that may be because he's only had it sated one way. Different people, places, toys cause different pain, he may have just got used to the feel of the razor and therefore it didn't ease his need, hence the reason why it was taking a lot more to make him feel fulfilled.

"It's something we will have to see when he is needy. The only one who knows what it's like, what it feels like, is Leo and he's never shared that with anyone. Now he's going to have to if he wants it gone, if he wants us to make it better. He will have to learn that he can't just have it, no matter how much fuss he makes, he has to give us something first."

"Is it going to hurt him?" I already knew the answer.

"Let's talk while I change, your time is limited, remember? Leo won't sleep forever."

I wasn't sure if it was a ploy not to answer my question but he was right, I was on a time limit. Layton moved towards a door and I looked around the basement once more before following him.

"This is mine and Isaac's room. I think it's his favourite place to be, no matter how he feels. If I allowed it, he would stay in here and never come out, it's the place he feels safest and the most secure. When he's here with me, he's different, I get to see a different side to him that no one else sees. I see happiness, you know, the one thing I said it's hard to see? I see it in Isaac when we are in here usually.

"I know you see Leo differently to others, you always have. If Leo has found someone that understands him like I understand Isaac, then I wouldn't take that from him. I didn't realise what I had with Isaac until he was gone and then it was a while before I got him back and realised my feelings were the same. It was a lot of wasted time. I regret not acting upon those feelings, not trying to understand them better but letting them simmer inside me for so long, trying to ignore them.

"Isaac and I had time to grow in our time apart, find our places. You and Leo can do the same but you get to do it together and despite what people say or believe, I know it can work. It's not going to be easy for either of you but at the end of each day, despite what you've both endured, you have each other and that is the most important thing isn't it? Sit, while I change." He gestured to the bed and I sat on the edge, turning to follow him as he went to the other side and started to undress.

"That's...deep but right, I guess. I have strong feelings for him, feelings I've never had for anyone else. I'm not sure I would be here if it wasn't for Leo, you know? That's what worries me though, seeing him suffering, I'm not sure I can watch that, feeling the way I do. I want to protect him, keep him safe. It doesn't matter how many times I tell myself he wants it, it goes against my feelings. Do you understand that?"

Layton, now naked, nodded. *Jesus, he was fucking fit.*

"I do but you have to give Leo a chance to show you what it means to him." Layton walked off and I stayed silent, not sure where he'd gone, then he returned with folded linens and started to dress.

"You mean show me what the pain means?"

Layton nodded. "Yes and show what it means to him to have you there, during and after and now, before it all becomes confusing. When his need asks, it will hurt him. Not the way you think, not the physical pain, although that does hurt." He smiled. "Leo's mental journey from independent street boy to being needy and learning that he has to be submissive to have his need sated is going to be tough on him. That will be his painful journey and that's going to be tough on you too.

"You are going to have to watch him endure all that, and then watch him have his fix, and there are times when things will not make sense or seem very right, but you need to hang in there for both of you because what Leo is enduring, it's just for a moment, when that moment passes it changes again and Leo will come back.

"That journey back from where he's been will be so much easier for him if you are there for him and you will see things differently too, him, his need, the whole suffering thing will be a little clearer. As bad as I know you will feel for him, give him a chance to show what it means to him and what you mean to him. He is stronger than he looks, even though he will have you think otherwise, you need to encourage that strength in him when the time comes, he will endure it for you, you only have to ask it of him." Layton slipped his top over his head.

"What if I'm asking for something he can't give? What if it's too much?"

"You know Leo, you love him. Those feelings will allow him to have his fix because you will want to give him what he wants, you will want to see it but it will also protect him because that is the strongest feeling you have, you told me that."

I smiled. "I did but I feel like I want to protect him now…from..."

"Us hungry junkies?"

Layton smiled at me and I smiled back. "I'm not going to be allowed to forget I said that, am I?"

Layton laughed. "It's funny, well Julian thought so. I'm not sure anyone's called him a junkie before, I find that hilarious." I laughed now with him.

He climbed on the bed, reached out, and pulled me towards him. I pushed myself back on the bed towards him. He kissed my mouth then held my face while he looked at me. "I like to see you smile but laughing is better, it sounds good."

He pulled me to him and kissed my cheek before wrapping his arms around me and pushing his legs on either side of me. I had no idea why I liked such simple gestures like this. "What do you want to do first? Have a cup of tea? Decide on where you're going to sleep? See the rest of the house? Meet some people?"

I smiled as I lay back against him. This was nice, like time out from the trauma of the last few days. "I…I'm not sure, but this is nice, this moment. I feel like I can breathe here."

Layton kissed me. "Well, that settles it then, tea and some breathing time. You fill the kettle, I will get the rest." He moved from me and I pushed myself forward to the edge of the bed again.

I waited to see where he would go and then watched in amazement as what seemed like room furniture, changed into a kitchen as sliding doors were opened and seemed to disappear into the wall. I got up and joined him and he gestured to the kettle which I picked up and filled as he gathered the rest of the stuff.

"Are you sure this isn't Isaac's favourite room just because it has a kitchen in it?" It wasn't a small one either, it was like a whole kitchen side with hob, microwave, and store cupboards.

Layton laughed. "You're probably right. He does have a food fetish." I smiled as Layton put tea bags in the cups. "Sugar?"

I nodded and then changed my mind. "Actually, no, I only have sugar because of Leo, I prefer it without."

Layton smiled. "Then no sugar. Are you missing the alley, Joe?" I half shrugged as the question took me unawares. "You can say, you were there a long time."

"I know but it seems silly to miss something that I wanted to get away from every day."

"Did you? Did you think about getting out?"

I half laughed. "Of course, everybody did. Who wants that for the rest of their lives? I never had a plan though, never thought about what I wanted. I never dreamed of anywhere like this, I never dreamed of anything really. Thinking about it, I don't think I did think about leaving every day, just now and again."

I wasn't even sure that was true either. I hadn't thought about it hardly at all, not for me. I had wished better for Leo.

The kettle boiled and Layton made the tea. "I miss...that it was simple, it was hard and cold most of the time but it was simple. I didn't have to care if I didn't want to." Layton picked up the tea and walked towards the bed, I followed him.

"But you did care, Joe, about Leo, especially about Leo, but you cared about the others too, Ginger?" He sat on the bed and held out his hand which I took and he pulled me to sit between his legs as he turned slightly sideways to allow me room.

He pulled at my leg and I bent it and he took my boot off and then did the same to the other and chucked them on the floor. I felt like a child but at the same time, it was nice to be made comfortable without the worry of whether it was right or not.

"Ginger looked after himself." He sat back pulling me with him and handed my tea to me from the side. He wrapped an arm around me and picked up his tea with his other hand.

"Yes, and when that went wrong and affected him, it affected you. You saw things, saw the consequences…you replaced his shoes."

"He needed them, he worked hard for them." I shook my head. "It was shit, every day was shit for every boy there." I smiled. "Except for Leo. I mean it was shit for him too, but he liked it. It was the safest place he'd ever had, which shows you how shit the rest of his life had been. Who rapes a fucking kid for fuck sake? Who does that? I've never known what to say to him about it and he's never mentioned it, not once in all those years. Then the other day, we were talking about sucking cocks and our first times and he spoke so matter of fact about it. Just out of the blue he said his first time had been with his stepfather.

"It made me feel sick. His first time sucking cock had been with someone who should have kept him safe. How do you live with something like that? I asked him then if he wanted to talk about it, that night but he said no, very politely, no thank you. He always says no. I'm kind of glad in a way because I still don't know what to say to him."

Layton kissed my head. "Breathe, remember. This was meant to be breathing time."

"I'm sorry, I get so angry when I think about it." I felt Layton nod behind me and I sipped my tea to try and quell the sickness I felt returning.

"That's because you care. It's a bad thing, Joe, and something Leo hasn't shared with anyone. No one knows what happened to him. There's a lot of stuff that only he knows and there'll be a reason he's not sharing. If he shares like that again with you, in a matter of fact way, then you should stay quiet and just let him see if he can get it out in his own way. How on earth did you get to the conversation of sucking cocks?"

I sort of laughed into my cup as I drank the last of my tea. "We were talking about the alley, what he missed and he said he missed watching the boys with customers. I couldn't understand it because he didn't like the customers but then he said he watched them to learn in the beginning, because he didn't know what to do, then he watched them because it was hot." I smiled. "He watched me too. He created his own sexual education. It never occurred to me that he didn't know what he was doing."

Layton put down his cup and took mine from me. He laid back and still with one arm wrapped around me he stroked his fingers through my hair with the other. I felt...content...loved? Did I even know what that felt like? These people here blurred the lines of friendships and relationships, I had no idea what I was meant to feel.

"Most boys who find themselves on the street learn from others and their customers. I expect Leo was traumatised by what happened before, that he couldn't learn anything from them, and he would never have taken the lead. He would have much preferred watching and learning that way. It would have felt safer. Considering what we believe happened from his past, he's shown amazing resilience, it's a show of his strength and your care."

I shook my head not understanding it all. "I'm not sure I had a lot to do with it, I hardly knew anything that was going on with him. The more he tells me things, the more I realise how much I didn't see. When he looks at me now...in the bathroom the other day, I saw desire in his eyes as he looked at me. I've never seen that before. He said he's been waiting for me but I've never seen that look. It makes me confused about whether it's his need or me that makes him look at me like that."

"Does it matter? If his need is asking and he's looking at you with such want, regardless of what takes him to that feeling, it's you he's asking to appease it. I know you want more from him, you want him to say the words, declare his love for you but like you, Leo does not understand his feelings. It's a hard time for you, I understand that you are giving him everything, you are showing him your love, comfort and care and he is showing you very little in return. You have to see other things he gives you as your return for now. Like the look of desire in his eyes when he looks at you. Have you seen him look at anyone else like that?"

I smiled. "No, maybe...one other, I'm not sure."

Layton twisted his head to look at me. "Who?"

I looked fleetingly at him before I answered. "Isaac."

Layton laughed a little. "Ahh. That's because they shared something new. You have to try and ignore his feelings for other subs, they have this silent bond between them. It's not something I fully understand but I'm trying to learn from Isaac. Jacob and Isaac desire each other and yet have never shared anything very much. Even Isaac has trouble explaining it, he just knows that he wants Jacob and he knows the feeling is the same for Jacob.

"I thought it was just about the need to come but yet when I allowed him to have some time with Elan, one of my slaves, it seemed it wasn't about that at all. They touched and sucked and pleasured each other and then it all seemed to slow down and they seemed just caught up in touching each other, sharing something deeper than an orgasm maybe. As I said, I'm still learning but I know that it's different for Isaac with different subs. That connection that Isaac and Leo have is just that, it's like a book club, they want to visit it but they don't want to stay there."

I laughed. "Book club?"

He smiled "You know, a place where people share the same interests and understand each other, beyond that, they are not people they want to stay with. The submissive bond thing is a little deeper than that but Isaac never wants to stay there, he just wants to feel that understanding for a while and then returns. I'm sure Leo is just feeling that when he looks at Isaac.

"You have to remember though, you said yourself, that Leo wants more, Isaac showed him something different, something more. He obviously liked it so he is going to want to do it again. It doesn't mean he has to do it again with Isaac." Layton looked at me and smiled.

I leaned into him and he kissed me and held me tighter. Things felt so clear when I was with him, I felt so sure. When I was away from him, I had so many doubts.

"Do you ever doubt things? You always seem so sure."

Layton smiled and stroked my hair again. "I'm sure of my feelings for Isaac. Doubt comes from a lack of understanding mostly. I don't doubt what I feel for Isaac or what I want from him. If I don't understand something then I try and learn by watching it and feeling it. You will have lots of doubts, Joe, everything is so new to you. It's the same for Leo. As you learn about his need and him, things will become clearer, for both of you. You need to hold onto the things you are clear about, your feelings for him, your knowledge that he needs you. Just those two things can guide you both for now until the other things become clearer, like his feelings for you."

"What if he doesn't feel the same about me?"

"I don't believe that is the case and I don't believe you do either, or you would have gotten in the car when you had the option to leave. You made a choice then based on your feelings and knowledge of Leo. Those feelings and that knowledge are still there, you just have to keep hold of them through these confusing times. Leo is going to rely on those feelings you have because he doesn't understand his own. He will be looking to you to keep him safe through his confusion so don't doubt them." I nodded.

Yes, I was sure that I loved Leo, that these feelings were love. They were the reason I was here now because I loved him, I wanted to do whatever I could to give him peace and make him happy.

"Okay, I think I'm all breathed out now. Can I see where Leo and I will sleep?"

Layton smiled and kissed my head. "Of course but anytime you need to do this today, have a little time out, have questions, you just need to say. There is a lot to take in, I understand that." I nodded. "Come on then, I have a few options for you to choose from." I moved from the bed and Layton followed.

He walked back through to the basement and stopped. "I know it doesn't look much but, there is the mattress over there. You probably won't choose it now but maybe when Leo becomes a little consumed with his need, it will be easier. This place is basic and simple and not so confusing for them, they don't have to worry about their surroundings."

I nodded. "That's fine, we'll sleep there."

Layton sniggered a little. "You haven't seen the other options yet. I have two more to show you, more private for you both."

I smiled a little. "Okay, but really, that mattress is more than Leo and I are used to."

Layton nodded. "I know which is why it might be somewhere that's easier on him as the days draw closer to when he needs to be sated, but you will need somewhere before then and somewhere you can have some time with him after."

I nodded. "Of course, after. I'm struggling to see beyond what I know is coming."

Layton laughed a little. "I promise there will be an after, Joe. The after bit, your care of him, will be very important to him. Your acceptance of what he endured, the things he did, they will all be very unsure to him. He may be angry or upset, those are all natural feelings but things he has never had to share before.

"Then after a time he will be a little high from his play, it will make him feel powerful and strong but he will still be healing so you need to allow those feelings in him but restrain them at the same time. His body will be tired and exhausted, his mind exhilarated. They usually sleep a lot but have waking times with high emotions. It is all natural and you just need to be there to comfort him while they run their course. I will be here if you need me, and at some point, I will come back and make friends with him again. As I am to be the Dominant giver, I need to show him that he pleased me and that I also give other things, not just pain. This healing time is best done in a private, quiet room."

I nodded, which probably made me seem agreeable to it all but, I just didn't know enough to do anything else. "It sounds intense, how did he go through that on his own? After Ginger?"

Layton shook his head. "Who knows. He may try and deal with it on his own like he's always done, so we may see. Your job is to keep your connection with him so he can see there is another way, a better way, an easier way for him to deal with it, with you."

I nodded again. Okay, so Leo needed a place to heal. "Okay, show me the other options then."

Layton smiled and took my hand. He walked me around the basement through some pillars and turned on some lights that lit up a huge room. I stood with my mouth open which made Layton laugh and took my attention. "Erm, wow."

"Come on, it's down the other end." I followed, stopping momentarily to look up at the windowed ceiling among the pillars, then looked around before looking back at Layton. He was waiting patiently, watching me.

"Is this the turret bit I could see from outside?"

Layton nodded. "Yes, it's the only bit of the basement that can be seen outside. It's my favourite place to play with experienced slaves, it makes them feel like they are on show and I can adjust the lighting to make their space bigger or smaller depending on their concentration and emotional state. A newer slave would be a little overwhelmed, so I usually stick to the basement. I can also do some extreme bondage here, in the centre of the pillars, it looks amazingly beautiful."

I tried to visualise it but fell a little short of beautiful, which must have shown in my face because when I looked back at Layton he was laughing a little. I smiled at him. "Come on."

He took my hand again and walked me down the room. I let him lead me while I looked at the array of equipment in the room. Some of it didn't look...friendly. I dragged back on his hand and came to a stop.

"Hang on." He looked at me. "This..." I gestured to the room and the stuff in it. "... It's, I'm guessing, for play times?"

He smiled and nodded. "Yes, bigger toys. If it worries you, I can curtain it off, so it's not so on show."

"I'm not sure what Leo would think of them. Do you think it would worry him?"

Layton smiled. "There's only one way to know the answer to that."

"And if the reaction is not good?"

"Then you deal with it, with him. You can't keep things from him because you don't know what he will feel about them. Don't you want to know what his reaction would be to seeing them? It's about learning about him, what makes him curious, what makes him hot, what makes him worry. You will never know unless you see it, allow him to show you. Doing things like this, seeing things for the first time, is a good bonding exercise for you both.

"He gets to explore his new world with you and know that when something makes him feel bad, you are there to share that feeling with him, move him from it or continue the unsure feelings until you have seen enough to understand where his mind is. He learns to trust you. If you say this is going to hurt, then he may well accept that and still want it to see what it feels like. If you say this will cause him no harm, then he will be more ready to accept being restrained for it."

"That's the problem, I have no idea what half of this stuff is used for, I can guess at some of it."

Layton smiled. "Maybe I will teach you both then."

I smiled at him as he gestured that we should move on. We walked to the end of the room and there was a large double bed and a small basic kitchen. I looked around the room and then back to the bed. There was too much in this place for even me to settle here.

"The mattress on the floor is looking more appealing. This feels a little…out of it, like a different place. I don't mean to be ungrateful."

Layton smiled. "You're not ungrateful, it was a choice. I think the playroom has put you off." I smiled. It had a little. "Right, well that leaves upstairs. We'll look at the room and then I'll show you my office and meet Bea."

"She makes the food? Kendal told me, I think that's what she said she did."

Layton nodded. "She does. She oversees all the cooking and cleaning of the house, with the help of Hazel and the Keepers."

"They clean?"

"Well, they are all responsible for their own slave's rooms and they like to help Bea out with other stuff, it keeps them busy if their slaves are on visits close by. They come back here to wait and Bea keeps them busy if she sees that they need it. It's an anxious time for the Keepers when their slaves are away from them."

"Aren't they used to it?"

"They are, but they still worry for them. They know what they are enduring, and they are not there with them, it's a testing time for both slave and Keeper. You will have more questions about the slaves and Keepers after you've met them. The Keepers may be able to answer your questions and give you more understanding. Come on, let's go look at this other place."

We walked back towards the basement's main room and then walked towards a door.

Layton stopped and looked at me. "This is going up to the main part of the house where the slaves live, so try not to be surprised if you see any. Some may be on a viewing day, so their doors will be open and they will be exactly as it says, on view for clients to see before they buy. If you have questions that may upset them or make them unsure, then please ask quietly or wait." I nodded.

I followed Layton through the door and up some stairs and through another door that took us into a corridor. He locked the door behind us. "I don't have my door locked usually but Orion is always coming down uninvited and it's not safe for him when I'm not there."

"Is he allowed to just walk around?"

Layton smiled. "No, but Orion makes his own rules for now, while he's still training. He always manages to give his Keeper the slip when the moment takes him so it's becoming a regular thing. Orion is different from the sort of slaves I keep here generally and he already has a place ready at a different house when he has learnt some manners, but for now, he stays here while he's training. Half the time he does it just for the punishment he knows he will get, which is throwing his need out a little. His Keeper is working very hard though to correct his behaviour. We may see him later, I will find out what mood he's in. This way." I followed him to the right, down the corridor to the end and the very last door. "This is it."

I looked at the corridor and then back to him. "A room with the slaves?"

"It doesn't mean anything, Joe, it's just a room. If you don't like it then it's the mattress in the basement or we'll try something else. The choice is yours."

I nodded and entered the room with him. It was sparse of furniture, a double bed in one corner and a few cupboards on the other side. There was a kettle and cups and a first aid box sitting on them. On the floor next to the bed was a black box, like a small trunk.

What took my attention though was the window. It was in the slanted ceiling and I could see the sky. I looked at Layton and he smiled at me before looking up at it himself. "Mm, I know, it was kind of made for him, wasn't it? We don't use these end rooms for the slaves, they are better without having the window to the world but I think Leo would like it. There is nowhere for him to sit outside here really, but he can still sit under the stars without leaving his room. What do you think?"

Leo would love it, the night sky over his comfy, warm bed.

"It's kind of perfect."

Layton grinned. "Well, I never thought of it. I was telling Bea about Leo and she came up with the idea. I'm two doors down if you need me and you are in the main house so it's completely safe. I'll get Bea to sort out bed sheets and clothes for you both and get one of the Keepers to bring a fridge in for you."

"It's okay, I don't want to cause a fuss or make trouble for anyone. The room is fine as it is."

Layton laughed. "You and Leo are my guests. I hardly think a fridge is making a fuss. Is there anything else you think Leo would like?" I shook my head. Layton moved across the room to an archway in the far corner. "Through here is the toilet and shower, there's no bath I'm afraid."

I smiled. "I don't think Leo is too fussed about having baths, they take too much time."

Layton smiled. "Well, everything you need for cleansing is there..."

"Cleansing?"

"Yes, cleaning his hole. There's a separate pipe... have you ever been cleansed?"

I grimaced at him. "Err…Kind of, we had that pipe thing that Ginger set up, it was cold water though and too big to...get up there so it was more about good aim. When Kendal asked me to clean for my medical, I just did the same with the shower. I don't think Leo will understand."

Layton nodded. "Okay, well that's something you and I will do today and then you can show him. Cleansing is very important for their wellbeing. They are cleansed before every visit, every viewing day, and anytime there is a possibility of any play. It's not healthy for them to do it every day but they are also checked every day by their Keepers."

"Their hole is checked?"

Layton smiled and nodded. "Their bodies are what we prize, so we have to take great care of them. A hole that is sore or damaged will cause them great pain, if they were then sent on a visit without it being noticed, it could cause serious repercussions. Slaves are taught to accept and deal with their pain, so they will not always be aware or share their discomfort. No slave here goes on a visit if they are in any discomfort or healing, whether it's minor or not. Their wellbeing always comes first, before anyone's needs or desires and before money. My slaves trust me to look after them, take care of them and see things that they might not be aware of.

"All the slaves are used to being checked every day, it's part of their daily routine to have their bodies touched. It helps the bond between slave and Keeper too. A Keeper who knows their slave well will be able to run their hand over their body and detect things like a pulled muscle or a bruise that may not be visible. They are checked after every visit too so that any medical attention can be given if needed. You should get Leo into a routine of being checked every day. Although he doesn't play with clients, it is not a bad thing for him to get used to. If you ever need to check him after play, he will not think anything of it, if it is something you and he do regularly." I nodded.

That made sense. I knew Leo didn't always tell me when he was hurt. Kendal had said his hole was sore and he never mentioned it, or the cut on his toe that she found.

Layton continued. "The slaves have poses they take for checking but it doesn't need to be that formal. Rubbing his feet, for instance, will allow you to see if his nails need cutting or if his toes and feet are sore from play. They never or rarely wear shoes so their feet always need attention. Checking is about their whole body, not just their holes and cocks. Learning about their bodies helps you understand them."

Cleaning Leo's back, I had learnt which of his marks were still sore to touch and which ones didn't bother him now. It also had become easier to check it and clean it, without him fussing about it.

"And the slaves accept being cleansed too?"

Layton nodded "Yes, some like it more than others. It's a strange feeling having your hole filled with water but they get used to it and usually, they know it means that a play is imminent and they always want that. Slaves like attention and as long as that attention is a positive thing, you can more or less get them to do anything for you, even if it's not to their liking. They will want the attention that comes from doing it."

"I think you may have to help me with cleansing Leo, teach me how to move him forward when he's unsure. Him and water don't go well together."

Layton laughed a little. "Of course I'll help you. Now, are you sure about this room?"

I looked back up at the window. "I don't think the room will matter so much. This was definitely made for him. We won't disturb anyone though will we?"

Layton shook his head. "No, not at all. Your neighbour is Orion and he can be quite noisy when he wants to be. He may disturb you, you have to tell me if that's the case."

I shook my head. "Leo is missing the street sounds, he says it's too quiet. I think hearing other sounds will soothe him a little."

"Good, well that's settled then. Let's go and see my office, then meet a few people." Layton turned and walked out the door and I followed, taking another look around the room before I left. I hoped Leo liked his room.

HUNTERS MOON

CHAPTER TWENTY-ONE

JOE

I followed Layton around the house as he told me about each room. He knew whose room was whose even though all the doors were closed. It was obvious he took great care and interest in his slaves. The house felt very calm, which surprised me. I thought having so many people in one place would be busy and chaotic, especially as they all had needs and…these cravings. As we walked down a corridor there was an open door up ahead. Layton stopped and looked at me.

"This is Finn's room. His door is open which means he is on a viewing day. Would you like to view him?"

I looked at Layton, unsure. "What does that mean? What do I do?"

Layton smiled. "Well, he is on show basically for clients to come and meet him and view his body. Each slave is matched to clients very carefully, depending on their needs...what they want from their slave when they play. Once a client list has been set up, they are invited to view the slave to see if they are to their liking and suited for them. Some just come and look, some want to touch. If they like him, they will book their visit with the Keeper.

"What you want to do when you see him, is entirely up to you. You can walk around and look at him, you can touch and talk but he's forbidden to answer unless requested to by his Keeper. Finn is still learning what it is to be a slave but he knows the rules, he knows what is acceptable behaviour."

I was eager to see my first slave but I wasn't sure. It seemed a bit like a...human shopping market, looking at someone.

"I want to but I feel bad looking at someone, another human, like a bit of...meat. It feels like a bit of a...cattle market? I'm sorry if that is offensive to you or them but it's what it feels like."

Layton frowned. "I'm not offended but please do not refer to them as cattle, especially in earshot of them. This is business and yes, what we are doing is showing them off. These are beautiful people who, for whatever reason, find it impossible to live in the vanilla world. Here they have a place where they can fulfil their needs openly but that place has to be earned. It's a circle of needs where each person, the slave and the client, each get what they want.

"The viewing day is just another one of the steps in place to make sure that the slave goes to a client who wants them, who's suited to them, and that their needs are similar. It would be no good if a client wanted some toned, muscle built body, and they got a small built slave. Viewing days are worrying for the slave but they are given to them as a task for that day.

"They are restrained in a pose which allows clients to see their full body and they may touch and look as the client wishes. The client has a code of conduct they must abide by. If the Keeper is not happy with the way the client makes the slave feel, then they will have their doubts about letting their slave go with that client. If, as you say, the client treats the slave 'like meat', then there would have to be some discussion about whether the slave should go with that client. The slave has no say in where they go, they are governed by their Keeper, trusting them to send them to clients that will take care of their need but also keep them safe.

"If the slave wants to have their fix, then they must submit their body on viewing day to be...viewed. They want things and the clients want things, the viewing day is to make sure that everyone is happy. If the slave misbehaves, then they will be punished. They have to learn that their need is satiated by the client and if they want to play, they have to earn the clients attention." I stood silently. I got it, I did, I understood, but it still felt uncomfortable.

"Maybe I shouldn't see him. I don't want to make him feel uneasy."

Layton smiled again. "I wouldn't let you for one and knowing you, Joe, I know you wouldn't do that. Now I'm eager to show you, it's not as you think. Come and watch him while I see him and if you still feel uncomfortable we can talk about it more?"

I took a deep breath. I was here to learn, for Leo's sake. I couldn't pick and choose what I learnt because I found it not to my liking. This wasn't about me.

I nodded. "Okay."

Layton smiled and pulled me to him and kissed me on the side of my face. "I won't abandon you, Joe, I'm with you. I know some of this is hard to take in but this is why I wanted this time with you. I want to change your feelings about what we do here and then you can decide if your thoughts on it change." I nodded again. "Good, come on. Finn knows me but he will still seem to you like he's worried a little. There are rules he must follow like, he's never allowed to look clients or Dominants in the eyes unless requested to do so, he must not speak unless requested, even if he is asked a question, he must wait for permission to answer."

I smiled. "Then why ask a question?" Seemed harsh to me.

Layton smiled. "It's about control. They have none and they must always be aware of that. It's annoying to be asked a question and not be able to answer it verbally. They have to learn to show their answers in other ways. You will see what I mean."

He stood behind me, wrapped his arms around me, and walked me forward to the open door. My stomach lurched and I thought it was just nerves but then I realised, I did feel a little excited at seeing my first slave.

It kind of threw me a little and I looked up at Layton unsure of my own feelings. He kissed the side of my face. "I have you, Joe, breathe."

As we got to the doorway, I could see into the room and saw there were already people, clients there. Layton stopped and whispered. "We will have to wait our turn but we can watch. The guy standing to the side is Finn's Keeper, Rae." As he said that, Rae looked fleetingly at Layton and gave him a nod.

He seemed to be standing to attention, off to the side of what I now noticed, was a hanging naked body. The slave, Finn, was restrained by his wrists from the ceiling, pulling his body taut. He could just about stand on the balls of his feet to keep himself balanced. He had leather restraints around his ankles too although he wasn't restrained by them, only to each other. There were two clients in the room, a man and a woman, they were obviously together, a couple maybe or...just shopping together. I had to stop an hysterical smile from that thought. They kissed each other and then both reached out and touched the hanging slave.

Finn jolted at their touch and his Keeper said something that I couldn't quite hear but I watched Finn take a breath. I wanted to watch everything, Finn, his Keeper and the clients, that seemed so taken with what they saw. I watched while they ran their hands over his body, not at all how you would treat a piece of meat, more like you would treat something fragile, something precious.

The woman stroked her hand over his bowed head and kissed him, then continued to stroke his face while she looked at his Keeper and spoke. "He's very beautiful, Rae, I want him." She looked at her male partner. "I want to play with him."

The man smiled at her and then looked at Rae. "You've been hiding him from us, Rae. Is there a reason why we've not been invited before to view him?"

Rae smiled back. "No, no reason. Finn is still training, still new. I always had you in mind for him but I wanted to make sure he could fulfil your needs."

The woman spoke again. "I'll look after him."

Rae smiled at her politely. "Of course, Tessa, the issue is having two Dominants, it will be new to him but I think Finn is ready to please you both."

The man nodded. "We would want to keep him a few days, obviously his needs will be catered for, food and rest. Is he passive? Both me and my wife like to give."

Rae nodded. "Yes, that wouldn't be an issue. I would like to discuss the time with you further, maybe a shorter visit to start, until he becomes accustomed to you?" The man looked unsure but the woman was clearly taken with Finn.

She looked at her partner. "Please?" She may have been Dominant as regards Finn but she was controlled by her husband.

The man looked at Rae. "Okay, I'm willing to discuss." Rae nodded his approval.

The woman smiled at her husband and then turned her attention back to Finn. She swept her hands up his body and his arms that were stretched above him. She put her face close to his. "Would you like to come and play, Finn? You're so very beautiful, I want to play."

As Layton had said, Finn didn't answer but I noticed that the woman's touch was making him breathe quickly and his cock twitched to show his interest.

The woman stroked her hand down his body and ghosted over his cock excitedly. "Mm, you do want to play with me." The woman looked at her husband and smiled and he smiled back. He was more controlled in his feelings but it was clear he was also excited at the prospect of playing with Finn and pleasing his wife. He held out his hand to his wife who immediately went to his side.

"Excellent. I will call later to discuss the day and times?"

Rae nodded. "He will not come with any restrictions of play but I must remind you that he is still training. Please take that into account when making your decisions and plans." The man nodded his understanding. "If you would just give me a minute, I will escort you back to your car." The man smiled and nodded, turned with his wife and walked towards us. Layton, who was still holding me, stepped us back to allow them to leave the room.

The man smiled at Layton as he joined us. "Hello, Layton."

Layton nodded in greeting. "Mark, Tessa." He moved slightly from me and kissed the woman, Tessa, on the cheek. He smiled at her. "I take it you like Finn then?"

The woman smiled at him and nodded. I was still watching in the room. I could just about see Finn and watched as Rae joined him and kissed him. He spoke to him but I couldn't hear what he said, then kissed him again before joining us in the hallway.

I looked back at the couple and the woman was looking at me so I smiled politely as Layton finished a conversation he was having with the man. "Finn will work hard for you but you need to be patient with him to start. He becomes unsure sometimes with new requests but with a little praise and persuasion, he will give you what you want. I'm sure you will become one of his returning clients."

Mark smiled at his wife. "I hope so too. He seems to have agreed with my wife."

Tessa smiled her agreement. "I love him, Layton, he's sweet."

Layton smiled at her. "Good, I'm glad you like him. I trust you to look after him while he's in your care."

"You know, I will." Layton smiled at her. Mark looked at Rae and Rae took that as his cue that they were ready to leave.

He looked at Layton. "I'll just be a moment." Rae looked at me and smiled and then looked back at Layton. "He's being exceptionally well behaved, you can go in and watch him. He hates being left alone while he's on view." Layton smiled and nodded. Rae led the way down the corridor and the couple followed, saying their goodbyes to Layton. I watched them leave and then looked at Layton.

He smiled back at me. "The Roberts, an amazingly nice couple."

"They have a..." I wanted to say strange but changed it. "...different relationship."

Layton sort of laughed, noting the change. "They do. Mark is the Dominant of their relationship, but he adores his wife. He likes to watch her play with others and tends to give in to her wants. Tessa is submissive to her husband but Dominant with the slaves they play with. Having the slave allows her to give in to her Dominant feelings without interrupting the relationship and place she holds with her husband. Mark gets to play with both as he wishes. They have been together a while so it works.

"They have been clients here for a while but Finn is new to them. Tessa is extremely loving when she plays so Finn will not find having two Dominants to please, too confusing. Let's go and see Finn."

Before I had a chance to worry, Layton propelled me into the room, still keeping his hold on me. My eyes were glued to the naked body on show in the room. It took my breath for a moment, and I settled it as Layton spoke to him.

"Hello, Finn. We've just come to watch you so breathe nice and easy. This is Joe, a friend of mine. He wants to look at you for a while." I could see the small, agitated movements that I often saw in Leo. Layton spoke again. "Rae will return in a moment when he has seen your new clients out. Did you like the new Mistress?" Finn's head was still bowed but he nodded. He adjusted the weight on his toes, moving slightly. "Settle now. Look at me."

Finn lifted his face and moaned out a little on a breath. He pulled his wrist in his binds, his arms were obviously paining him, aching.

Layton spoke again, answering a question that I hadn't heard asked. "I know, Finn, but you are still on view. This is not new to you, I have seen you hold this pose for longer." Finn looked at me. It was easy to see he was not happy about my presence in his room and Layton gave him a word of warning. "Finn!" Finn dropped his face from me. "For that behaviour, you will hang now until I give permission for you to be released."

Finn moaned and stamped one foot against the floor making the connecting chain on his restraints clink and rattle.

Layton shook his head. "This is not acceptable behaviour, Finn, it's disrespectful to my guest."

I shook my head. I felt like I had caused his unsettled state. "It doesn't matter."

Layton frowned at me. "No, it really does. He is attention-seeking."

Rae returned to the room and walked up to Layton and kissed him. Again Finn stamped one of his feet against the floor as Layton introduced me. "This is Joe."

Rae smiled at me, leaned forward and kissed me on the cheek. "Hello, Joe." He looked back at Layton. "He's being rude isn't he?"

Layton nodded. "He is. He has made Joe feel uncomfortable and clearly shown him he is not welcome."

Rae shook his head. "He has been so good today, I'm sorry, Joe."

I shook my head again. "No really, I'm a stranger to him...it's...it's fine."

Rae smiled. "You are and that is very understanding of you but Finn knows better than to disrespect anyone, least of all a guest that Layton brings." Rae looked at Layton. "I think maybe he's a little jealous."

Layton smiled. "He's not making me look good though. This is Joe's first look at one of my slaves."

Rae smiled. "Oh, Finn." They both seemed to be taking this all in stride and quite light-heartedly. Rae looked at me. "He is usually very well behaved, Joe, but he has been on view for a good part of today. I arranged more viewings than normal for him but he knew this, we spoke about it yesterday. Usually, when Layton comes to visit he's on his best behaviour but I think your presence has thrown him a little, he likes Layton's undivided attention." Rae looked at Layton. "Have you administered his punishment?"

Layton shook his head. "No, I told him he was to hang for longer but I think we should make him a little more uncomfortable and stop the rest of his viewings for today. We cannot have him being rude to the clients. Does he have many more?"

Rae shook his head. "No, just one, I will call them and postpone the viewing." Rae shook his head. "It was all going so well. What would you like to see?" Layton looked at Finn, who, since Rae's arrival, had again been on his best behaviour. He hadn't made a sound or movement.

He looked back at me. "I think Joe should be the one to give the punishment, it will teach Finn to be very careful in the future about who he decides to disrespect." I shook my head and Layton smiled and leaned in and kissed me. "Don't panic, I shall give it on your behalf."

I felt little relief at that. Not only had I caused his strop, but I was also now going to be the cause of his punishment. I felt bad. I looked at Rae. "I'm so sorry."

Rae smiled at me. "Don't be, he's not sorry. He demanded attention and now he's going to get it." He looked at Layton. "He's all yours."

Layton spoke to me. "Stay here, try and look unhappy." Layton left me.

His request wasn't hard to do. I was a little pissed...with him. Rae smiled at me before turning and following Layton to stand in front of Finn.

Layton stood and watched him for a moment. "Well, Finn, you seem to have got yourself into some trouble. My guest is not happy and requests that you are punished for your disrespect." Layton looked at Rae. "A spreader bar please and the cane." Rae nodded and left them.

Layton stroked his hand down Finn's body. "I know you know better than to behave in such a manner, Finn, but Joe does not. Now Joe wants to see that you are sorry for your behaviour. He has stopped the rest of your viewings for today, he's concerned that you cannot be trusted to fulfil your duties as a slave." Finn moved uneasily again. Layton's words were making him agitated. "He's requested that you are punished to show your apology. Do you understand? Speak your answer."

Without looking up Finn answered. "Yes, Sir. I'm sorry for being disrespectful, Sir."

Layton reached out and tipped his face to look at him. "Very nice apology, Finn, but you earn your forgiveness for your rudeness first and then maybe Joe will accept your apology."

"Yes, Sir." Rae returned with a wooden bar and a cane. Layton took the cane and bar and showed them to him.

"You will hang as I requested until I feel you have learnt your lesson and as a reminder of my own displeasure, your hanging pose will be made more uncomfortable." He gave the spreader bars to Rae who then bent and started to attach them to Finn's ankle restraints. Layton showed Finn the cane, which I could tell worried him. "When you have suffered for me and pleased me, you will then receive Joe's punishment of the cane. How many strikes do you think it will take to pay for your rudeness today, Finn?"

I was thrown by the question. I thought this was about giving him what Layton wanted, now it seemed he could choose his punishment? I watched as Finn struggled to answer, as his legs were drawn widely apart by Rae, as he connected the wooden bar between his feet.

"If you cannot decide then I will ask Joe."

"Six, Sir." The answer was given in panic.

Layton turned and looked at me. "Six?" I wasn't sure what to say. Did Layton want more? Less? "Is six sufficient, Joe?"

He wanted me to answer? I had expected Finn to say one or none but he had chosen six. I nodded my agreement feeling really uncomfortable for my part in this…torture.

Layton smiled at me and turned back to Finn who was now struggling to stand. The bar had spread his feet so far that now he was standing on about three toes, the rest of his weight was on his arms and wrists.

"Open your mouth." Finn opened his mouth and Layton placed the cane across it and Finn bit down on it to hold it. It was obviously a common request as he did it without thought. "You will hold the cane until we return, it will serve as a reminder that your punishment is not over. If you drop the cane, the strikes double, do you understand?" Finn, who was clearly already suffering, nodded. "What do you say to Joe for teaching you this valuable lesson?"

Finn looked at me. "'hank 'ou, Sir." Again, not liking my part in this, I nodded at him silently.

The boy was stretched out uncomfortably tall and wide, with no room for manoeuvre to make himself more comfortable. He had to suffer his pose. Again I felt the pang of responsibility. Layton reached out his hand and stroked it over his head.

"You will not forget your place again, Finn, I'm sure. Breathe nice and slow and keep hold of the cane, Rae will stay with you while you suffer. Joe and I will return in a while to complete your punishment." Layton leaned forward and kissed his forehead. He turned and looked at Rae, then kissed him. "Watch him closely for me, message me if there's an issue, we will return in a while."

Rae nodded. "Of course." Layton looked at me and held out his hand and I joined him.

I looked at Finn concerned and Layton pulled me from the room and shut the door. I immediately took my hand from his and threw my back against the wall. I needed the support, I suddenly felt weak and a little sick. I closed my eyes and tried to ignore it.

"Fuck, Layton..."

I opened my eyes to look at him as he spoke. "I know, I've upset you, that you don't understand, Joe, but I could not let that behaviour go unpunished. He not only disrespected you but me as well. He will have to learn better manners than that if he wishes to stay in my house. If you're going to get loud then please wait until we get to my office, I do not wish him to be upset." I sort of laughed at that. Layton looked at me. "Come on, we'll have tea and talk about it." He held out his hand and I looked back at Finn's door. "Finn is safe and secure with his Keeper. Rae will make sure no harm comes to him while he suffers his punishment. He will talk to him while it hurts and empower him when he struggles. He is not alone."

I sighed and pushed myself away from the wall. Layton again offered me his hand and although I wasn't comfortable with what I had just seen him do, I needed his support while my thoughts were in turmoil. I felt sick and was already trying to figure out other options for Leo.

CHAPTER TWENTY-TWO

JOE

We walked silently to his office, which wasn't far from Finn's room. There was a desk and a sofa and I didn't notice anything beyond that as I sat down. My mind was with Finn and the extreme pose Layton had given him to endure...because of me, because my presence had upset him. I sat down and drew my leg up, putting a foot on the sofa and leaned my head against my knee, I felt sick again.

"Do you have a… bathroom please?" Layton turned from standing at his desk with concern on his face and nodded to a door behind the desk.

"Through there."

I got up and walked in and then threw myself on the floor in front of the toilet. I waited as wave after wave of sickness churned my insides until it finally made my stomach convulse and empty. I gripped the toilet as my stomach contents emptied into the bowl. What did I think I was doing here? Making things better for Leo? At this moment, it didn't feel like it. If I couldn't watch a stranger get punished then how was I ever going to be there for Leo? This was the craziest thing I had ever done, watching another naked person strung up and…punished.

I wasn't stupid, of course I'd seen some things on the streets, unbelievable things, I even had customers who liked it a little bit…kinky but that was just for kicks, just a little extra fun. The drive-by customers, they usually paid well for a little extra… stuff, a bit of rough fucking, bit of tethering with the odd necktie and maybe a bit of arse slapping, even handcuffs weren't unusual. Nothing like this. This was totally different.

I heaved over the toilet again aware that Layton had entered the room but not particularly caring as the sickness continued until I was just heaving with an empty stomach. I heard a tap running and then felt him sit next to me.

"Okay, Joe that's enough now." He wrapped his arms around me and pulled me from the bowl but I was still retching and I tried to pull away from him.

He pulled me against him and held me. "Enough, breathe, breathe, Joe." I gripped his arms with my hands as I tried to take my breaths, gasping them at first and then more settled as the sickness abated and allowed me to breathe easier.

Slowly my body gave up its fight and I leaned against Layton. He washed my face with a cool cloth and then dried it.

I sat for a moment before speaking. "I'm not…I'm not going to be able to help him, am I? Is that what you wanted me to see? To show me? Is that why you brought me here?"

"Stop, Joe. Your sickness has nothing to do with it. This is just a build-up of your nerves and anxiety and leaving Leo alone and visiting here. It will pass in a moment. This didn't go as gently as I planned but that's slaves for you, they don't always do what they're supposed to, that's what makes them interesting. We will talk about Finn in a moment, once you have had time to settle your thoughts."

"I don't think they're going to settle, they've pulled up their petticoat tails and they are running…full speed, in a different direction."

Layton stroked his hand over my hair, kissed me, and smiled. "A sense of humour is always good."

I half turned and looked at him. "It's not funny. I have visuals that aren't going away any time soon." Layton half laughed again. "You finding it amusing, is not helping."

"Okay, let me help you then. Go back to a conversation we had about Leo. Your fears are coming from your lack of understanding but there are things you know and are sure of. Talk to me, tell me about Leo." I thought about him and sighed. How did you explain Leo?

I shook my head not knowing where to start. "He…he likes the stars and the night sky, which I never understood because the night was when customers came and he didn't like them. He likes new things, like clothes, well things that are new to him, and pretty things, things that look nice, that shine…or sparkle." I sort of laughed. He wasn't like other boys. "He spent a few hours once telling me about a birthday cake he'd seen a person carrying, he just talked, I never had to say a word. He strops when things don't go his way and because he doesn't like those feelings, he tries to hide, move away from them. He daydreams a lot.

"He's not shy about his body or mine, he makes me feel comfortable about being naked with him. He has the most…softest male body, which I could look at for ages and the roundest, curviest arse, which I always want to touch when it's on show." I smiled thinking about it. "When I go quiet, he knows I'm thinking about things and it worries him sometimes. He says he doesn't like the marks on his back but I caught him trying to look at them, so I think he does…I know he does. It's just me, I make him feel unsure of them. He asked me once if holding my hand is what love felt like." I turned and looked at Layton a little. "He fell asleep before I could answer him."

Layton kissed me gently. "That's a beautiful thought and feeling for him. He must like holding your hand very much."

I nodded. "It's the one thing we did on the street. When we were alone, we held hands. We hardly kissed, which is strange but we did hold hands. I think it was like kissing to us, it meant the same." I smiled as I spoke. "It didn't have quite the same reaction though as when I did kiss him."

Layton smiled softly. "You can do this, Joe. For now, you will do it for Leo because you love him but soon, you will do it because he'll help you understand and feel the depth of love and feeling that comes from sharing these deep and intimate moments with him. The more you can share with him, the more sure and confident he'll become of his feelings."

I closed my eyes fleetingly. "I have to be stronger, don't I? I have to be stronger for him."

"For now, yes but soon you will feed off each other's strength. He just hasn't found his yet, he can't see it. He needs you to show him and then he will show you back what it means. You can empower him but you have to understand and believe he can do it, you have to want to see it. If you want him to show you what it feels like to have this need inside him, what it feels like to have it satiated, you have to ask him to show you. It does mean you will have to watch him suffer but there is more beauty in watching that suffering than there is in watching him suffer the confusion you see in him now. The more he sees that you control it, the easier it becomes on him."

"But this thing with Finn, you made him suffer, you are making him suffer and that has nothing to do with his need. I found it hard to watch."

Layton nodded. "Okay, we'll talk about Finn. Is your stomach settled now? I would prefer to move from the bathroom and sit somewhere more comfortable." The sickness had gone. I nodded and Layton kissed me before pushing me forward and getting up. He held out his hand and I took it and he pulled me up. "I made tea while you were throwing up."

I sort of smiled at him. "You weren't concerned then?"

Layton leaned forward and flushed the toilet. "Of course I was, that's why I was making tea. It's more productive than standing and watching you throw up. I came for you when your sickness was not being productive, when you were just stuck in your thoughts and... the retching."

"Err... thanks, I think?"

Layton smiled. "You're welcome. I don't like unnecessary suffering, only productive suffering." He smiled at me and I sort of laughed. He took my hand and kissed it. "There's mouthwash above the basin."

I walked over to the sink and opened the cabinet, poured some into a glass and swilled my mouth out, which helped get rid of the vile acid taste. We walked to the sofa and Layton picked up our tea and we sat together again.

He pulled me to him again and handed me my tea. "If it's not going to stay down, please warn me."

"Don't you care about anything?"

"Ow, that hurts, of course I care."

I sipped my tea and shook my head. "No, I mean, does anything bother you?"

"I'm very bothered about not seeing Isaac for the last two days."

"Well, it doesn't show."

"Well, I know Isaac is completely safe and secure with Peter. They have issues to sort out, issues that I cannot solve for them if they wish to have a relationship that will make them both happy. When Peter is happy that Isaac has found his place with him, then I will get him back, until then, Isaac's wellbeing is out of my hands. I have to be patient, Isaac can be stubborn, I know that. I will get him to make it up to me when he returns."

I looked confused at him. "Shouldn't that be the other way around? Shouldn't you make it up to him?"

Layton smiled and nodded. "Yup, and it will be like that, but I will make him think he has to make it up to me. Now he has two Dominants in his life, he will have to work hard at making us both happy. Peter's rules and mine may differ slightly, he will have to learn the difference but I can't have him coming back and feeling that his work is done. Of course, that's in theory, I may change my mind when I see him and just love him silly." I laughed a little and Layton smiled. "He'll be back when Peter says he can come back. Some things cannot be rushed with subs, it takes as long as it takes. There are other people who I can help, who need me."

"Me?"

Layton smiled. "You, Leo, my slaves, my Keepers. So, while I miss him and it hurts to not see him, I will be productive with my time."

"I'm sorry that you miss him, that it hurts but I'm glad you're here. I feel like you're my only friend, my only ally in this world. Well, you and Leo, but he's not helping much."

Layton laughed and kissed my head. "That's not true, either of them. Leo is helping, in his own way and you do have friends here. Peter and Kendal... Julian."

I huffed at him. "Now, I know you're making it up."

Layton laughed. "Believe me, Joe, you have friends you haven't met yet, most of them live here."

"Yes, well I haven't got off to a good start have I? Finn and Rae have reason now to dislike me...I kind of think that's your fault."

Layton laughed again. "Actually, it's Finn's fault and he is working very hard, as we speak, to make it up to you and me. Something was not to his liking but it is not for him to decide who comes into his room at any time, let alone when he's on view, and that is certainly not the way he should communicate his unhappiness. If you had been a client, he could have caused a great deal of upset and would have been punished more severely. He will feel differently about you when we return."

I looked at Layton a little shocked. "We have to go back?" Now *I* was being tortured.

Layton nodded and stroked my face with his fingers. "We do, to see the completion of his punishment and to let him show you he's sorry and show you his place."

"Oh dear, I'm not sure my stomach has anything left to give." I sunk against Layton dejectedly.

"If you don't go back, Joe, then Finn will be unsure of his punishment, his suffering. He's showing you his apology, he can't show you if you're not there to see it. He will want to show you, suffer the cane for you, it's a spiteful punishment but the harsher the punishment, the harsher the suffering, the quicker he is forgiven, that you get to forgive him."

I shook my head. "But, he doesn't like me."

"You have just punished him, your dominant status would have risen somewhat, while he suffered."

I shook my head again. "I don't understand, why would he like someone who makes him feel pain?"

"Because he has a desire to be in that place, to be punished for the things he does wrong, that's why he came to this world and you have shown him that you can fulfil that need when you wish. You controlled the punishment. You are my guest and just the fact that you walked into his room with me, should have immediately shown him that you were someone to be respected, now he knows. He'll be sorry and want to make it up to you. If you don't let him then he will worry about his place." God, I didn't want to cause him more distress. "We will leave him a while though and return when he is ready to show some manners. Rae will watch him."

"Won't Rae hate me for making his friend suffer?"

Layton shook his head smiling. "Rae and Finn are more than friends, they love each other. When Finn suffers, Rae sees his strength and his beauty. When someone endures such feelings and shows them to you, shares the suffering, it opens the door to a deeper relationship. Rae will encourage him to breathe in the pain, feel it, show it to him and he will praise him for his suffering. He will love him while he suffers and take care of him when the punishment is over.

"Finn wants that attention from him so, he will share his suffering with Rae, earn his comfort. If his actions went unpunished then Rae would have to spend the night trying to quieten his worry over his place. From you, he gets approval of his suffering, and acceptance of his apology and his place. From Rae, he gets love and comfort and care for his suffering.

"It's not very often that a Keeper gets to see their slave work, they usually just get the after bit, so Rae will be very keen to watch Finn, encourage him, learn from him and teach him at the same time. The cane that I made him hold in his mouth was not just to remind him of what is to come, it's a focus point for him. When the pains become too much, Rae will focus his mind on holding the cane, it keeps his thoughts busy while his body suffers."

"And asking him to choose how many strokes of the cane he gets? That's rough…I thought he would say one?"

"He wants to show he's sorry, he has said that six strikes will appease him, make his bad feeling go away. I'm sure that he would have liked only one but he wants to please you."

"So he's kind of making himself feel better too?"

Layton nodded and smiled. "Something like that. He offered six to you, you could have asked for more, you didn't, which means his offer was accepted. It means that when the punishment is over he doesn't have to worry that it wasn't enough. What did you think of his clients? Hungry junkies?"

Layton smiled while he spoke. "Well, yes but not for meat, for something beautiful, adored. Like they wanted to cherish him. Well, the woman especially."

"Yes, Tessa does have a way with them. Maybe that's what worried him. He's never been with them before, maybe two clients at once is what actually bothered him."

"Then shouldn't he have shown them and not me?"

Layton smiled. "Well, when they were here, Rae was here and he was behaving for Rae, following his wishes. They left and we entered, his feelings were maybe confused and without Rae here, he became unsettled."

"So, he can just be forgiven now?"

Layton shook his head. "Certainly not. Bad behaviour cannot be ignored, even if there was a reason. He will show his place and then Rae will talk to him about what happened. Tessa and Mark like to play together and they like to add another submissive into the mix for both their pleasure. Two Dominants can be confusing for a slave but Rae thinks Finn is experienced enough now to cope with it. Once he's spent some time with them, he'll be happier.

"Because Tessa is a submissive herself, she has a lot of understanding of their minds, it will help soothe his fears when he's with them. Mark is the overall Dominant; Finn will learn that through Tessa. It still does not excuse his behaviour. He knows me and knows that I am to be respected if he wants to have good things, good feelings given to him. He should have shared his bad feelings with Rae, not with you.

"This is not what I wanted you to see, Joe, I wanted to show you a well-behaved slave that was adored by his clients and was rewarded for his submission to them but these things happen. It's important now that Finn is put back firmly in his place and I'm sorry if that upsets you but Finn's needs must come first, I must make sure he is settled again regardless of your feelings."

I nodded. "I understand." Did I? "This is your world, your house, I'm just a visitor. Of course, you must do what you know is right, what you always do. I'm trying to understand, to learn I...just wasn't ready to be part of it yet, to have an active part. I feel like I caused this trouble and I want to put it right but I don't know what I'm doing. I don't want to make things worse for Finn or Rae...or you."

Layton kissed the side of my face. "This is not trouble, Joe. This is just everyday life with a submissive slave. They are very emotional people and their feelings are intense. Because you were the one he disrespected, I had to make you part of his lesson, his punishment. I am not expecting you to actually punish him but it must be seen to him that you want him to do this for you. I will guide you, Joe, all I ask is that you follow my lead, for Finn's sake."

I nodded and turned sideways. I had that feeling again, that need for him to hold me, to feel him close.

"So this is what it's like then? With slaves? It wasn't just me being here that caused it?"

Layton laughed a little. "Yes, this is what living with the slaves is like. It's hard work and twenty-four-seven, to keep up with their ever-changing feelings but it's also extremely rewarding. To have another show you such intense feelings, to trust you enough to share them with you when they feel so vulnerable, is not something I take lightly. To have them lay quietly with you and know that you have helped them find that peace, even if it is just for a while. Maybe, as well, to get a smile from them now and again.

"Their need is a destructive need, like any hungry junkie, they will do whatever it takes to have it sated, to have the feeling of pain and lose themselves in it. Here, we give it to them in measures that their bodies and minds can deal with and take care of their other needs, their intense need to be loved and adored and accepted for who they are."

I couldn't believe I was about to say this. "They're the lucky ones then? To be here? You found them and you save them from themselves, you save them from their need?"

Layton lifted his hand and fiddled with the front of my hair. "Initially they make that first step, they save themselves by giving themselves to us. To make that sacrifice, to give up your life to keep yourself safe, is not taken lightly here by anyone. Everyone here understands the pain and anguish of such a decision and the fear that goes with it...much like you have now. We would never forsake our side of that commitment, to always keep them safe. It is us Dominants that are the lucky ones, to find such open and beautiful people, who allow us to share our need with them."

It was so deep, so amazing that these people understood each other...at least, I hoped that's what they did and it wasn't one-sided.

"What do you think would have happened to Leo, if you and Isaac had never come by that day? We're both here because of you, and Leo is safer here, I know. I look at his back and don't know where it would have taken him if it had continued. My time in that alley was over and I was hanging on... I'm not even sure why now, but I was on borrowed time there. What would have happened to him? Ginger was losing patience with him so do you think he would have turned to the customers again?" Layton tipped his head to the side and I saw a little sadness in his eyes.

He sighed as he answered. "Leo's need is very strong, very powerful. If his back had gone untreated, it would have been severely infected within a few weeks and as that's not the sort of pain that quenches his need, he most probably would have continued to ask Ginger. If Ginger had continued, then eventually he would have been so ill, he probably wouldn't have been able to move. Would anyone have noticed if Leo was not around? I very much doubt it. Only you would have missed him…Ginger would have enjoyed his peace.

"His life could have gone several different ways but the only way he ever had a chance was with you around. I believe that still holds a little bit of truth, even here. We can salve his need, keep him safe here and love him for what he gives us, but it will never be what you give him, the peace that you give him. I doubt we would ever see his smile."

It would have killed him. Layton was right, no one, not even Ginger would have noticed if they hadn't seen Leo. He crept around the alley spying on them, he knew them, they knew nothing about him. I would have noticed…but I could easily have been gone. Layton's and Isaac's arrival had come when we were on the brink of changes that could have taken Leo's life. It didn't bear thinking about. Just Layton bringing Isaac with him had changed everything because, without him, Leo's need would still have been a secret from us all.

I had always known that Leo didn't belong there, that every day he struggled but I never stopped fighting for him. Now it was he that was fighting for me to stay with him and me that was struggling. He never gave up, as hard as he found it, as difficult as it was for him to step in front of those customers, he never stopped trying for me. Now it was time for me to prove to him that I would also never stop trying for him, no matter how hard it seemed.

If he was going to take punishment like Finn, then I was bloody sure that I was going to be right there by his side watching and sharing it with him. Thinking about it, it was no different to what I had always done. I sent him off with his customers and watched him while he suffered them and then comforted him after. Maybe I did have some sadistic need because I didn't remember ever feeling sorry for him, merely willing him to get through it.

"Have I made you sad, Joe?"

I came back from my thoughts and looked at Layton. "No, not really, because it didn't happen, did it? I have a chance here to make Leo's life more...peaceful. I think I can do it, I mean I think that's what I've been trying to do the last four years, only I didn't know how to.

"I watched him with customers, he was sort of suffering then but I watched him. I never once felt sorry for him, I mean I felt for him because I knew he didn't like it but I didn't show him pity. Sometimes, I think he wanted to like it but he couldn't because his fear wouldn't let him. I just have to think street...but a little bigger. Everything here is a hundred times more magnified but I think the basis of what Leo and I were doing was the same. I just have to understand that that also means emotions are also more intense too." I looked at Layton unsure. "Am I talking rubbish? Am I thinking too much again?"

Layton grinned at me a little excitedly. "I think your thoughts are a little hectic, but you are so on the right lines. Tell me something? Was Leo aware that you watched him?"

I shook my head. "No, I don't think so. I didn't want to disturb him, having gotten him there with the customer. I used to go to him after. Why?"

He scrunched his face a little thinking. "I wonder if the fear would have dissipated some, if he knew you were watching? He probably wouldn't have worried so much. He may have even tried harder to please you. We can test these things when he's here."

I looked at Layton. I had never met anyone like him. Whether he knew it or not, he had saved Leo and me from a path or paths that didn't bear thinking about. Well, him and Isaac. I knew he was trying so hard for us.

"I'm not sure where Leo and I are heading, what our future holds but I know you've made it different, better different. I don't understand what that better different is yet, but I'm going to try hard to. I'm not going to throw up anymore." I smiled at him. "Well, that's one of the things I'm going to try hard not to do."

Layton laughed and kissed me. "I like you, Joe, you make me smile."

I frowned at him. "Does that mean you're laughing at me?"

Layton laughed a little more. "No, it means I like your company very much." There was a knock at the door and I went to move away from him but he grabbed me back. "Where are you going?"

"Someone's here, so I thought I would sit sensibly, not be so... clingy."

Layton smiled. "I like clingy. Sit. Stay." I wasn't about to argue. "Come in." He wrapped his arms around me and kissed me again as the door to his office opened and an older lady walked in carrying a tray. "Ah, Bea. I was just about to call you."

"I don't need a phone call to know where you are and what you're up to when you're here. Word spreads like wildfire. Hello, Joe."

I smiled at her. She was Bea, the lady who made nice dinners and looked after the house, so I wasn't surprised she knew who I was. "I thought you might need a cup of tea and some sandwiches to settle the nerves a little. The house is very annoyed with Finn for giving you such a terrible welcome."

Now, I was surprised that she knew so much about what had just happened in Finn's room. She had put the tray on the desk and was moving a small table towards us.

She looked at Layton. "I have messages for you from about every Keeper."

Layton smiled and looked at me. "Word spreads quickly here, I'm not sure how but it does."

I looked at Bea. "I don't want anyone to be angry with him. Can you tell them, please? I don't want him to have to make it up to everyone, I would feel awful."

Bea picked up the tray and put it on the small table as Layton spoke, smiling at Bea as he did so. "Joe is a little unsure of Finn's apology to him. It's the first time he's witnessed a submissive being punished."

Bea took our empty cups from us and put them on the tray and handed us fresh ones. More tea!

"Thank you."

Bea smiled at me as Layton spoke to her. "Sit with us, Bea. Share the messages, although I'm sure they all say the same thing."

Bea smiled amused and sat down patting my hand to quell my worry. "Don't you worry about Finn. It's not the first time he's misbehaved and I'm sure it won't be the last. A little uncomfortable for you though, I'm sure. I made plain cheese and plain ham as I didn't know what you liked, you'll have to let me know. Most people like at least one of those."

I shook my head. "No, that's fine, thank you, I'll have one in a while...maybe." I wasn't sure if I could manage to eat yet or if it would stay in my stomach.

Bea looked concerned and then looked at Layton. "Not quite going as planned then?"

Layton smiled and shrugged. "It is as it is. Joe's doing okay. I'll make sure he has something to eat before we head back for Leo."

Bea smiled and looked at me. "Did you like the room? Will it be suitable for him? When Layton told me about Leo's like of the stars, I thought of it straight away. On a clear night, the moon lights up the whole room. There are blinds, mind, if you want to shut it out. I and the rest of the house are eager to meet him, don't let them bother you though. Keep your door shut if you don't want company and no one will bother you."

I smiled at her again. "Thank you, Bea, for the room. It's perfect. I'm sure Leo will like it."

Bea smiled at Layton smugly. "See, I told you it would be better than that cold basement bed you were going to give him." She looked back at me. "I'll get it ready for you, warm it up and get one of the boys to put you a fridge in. I'll fill it with fruit and bits but if there's something Leo and you like, just let me know. Does he like food?"

I smiled and nodded and Layton spoke. "He's like a mini Isaac, just quieter. Kendal says he woofs his food down so quickly that she's not sure he even tastes it."

Bea laughed and I felt like I had to explain, what seemed like, Leo's bad manners. "I will teach him..." I looked to Layton. "I will teach him to appreciate it more, it's just that he's been hungry for four years and if Leo didn't eat his food quickly, the other boys took it from him if they got the chance, if Ginger and I weren't around. I will teach him some better manners."

Layton smiled softly and shook his head. "It's not bad manners, Joe, we understand that. He's doing what he's always had to do, he's trying to look after himself, survive. The concept of food being there when he gets hungry is new to him. He's in a strange place and is still unsure when his next lot of food will come so he's just making the most of it when it does. No one is judging him, or you. The fact that he eats is always a good sign, a sign that at that moment, his thoughts are of hunger, which means no thoughts are overriding that basic need."

I smiled at a thought. "He stole Isaac's tea at the breakfast table, I'm sure that's bad."

Layton laughed a little. "For Isaac, I'm sure. What did Isaac do?"

"He was a little put out but he asked for another tea for Leo so he could have his back."

Layton laughed again. "Bless my Baby Boy, looking out for the newbie. Leo's understanding will come when he realises that hunger is not something he has to suffer here. There will be times when food will not be given and at first, that will be because you say, but he will soon realise that there are other reasons. No food is given directly before play so as not to encourage any sickness during their physical and mental exertion. There are also times when eating will not be important to Leo, when other things are on his mind. We do not offer food during these times so as not to add more upset and confusion, usually just water. Food is always offered as soon as possible after play though."

"You mean when he's needy? Is it a bad sign if he doesn't eat something that is given to him?" Kendal had given him biscuits and he hadn't eaten them.

"Not bad, but it's information. When he's needy he will not want food and so it is not offered. When he's needy, the not eating is understandable so no, it's not bad but if he doesn't eat when you believe things are okay with him, then it usually means that something is not right. It may be a thought that he's stuck in or it may be that he's sick. They just need to be watched closely and something usually comes to light, a reason."

"Kendal gave him biscuits and he didn't eat them. I think he thought she was trying to bribe him to look at his back."

Layton nodded and smiled at Bea. "He's a clever one, Bea. Kendal bribed him once with a lolly, back on the street, to look at his back as it was urgent. It wasn't pleasant for him." Bea shook her head. She was not happy about that. "The pain he remembered overrode the want of the biscuits."

Bea spoke to me. "We never use food to control or bribe the slaves here, Joe. Food is a basic need and does not get earned, it is given freely." Bea scowled at Layton. "Layton makes up his own rules for Isaac though, I know."

Layton laughed. "Sometimes it's easier, Bea, just to move him on from something. You know that Isaac sometimes struggles to put anything beyond the importance of food, even me."

Bea smiled. "Aw you know that's not true, you're soft on him sometimes. When is my baby coming back anyway? I miss him. He says nice things to me, appreciates me."

Layton laughed again. "He butters you up, so you'll always feed him. He's with Peter, learning his place. We can't have him back until Peter is happy with him. He's stubborn, you know that. I'm sure he will be testing his boundaries often, testing Peter."

Bea smiled. "Well, as long as he's feeding him. Let me know as soon as he's on his way back, I'll make him something nice." It was obvious that it was Bea that was soft with Isaac. I liked listening to them talk about Isaac though, it felt normal. "Right, I must get on and ready your room... Oh, the messages." She smiled at Layton. "Word got around about Finn's behaviour and so the general message is that all the Keepers would like you to take Joe to visit them."

Layton smiled and shook his head. "Tell them, thank you, but our time is running short, we can't possibly see them all."

Bea smiled. "I already told them that, told them to be patient." She looked at me. "Your visit has created a stir, Joe."

"Really? I'm sorry." I looked at Layton. "I'm sorry, maybe Leo shouldn't come then, maybe there is somewhere else we can go?"

Layton laughed a little. "And disappoint them?"

I was confused. So far, I had upset one slave and made extra work for his Keeper...and thrown up in Layton's toilet, not to mention, turning down Bea's food.

Bea took my hand and held it in both of hers. "You're a sweet boy, Joe. You have a big heart and you are most definitely a welcome addition to this house. I will have your room ready and waiting for you and Leo, along with something nice in the fridge for him, to help soothe him a little. Now, give me a hug." Layton grabbed the cup from my hand just in time, as Bea pulled me into her body and hugged me tightly. She kissed my face. "Listen to Layton, he'll guide you right, Joe."

I nodded against her, a little overwhelmed with her open friendliness. She got up and looked at Layton. "Leave the cups on the tray, I'll collect them in a while. I'll leave dinner until you and Joe have done your visits, you're still visiting Elan and Sim, aren't you?"

Layton smiled warmly at her. "Yes, maybe Orion. Has he been behaving today?"

Bea smiled. "Well, he went on a walkabout earlier but he ended up in Kye's room. Harris kept hold of him until Michael got there. As far as I know, he's been quiet since then. Are you going to intervene? It's becoming a regular thing."

Layton smiled and handed back my tea. "Nope. For one he has to learn Michael's way, Michael is no soft touch, I'm sure they will come to an understanding when Orion's ready. And for two, I'm interested to see how far Orion is prepared to go from his Keeper. He's doing something, trying to understand something, work something out, gain something. I'm not sure what it is.

"I know he doesn't want to go back to the street so I'm not too worried about his safety and everybody is aware now of Orion's little walkabouts. Until I work out what it is he's doing, or until it becomes a danger, I'll let it continue. I hope he doesn't stop doing it without me finding out though, that will be so annoying."

He laughed a little as Bea shook her head. "Always wanting to know more."

Layton grinned. "They have reasons for doing things, you know I won't be happy until I find out what it is. It's intriguing, interesting, keeps me on my toes."

"Yes and everyone else in the house. Next time I'm shopping, I'll buy you a puzzle book, I heard they give similar feelings." Layton laughed and Bea left the office.

I was still sat, holding my tea and Layton took it from me and turned my face to look at him. "You okay?" I nodded and Layton smiled and leaned forward and kissed my forehead.

"I don't want to create a stir or trouble for you. If you're having second thoughts, then I understand."

Layton looked amused. "Do I look like I'm having second thoughts?" He didn't. He looked relaxed and happy.

"No, but now you know I'm upsetting the house, maybe you should be?"

Layton smiled. "Oh, Joe. The stir that Bea was referring to is not trouble or upset, it's excitement. I spoke to all of my Keepers about you and Leo. I wanted to know their views and feelings surrounding you and Leo. After hearing your story, the first thing they all said was to bring you both here. And before you think it, it's not out of pity for you and Leo. They want to meet you and Leo, you especially. They want to meet the person who kept Leo safe and secure without help for so long and who is now willing to learn with him about his need. They think you're amazing, Joe, because you know very little and yet you have opened your mind to Leo, you are willingly taking on something that comes so naturally to them. They were born with their need, you are making yours out of your love for Leo.

"It's never heard of here, which is why Julian has a hard time with it. I, and they, believe that it's possible because of your past. I saw it in you, way before I even knew about Leo, now all that has changed is the stakes are a little higher and you have to learn a little faster. The stir in the house is about you actually coming here and with Leo too. I wasn't sure that you would, it was always your choice and I knew, to you, this was not going to be the easiest option, for you anyway." I felt overwhelmed again and could feel the tears starting to prickle at my eyes.

"You can change your mind. If you are not happy about coming here with Leo, if you believe you can't do this, then we can come up with something else to help him but I wanted you to see how it is. You've seen Finn and how quickly their thoughts and feelings can change, I was going to show you that bit later but slaves don't always want to do things my way." He smiled at me.

"They could all react like Finn?"

Layton nodded. "They could, but I'm sure I have at least one I can rely on to show you something different. One of my slaves that is more settled with his place and very smitten with his Keeper and rarely misbehaves, well, not what I call misbehaving anyway."

I felt a smile break my mood a little. "Do you make up your own rules?"

Layton smiled back. "A little...maybe but it keeps them on their toes. Elan is probably the most balanced slave I have. I want you to meet him. He's Isaac's friend, the one Isaac likes to spend time with and Anton, his Keeper, is very knowledgeable. You can ask him anything and he'll be honest with you."

I smiled at Layton. "It's okay, I'm still with you, still coming. I'm excited to meet him too and a little nervous after Finn but mostly excited. I just got a bit overwhelmed. Bea was so nice and then people wanting to meet me. I'm not that amazing, can you tell them, I don't want them to be disappointed." Layton held my face and wiped my eyes with his thumbs, nothing escaped his notice, not even unshed tears.

"You are amazing, Joe, and already very loved. No one is going to be disappointed. Everyone here understands how hard this is for you and they certainly understand Leo. They know that at this moment you are not getting any love returned from him and that is hard to work, they've all been in that place at one time or another with their submissive slaves when they were new. All the Keepers here are with you, not pitying you but ready to help you if you need it." He leaned forward and kissed my lips. "Do you feel up to meeting him now?"

I half smiled and nodded. "What about Finn? He's still being punished, I feel bad."

Layton smiled. "Would you like to finish Finn's punishment?"

I wasn't sure what was the right thing to do. "What would you do?"

"I would let him suffer a little longer but if you are worried then we can shorten it?"

I wasn't here to change things, I was here to learn.

I shook my head. "No, don't change what you would normally do, he'll know, won't he? He'll be bothered if he knows it's different and that will be because of me."

"He will know something is different, yes, if he is not made to earn his apology and his place again, but Rae can settle him. I don't want you to worry."

I shook my head. "If you're not worried then I'm not...after Elan maybe? Will that be enough?"

Layton smiled. "Yes, after our visit to Elan will be plenty of time for him to see the error of his ways."

"Okay. Let's go then, I'm ready." I sounded positive and keen…didn't I?

Layton laughed a little and kissed me again. "Your thoughts are in chaos, I know, but you are still very beautiful. I can see why Leo loves you."

I smiled at him unsure. I wish I could see it too but it was a nice thought.

CHAPTER TWENTY-THREE

JOE

Elan's room wasn't far but then again, I wasn't completely sure of that. The corridors all seemed the same. We passed a few doors, all closed but it was still quiet and calm.

"Are there slaves behind all these doors?"

Layton nodded. "Yes. If the door is closed then the slave is in their room. They will be healing or just having, what we call, quiet time with their Keepers. A wide open door means that the slave is on a viewing day, if it's just ajar then the Keeper and slave are open to visitors. That's a new one I'm trialling at the moment. Most slave houses keep their slaves separate all the time, it's easier on their minds but here I allow the Keepers and slaves to visit each other if the slave is in a balanced state of mind and calm.

"It's rare but there are moments when, for a short time, they can emotionally manage being beyond their room with their Keeper. It's something new still, here, something I introduced recently and there are only a few slaves who can manage it at the moment. It's something Isaac taught me really, he showed me that the slaves can have friends, well contact with others, and it does not screw with their mind and emotions too much.

"If the room is empty, if the slave is on a visit, then the door will just be open a little, to show Bea and Hazel it's vacant and they can clean the room and change bedsheets. Mainly Hazel, because Bea usually knows who's where and what's going on.

"All the Keepers have phones, for emergencies and to keep in touch with each other, clients, and me, and there is an emergency walkie talkie in every room. Any business is conducted when they are away from their slave or when their slave is sleeping. It lessens any trauma caused by conversations overheard by them. Bea has a phone too but she rarely uses it, she doesn't like them very much."

"Bea's nice, I liked her. She does a lot of work here doesn't she?"

Layton nodded. "Bea, or Beatrice as she likes to tell me, is one of my most cherished friends. She says it like it is, to me and everybody else. She was a slave, a long time ago, when there were no rules and boundaries for anyone and no Keepers. She understands the slaves very well, she has been there, felt those intense emotions that they have trouble understanding and dealing with. She dealt with hers alone for a very long time. A few years back, I found Hazel, kind of like I found you and brought her here to be a slave but it didn't work for her. Bea took her under her wing and looked after her and she's been helping Bea ever since.

"The place is a lot to look after, the meals alone take some organising, who's here, who's not, who's eating, who's not. Bea manages it so well but she's not getting any younger and will soon need to slow down some. Very soon I will have to think about finding someone else to help her but she won't like it so I'm putting it off as long as I can. It's not like I can advertise the job with the vanillas." He smiled at me and I returned it. "Between her and Hazel and the help of the Keepers, we have a very organised house. It means my time is freed up to concentrate on other things. This is Elan's room." He gestured to a closed door.

"It's closed?"

Layton smiled. "It is, but as the owner of this house and the slaves, I have special rights. I am free to enter any room...and bring whoever I wish."

I looked unsure at the door. I couldn't work out if my heart was missing beats or my stomach was somersaulting, my earlier eagerness had left me.

"I'm worried." My first meeting hadn't gone so well. What if the slaves just didn't like me? "If this doesn't go well, can you not make me punish him, can you just do it?"

Layton smiled. "I know you're worried but I can't promise that. I have to do what is right for the slave, Joe. If it helps, I can't remember the last time Elan was punished for bad behaviour." No, It didn't, not really.

"Maybe they just don't like me, in which case, I don't think that matters."

"Joe, of course, they like you. I would never have brought you here if you were not... likeable. Finn will show you differently when we go back to see him, I promise. Elan will be a little unsure of your arrival, but he'll also be curious about you. Anton and I will encourage him to make friends. He is very sure of Anton, trusts him, if Anton says you are a friend he will feel more sure of you. You may hear Elan call Anton Daddy, their relationship is transitioning into something new and sometimes Elan's feelings, feelings of being vulnerable and little, will just happen naturally. It's not always though, but just in case you hear it."

I frowned at him. "Daddy?" Layton nodded as I ran what that meant through my head. "Like...it's his dad?" Layton nodded again. "Err... is that not... a bit twisted?"

Layton sort of huffed as he smiled. "Not here. Here we accept peoples' deeper feelings and wants. Anton and Elan have been together a while now and Elan loves the whole being protected and loved feeling. Being a little, as in taking a place as an adult little/young person, means he can immerse himself into the vulnerable, needy feeling he craves. Who better to look after him than his 'Daddy'? This is not a role he plays, it's a feeling that draws him. It's not anything that anyone asked him to do, it's something he's slipped, is slipping into, naturally. It's beautiful when someone can just follow their feelings and find their place, somewhere where they feel they fit and gain comfort from it."

Whoa, whoa, whoa…this was…this…was crazy. Okay, yeah, I'd had a few kinky meets where the customer had asked me to call them daddy… it was just dirty talk to me and of course, I had. The paying customer got what they wanted, within limits, and a bit of dirty talk was nothing. This though, this was…

"Do they…have sex?"

Layton nodded. "Yes, Elan wants to be completely loved by his Daddy, sometimes that means being put in his place and sometimes that means feeling completely loved and cared for. As I said, they are transitioning and the places are not set yet, Anton believes Elan has him on trial for the position." He laughed a little.

"But he's still a slave?"

Layton nodded. "Yes, very much so, although his client list is small and unique to him. He has regulars he plays with who understand him and his needs very well. He's extremely emotional when he plays so he cries a lot, it doesn't mean he's not wanting or liking the play, it's just how he manages it. It wasn't a surprise when he started slipping into his little place with Anton. Being a little will open up his client register more if he takes the place permanently and even more so if he slips into being a baby but there is no pressure on him. We just allow him to slip into his feelings and make him feel very safe while he's there."

I took a deep breath. "I'm...I'm struggling to understand, to accept...this."

Layton nodded. "Okay, let's just meet him and see if it helps? Every time you meet them, regardless of what happens, it's a learning experience for you. I won't let it go bad for you or them." No, he wouldn't and he was right, I needed all the contact learning I could get.

"Can you stay close? I don't want to do anything wrong." He smiled and held out his hand which I took and he pulled me into his body and kissed me.

"Nothing you do will be wrong. Be guided by what you would do with Leo and let Elan guide you. He will be clearer than Leo in what he wants from you."

"Will he be allowed to speak?"

Layton nodded. "Yes but he may not, not if he's unsure, he'll be worried like you. Like Leo he can be non-verbal sometimes, so will communicate in a different way."

"Can I talk to him?"

Layton smiled. "Of course but keep it simple, you don't want him to think you're here to confuse his thoughts." I nodded and took a deep breath to settle my nerves. Layton smiled. "Elan has been healing these last few days so he's not needy and should be quite settled." Layton held me tight and knocked gently and opened the door. The room was very similar to Finn's and the room that Leo and I were to have. There was a bed on the left, which a man sat on. He was extremely well built, very muscled like a bodybuilder, just his size drew my attention from the rest of the room. It fleetingly worried me that he was the slave and then I realised he wore black linen trousers.

He turned and smiled. "You've come just in time, Elan is a little bored. Hello, Joe."

I smiled and Layton kissed the side of my head as he stood behind me. "Hello."

Layton spoke to Anton. "He's feeling better then?"

Anton smiled. "Yes, definitely. I believe you have averted a trauma of some sort. Take a space for a moment, worry will bring him out."

Layton guided me back and sat on the floor with me between his legs as I frantically searched the room for him. The room wasn't that big but I kept scanning it in case I was missing him somewhere.

Anton spoke, bringing my attention back to him. He was looking at the floor while he spoke which threw me even more. "Elan, Layton has come to see you, he has brought a friend."

There was silence and no movement from anywhere in the room and then I heard a soft moan coming from what I thought was Anton.

When Anton spoke again, I realised where Elan was. "Hush now, you know I'm here, you can see my feet, come on." He hung his hand down between his legs and a small hand with a leather restraint around its wrist, came from under the bed and grasped it.

I looked at Layton who was smiling, he looked at me as I whispered. "Is this...usual?" I was careful to keep my low.

Layton shook his head. "Not that I know. Anton?" Anton looked up. "We're intrigued, is there a reason Elan is...under the bed?"

Anton smiled. "I'm not quite sure but I think it has something to do with him wanting the night to come. He got restless when sleep wouldn't take him and he wanted the light off. He's not tired, he's been sleeping on and off for the last few days, he's just at that in-between stage, feeling better but not needy yet. It makes him restless because he's got nothing to focus on. Now he has. Give him a moment and curiosity will get the better of him."

I looked from Anton to Layton again. He was smiling, not worried by this turn of events so I decided not to worry either and looked back to the bed. I was eager to see Elan, so far I could see his hand and the outline of him and then as I watched, a blond slim boy moved quickly out and sat on his knees at Anton's feet.

Against Anton, Elan looked even smaller but the more I looked at him, the more I could see his adult male curves, similar to Leo's, svelte but definitely a man's. He was naked apart from the black leather restraints on his wrists and ankles, the same restraints that Finn had.

I looked at Layton as Elan held his hands up to Anton. "What's he doing?"

Layton looked from them to me. "He's worried about you in his room, so he's asking Anton to keep him safe. It's a natural course of events and once Anton has reassured him, he will settle." Layton looked at Anton as he stroked his hand over Elan's blond hair. "Did you speak to him about our visit?"

Anton pulled Elan onto his lap and nodded to Layton. "I did and he was interested but I think the waiting got to him a little, as it does. I'll put his linens on so he doesn't feel so vulnerable. He knows you would never do anything to harm him so he'll move on in a moment. He was excited to see you, you know he likes to have time with you." Layton nodded.

Anton helped Elan into his linen trousers and I saw the first signs of Elan's interest in me. He craned his neck to see around Anton's arm to look at me and I smiled at him.

It was like Leo had done in the kitchen with Julian. He had held on to me tightly but strained to see him, curious about the new face. Once dressed, Anton wrapped his arms around him and he almost disappeared in Anton's body. They looked like an odd pairing but I could see the trust that Elan had in Anton and knew that that was not an easy thing to gain. Leo trusted no one except me and it had taken four years to get that.

I could also see that Anton cared about Elan, his gentle soft touches went against my initial view of how they were treated. It was clear that they loved each other and were both sure of each other.

Anton spoke again. "I heard, Joe, that Finn was a little rude to you. You shouldn't take it badly, viewing days are still a little worrying for him, especially when his Keeper is out of sight. It was just an off moment."

I nodded. "He's apologising."

Anton smiled. "Good. Rae will get him back in his place, he's usually pretty good." Elan slipped between Anton's legs to the floor and Anton smiled at me. "He wants to come over and see you and Layton, he's just a little unsure."

"I can come over to him."

Anton shook his head. "No that's okay, it's his place to come to you and ask."

Layton tapped my arm and I looked at him. "Sit beside me." I moved over his leg and sat with my legs crossed, copying Layton. He looked at Elan and held out his hand.

"Hello, beautiful Elan, come and show me your wounds."

I looked at Elan's body and couldn't see anything, nothing that stood out like Leo's anyway. Elan was looking at me and kept his eyes on me, unsure, as he made his way across the floor to Layton. He took Layton's hand and sat in front of him, offering him his other hand.

Layton smiled and took it and kissed it and then welcomed him onto his lap. He kissed his face and held him, stroking him. "You're quite safe, Elan, Joe is a friend. You are free to speak."

Elan sat up and touched his fingers to Layton's lip ring, in a gentle movement and Layton kissed his fingers which amused Elan and I saw a small smile take his lips. Elan moved and sat with his legs on either side of Layton and stuck his chest out. It was strange but then I realised he was drawing attention to what I could now see were sore, red nipples. He also had marks on his back, small pink welts that disappeared into the back of his linens.

Layton reached out and touched his nipples, squeezing them gently between his fingers. Elan sucked his breath in and looked at Layton. "Oh, that's beautiful, Elan, good boy for showing me."

"I cried a little bit when they pulled them off and touched them."

Layton leaned forward and kissed each nipple. "It's okay to cry, it's good to show your feelings when things feel difficult."

"I don't like crying but I can't stop it."

"What feels worse, Elan, the play or the crying?"

"I like playing, I don't like crying."

Layton smiled and stroked his fingers over his face. "But you clients, your friends like to see you cry, it's very beautiful to watch. When you cry they know that you are trying hard to please them and you know I like that and Anton likes that." Elan nodded.

Anton moved off the bed and came and sat beside me on the floor. He kissed the side of my face in greeting. Kisses all around. When you came from a place where you were greeted with silence or usually aggression, it was a bit off-putting.

"I wanted to say hello properly." He smiled at me and I half smiled back. "Elan struggles with his emotions when he plays. It is not the play that upsets him, it's the way his body and mind react to it that he finds difficult. It makes him appealing to clients. Crying is a deep emotion and not many slaves show their suffering in such a manner."

"Is it hard for you to see him like that?"

Anton shook his head. "I have to see his strength in what he's doing, giving, rather than the upset that is caused by his emotions. Elan suffers beautifully with the punishment he is given, but that is not what upsets him. He dislikes crying in front of people but that is how he shows his suffering so that feeling is encouraged. If the punishment stopped when he shed his first tear then his need would go unsated and he would be needy very quickly. It would not give him days like this where he has some peace and can come back and feel part of the world. Once he's back with me, he settles very quickly."

Elan looked at Anton and sort of smiled. "I like being with you."

I smiled at him as did Anton. "You do and I like being with you."

Elan smiled and looked back at Layton. "Is Isaac coming today? I've been waiting."

Layton smiled at him. "Isaac is with his Keeper, learning to behave. When he comes back I will bring him to spend some time with you." It must have pleased him because he stroked Layton's face.

I looked at Anton. "What are the wrist and ankle bands for? Restraint? Finn had them too."

Anton nodded. "All slaves are given them by their Keepers. It is their first...gift, like showing them they belong to you. The restraints are used for restraining them, not just when they behave badly or are punished, but it's used for comfort too. It quietens their movements and in turn, their thoughts, it makes their world a little smaller so they can cope with it better. Elan, show Joe your wrist so he can look at your restraint."

Elan looked at me unsure and leaned into Layton to have his feelings salved. He hid his hands between him and Layton, which made me smile. Layton unwrapped his arms from around Elan and lay his palms on the floor and Elan pushed himself further into his body, burying his face into him.

"I can show you something, Elan." Elan turned his face to look at me. "Something nice, at least, Leo thinks so."

He looked at me, cocking his head as he asked. "Who is Leo?" He was sweet, soft and…sweet.

"Leo is my friend, he's like you and Isaac."

"Is he a slave? Do you own him?"

Anton spoke. "Elan, it is not for you to ask so many questions."

Elan looked apologetic at Anton. "Sorry, Anton."

I looked at Layton. "I don't mind." Then looked at Anton. "Really, it's okay…if it's okay with you." Anton nodded and smiled.

I turned back to Elan. "Leo is not a slave and I don't own him but he does like to be with me, he likes this thing I do to his hand."

"What thing? I want it."

Again Anton jumped in with a warning. "Elan! That's not nice asking."

Elan glimpsed fleetingly at Anton. "Please? Please may I see? I like nice things."

I smiled at him and held out my hand. "If you show me your hand."

Elan took his hand from between him and Layton and held it out towards me. I moved to touch it and he closed his fingers and drew it back.

"You can't have it, it's mine."

I dropped my hand smiling. He was a lot like Leo. "Okay." Elan moved over Layton's leg closer to me and I ignored him and looked at Anton. "Is this a good day?"

Anton smiled. "It depends what you mean. This is Elan when he feels able to take part in the world around him, it can be entertaining, interesting, and tiring. Tomorrow or maybe later it will change and he will be less sure of his surroundings and his thoughts. I love and know all of him, see him at his worst and his best."

I frowned at him. "What's his worse?" Anton smiled and reached out and touched my split lip that was still healing.

"I'm guessing something like this? Even that is a good day, if he shows me something that feels like that, he's just being honest with me"

I nodded understanding. "Mm, I upset him. He made me feel what he was feeling. I deserved it, I forgot his feelings because I was wrapped up in my own."

"It's not just about him, Joe, it's about the both of you. It's not about putting his feelings before yours. The more you share with him, the more he'll share with you. How you share your feelings will be how he shows you his. You must be very strong to have got Leo this far without help and this is a difficult time for you both. If you need my help with anything, you just need to knock. Is this the worst Leo has ever shown you?" I nodded.

Anton smiled. "He will feel these rush of emotions that he's never felt before, anger, upset, a little of both because you have taken him from the place he was safe and he knew so well. You are unsure of where you're going and he will sense that so his world will seem a little out of control and that won't sit right with him. Don't be worried if you see a few more of them."

"Does Elan...strop?" I heard Layton laugh beside me but didn't look at him.

"Not so much now, I can usually see them coming and avert them to something more manageable. When he was learning the rules though, we had many but he's happier now, in a better place, more accepting of his wants and feelings and more secure. The bed thing was a kind of strop, he wanted the light off and I refused him. Everybody needs to vent sometimes so as long as he's not harming himself or anyone else, I try and let them run their course.

"Usually, he doesn't like the place he ends up, he doesn't like his thoughts so he will eventually come and ask for help from them. Sometimes that's talking about them, sometimes he can't put them into words and he made need comfort from them or he made need to have them taken from him. I know him quite well now so I usually know what he needs and he has learnt to trust that I take him to a better, safer and secure place, even if it seems difficult at the time."

"You mean, he doesn't like it sometimes?"

"Every feeling is a journey, like all journeys, some are easier than others. It's always nice though to reach the place that feels safe and secure, to feel like you're home."

Elan spoke, taking my attention and Anton's. "We're home, this is home. I always like being home."

I smiled at him. In some ways, he hadn't understood our conversation but he did understand his answer. Anton was important to him, Anton and this room were home, his comfort, his safe place.

Elan had moved off of Layton's leg now and was sitting between us. He moved across to Anton, who took him in his arms but he never took his eyes from me. I could see so much of Leo in Elan but Elan was more confident which was a little confusing, as it was he who was the slave. Leo the street boy, who should have been the more confident and sure of himself, was not.

Even when Elan was unsure of his surroundings and people there was a confidence about him, which I gathered came from Anton and Layton and the people around him. That confidence allowed him to go to clients and play, to share his need, something that would cause Leo a great deal of distress.

Layton put his hand to my neck and stroked his fingers over it. "He's special, isn't he?"

I nodded. He was. I could easily spend the day with him because I could see there was so much more to know about Elan than I could see here. Like Leo, he saw the world differently.

He hadn't made friends with me but he had shown me it wasn't all hanging from ceilings and getting punished, and as I thought that thought, Elan stretched one hand out across my knee. He was still sitting with Anton, still safe with his Keeper but he was asking, testing the friendship request and seeing if he could trust me.

I slid my hand over his to his restraint and was surprised at how thick and heavy it felt across his wrist. I then slid my hand back over his and tickled his palm with my fingers, gently stroking and touching.

He moved a little closer, stretching Anton's hold and then finally he offered his other hand to me, wanting the same for that palm. He left Anton completely and my heart jumped a little as I realised he was giving himself to me, trusting me, letting me have him. I knew it was a big thing, like going with a client, like Leo going with a customer and trusting that customer to look after him while he was with them. They never did, they never understood. He was watching my fingers on his palms, connecting the action to the feeling. I wanted him to look at me, I wanted to talk to him.

I put my other hand to his and stroked both his palms. "Hello, Elan. That is such a nice name."

Elan looked at me. "I don't want it to be nice, I want it to be beautiful." He looked at Anton. "It is, isn't it?"

Anton smiled and nodded. "You already know it is, Elan, I tell you every day."

Of course, constant reassurance, constantly made to feel adored and revered, treasured, like Isaac in the kitchen. Nice was not a high enough admiration for what he gave them. Like his emotions and feelings, their adoration also had to be high and intense. The more they gave, the more he gave them to have it, feel it from them. Leo liked nice things, he liked nice touches, nice words. We hadn't moved beyond nice because he found anything more hard to understand and overwhelming. I was going to have to work on that if I wanted to make him happy because I could see that Elan was happy. He wasn't laughing, and only smiling now and again, but it was clear that Anton, Layton, his room, the adoration he received made him happy.

I smiled at him. "I'm sorry, Elan, it is beautiful, sometimes I don't know the right words." I could see understanding in his eyes as he edged a little closer.

"Sometimes I don't either. Were you punished?" He took his hand from mine and touched my lip. His action kind of mimicked his Keeper's earlier but he hadn't understood.

I shook my head. I wasn't sure what to say so I tried to explain it so he would understand. "No. Leo was misbehaving. Do you know what that feels like?" He nodded and fleetingly had a look of confusion on his face and looked to Anton for reassurance.

Anton smiled at him and reached out and stroked his cheek briefly and Elan looked back at me before speaking. "It's a bad feeling inside, something quick. It doesn't give me a chance to behave even though I want to." He looked at Anton again. "You make it stop don't you?"

Anton nodded and reached out and caressed his neck. "I just make it slow down a little, so you can share it with me."

Elan nodded. "Yes, that's what you do." He looked at me. "You should make Leo's slow down. Can I see him?"

I smiled. "Leo's a little shy."

Layton spoke. "He's new, Elan, very new. He gets worried. Maybe when he's settled Anton will take you to see him."

Elan looked at me and touched my face again. His touch was so gentle, soft. "That's why he misbehaved. I did it when I was new, didn't I?" Again he looked for confirmation from Anton.

Anton nodded. "You did, a little, just while we were learning trust."

Elan stroked his fingers all around my face. "Leo and I can be friends if you and Daddy say."

Although taken aback by his use of the word Daddy in regards to Anton, I smiled. I got what he was doing, I understood. He wanted something, he wanted to see Leo and the stroking and caressing of my face was him trying to be extra nice so he could have it.

I took his hand and without thinking, I kissed it. "I will think about it."

I saw a little excitement in his eyes and he turned quickly, putting his back to me. "Do you want to see?" The offer was to see his back and I smiled at his confidence in me now.

I wasn't sure who was entertaining who but I felt pretty good that I was allowed to, not only look but touch his wounds. Having seen to Leo's back the past few days, I wasn't worried now about touching his small pink welts that were virtually healed. I rubbed my fingers gently over them, increasing the touch when I got no response. When I saw the first twitch from him, I kept my touch like that for a bit before rubbing my hands all over his back and neck.

He obviously liked it because he sank back against me and I transferred my touch to his chest and stomach. I was careful not to touch his nipples though, which I could clearly see had had their fair share of play during his time away. They were sorer than I had first thought and it showed me once again, his trust in Layton that he had allowed him to touch them. I was not offered them for touching, which I was grateful about. The back wounds I was beginning to understand, I understood how they got them.

I wasn't sure what sort of play made nipples red and swollen like his were or why he would want such play. I swept my hand over his face and his forehead brushing his short hair back over his head. He slipped down further until his head was in my lap and he lay across the floor looking up at me while I repeated the touch. He was content, which made me feel good, I had made him feel content. It was completely different to the feelings I had evoked in Finn.

I looked at Layton a little breathless and smiled. "This is better."

Layton reached out again and stroked my neck, smiling. "Elan is very clever, he knows his place very well and will stay there happily when he gets this sort of attention."

"Isn't it a bit like bribery?"

Layton half laughed. "Maybe but who is bribing who?"

I smiled and looked back at Elan. It was true. Elan had instigated this. I also knew that, if like Finn he felt unsure of his place, then no bribery would move that feeling. This was definitely about his want of it too, to be kept here, to have his control taken, to do their will. He had found people who were willing to do that for him. It made me view Leo differently. He was different but he wasn't different alone. He was part of a…secret group of people who felt and viewed the world the same as he did and who was I to say that it was wrong to feel like that? Even Elan's use of the title Daddy didn't feel so out of place coming from him. I fleetingly wondered if Leo was…little?

If I compared Elan and Leo, it was clear that Leo was not in a happy place, well, certainly not content and hadn't been for the time that I had known him. I could count on one hand the moments when he had seemed content, they were rare moments. He hadn't found anyone who could help him find his way, he had found me and we had become friends, more than friends, I had fallen in love with him. I wanted him to find peace and contentment. I wanted him to be happy.

Elan moved from me suddenly, he went to Anton and sat in his lap and snuggled against his body, whispering his need for his Daddy. Was it wrong that I found that sweet? Endearing? And also still a little twisted. I looked at Anton, concerned that I had done something wrong, but Anton shook his head.

"It's okay, Joe. He's tired, you've given him some beautiful thoughts and he can feel himself drifting with them. Elan is a very capable slave. He knows that being, feeling, submissive makes him vulnerable. He was a little bored earlier but you have filled his day. It happens when they are feeling part of the world for a while. His thoughts will soon be filled with other things. It was nice to meet you, Joe, and I know Elan thinks so too." I looked at Elan who was looking at me from the safety of his Keeper's arms.

"It was nice to meet you too, Elan."

Elan whispered. "Is Leo coming now? Can I sleep with him?"

I smiled and Layton spoke. "Leo's not here, Elan. You can stay with Anton and sleep on the bed this time okay?"

Elan nodded. "When he's not new can I sleep with him?"

Layton smiled. "Joe is going to think about it. He told you that." Elan sighed heavily and Layton smiled again. "Say goodbye to Joe now before you sleep."

Elan looked at me. "Bye, Joe. Can you talk to Leo about me? So he will know that we're friends."

I leant forward and brushed his cheek with my fingers. "I will, Elan, I will tell him how beautiful you are."

Elan smiled shyly. "You remembered." He closed his eyes. "Daddy, I like Joe."

Anton kissed him and smiled. "Good boy, nap time now I think."

Layton wrapped his arm around me and kissed me as I watched Anton and Elan's interaction. His words brought me from my thoughts. "It's time to release Finn from his punishment."

I watched as Anton got up, carrying the almost sleeping Elan, who now had his thumb in his mouth and was suckling on it. Just like a Daddy would carry a sleeping child, with his arms scooped under his legs, he took him to the bed and laid down with him. Watching their connection, their care made me breathless and hurt with the want of it for Leo, but he was so far away from having this sort of peace.

I looked at Layton. "I want Finn to find this place that Elan has."

Layton smiled. "Well, he has a slightly different relationship but he's just as beautiful and has been working on it. Shall we see if he has remembered it?"

I blew my breath out, a little nervous again. I looked over at Elan and Anton.

"Okay, I'm ready...I think." Layton kissed me before getting up and pulling me to my feet.

He walked over to them on the bed and kissed them both before taking my hand and leading me from the room.

CHAPTER TWENTY-FOUR

JOE

As he closed the door quietly behind us I turned and looked at him.

He smiled at me. "Different to how you imagined?"

I nodded. "He's happy, I can see he's happy and content. It makes me see how unhappy Leo is."

Layton nodded. "Elan is happy with his place. I don't think Leo is unhappy. He's just not content with his lot but he's not unhappy with you. I think moments with you are the times when he is happy with his…uncontent feelings."

I smiled at him. "I think you make things up to make me feel better." I shook my head. "No, he's not happy, I know that, I've known for a long time, I just wasn't sure how to put it right. I thought it was what happened, you know, back at his home. I thought he was hung up about it, which I understood, it was a big thing, a not very nice thing but now I'm not so sure. He's not over it, I know, but he's not going to get over it while he's constantly suffering this feeling of not belonging somewhere. He's missing something, he knows something's missing, something's not right and he doesn't know what it is because he's never known it and had no other options.

"I have a chance to make things so much better for him, easier, make him happy, I think. He's not going to let anyone else show him because he's learnt not to trust anyone. It's why I know he will struggle to become a slave. He's been with customers, they never looked after him, they scared him to the point of him letting them take his life. I'm not sure he'll ever be able to get over that fear and I never want to put him in a position where he's alone with a customer…client. I did enough of that in the alley."

"This is not just about Leo, Joe. You have to be happy too. Looking after Leo will be hard work without help."

I nodded and smiled at him. "Isn't that what friends are for? I can see what lies ahead. I can see that what Elan has is so far off from what Leo could even think of having and getting him there is going to mean a lot of ups and downs for both of us. My wish is for him to be like Isaac. To have the safety and security of the people around him to be himself and to know that when he needs to, he can also have the place and peace that Elan has.

"I know for that to happen, he first needs to find that confined space, where everything is taken from him, his will, so he will know that he can have that and be safe whenever he needs it, so even when he's needy and unsettled he knows he's got people around him that will protect him...not send him away to strangers. I know it's not what you do here but I know Leo and I know sending him to strangers when he feels like that will not make any sense to him. That is the time when he needs to be around people he knows and trusts. That may change but I need to stay within his limits while he learns."

Layton took my hand and walked along the corridor. "You learn quickly, Joe."

"Do I? I don't feel like I'm learning quickly enough. I don't understand it but...do you think Leo is like Elan? Do you think he wants to be a...adult child? A...little...young person?" I mean he kind of was sometimes but I thought that was just Leo, I didn't know it was a thing.

He looked back at me. "Mm, I couldn't say for sure. All I know is he's a masochistic submissive, if there are any other facets to his nature, they're not clear yet. It could be possible. It's good you're taking your lead from Leo, from your knowledge of him and until you understand more, don't try and lead anything. Are you still happy about bringing Leo here? It's going to be a confusing time for both of you."

I nodded. "Yes. He needs you, I need you, to get us started. I kind of want to give him to you but be around to learn, do you think that's possible?" Layton nodded and we stopped outside a door. "Are we here?"

Layton nodded. "Yes, this is Finn's room. When we bring Leo, he will be wide awake, having slept most of today and fear will add to that. We will spend the night soothing him and just letting him feel safe and seeing that you are not about to run off and leave him. You have to trust me, Joe. Finding his place is not an easy journey, it goes against what he's been doing for the last few years. Letting go of that independence, letting someone else have you is frightening until he learns that no harm will come to him, only good things.

"We will set some ground rules…you will before you leave his room, where he is now. Some basic things. If he wants you, if he feels overwhelmed he has to drop to his knees and hold his hands out to you in a silent request. This will give you a moment to evaluate him and the situation before taking him back. The first time he asks, you need to take him back so he can see that you take note of his request and then from then on, I only want you to take him back when you feel he's had enough, that he's overwhelmed and needs some time.

"If you think he can move through his feelings, accept them, and he's safe, then you need to ignore his request. This then shows him that you want more from him, you want to see more before you will allow him back. Do you understand?" I took a heavy breath and nodded. "When you ignore his request, I will then take him back with me. This way you get the overall control and Leo will see that and start to understand that he has to show you things, earn his time with you. You and I have to set some boundaries too. You have to tell me what is off-limits?" I looked at him, not understanding. "Leo's idea of play is very limited, he knows no pleasure with his pain, he's never had toys to play with." Layton smiled.

Oh, of course, this need was a sexual thing or supposed to be. Leo didn't know that. Well, he hadn't been shown, although he had told me that he felt things in his cock. His orgasm had always been a separate thing, never part of his play.

"What sort of boundaries?"

"Well, you have to decide whether it's acceptable for me to play with him and how far that play will go. Is it acceptable for me to pleasure him? Get him to pleasure me? Can I fuck him? It's up to you to decide what you want to see. I will abide by any boundaries you say. I am working on behalf of you, you are still the controller, you know Leo better than anyone.

"Playtime for Leo will always be about what you want, that way he always stays safe. For now, while you learn, you have an extra player in the mix, me. It doesn't take away from the play being about what you want but you have to let me know if there are boundaries. Leo has to be completely confident in what he's doing, that he's doing it for you." I wasn't sure.

Watching Leo play sexually with someone else, I wasn't sure how that would make me feel. It was something we hadn't even shared ourselves.

"You don't mind playing like that in front of me?"

Layton smiled. "If you're asking if I mind being naked and having fun, then no, I don't mind. I'm not shy." He laughed a little. "The play would be very controlled anyway, I will be concentrating mostly on Leo and you. Will I gain some pleasure from it? Of course, I always enjoy watching someone suffer and earn their pleasure, even if I am teaching."

"And that's your need?"

Layton nodded. "Yes, basically, it never leaves me. It's a little addictive but one that Dominants keep control of. Someone always has to be in control and it can't be them. You've seen where Leo's control of his need got him. Would I want to see another man suffer those wounds given by me? No, there is no fun in that. It's no fun if they never want to do it again or get so damaged that they can't come back from it. Whatever you want to see, I will abide by."

I thought about it. I couldn't decide. I had no knowledge of which to base my decision on. "Can I think about it?"

Layton smiled. "Of course but I need to know before Leo comes here later. You can tell me just before you walk in the door if you like but I need to know before we start the journey with him so I can clearly show him my expectations from the beginning." I nodded. "Now are you ready? I think Finn has suffered enough. I think it's time that he showed you some love and a proper welcome to my house." I looked at the door and nodded.

"Guide me though, okay? I'm still feeling a little shaky about this." Layton smiled, leaned over and kissed my forehead.

"I have you, Joe. When we go in, Finn will be hurting, suffering. You have to remember that he's doing that for us. It makes the pain of it feel a little different to him. We will watch him for a moment so he can show us and then we will put an end to it."

"And the caning? I don't want to do that."

Layton smiled. "Don't worry, I would not let you touch one of my slaves with a cane until you understood its feel yourself. Rae will conduct his punishment." I felt a little relief and Layton smiled and kissed me again. "Come on, you get your first look at what it means to Finn." He opened the door and guided me through in front of him as my heart thumped loudly inside me.

Finn was still hanging where we had left him, although his stance now was completely different. Layton pulled me back against him and wrapped his arms around me as I stared at Finn. He was now hanging from his wrists, with them taking most of his weight and his toes were dragging on the floor, attempting now and again to take some of the weight from his wrists. He still held the cane in his mouth and his spit drooled down his chin and down onto his body. He was breathing hard and heavily with his endurance of the enforced pose and he was looking at his Keeper, who was standing in front of him, stroking his hands over his thighs.

Finn moaned and Rae spoke to him softly. "Okay, Finn, just a little longer. Layton and Joe have come to watch your apology. You show them and they will decide when you can come down." Rae stepped to the side but he kept his hand on Finn's body, gently stroking. He looked at us. "Finn is ready to show you his place now. May I request that his punishment is given quickly and finished here where he hangs? He will not be able to hold himself for his caning in another pose."

Layton nodded. "Thank you, Rae. Let us watch him for a while."

"Yes, Sir."

Layton put his mouth to my ear and whispered. "Rae is aware that Finn's body has had enough. When a Keeper puts in a request, I always take it very seriously, they know their slave better than anyone. Usually, the slave would hold themselves for the cane, to show their willingness to please but Rae has informed us that Finn would find that difficult. If you wish, we can ignore the request and have Finn hold himself. The decision is ours, we can have whatever we want. It may seem harsh to punish him while he hangs but we would actually be making it easier for him." I stood in silence still not sure I'd moved past that an actual person was hanging in front of me. "Let's show him a little praise for what he's showing us."

Layton walked me towards Finn until we stood in front of him. Layton reached out and wiped the drool that hung from his chin. "Look at us, Finn."

Finn lifted his eyes to Layton and then looked at me. He moaned a little. "Oh, good boy, Finn, that's very beautiful. Would you like Joe to show you some mercy?" Finn didn't answer and Layton reached out and squeezed his nipple. "Finn? Pay attention. Would you like to show Joe your place now?"

Finn flinched and he nodded to me. His look was asking. I reached out and stroked his wet face and he tilted his face into my hand. Layton continued to speak. "I want to see six welts across your arse as proof of your subservience and apology for your rudeness to my guest and then you can have your release and spend some time with your Keeper."

Finn nodded again. Layton looked at Rae and nodded. Rae stepped forward and took the cane from Finn's mouth. "What do you say, Finn?"

"Thank...you...Sir."

Layton swept his hand over Finn's head. "Good boy, Finn. Now take six good ones and show Joe your apology."

"Yes, Sir." Layton nodded to Rae, who stepped behind Finn and stepped into his back and kissed him.

"Okay, beautiful boy, breathe for me." I watched Finn blow out a breath at his Keeper's request and lift his chin, readying himself for the punishment he was about to receive.

Layton wrapped his arms around me again and put his face next to mine and it took every ounce of strength and thought, for me not to grimace at what was just about to happen. Worse was, Finn looked directly at me. I found myself breathless with expectation.

"Count them out for us, Finn." Rae touched the cane against his arse and tapped it gently and then I heard the first one connect hard with his arse. I watched the pain in his eyes and it took his breath but he never took his eyes from me. "Count Finn, or we will forget."

"One, thank you, Sir, for showing me my place."

I was a little taken aback by his words and I heard Layton's breathy smile beside me. "Very nice, Finn, very good boy."

His breathing was quick as he recovered, ready for the next and as he took each one and showed me, I was transfixed to his face. I could see his pain clearly but there was also something else. After each one, he seemed to relax a little more, like a weight was being taken from him.

As he took his fifth he moaned out to me. "I'm sorry, Sir."

I was willing to forgive but Layton spoke. "No, Finn. That is not how you ask for your place or forgiveness. You show it and we will decide if you have learnt your lesson. Now you have earned another for not counting like you were asked to." I moved, uncomfortable and Layton held me tighter and kissed me. "Two more, Finn, look at me." Finn moved his eyes to Layton. "Two more and then you will have earned your release from this punishment."

Finn nodded to him, accepting his mistake. Rae stepped forward and stroked his hand over his arse, he looked at Layton. "Two more, Rae, and he will be given time to heal before his visits."

Rae nodded and stepped back. "Yes, Sir. Breathe, Finn, two more, count like you have been asked."

Again his Keeper's voice seemed to spur him on, giving him energy that his pose seemed to be sapping from him. He took the last two, counted and gave his apology and now his body was completely sapped. The last had made him completely lift his feet from the floor and now he hung exhausted. But he still looked at me and managed to speak again. "Thank you…Sir."

I wasn't sure what to do so I nodded at him as Rae released his legs from the spreader bar and then lowered him slowly to the ground on his knees. His hands were separated from each other and Rae touched his fingers and stroked them, massaging life-giving blood back into his body. Layton told me to sit down and I did, watching Finn as he worked through the pain of being released. Rae, I could see, was fussing around him checking hands and feet until Layton called his name.

"Rae." He looked up from Finn to him. "He's good?"

Rae nodded. "A little numb but he's okay."

Layton nodded. "Then leave him, his apology is to Joe."

Rae, was unsettled and swept his hand over his head and left him kneeling on the floor in front of me, as he joined Layton, who kissed him and held him. Then we all seemed to wait, just looking at him.

I turned and looked at Layton wondering if I should do or say something but he shook his head at me. "If he wants it then he has to come and ask for it."

I looked back at Finn who didn't look like he could ask for anything. His hands were shaking, his body half folded over his knees and he was still breathing heavily. Then I saw him look at Rae under his lashes. He wasn't quite as out of it as I had first thought, a little subdued but then that was to be expected after what he had just endured. I fully expected him to move quickly to Rae, as Elan had done when he'd been unsure but instead, he just sat and a moan left him.

He was hurting, his arms and legs and no doubt his arse were all paining him and he wanted his Keeper to make it better but Rae, on Layton's request, was ignoring him.

He looked at me and I wasn't sure if I should or not but I spoke. "Hello, Finn."

Speaking to him seemed to have an adverse effect and he looked away from me, then just when I thought I had made a mess of it all and upset him again, he edged towards me. I took this as his asking, my sign that I was now free to touch him without him fretting and trying to run off. It made sense to me now. If he asked then he wouldn't worry so much, whereas if I had just tried to touch him and make him better it would have overwhelmed him, as Julian had done to Leo in the kitchen.

I reached out my hand to him. "It's okay." He slowly and shakily lifted his hand and then dropped it again. His shoulders must have been hurting him, he had been up there a few hours that I knew of and also before I had arrived earlier.

I thought about Elan and couldn't imagine him hanging for so long but I was starting to realise these slaves, subs, were very strong, regardless of their stature and size. Finn was quite well built, toned but Elan and Leo were not, their strength came from their minds. Leo was looked upon in the alley as being one of the weaker boys but I knew that every day had been hard for him. It was just a different fight from what the other boys had.

Thinking about Elan made me remember how intense these feelings they had were and I had to make Finn's forgiveness equally intense. A pat on the back and a hearty well done was not going to cut it. He had suffered for me and I had to show my appreciation for that and the fact that he was still suffering even though the punishment had finished.

I edged towards him. "Turn around, let me see." Slowly Finn manoeuvred himself around so his back was to me and I reached up and put my hands on his shoulders and began to rub them.

I looked at Layton for approval but he had taken Rae across the room by the door and was sitting on the floor, talking to him. They were holding hands and smiling and it reminded me of what Layton had said about his Keepers also needing to be loved.

I turned my attention back to Finn. He was sitting on his knees which made him a little higher than me, I got up on mine and moved closer to him. I rubbed his shoulders and arms and I kissed the back of his neck. "That was very beautiful, Finn, thank you. Did I frighten you when I came into your room earlier without your Keeper?" He nodded.

I wanted to say sorry but remembered what Layton had said. Only say sorry if you want them to know. I did want him to know but I didn't want him to think it was okay to react like that to me. It was all very complicated but I had to stay ahead of the game, something that wasn't happening with Leo right now.

"I liked watching you." I continued to rub his shoulders and eventually, he leaned back against me. I stroked his hair and kissed him. "I like this, this is how you should say hello, okay?"

He nodded and turned into me. "Would, Sir like to play with me again?" His request took me off guard.

He was sorry, that was clear. He had reacted to a momentary feeling of fear and it had gotten him into a heap of trouble. I was sure it was a lesson that he wouldn't forget but that was the point of it, to remind him of his place. I had to remember it was a place he had chosen to be and that he wanted to be kept in. It was the place that I was going to take Leo for a while until he understood.

Finn turned a little more into me and I understood then what he was doing. He was trying to move his weight off of his welted arse. I looked at them for a minute and then reached out and touched them gently.

They looked different to Isaac's that had been made with the whip, these seemed more intense but I wasn't sure if that's because they were fresh. They had criss crossed over his arse more on one side than the other.

"Finn?" He was listening, I could tell but I wanted to see him. "Look at me." Finn raised his face. He looked unsure and I stroked his face with my fingers. "Are your welts hurting?" He shook his head. I was a little confused. "I think you need to tell me."

"Erm..." I saw his eyes sweep to his Keeper. He wasn't sure what to say.

I smiled at him. "It's okay. You can tell me. They look beautiful…I think." I saw the semblance of a smile and I smiled back.

"I say I think when I'm not sure too." Oh. "I think they feel beautiful." I needed to backtrack quickly before he panicked, although I kind of felt like I was the only one doing that.

"Then I think we're both right."

"It only matters what you think...and Rae. I was good wasn't I?" Hadn't I said that? No, I hadn't told him.

"You were very good and you are very much forgiven." I saw his eyes sparkle. "Rae will see to your welts. I don't want you to think of me and have bad thoughts."

I felt his body shake and I thought he was worried or cold but then I realised he was holding in a laugh. I was amusing him which made me smile. They weren't completely devoid of other emotions then.

"Let me have your feet and I'll rub them for you." He laid across my lap and lifted his feet behind him and I rubbed them while looking at his welted arse.

I watched him relax and smile when I touched a sensitive part of his foot and then I rubbed his back and shoulders again once I was finished. "Does that feel better?" He nodded. He was done talking. I understood that. Leo, after a few hours of nonsensical words, often would sit quietly for hours.

I was glad I had come back now. This time with Finn had made it right for both of us and I kind of got the feeling that he understood that too. He had already picked up that my thoughts were unsure and that was something I would have to be wary of in the future. There was no room for doubt with Leo. Finn had accepted it but his Keeper was right over there. Leo had me, no one else was waiting to have him. I smiled. That wasn't true, there were lots of hungry junkies who would have him but they wouldn't know how to soothe him, even if that's what they wanted, which I doubted.

"Joe?" Oh, and there was Layton. The only person I trusted to give Leo to. I looked at him. "Rae needs to see to his wounds." I nodded.

It wasn't nearly enough time to get to know the things I needed but I had learnt a few things. Never say *I think* when you wanted them to feel something, the bottom of their feet were as sensitive as their palms and that Layton was right of course, they were all beautiful.

I also saw that as willing as Finn had been to suffer, he was just as ready to be brought back and hold no grudges against the person that had caused his suffering. I wasn't sure that Leo would feel the same way. Maybe that was something he had to learn. I looked back at Finn and stroked my hand over his head as he looked at me. I wasn't sure if we were friends but we had found a little peace. I still had the feeling that I amused him but that was okay.

I smiled at him. "I have to leave now. You can go to your Keeper."

It was the quickest I had seen Finn move and reminded me again of Elan. It was very clear when they were sure about things. Not any ache or sore arse would keep them from their trusted friend. I watched as he knelt in front of Rae and offered him his wrists, which Rae took. He bent and kissed him and whispered something to him.

Layton walked over and held out his hand. "Okay?" I half smiled and nodded as he helped me up.

Layton kissed Rae goodbye and then swept his hand over Finn's head and kissed him.

I looked at Rae. "Thank you."

Rae smiled and leaned forward and kissed me. "Thank you, Joe. I'm sorry that it was not the welcome you deserved. I hope Finn has put that right?"

I smiled and touched Finn's face, nodding. "For both of us."

"Good. You come by anytime you like and bring Leo. I would love to meet him."

I smiled. "Thank you." Offering friendship and help to a stranger was new to me.

As Layton and I left the room I looked back at them to see Rae bend and kiss Finn. It was kissing with tongues and I wished I could stay and watch them cement their friendship again after the days' trials but knew that would be imposing on their time together. Layton closed the door.

CHAPTER TWENTY-FIVE

JOE

As Layton closed the door, I took a deep clearing breath.

Layton looked at me and smiled. "Well? How did that go? What do you feel?" I leaned back against the wall, feeling emotionally exhausted.

"Relief." I smiled at him. "I think it went okay. I think he found me amusing. I wasn't sure about things and he knew it. I mean asking him to speak, is that allowed?"

Layton nodded and smiled. "You can do what you want. I saw him look for Rae once and you got him back to you so that's pretty good going considering you don't know him."

I nodded. "Yes, I made him feel unsure about his welts, then we seemed to come to an understanding about them. He wasn't put off by the fact that I had caused his suffering, he didn't hold it against me. Do they learn that?"

Layton shook his head. "There is nothing to learn for them. He caused his own punishment and suffered it for you. You rubbed his sore body and eased his aches and pains, you didn't have to do that, you did it because you wanted him to have better thoughts. When he's in the place you want him to be, he has nice things given to him, regardless of what his feelings were before. It moves him on. You are not holding his bad behaviour against him so why should he hold his punishment against you?"

I nodded. "And Rae? He gave the punishment, the cane. He looked unsure?"

"Rae was concerned for Finn, the love they share can sometimes cause a hurdle and he'd watched him hanging for a while. I took that into consideration. Getting Finn to count out his punishment was a good way of assessing his mental state. He was very clear about why he was receiving them, a little unfocused at the end as the pain seeped into his thoughts, but he worked through it. The cane was held by Rae. The punishment is given by you. You have made your peace with him and Rae will make sure that Finn knows how proud and…hot it made him feel to give it to him." Layton smiled, conveying his thoughts on where that would take them.

"Can I see Orion? I know I have to get back but just for a moment?"

Layton looked unsure for a moment. Then nodded.

"Okay…but Orion is not like Elan or Finn. He does not find his place easily or very often. I have no idea what sort of reception we will get or knowing Orion, if he's even there." Layton laughed a little and I smiled.

"Mm, I remember him, what he was like. That's partly the reason I want to see him. I want to see if he's changed."

"Orion has a need for pain, he's a masochistic bottom but does not have quite the same need to be submissive to those around him. The only time he's ever quiet is when he's playing or being punished, it's the only time he submits willingly. I took him in because I believe he can find a place here, not one like Elan or Finn or even Isaac but a little peace of mind that he is safe.

"He is very unlike the slaves I have here and I doubt that as much as we try, we will ever change that. He knows he's better off here but he pushes the boundaries he is given to the point that makes everyone doubt if he should be here. Everyone except Michael, his Keeper, and myself...oh and Isaac, believe he belongs here. I'm not sure Isaac counts though, he thinks every street boy should come here and be loved."

He smiled, thinking. "Now and again, for a moment, Orion shows what's inside him and it's beautiful. Sometimes you have to look hard to see it. He's a boy with an insatiable need for pain and he will do things to get what he wants, he will misbehave to be punished but he also misbehaves when he wants to be loved. He seeks attention just like the other slaves, he just does it differently and as Isaac will tell you, it's not wrong, it is just different. Will he remember you, do you think?"

I nodded. "Possibly. Our paths crossed. Not often but enough for us to know each other's names. If there's an issue with me knowing him, then we can leave it?"

He shook his head. "I'm concerned about his reaction to you and yours to him but intrigued too. Your paths crossed? Is there more to that?"

I smiled. "Not really, nothing that was bonding. I think he was healing, I didn't know then, well, I didn't understand it. He hadn't moved from his sleeping place for a few days so I went to see if he was...dead. He wasn't, so I got him a tea from Manni's and sat with him a while."

Layton stared at me for a long moment as if trying to hear my thoughts. I held his gaze as if it stopped him from looking further into my head.

"Okay, let's go then." He started walking and I followed in silence. He knew there was more, I could tell.

We reached the corridor with Orion's room. I recognised the door to Layton's basement home and looked beyond towards what would soon be Leo's room. We reached the door and Layton turned and looked at me. "Ready?"

I paused for a moment. "There's more."

Layton smiled. "Mm, I gathered."

I shrugged my shoulders. "I'm not sure how I feel about it, whether it was right but he asked me, wanted it. I fucked him... I wanted it too. Leo was with Ginger and maybe...I was feeling a little jealous or something, I don't know. I did get him tea... after... and I did sit with him, while he slept. I felt bad, like I had taken advantage of him, used him. We never spoke about it and the next time I saw him, he was getting in a customer's car, he just smiled at me. It was just the one time and after that things were as usual between us, street boys living in the same space again."

I fell silent and looked at Layton, waiting for him to tell me I had taken advantage of Orion, that I had used him. I didn't know then what I knew now. I probably wouldn't have done it if I'd known he was healing, that his body was...recovering.

"Why did you ask to see him?"

I shrugged. "I... I think I just want to know he's alright, that I haven't... hurt him. I don't think I did, maybe a little... I wanted to fuck... I wanted to fuck Leo I suppose, and he was with Ginger and so I was a little..." I couldn't think of the word.

"Needy?"

Had I been? I suppose I had been... for something. I had wanted to feel something other than that bad feeling inside me.

I sighed. "Maybe... yes, for something."

"There's nothing wrong in that, Joe."

"Isn't there? I took advantage, he was... unwell."

"He wasn't unwell, he was resting. It's different. He wasn't sick. You said he wanted it. If anything, he took advantage of you to have it. I assure you, your crossing of paths has not damaged Orion." He smiled at me. "This is going to be more interesting than I first thought." With that, he turned and opened the door, then looked back at me. I hesitated a moment then walked forward and entered the room with him.

The room was empty. Layton closed the door behind us and I looked at him.

"Has he gone on walkabout?" Layton smiled and shook his head.

"No, they're in the back. Wait here." He walked towards an open door at the back and stood looking in. I did a quick sweep of the room with my eyes before looking back at Layton.

"Hey, Michael, Orion."

Another voice spoke from inside the room. "Hello, Layton. Have you come to check on the boy after this morning?"

Layton smiled and shook his head. "No. I've brought company. The boy I was telling you about, Joe?"

The man then came into view, kissing Layton and then turned and looked at me. "Hello, Joe."

"Hello."

Layton spoke again. "Is this a bad time? We don't want to intrude?"

The man smiled and shook his head. "No, no. This is just me practising my rope work, Orion's helping. It keeps him out of trouble and in one place."

Layton laughed. "Mm, I heard he gave you the slip again."

Michael smiled. "Actually, he's not even trying to be sneaky about it now. When the moment takes him, he heads out the door. I followed him this morning to see where he went. He tried your door and when he couldn't get there, he went off to Kye's room. Kye was sleeping, so no damage was done there but he just got in the room and stood and watched him. He was glad to see me when I took him back as always. It unsettles him when he does it so I'm not sure why he continues. He's been punished for leaving his room but he says he doesn't want to share. We're working on the sharing of thoughts, it's slow but I think the trust is beginning to grow. His quieter moments are growing."

Layton smiled. "Good, that's good to hear." Layton reached out and touched the side of Michael's head, tracing his fingers over a shaved line. "Isaac will be pleased to know that your feelings are too."

Michael smiled. "Where is he? I haven't seen him for ages. I wanted to show him. I know he was anxious."

Layton smiled. "He is spending some time with his Keeper. They need some bonding time. I will withhold what I know and bring him by when he returns." Michael laughed and Layton looked at me. "It seems Joe and Orion have crossed paths before, they're from the same neck of the woods. Joe was interested to see Orion. I wondered if it was a suitable time?"

Michael smiled as he threaded some rope through his hands. "I've yet to work out what is a suitable moment for anything with Orion." He turned and looked at me. "Were you friends?"

I wasn't sure how to answer that. I was thankful when Layton spoke. "They shared... a moment."

Michael nodded. He was still looking at me and I felt I needed to say something.

"I just wanted to see him, just for a moment. If it unsettles him then I will leave, immediately. I just wanted to say hello... or goodbye."

Michael sort of laughed. "Not good friends then?"

Layton laughed a little and I smiled. "It's hard to tell who's your friend and who's not on the street and I'm sure he would feel the same. It's different here, I understand that."

Michael looked at Layton.

Layton smiled and sort of shrugged. "He walks the corridor searching for people, he doesn't do anything when he gets there, but he still seeks them out. I'm intrigued to see what he does when someone visits him, someone, he knows. If he stresses out though, you have to be able to get him back. It's your call, Michael, do you think he will come to you if he's unsure?"

Michael smiled. "Well, let's test it, shall we? I'll go and get him if he doesn't." Michael looked at me. "Just give me a moment, I'll get him down. I don't want him to feel too vulnerable." I nodded and Michael went back into the other room.

I couldn't see in from where I stood but Layton could. I stepped towards him and he turned and looked at me. "I'm not going to come into the room, Joe. I want to observe, not be part of it. Michael will stay there with you if you need him. Plus, I can hold the fort at the door in case he decides to bolt." He smiled at me.

"Where's he getting him…down from?"

Layton looked into the room and smiled. "Michael is a highly trained Dominant, not just a Keeper. He has expert rope skills but those need to be practised continually by both Dominant and slave if you wish them to hang off the floor for any length of time in rope bondage. He's down now, Michael is just letting him catch his breath and rest a minute. It's extremely tiring but the sort of training Orion needs to keep him balanced."

I stepped forward again. "Can I see?" Layton nodded and I walked over to him and stood at the door. Layton wrapped his arm around me and kissed me as I looked at Orion sitting on the floor. "God…"

"Joe?" I looked fleetingly at Layton before turning back, shaking my head.

"Sorry…He looks... he looks so well."

Layton rubbed his hand over my shoulder. The boy that sat tired and exhausted on the floor looked nothing like Orion and the way I remembered him. His hair had been cut and was in short curls now instead of the shaggy mess he used to have. His skin looked clear of the many bruises I always saw and although it was pale and adorned in rope, it sort of glowed. He was holding a water bottle and Michael was kneeling in front of him, talking to him, while he fiddled with some rope. I was nervous now. This did not look like the Orion I knew. He was always full of energy and confidence.

I looked at Layton, unsure.

He smiled and kissed me. "He's not as submissive as he seems. Sneaky little fuck applies to Orion more than most."

I looked back, as Michael kissed Orion on the head. Orion shrugged him off which made Michael smile. I hadn't heard what Michael had said to him but as Michael stood, I could hear him speaking. "You have a visitor, Orion, someone you know, I believe?"

Orion's head was bowed but I saw a little turn of it at Michaels words, a little interested. Michael patted his head which again was met with an aggravated movement from Orion. "Behave and you can rest awhile with me." Michael nodded for me to come in and he walked and sat on the floor against the wall by the door.

I took a deep breath and made my way towards Orion who was still sitting on his knees. His body was covered in rope, all ornately twined and knotted around his body. There were marks where a rope had been but it was now gone and I fleetingly looked up to see where he had hung. I wished I had seen it, seen him hanging. I looked back at his downturned head and looked at his body.

The ropes extended down his arms to his wrists and I could see the rope around his ankles that were tucked under him. Even through all the rope, it was easy to see how well he looked. He had been well looked after that was clear.

I sat on the floor in front of him and just watched him a minute before reaching out and touching his face with my fingers. "Hello, Orion."

He recognised me, I could tell by the small movement his body made. He was also surprised. I smiled. "Strange isn't it, that we both ended up here." He was looking at me under his lashes. "Do you remember me?" He nodded. "Look at me."

He raised his face and I saw the look of confusion in his eyes but also a little amusement. No, he wasn't as submissive as he seemed. "You are free to speak."

He spoke straight away which surprised me a little. "Have you come for seconds?"

I smiled a little and shook my head. "No, although you do look very tempting in those ropes. I'm here with...Leo. Do you remember Leo?"

He smiled a little. "The little rat kid?" I nodded. "No fucking way!" I tried to stop my smile.

Yes, I was here with the quiet street kid that never made a sound or impression on anyone. I was also smiling because Orion was still…Orion. This world had taken nothing from him, he was still funny and had that air of energy and confidence and fight.

"I wanted to see if you were... safe."

Orion smiled and lifted his hands which were still bond together in the rope at his wrists. "Safe enough for you?"

I reached out to touch his hands and I saw the first signs of vulnerability from him, he edged back a little and I dropped my hand.

He looked at me defiantly. "I really want a smoke, do you have one?"

I smiled and shook my head. "I think I gave up." I hadn't smoked in a few days and I would usually be tetchy without them but the days had been so busy, my thoughts so full of other things, I hadn't had time to think about it. Orion obviously hadn't given up the want of the thing that had been a daily staple and respite in our alley days. "Besides, smoking is forbidden here."

"You can fuck off, now that you've seen me then."

Michael spoke which made Orion drop his head. "If you can't speak with any respect then you shall be forbidden for the rest of the day, Orion."

He may still have had fight in him, but he had learnt a thing or two here. Michael, his Keeper, was to be respected. I looked at Michael quickly. He was smiling a little, not at all worried or angry with Orion.

I looked back to Orion who looked at me under his lashes and smiled. He was kind of happy here. He let them have him because it's what he wanted and when he didn't want it he tried to do what he wanted. I wasn't sure they would ever train that out of him. Orion liked mischief and trouble. It amused him, kept his mind busy and Michael and Layton seemed to enjoy watching him. He was definitely different from the other slaves I had seen today. Their willingness to serve, to submit was obvious and they could do that safely here when they felt vulnerable. Orion's reason for being here was not so clear.

"Why do you want to be here, Orion?"

"The same reason you're here with Leo."

I shook my head. "No, Leo is different, you know that."

"Maybe on the outside, but inside we're the same. He likes to be led, I like to be pushed, but we want the same things. We both want to feel it. It doesn't scare me, not feeling it scares me. Every moment I feel release from the fucking thing, I can feel it asking again. I fucking hate it, it rules my life. It's different here, they rule it, whether I like it or not and it doesn't matter how hard I fight it, or them, they always rule it. They do things here that people in the vanilla world would be arrested for." He smiled. "Leo will be safe here, it'll scare the hell out of him but he'll be safe. Is that what you wanted to know?"

How different he and Leo were. Leo was frightened and ashamed of his need, hiding it away, constantly trying to ignore it. Whereas Orion was constantly throwing himself at his, like if he fed it enough it would disappear. He had tried to rule it and it had become a constant battle, the more he gave it, the more he wanted. At least here he could fight for all he's worth and still be breathing at the end of the day. Their personalities were different, their need the same, they dealt with it in different ways. Either way was okay in this world.

"Maybe. Are you ever going to submit to them?"

"I submitted to you, didn't I?"

"No, I don't think you did, I think you were still fighting."

Orion smiled. "Whatever. You needed it. That ginger one had run off with your rat and you needed me to make it feel... different. I get that, wanting to feel different."

I shook my head, smiling. "Why do you leave your room, when it's forbidden?"

He looked at Michael and then back to me and shook his head. He wasn't going to say. I guess that was something for Michael to find out. Orion was rarely vulnerable, he never felt the need to submit or ask for help. Here he got it, he got help and he was made to feel vulnerable to them. It was something new to Orion.

I couldn't imagine the force it took to make him feel that but Orion needed that, he needed to feel something else other than his need. That's why he needed to be here, these people, this world was the only place that was willing to do the extreme things that Orion needed to make him feel that vulnerability so his other feelings had a chance to be heard.

It was kind of the reverse of Leo. He needed help in accepting his need, he was already vulnerable to people, their feelings, and his own, but feared the craving he had of the pain and of the pain itself. Orion was so open and accepting of his need that it smothered his other emotions, shutting him off from forming any relationships with people. Watching him now properly, I could see that he was just as lost as Leo.

I moved to get up and Orion panicked and moved towards his Keeper. "Are you going?"

I smiled at him. Not wanting me to be here but at the same time not wanting me to leave.

I nodded. "I have to get Leo and bring him here. I'm glad you're safe, Orion."

"Can I see him?"

I wasn't sure. "Maybe, it's up to Michael. I hear you don't do visitors." He looked agitated. "I'll come and see you again. If Michael allows it."

Orion looked at Michael. "Everything has to be earned Orion, you know that." Orion sighed.

I walked over to him and he edged back a little but managed to stay put. I crouched down and held my hand loosely out to him. "You were always good, Orion, but you glow here." I went to move when he spoke.

"Joe?" I settled back and waited for him to say more but he reached out his joined hands and touched his fingertips to mine. The touch was fleeting and hardly at all and then he made a very sure movement towards Michael and sat by him.

I got up and smiled at Michael. "Thank you, Michael."

Michael nodded and reached out for Orion as I left the room.

I stopped in the middle of his room and turned to wait for Layton. He was watching Orion and Michael at the door and seemed in no hurry, which suited me. I needed to breathe and try and take in everything that I had seen today. A few days ago, I had no idea this place existed. They called it their world and it was certainly different to the world I knew.

I looked around Orion's room, it was a little bigger than the other rooms and the one Leo and I were going to be staying in but it was still basic. Not as basic as the broken building Leo and I had been sleeping in for the last four years. Would Leo be able to adapt? He had been fine so far, away from the alley, a little shaky at times but he had coped. Another move to another new place was going to upset him, I knew.

He still clung to the thought of going back to the alley and I couldn't blame him. The only place that he had felt safe, ever, he couldn't see beyond it. He had been invisible to everyone, no one worried about him stealing their customers, no one saw him coming and going because no one cared. Yet he knew the alley and the people in it better than anyone. He saw them, knew them, knew every brick and rubbish in the alley. He had made his own space safe. He was going to have to trust me now to keep him safe.

I would give him to Layton to learn but I would stay with him, watch him every moment and take him back when I could see he needed me to make his world safe again. That was the plan.

I had to change though. I had to take on board everything I had learned about Leo's needs, about being submissive, about wanting pain. A few days ago, the concept of wanting pain, wanting it to hurt, had seemed ludicrous, insane; now I was thinking and talking about it like it was the most natural thing in the world...which it was, in this world, to these people. I had no doubts that bringing Leo here was right for him. Even after seeing Finn take his punishment, which had been difficult to watch. I had been amazed and astounded at how settled he had been after, he had even found me amusing at my lack of understanding.

Then there was Elan, the one that cried. The one that they encouraged to cry because that was his natural reaction to the pain and it was, he was praised, because clients liked it. For every client, there was a slave to match their needs. Not people who were forced or coerced into doing these things but people whose natural needs were nurtured and worshipped, and in return they were looked after, adored and loved. Orion was proof that they were indeed precious and even the most difficult slaves were respected in their way and their wellbeing always put first before anything else, regardless of their feelings on that.

To be on the outside of this world and be told about it, made it seem harsh and, if I was truthful about my first feelings, a little sick but to come inside and see it, feel it, it was sort of good...beautiful. I could see why they used the word so much. None of the feelings here were man-made, they were natural, all they did here was feed those feelings.

I sat on the bed feeling a little exhausted. This time tomorrow, Leo and I will be here, starting our new journey together. I was nervous and a little worried but I was also eager for it to begin. I could see a place where Leo could finally be happy and I wanted that for him. I looked at Layton who was now leaning against the door frame but he wasn't watching them anymore he was watching me.

"You okay, Joe?"

I smiled and nodded. "Is Orion alright?"

Layton smiled and nodded. "Yes, I was just watching them share a rare moment of understanding. Your visit touched something inside Orion and when he feels something different from his need it makes him unsure. It's the first time I have seen him ask for reassurance."

"I didn't mean to unsettle him."

Layton shook his head as he walked into the room. "You didn't, you gave him a moment of balance. The moment has passed and he is now trying to cover his insecure feeling by asking Michael to fuck him." Layton smiled and I smiled back. That sounded familiar.

"This room is bigger than the others and he has the other room back there?"

Layton nodded, looking around. "Yes, Orion's needs are bigger than the rest of my slaves. He does not go to clients yet but he needs to have room to play with Michael."

"When will he go to clients?"

"When he's old enough and when Michael and I decide he is ready. He hides behind his need, most of the new slaves that come here, are hiding from theirs." I nodded my understanding. That's what Leo was doing. "He still has a lot to learn and as I said, these things can't be rushed. Are you ready to leave?"

I nodded and stood. "Yes, I need to get back."

Layton nodded. "You still have some time. I have spoken to Kendal and she said Leo is still resting so there's no rush. He's quite safe."

"When did you speak to her?"

He smiled at my doubt. "When you were talking with Orion. I'd like to spend a little time with you before you bring Leo here."

I thought about it. I was eager to get back to Leo but time with Layton was inviting. I felt so at ease when I was with him.

I nodded. "Okay." He smiled at me and held out his hand which I took. He pulled me into his body and kissed my face.

"Good, I need a little sugar too." We left for the basement.

CHAPTER TWENTY-SIX

JOE

I felt a little relieved as we entered the basement. Layton took me into the bedroom and I sat on the bed and watched as he filled the kettle and put it to boil before taking off his top and joining me on the bed. He sprawled out beside me then raised himself on his hand and pulled at my top, gesturing for me to take it off, which I did. He ran his hand over my body watching me.

"Are you hungry, Joe?" He brushed his fingers over my nipple and I knew that that question had a double meaning. I wasn't quite sure how to answer it. He smiled and touched my hand, lacing his fingers through mine. "Are you worried?"

Again, I wasn't sure what he was asking. Was I worried about upstairs? The slaves? Bringing Leo here? Or the soft inviting touches he was giving me? All made me a little unsure, nervous.

"I'm... It's all new, I'm not sure what I'm doing." That covered everything.

Layton smiled. "I know. I have you."

God, why did that sound inviting? Why did I feel the need to lay down next to him and let him 'have' me? He pulled my hand towards him and raised himself a little more and kissed my hand, then he trailed the kisses up my inner arm to the crease of my elbow. My breath caught and I let out a small sigh.

Layton pulled me down to the bed and took my mouth with his and kissed me. The kiss was gentle and tender but full of passion, making me feel hot and needy. He wrapped a leg over me, pinning me to the bed under his weight while the kiss continued. I joined his asking tongue with my own and felt my stomach flip flop inside. When he pulled away and looked at me, my sane thoughts returned.

"Do you want me to submit to you?"

We were both breathing hard and he half-smiled while he stroked my face with his fingers. He wanted something from me and I wasn't sure what it was. I wasn't even sure what I wanted. He drew out this needy feeling in me that made me so uncomfortable, but I couldn't deny its pull.

"Do you want to?"

My heart was racing with nervous excitement. Should I be feeling these things when my feelings for Leo seemed so strong? It made it all confusing like I was cheating on him.

"But Leo?"

Layton smiled down at me. "What we share is between you and me, Joe. It has nothing to do with your feelings for Leo or mine for Isaac. They will remain untouched and still as strong. This is about our wants, our desires and what we want to share, at this moment." Shit. Why was it hard to breathe?

"If I submit to you…how far will that go?"

What was I asking? Did I desire to? Want to? I was unsure about what submitting to Layton meant. Would it mean being punished? Experiencing pain? I was unsure about that, a little scared, but what scared me most was there was a small part of me that wanted to know what that would feel like. *Jesus, my cock was lifting in my linens.*

Layton kissed my mouth before pulling away. "It will go as far as you want it to. You are not a slave, we are just sharing a moment, I am not going to force you to share things you are not ready to."

Why was I disappointed? It was so confusing; my feelings were all over the place. I was meant to be the controller, the Keeper to Leo, so why was I feeling like I wanted to give myself to Layton? I didn't have a need, did I? Wasn't this what it was about? Finding my way so I could lead Leo? I could hardly lead him to a place I didn't understand; that I had no clue about, what it felt like, not even a little.

"Talk to me, Joe." I was breathless, panting at my own thoughts.

I shook my head, trying to shake the confusion away. "I'm meant to be the strong dominant one. Can I do…things with you and still be that for Leo?"

He smiled softly, but I sensed his amusement at my question. "Yes, this is just a moment. Just because you learn about it doesn't mean you have to major in it." He smiled at me. "Do you trust me?"

I looked at him. Did I? Yes, yes I did. Just today had shown me how much he cared for his slaves, these people that gave themselves to him completely. Elan had loved him and willingly gone to him, gone to the people that made him cry with pain. Just seeing that showed me that he could be trusted but…I couldn't remember the last time I had trusted anyone.

"Y…yes." My heart was pounding in my chest. "I want to. I'm scared."

Layton looked at me for a moment before kissing me softly. Every touch reassuring, drawing me in.

"I know, it's okay to be scared. We're just going to taste it a little, see where it takes you. I'll have you the whole time."

I took a deep breath and nodded. It was done. I had given him permission to do what he wanted with me. I lay looking up at him waiting for it to begin.

Layton smiled and kissed my lips. "Oh, dear."

"Wh…What?" Had I done something wrong already?

He smiled down at me. "That is not the look I want to see. I want to see that need in your eyes, the one you had when we were kissing, the one where you wanted it." He swept his hands down my body and back again.

"I'm sorry…"

He put his finger over my lips and smiled. "Shh, no speaking. I can get it back." He sat up and pulled at my hand. "Come on." I was just about to ask where we were going when he looked at me and smiled a little. "Shh, no speaking." I closed my mouth as he took my hand and led me through to a bathroom.

I stood waiting in the bathroom while he turned on the shower and gathered some bits and pieces together. I was so nervous and worried, I stayed exactly where he had dropped my hand, watching him. He took off his linen trousers and stood by the shower, testing the warmth of the water. He looked at me and smiled.

"We're just going to do some preparation, don't look so worried, it's painless." He adjusted the temperature of the water and then joined me.

My heart missed a beat and then raced fast in my chest. Is this what it felt like for Leo when a customer took him up the alley? I guessed it was, not knowing them, not knowing what was to come, what they wanted. I felt a little sick and looked at Layton, unsure now whether my decision to let him lead me had been the right one.

It had been made when my blood had been flowing hot and needy through me when I could feel his body next to mine, when his mouth had been on mine.

"Aw, Joe, it's not so bad." He reached up and stroked his fingers around my face. "This is what waiting feels like to them. It's a little uncomfortable isn't it?"

Breathing heavily, I nodded and he smiled. He leaned forward and kissed my lips, letting them linger there before kissing them again and then whispering. "I like it."

He ran his studded tongue across my top lip and whispered again. "I can feel it in you." He ran his hands up my body and over my neck and held my face as he deepened his kiss.

I was completely breathless from the waiting, the fear, his words and his touches and I half joined him in the kiss, unsure of whether I was allowed or where it was going. He pulled away and looked at me as he swept his hands down my body, pushing my linens to the floor.

"I can take it away, the bad feeling. Would you like me too?" I nodded. Yes. I wanted it to go away.

He smiled at me and took my hand and kissed it. He stepped backwards still looking at me. "Come on then, you'll have to come with me if you want me to take it away." Without much coaxing, I stepped out of my linens towards him and he smiled.

"That's it, Joe, I have you. You don't have to be scared of me, I'm the one that's going to make it all feel...beautiful." I gripped his hand tightly and he led me under the shower, the water was warm and inviting and I felt my breathing slow a little.

He washed me, slowly and gently, he cleaned every part of me, stroking down my body, down my sides. He held me close and wrapped his arm around me while he sucked and kissed my neck. I felt his other hand run down my back and over my arse and then I felt his fingers run over my hole.

"Breathe now, Joe, while I cleanse your hole. It will feel a little strange at first, just like you're full. Don't bear down until I release you." I nodded as I felt the cold plug slide inside me, making me catch a breath.

It was a strange feeling having something just sitting inside me. I tried to spread my feet but Layton stilled me. "Settle and breathe through the feeling."

Cleaning my hole had always been intense but that was because the water had been bloody cold most of the time. It had been a case of shooting the water up there rather than having the pipe inserted, it was too big and not clean and then it was emptied as quickly as possible. It was too cold to keep inside for any length of time, so you emptied while you washed over the toilet, it was not as thorough as this but it had served its purpose for a clean fuck.

This was intense but in a different way. I could feel the warm water running inside me, filling me, which was uncomfortable but it was coupled by an intensely pleasurable feeling too. It was confusing and I couldn't decide whether to like it or not, then came the intense feeling to bear down as my insides told my brain my hole was full. It was hard not to follow that feeling, it was natural and a life habit. Your hole was full, you needed to empty. I shook my head against Layton's shoulder and growled the new feeling away.

Layton stroked his hand over my arse and held the plug as I pushed against it. "I know, just ignore it a little longer." I shook my head again. "This is proper cleansing, deep inside you, you can override the feeling, breathe it away." I pushed my breaths out over and over. "Good boy, now hold it while I remove the plug and you may empty in the toilet." I felt him pulling at the plug and I moaned as I felt like the whole contents of my hole was going to follow. "Hold it, Joe. It is not my wish to upset you." The plug was removed and Layton released me. "Okay go and empty."

I lifted my face from him and looked for the toilet in a slight panic and he smiled and pointed, enjoying my discomfort. I was relieved to empty, it took me a while, there had been a lot of water. I returned to him and the cleansing continued another three times.

As I held the last one waiting to be told I could leave to empty, Layton kissed my moaning mouth. "Kneel." I dropped to my knees, looking at him, waiting for the instruction that I could leave for the toilet. He smiled at me. "Mm, that's nice, Joe, silently asking for release." He stroked his fingers around my face. "Okay, you may empty." I went to move and he shook his head. "No here, you can empty here. It will just be water."

I shook my head and he smiled. "This is what submitting is, Joe, following my instructions regardless of how it makes you feel. I am making you feel them because I want to see them, I want you to know them. Now bear down for me, and empty."

I bowed my head in turmoil, in confusion. Humiliation was what this was…fuck! I held it as he caressed my face, pulling it up to him so he could watch. I closed my eyes and followed the feeling to empty.

As the water left me, I opened my eyes to look at him, showing my upset, as he watched my discomfort. When I was empty, he bent forward and kissed me, taking my mouth gently before pulling away and wiping my tears from my cheeks. "Good boy, now I can take that feeling away. Would you like me to?" I nodded.

It was awful, the degrading feeling of emptying my hole on the floor in front of him and have him watch me. I wanted it gone. He put some soap on his hands and rubbed my hair, massaging my scalp as he washed it, then moved behind me to kneel with his legs around me. He kissed my neck under my ear and I tipped my head a little to give him room. I could feel myself relaxing as he rinsed off the soap from my hair until I was leaning against him.

He kissed the side of my face and stroked his hands over my body under the cascading warm water, it felt glorious. It felt even more glorious when he swept his hand over my cock, it brought me out of my relaxed state a little, as I felt the blood start to rush urgently round my body ready to feed the new feelings. He stroked my body again and now and then he would sweep his hand over my growing cock, this continued until I was hard and erect, waiting, begging for the next touch.

Layton turned my face to his and kissed me. It was like the first kiss we had shared. It was gentle and coaxing and then turned more urgent as he stroked my cock continuously with one hand and devoured my mouth with his.

It was like being on a rollercoaster ride. First feeling utterly ashamed and humiliated and now blood was racing around my body, I was so turned on. Layton pulled away and looked at me. "Come back a little, Joe, come back and talk to me."

I was breathing heavily again and I opened my mouth to say something but the words escaped me, all thoughts escaped me. I couldn't form a thought long enough for my mind to register it and my mouth to speak it.

Layton smiled at me and I tipped my head into his body. He kissed the top of my head and held me close. "You're alright, Joe, I have you. Your feelings are overwhelming you."

He held me close as he leaned over and turned off the shower and we sat for a moment. The cleansing and emptying had been awful but this was good, this warm safe feeling I had, being close to him. I felt desperate for it, even though I had never felt anything like it before.

Despite the bad feelings he had caused, it was hard to hang on to them when I felt this…warm, this safe. He played his fingers through my wet hair and kissed me again. "Come on, let's get you dry before you catch a chill."

He pushed me forward and stood and the next thing I felt was a towel being wrapped around me and I was pulled to my feet and led to the bedroom. We sat on the bed where he dried me. He dried me. Like I was some kid or something who couldn't be trusted to do it properly and...I liked it. I liked it so much, I felt overwhelmed and I felt stupid tears stinging my eyes—again—but I never said anything to stop him, I could hardly look at him. Then he was gone and I was just sitting there alone.

When he returned I looked at him anxiously and he smiled and held out a bottle in his hand. "It's just moisturiser. I thought it would soothe your thoughts a little, calm your nerves."

He pushed me back on the bed so I was lying flat and squeezed some of the lotion into his hand and spread it over my body, then he began to massage it into my skin. The feeling was beautiful, being touched, having my body sort of worshipped. If I had earned this, if my uncomfortable feeling about being cleansed had earned me this, then it was, I thought, a fair trade.

Layton put away the lotion and crawled onto the bed until he was leaning over me. He kissed me and then worked his mouth down my body, sucking at each nipple and then lower, until his mouth was just above my cock. I wanted him to suck me, I wanted to feel his mouth around me, instead, he rubbed his hand over it, making it beg to him.

He crawled back up my body and pinned my hands to the bed. "I think it's time you showed me what that beautiful mouth can do." He released my hands and pulled me up the bed a little to lean me against the headboard, then moved forward, kneeling astride me so his cock was right in front of my mouth.

I opened my mouth to have him and he pulled away. "Do you think I'm one of your customers, Joe? Do you think you can just say when you have it?" He shook his head at me. "I say when you can have it and how much you have. Open your mouth and put your tongue out."

So wanton and desperate, I did as requested and he put two fingers on my tongue and slid them slowly over it to the back of my throat, making me heave a little. The reaction made me anxious and I moved under him, agitated.

He stroked my face. "You're okay, settle now." I was breathing heavily with a little fear, with a little anticipation at having his cock.

He held my head in one hand and held his cock with the other. He was hard already and he stroked his cock in his hand. "Open that beautiful mouth and look at me." It was open and I stretched it open further as I raised my eyes to him. He rubbed his cock head over my tongue.

"Mm, that's it, nice and wide." He pushed his cock into my mouth and out again. "Suck it for me." I closed my mouth around him and sucked him.

He was still holding my head back to the headboard so he directed the movement, with each stroke he thrust a little deeper and I put my hands against his body ready to restrict his thrusts. He let go of my head and took my wrists in his hands and held them away from him while he continued to thrust. "Just keep sucking, Joe. It feels fucking amazing." I did as he asked.

Sucking cock was my trade. I knew I was good at it, I knew how to make him feel like he wanted to spill his load and I worked his cock with my mouth and tongue until I could hear him moaning his pleasure. He moved my hands under his knees and knelt on them painfully. I tried to pull them away from under him but he increased his weight and looked at me, shaking his head.

He leaned forward putting his hands on the headboard above me and thrust into my mouth while I sucked him. I had never felt so defenceless, so vulnerable while giving head. It was scary and hot all at the same time. His thrusts became deeper, touching the back of my throat so I would half gag on him but it wasn't until he thrust it in and kept it there, that the fear part took over and I struggled to free my mouth. He used his hands in my hair to hold me there and made me choke and heave on his cock, while he praised me and moaned his pleasure. Every time I turned my face from him to get away, he would turn it back and continue until I was moaning to him of my discomfort.

I retched and heaved as my spit was pushed from me over and over, my eyes full of tears and my fear became so immense, that I almost felt like I was crying. This was not how I sucked cock. I took their cock, I said when and how much. He held my head in both his hands and looked down at me, watching my distress. He stroked my face and then held me again while he again thrust into my throat and held himself there, watching me as I struggled and retched. "You're okay, just let it happen, just let it out around my cock."

I looked at him, panicked as the spit and the bile was pushed from my body and drooled out of my mouth around him. I fought for air, panicked, then I was released.

He pushed himself down my body quickly and took my cock in his mouth as I moaned my distress. It was short-lived as his lips wrapped around my still rock hard cock. My initial thoughts were to move from him to get away but as I did so the need for his mouth on me took over and I found myself lying helplessly on the bed and allowing him to have me, even spreading my legs wantonly.

He continued to suck me, dragging his wet mouth and that small metal piercing he had on his tongue, up my shaft over and over, until I was writhing under him, thrusting my hips at him. The last person to suck me off had been a new street kid a month or so ago, he needed money and I needed to come, so I fed him, literally, pretending it was Leo. It had served us both.

Back on the bed with Layton, my body and mind were both confused as to what it wanted so when he crawled back up to look at me, I moaned and turned on my side away from him, grasping at the bed covers. He turned me back and took my mouth with his and I joined him, kissing him back hungrily, wrapping my arms around him. I was horny, hot and needy for him but I also needed him to reassure the confused feelings in me. He wrapped his arms around my body as we continued to kiss and then I was scooped up from the bed and I found myself on top of him, straddling his body as he lay under me. I pushed my hands against his chest and pushed away from him a little so I could look at him. His eyes were like fire, the flecks of gold caramel were dancing against the darker brown.

I wiped the back of my hand across my mouth and chin, which made him smile a little at me, and I shakily put my hands to his body. The small niggling fear I had should have made me move but I couldn't seem to engage it, not when my body felt so hot and my cock stood proudly wanting attention.

I sat looking at him, not knowing what to expect. He was watching me back, stroking his hands over my body, his fingers leaving trails of expectation across my skin. He took my nipples in his fingers and played with them, pinching and pulling them while he rubbed his hard cock over my hole, teasingly.

"Fuck, Joe, you're beautiful. Everything is so new to you, it makes me hard just to watch you. I want to be inside you, I want to show you something amazing."

He pushed himself up and kissed my mouth and then spoke breathlessly against my lips. "Would you like me to?"

I was unsure. I was already consumed with feelings and thoughts that I had never known could exist together, that could play off each other and make a more intense feeling inside me.

Layton kissed my mouth again gently. "I know you're feeling a little spaced out, a little lost. you're okay, I have you. I'll bring you back."

He took my mouth again, deeper this time and I joined him, losing myself in his mouth, letting it fuel the need that was already burning in me. He kissed my neck and I moaned as I felt him thrust his cock again over my hole, inviting me to take it.

"Would you like me to show you, Joe?" I nodded and kissed his face, holding on to him to stop me from falling from this dizziness and he turned and kissed my lips fleetingly.

He lay back and twisted under me to get something out of the bedside drawer. It was a bottle of lubricant and something else, something silver and shiny in his hand, like a chain. He smiled at me as my eyes followed his hand but he didn't show, he kept it wrapped inside his fist as he squeezed some lube on his fingers and leaned forward, stretching behind me to coat his cock in lube.

He kissed me as he spread my arse and rubbed lube over my hole and then pushed his finger inside me. "Fuck, Joe, you're so tight."

Just having his finger inside me was so intense and I leaned forward on him and moaned out on my breaths. No customers wanted me like this anymore, just him, and I wanted him again inside me, stretching me open, around him, I wanted it. I clung to him while he finger fucked me into a needy whorish frenzy, wordlessly begging him for his cock.

He wrapped his fisted hand around me and held me, kissing my neck before whispering close to my ear. "It's going to feel a little intense, to begin with, I promise the amazing part will come okay?"

I nodded against him, totally lost in the feelings he was creating. He could have asked me anything, he had me. He pushed me slightly back to sit and rubbed his cock over my hole and I matched his wanting by thrusting my hips and grinding my hole over him. Then felt the burning pain as he pushed his cock head against the protesting ring of muscle. I whimpered out to him as he thrust up and into me, not allowing the feeling to settle until he was seated inside me. Then he started to stroke his cock over my insides slowly, drawing out the pleasure.

He stroked my cock in his hand increasing my need for it. "That's it, Joe, chase it, let it burn inside you."

I pressed my hands into his chest as I rocked and thrust over him, as the orgasm seemed to draw closer and closer. He took his hand from my cock and swept it up my body, feeling my body writhing and quivering on top of him. He moaned loudly as he let the chain slip from his hand a little and hang, he rubbed it over my body, my nipples, it was cold and sent a chill through me and then…my orgasm was ripped away from me by immense pain. It made me cry out and I shook my head at him but it seemed it was ignored as I felt another pulse of it.

My hands flew to my chest as I looked down at the clamps that were gripping my small buds, squashing them tightly, making them throb. I went to remove them and Layton took my wrists and held them down either side of me.

"Look at me, Joe." I looked down at him and let out a half cry to him for it to be stopped. "I know. I know it feels bad. It won't feel so bad in a moment. I can make it feel better but you have to promise me you will not remove them." I looked at him consumed by the throbbing through my body. "Promise me, Joe, and I will make it feel different. Would you like me to?"

I nodded and moaned. I wanted it to stop. He slowly released my hands and I shakily moved them to my chest. I touched the chain that joined them and let out a small cry as I intensified the pain.

Layton smiled at me and shook his head. "Don't touch them." I put my shaking hands to his chest and moaned at him.

My thoughts were in turmoil and I spoke out, breathless. "I don't like them…I don't want them."

He smiled again and rubbed my cock. He sat up and wrapped his arm around my back pulling me towards him. I was careful not to let the clamps touch his body as he swept his other hand over my back and my arse. He swept his hands back up my back and held me while he thrust into me over and over and I cried out again and tried to move away as my body became overwhelmed with pain.

He held me tighter, forbidding any movement and kissed the side of my face before breathlessly speaking to my ear. "Shh, breathe, Joe."

There was no escape and I gripped at him desperately, as the pain of my hole and my nipples all mingled together to create an intense throbbing through me, each trying to outdo the other until they seemed to pulse in unison. I sunk forward, unable to use my strength to hold myself from him, not caring now that it squashed the clamps.

He was still holding me tightly whispering in my ear. "Good boy, relax and give me your hole, take me all the way in," I growled into his body as he pushed his cock inside and then just held me there stroking my back and kissing my face.

"That's it, Joe, just breathe and relax. I'm going to make it all feel beautiful." He started to thrust his hips under me, pushing his cock in and out slowly and I moaned with every movement, shaking my head against it.

Layton released his hold on me and dragged his hands to my arse, pulling my arse cheeks apart so he could go deeper with each thrust. The feeling intensified and I pushed my hand against him, pushing my upper body from him but keeping my arse there for him so he could have it. With every thrust came a flickering of pleasure, over and over like touching my orgasm but then taking it.

I looked at him, my mouth open to take my breaths and he pushed himself up and took my mouth, kissing me roughly and deeply. I joined him again, tasting him with my tongue urgently, wanting him to make it all feel better.

I took my mouth from him and whispered my need against his lips. "Fuck me, deeper...harder." He laid back and pushed me up so I was sitting upright and held my hips tightly while he thrust under me.

I began rhythmically moving to have him deeper inside me, leaning slightly back to support myself on his thighs and he stilled his movements and let me slide my hole over him. With one hand he rubbed my cock, which swung in front of me begging, while he watched me and I looked back at him, totally lost in the building pleasure and orgasm that seemed so close.

"I want to come, fuck me, make me come." Through my haze filled mind, I saw him smile.

He took his hand from my cock and stroked it up over my body as it flexed under his palm, I was still fucking myself, thrusting my hips greedily over him.

"I think we've had enough fun, Joe. It's time to slow this down a little." He pushed up on one hand and then took my mouth.

My orgasm was still racing around my body and I was still chasing it, it was so close. Then he pulled at the chain that hung from my nipples and I stopped riding his cock and cried out, my hands flying to his, gripping his wrists to still him. They were bearable if they weren't touched, the pain just sort of humming through me but when they were touched, it was too much to ignore, ripping my pleasure from me.

He released the chain and I shook my head at him. It was too much, too overwhelming, not just the clamps on my nipples but the fucking also, the pleasure of having my hole filled, the hot burning kisses and Layton's need of me. No one had ever made me feel so hot and needy for it, not in a long time…maybe not ever, not like this.

He stroked his fingers around my face and kissed my lips gently. "Shh, wrap your arms around me."

Shakily, I put both arms around his neck and he kissed the side of my face before picking me up as we were, with him still inside me and turning me so I was under him, my back now on the bed. His face was still close to mine and I released his neck from my hold but he stayed there curled over me. He lay his elbows on either side of my head and stroked his fingers on either side of my face. "No more chasing it, let it come to you nice and slow."

He started to thrust slowly inside me again but this was different, this was gentle, drawing out the feeling so much so that I found it difficult to breathe through it and kept holding my breath.

He kissed my face, small gentle kisses, letting his lips linger against my skin. I could feel his quick breaths across my cheek as he got deeper and quicker, as the intense feeling built in both of us. I could feel my orgasm gaining speed again and I started to moan with every slow thrust as it seemed teasingly close. I gripped his arse in my hands, trying to ease the painfully slow pleasure, trying to make him fuck me quicker. When that didn't work, I moved my hand between us to my cock, it was wet with pre-cum, a clear silken line drooling to my stomach and as I took it in my fist, Layton took my hand and took it away.

He put both my hands on the bed beside my head and laced his fingers through mine. "Not yet, Joe."

Breathless, I spoke. "But...I need to come."

Layton smiled a little. "I know, breathe into the beautiful feeling, let it come a little closer."

He continued his slow thrusts inside me and I moaned and whimpered while he watched me, kissing me now and again on my open mouth. My legs were spread and curled up into my body as tight as I could pull them, to raise my arse for him, to give him all the access he needed. It was like drowning in an orgasm, being surrounded by it, consumed with the feeling of it. I was panting with the intensity of it and I looked at him.

"I'm going to come...I'm going to come." I repeated over and over.

I wanted to, I felt like I would with every thrust of him but it seemed to hit the point where it felt like it was going to explode inside me and then recede just out of reach. It was like sweet agony...if there was such a thing, then this was it. I had never tasted an orgasm for so long.

"Breathe it away, nice slow breaths, it's coming to you, Joe."

I made an effort to breathe through the feeling, trying to keep my breaths slow but the feeling was so intense they became whimpers of need. Layton took my mouth and kissed me deeply and I kissed him back whimpering into his mouth each time the orgasm asked. Layton moaned his breaths back, he was as close as I was and his thrusts started to increase in speed a little. He released my hands and knelt up a little. He wrapped one hand around my cock and stroked it in time with his thrusts inside me and the other he lay on my chest, covering the chain with his hand.

He watched me through glazed eyes as my orgasm now got the fuel it needed to ignite. It rushed at me and I did a few quick moans before my breath was taken and it exploded through my body. I watched as, in one swift movement, he ripped the clamps from my nipples and I tried to cry out but the orgasm seemed to just intensify another notch and rob me of my voice. I felt my body jolting over and over as wave after wave of pleasure pulsed through me, even my throbbing sore nipples seemed to join in the pleasure. I could hear Layton moaning his orgasm, feel the pressure as he thrust deep, pumping his life inside me. I had never felt anything like it before, never felt such intense lingering pleasure.

Orgasms were always good but they were always short-lived, this one, even now while it receded, was still burning inside me. I almost felt like I could come again. I felt Layton withdraw and then I felt his hands stroking my body, he rubbed my nipples and I cried out and jolted under his touch, the soreness of them mixing with the last of my pleasure. I felt frozen in the aftermath of the pleasure, which still twinged inside me, my legs were still pulled tight to my body as if not wanting to give up the chance it might ignite again.

I had never felt anything like it.

CHAPTER TWENTY-SEVEN

JOE

I felt the tears rolling down the sides of my face and he came and kissed them away, lying beside me, holding me while I…sort of cried? I didn't feel like I was crying but the tears just kept coming. That on its own unsettled me and I finally relaxed, dropped my legs and turned into his body for him to…love me? Reassure me a little? I wasn't sure what I wanted or expected, but I needed something. As my thoughts and body started to settle I started to feel the aftermath of our…lovemaking? It hadn't started as lovemaking, it had been lust and need that had turned into fucking but then he had changed it, he had taken control and changed the whole feeling around to be gentle and tender.

I could feel my hole protesting the assault it had just suffered and my nipples were joining in on the protest. It's like they were both trying to get my attention, my nipples were winning. The throbbing was making my breath catch and then I remembered Isaac and his nipples and Elan and his. I had no idea how they had endured such pain, I didn't even want to look at mine, a little fearful that they would look how they felt...mutilated. Layton's breathing had settled now but he wasn't saying anything, just holding me and stroking my hair with his fingers.

I did not doubt that I had been a rubbish submissive. My thoughts had been all over the place, my fear so strong that I felt like it had prevented me from giving myself completely. I was sure my report card would say 'could do better'. I felt a smile but it was taken by yet another throb from my nipples and I moaned quietly and looked up at Layton.

I wanted him to say something, even if it was 'could do better'. He looked down feeling my movement and kissed my forehead. He smiled at me.

"Hey. Are you with me? You look like you're back?"

Back? Back from where? Had I gone somewhere? I thought about it. I had felt like I was on some kind of a rollercoaster, being swept along, sometimes going faster than I could keep up with.

"I think I am. I think I fell off the rollercoaster and hit the ground."

Layton laughed a little. "Ouch. I was aiming for a slow boat ride but you wanted faster."

I closed my eyes, feeling slightly mortified, remembering now that I had asked for it, faster and deeper and harder. I was a little embarrassed and I screwed my face up, covering it with my hand to hide from him.

Layton kissed the top of my head. "It was beautiful, like watching a flower bloom for the first time."

I lifted my face to him again. "Really? I didn't feel like a flower, more like a...rampant weed."

Layton laughed. "Oh Joe, you're funny." He kissed my face and swept his fingers around it tenderly. "Believe me, from where I was, you were definitely a beautiful flower...maybe a...rampant beautiful flower."

I smiled and then sighed. "I think you're being nice. I was rubbish, wasn't I? It was all confusing, I was scared, the whole time...except when I wanted to come...then I don't think I thought about anything else. It all seemed to move so fast, one feeling to the other." I looked at him. "I didn't mean to cry...at the end, I couldn't seem to control it. The orgasm was..." I couldn't think of a word that described what I had felt so I went with the word that now held a different meaning, "Beautiful." I shook my head of the word, this wasn't about me and what I wanted or even felt. "I think I need to get back to Leo now. I feel like I forgot him."

Layton laid his hand against my face. "Your thoughts are still racing, your emotions are still overwhelming you. This is all part of what it feels like to give yourself to someone. This is sharing time and it's very important. We'll talk about it. You never forgot Leo, this was all to do with him. You now have an inside understanding of what it feels like and that can only help him. It also gave me a chance to see how new it all was to you and that will be no different for Leo. I pushed you a little, I will work slower with Leo. You may have lived on the street but it has sheltered you from basic feelings and emotions." I was a little hurt.

"Are you saying I'm emotionless?! Because on the street you know, there's no room for love and beautiful things and tears. Even this, lying here with you, I don't even know what to call it or what to feel about it. I've never done...never had such..." I pushed myself away from him a little angry at not knowing the words. Moving made my aching body twinge and I scowled at him, blaming him for that too.

Layton pushed himself up a little so he was half sitting and held out his hand. "Come back to me, Joe. We will work through these feels, they are quite normal despite how they feel to you. I know very well what is allowed and accepted on the street. No one is emotionless but the street suppresses feelings, it's kind of like a safety thing. It stops you from getting stuck in bad feelings."

I felt tears again and I bit my lip and wiped my hand across my face. "Fuck! I don't know why I'm crying again. I think I've cried more than Leo ever cried on the street...he's stronger than me..."

Layton smiled and offered his hand again. "Come on, Joe. All these thoughts and feelings will settle in a while, let me look after you while it all feels confusing."

Look after me. Yes, I wanted that, I didn't like feeling like I was alone and that was the whole point of being here, bringing Leo here, so Layton could help him…and me. I reached out and took his hand and he pulled me back to his body, wrapped his arm around me and then covered me with a blanket. I hadn't realised I was cold.

"Is it a bad thing that I need this?"

Layton smiled and kissed me. "What? You think that the other Keepers never need me?"

I looked up at him. "Do they? Do they do this?"

He smiled. "Of course they do. They need to remember what their slaves feel, it's very important. They also need to feel comforted and loved. That's what this is, Joe, it's feeling loved and sharing that with me, regardless of what else we shared. Theirs is a little more intense because they already understand a lot but the feelings that come after, are the same. It's okay to feel this, Joe, it doesn't mean you feel any less for Leo. You don't have to submit to me to have this. I give love freely."

I smiled against him, finding that funny and so very true. "You are pretty free with it. I didn't submit to have this, at least I don't think I did. Maybe, maybe a little but I just wanted to see what Leo was going to have. I wanted to see where I was taking him."

"And?"

I shook my head. "I'm not sure. I felt so scared, I know that's going to be the same for him. The bad bits were...bad but the good bits, they were really good." I smiled. "The orgasm was a little intense though, I'm not sure Leo will cope."

Layton laughed and kissed me. "Leo is naturally submissive, he will easily be led to feel whatever you want him to feel once he learns that letting you do that takes him to beautiful places. Like having orgasms that blow his mind. That was the point I was trying to make to you. I made you feel the things that you felt. I made you worry and I made you feel safe when you needed a little push. You wanted nice things so I made you earn them.

"I was trying to give you a quick lesson, Leo's will not be so rushed. We will give him time to understand for himself that he earns nice things when he follows requests, when he behaves in a more appropriate manner and when he shares things in a way that is more acceptable. Like you are now."

I leaned into him more. "I'm sorry about that. I was confused and then when I moved it hurt and I felt like it was your fault. I didn't mean to blame you."

Layton laughed a little. "It's all normal, Joe, and it was my fault so I can't feel bad about you because you feel that. I understand and make it feel better. What hurts?"

I screwed my face as I thought about my nipples. They were just a dull ache now not out and out throbbing like before.

"My nipples, I don't want to look at them because of how they feel. They feel broken. Is that how Isaac and Elan got their wounds on their nipples? With things like that?"

Layton kissed me and moved a little. "Mm, a little bit more intense play than that." I blew a breath out, unable to contemplate anything more intense than what I had felt. "Your nipples are connected to your cock and give pleasurable feelings, it takes a bit of time to learn but once understood a slave will allow you to play with theirs for a few hours."

"I know the connection…I've never had anyone try and rip them from my body before!" Layton laughed as I scowled at him.

"They will suffer the pain to have the pleasurable feelings. Let me see." He lifted the blanket and looked at my nipples.

I looked at him, wincing, hoping he wouldn't touch them. He looked at me and smiled and kissed my lips. "They are not broken, a little pink but not broken. Now you understand why Leo doesn't want to look at his back when it's so raw and new.

"It's hard for him to understand that he wanted what he feels. His back feels broken, probably like your nipples do and that must be a little scary."

Of course. I looked down at my nipples now and seeing they were intact I put my fingers to them and touched them. It didn't feel as bad as I had thought.

"I'm being a bit of a wimp, aren't I? What you did was nothing was it? It doesn't even compare to what the slaves have or Leo's back."

Layton pulled me towards him and held me. "There are no wimps here, everybody has their strengths and limits. Playing, and using your body is something you learn using your natural desires and wants…which I doubt you've even begun to know about. Your life has been about staying alive to take your next breath…for both you and Leo. I don't know anyone who would call that being a wimp. Isaac and Elan have been slaves for many years, they understand their body, their need, they understand what each toy makes them feel. They can play for many hours and endure a lot.

"You allowed me to show you something new, that you didn't understand, that took a lot of strength. Leo's back is not a good comparison, not for any play. He will not have that again, not like that. That is dangerous play, harmful. I can make him feel that sort of pain but in a safer, more controlled way. It will all be new to him, the toys we use, the emotions and feelings he will have. Like you, he will be overwhelmed so we will move slowly. We will take him there and bring him back so he learns that nothing he feels is permanent.

"You will have to encourage him when he feels unsure because he won't want any of it, to begin with. He won't know what the flogger feels like or the ropes that bind him, or the dildo that he knows is going in his hole. They will all just be scary. You also have to be honest with him. If it's going to be painful then you need to tell him, take away some of the shock for him but you can also push him a little by telling him how it would make you feel to watch him suffer it just for a while. He wants to please you so it may be all he needs to taste something new. If he's too distraught or too overwhelmed then you must bring him back straight away.

"We want to play with him and we want him to play with us so we never keep him in something that would make him feel he couldn't go there again. I will spend the first day gaining his trust and getting to know him before we move to anything more. The idea is to make Leo feel secure about being with me, feel safe. When he understands that he can be with me and you're not going to leave him, he will be more relaxed about coming to me of his own accord. Then I can start being a little more demanding of him. I'm not going to throw clamps on his nipples the minute he walks through the door, Joe, slow and steady is how we will move.

"You have to remember that Leo has a want and desire for it, he may be anxious and want to hide but he will also be curious and that will make him more open to requests to show you things." I nodded. "Where else do you hurt?"

"My hole is sore, well, actually not so much now, it was, and my legs."

Layton laughed. "Well, I'm not taking the blame for either of those, you were the rampant flower remember? Your hole will feel a little tender for a while but no damage has been done and your legs are just aching muscles that you haven't used in a while." I smiled against him. I guess they were my own fault. "It was beautiful." He kissed me and stroked his finger through my hair.

"What, even with drool and retching?"

Layton smiled. "It's exactly what I wanted, it made me hot to see you struggle a little. When you became unsure, I made it better, didn't I?" Yes, he had. He had sucked my cock and made me want him.

"Yes, but now I am covered in drool and cum."

Layton pulled me onto his lap so I straddled him. After looking at me for a moment, he took my mouth with his, while stroking his hand round my neck and face and I kissed him back. He smiled as we parted, looking at me again.

"None of which bothers me. You can shower quickly and I will make tea. Now that you are back properly, we need to talk. I have something I need to tell you." I looked at him concerned and he smiled and kissed my lips. "I'm not sharing now and you don't have to look so concerned. Go." He wasn't worried so I decided not to worry. I slipped off the bed and went to go but he didn't release my hand. I turned back to look at him. "We will do this again, Joe, you were quite beautiful to watch."

I smiled a little shyly. "Maybe next time you can stop the rampant flower and make me stay on the slow boat?"

Layton grinned. "Of course, as you wish."

I smiled and turned to go then a thought occurred to me and I turned back. "Am I going to regret that I asked that? Is it going to hurt?"

Layton laughed a little. "I can be nice, Joe, you know that. I would never want you to regret any time spent with me." I smiled at him. I don't think that was possible.

"I don't think I'll ever regret being with you, I think I sort of…love you. Well, that's what it feels like when I'm with you."

Layton pulled me back to the bed and sat forward and held my face while he kissed me. "I like that, I feel the same. I love you too."

I smiled as I turned and left for the bathroom. I didn't think for one moment that I was any more special or loved more than any of his other Keepers, but it was nice to hear and feel it, even if it was just words. It filled the empty void that I had carried for so long and not quite understood.

While I showered, I decided that it was just having a friend, someone to trust, someone who I could be honest with and tell anything to and know that they would still be there the next time I needed them. I had never had anyone like that in my life. The closest person to me was Leo and while I loved him and we shared things, he couldn't take any of my worries, he had enough of his own. I smiled thinking about him. I was missing him and a little anxious now to get back to him. I had liked my day here and it had taught me a lot, more than I could have learned if he had been with me but he had been in my thoughts for four years and I didn't feel whole without him.

I felt a little freer and lighter as I headed back into the bedroom. I felt ready to start this new journey with Leo. Layton was sitting on the bed, still naked and he had made tea so I sat next to him as he handed me a mug.

"I feel a bit more confident now about coming here with Leo…" Layton looked at me and sighed.

Something was wrong.

I looked at him questioningly. "What's going on?"

"Yes, but now I am covered in drool and cum."

Layton pulled me onto his lap so I straddled him. After looking at me for a moment, he took my mouth with his, while stroking his hand round my neck and face and I kissed him back. He smiled as we parted, looking at me again.

"None of which bothers me. You can shower quickly and I will make tea. Now that you are back properly, we need to talk. I have something I need to tell you." I looked at him concerned and he smiled and kissed my lips. "I'm not sharing now and you don't have to look so concerned. Go." He wasn't worried so I decided not to worry. I slipped off the bed and went to go but he didn't release my hand. I turned back to look at him. "We will do this again, Joe, you were quite beautiful to watch."

I smiled a little shyly. "Maybe next time you can stop the rampant flower and make me stay on the slow boat?"

Layton grinned. "Of course, as you wish."

I smiled and turned to go then a thought occurred to me and I turned back. "Am I going to regret that I asked that? Is it going to hurt?"

Layton laughed a little. "I can be nice, Joe, you know that. I would never want you to regret any time spent with me." I smiled at him. I don't think that was possible.

"I don't think I'll ever regret being with you, I think I sort of…love you. Well, that's what it feels like when I'm with you."

Layton pulled me back to the bed and sat forward and held my face while he kissed me. "I like that, I feel the same. I love you too."

I smiled as I turned and left for the bathroom. I didn't think for one moment that I was any more special or loved more than any of his other Keepers, but it was nice to hear and feel it, even if it was just words. It filled the empty void that I had carried for so long and not quite understood.

While I showered, I decided that it was just having a friend, someone to trust, someone who I could be honest with and tell anything to and know that they would still be there the next time I needed them. I had never had anyone like that in my life. The closest person to me was Leo and while I loved him and we shared things, he couldn't take any of my worries, he had enough of his own. I smiled thinking about him. I was missing him and a little anxious now to get back to him. I had liked my day here and it had taught me a lot, more than I could have learned if he had been with me but he had been in my thoughts for four years and I didn't feel whole without him.

I felt a little freer and lighter as I headed back into the bedroom. I felt ready to start this new journey with Leo. Layton was sitting on the bed, still naked and he had made tea so I sat next to him as he handed me a mug.

"I feel a bit more confident now about coming here with Leo…" Layton looked at me and sighed.

Something was wrong.

I looked at him questioningly. "What's going on?"

"I don't want you to freak out..." Too late for that now. "...Leo woke up and became unmanageable for Kendal." Oh god. I reached across him and put down my mug.

"You said he was still sleeping..?! Did...did you lie?"

"No, I didn't lie. I said he was resting, which he was...is... with Julian."

I felt sick. They had deceived me, gained my trust and...

"Julian's got him?"

Layton sighed and nodded. "Yes."

Motherfuckers!

They had split us up and taken him. Of course. I had made it easy for them. I had let my guard down, become needy for...something more, and Julian had taken his moment.

Easier, he had said. It would be easier if we weren't together. I could feel the rage building in me and I stood and closed my hands into fists.

I heard Layton get up and step towards me as he spoke. "He's going to be…"

I turned and swung at him and connected my fist with his face, the surprise knocked him back to sit on the bed with his hand on his face.

Four fucking years I had fought for him, to keep him alive and breathing, to keep him clothed and fed, to keep him from the bad people...the hungry junkies.

I wasn't going to stop now, they couldn't stop me. They couldn't have him.

To be continued...

ACKNOWLEDGEMENTS

As always, a huge thank you goes to Wendy for keeping me on the straight and narrow; to Leigh for her unwavering support of my words; and to Abrianna for her tireless corrections, commas and her little comments that make me smile. Most of all, as always, I thank them for their friendship.

The most important thank you, goes out to my readers, without whom, my characters wouldn't live.

AFTERWORD

Many thanks for reading my books. I hope the characters are drawing you in and you grow to love them like I do.

If you would like to leave me a comment or feedback or just drop me a line saying hi, then please head over to my website or catch me on Facebook where I usually hang out.

BOOKS BY THIS AUTHOR

THE ISAAC SERIES

ISAAC – The Isaac Series Book 1

LAYTON – The Isaac Series Book 2

SLAVE – The Isaac Series Book 3

BABY BOY – The Isaac Series Book 4

PETER – The Isaac Series Book 5

JUST BREATHE – The Isaac Series Book 6

OTHER BOOKS FROM THIS AUTHOR

JULIAN – A stand-alone book (these characters return in The Isaac Series)

SECRETS AND PROMISES – This book features characters from The Isaac Series

ABOUT THE AUTHOR

Taylor J Gray is a self-published author of Dark erotic and taboo stories. She was born in the suburbs of London and although she's moved about a bit she hasn't moved far from where she started. Taylor is married and lives with her partner, two dogs, and two cats. Her husband is very supportive of her work. She has worked in various roles and one of her favourite jobs was being a cinema manager but, even in school, where she used to write for her friends, her passion has always been writing stories and poems.

She has always loved the worlds of fantasy and fairy tale and reading and watching stories that don't quite fit into the normal. She's always wanted to write a romantic love story with a twist of something a little bit spicey hot and ended up with her first story Julian. Her interest and role in the BDSM community and the deep and trusting relationships they share led her to write stronger and more powerful stories about their desires and needs and her second story Isaac was born. She loved him so much she made a series!
She still considers what she writes as a love story.

She is an ardent supporter of gay rights and the LGBTQ community and totally believes in love is love.

"The human mind and body is such a beautiful thing."

Printed in Great Britain
by Amazon